DESERT BORN | BOOK ONE

Desert Brave

GIN COLEMAN

Black Rose Writing | Texas

ISBN: 978-1-68513-442-6
Library of Congress Control Number: 2025939003

PUBLISHED BY BLACK ROSE WRITING
www.blackrosewriting.com

Printed in the United States of America
Suggested Retail Price (SRP) $25.95

Desert Brave is printed in Minion Pro

*As a planet-friendly publisher, Black Rose Writing does its best to eliminate unnecessary waste to reduce paper usage and energy costs, while never compromising the reading experience. As a result, the final word count vs. page count may not meet common expectations.

PRAISE FOR
Desert Brave

"This book checks all my boxes: mystery, romance, drama, archaeology, horses, and the vast desert. Well-written, suspenseful, and descriptive, I felt I was inside the story peering from behind a diaphanous curtain, my heart pounding!"
–Linda M., Education Administrator

"Gin Coleman tells a terrific story! A great read for vacation, travel, or just sitting by the fire on a cold winter's night. Can't wait for the sequel!"
–Trish W., Educational Consultant

"5 STARS FOR DESERT BRAVE! Author Gin Coleman expertly blends adventure with rich cultural detail and emotional depth, creating a story that is both thrilling and educational. I loved the natural way that we learn about Kira's heritage through her whole ethos and way of viewing the world, with a beautifully up-close narrative that shows her every thought and feeling. The author's vivid and sensory descriptions of the Arabian desert immerse readers in the harsh yet mystical landscape, enhancing the novel's sense of adventure by letting us feel the moments of struggle and wonder that Kira goes through. She's also highly resilient and resourceful as a heroine, and this warmth and confidence is carried through into the narrative voice and command of the plot, making readers feel that they're in safe hands from cover to cover with an inspiring tale of adventure and bravery. The intricate storyline is well-paced and filled with mystery, danger, and romance, keeping readers engaged until the highly satisfying conclusion. Overall, Desert Brave is a must-read for fans of moving personal journeys of discovery, nature, and survival.
–*Readers' Favorite*

This book is dedicated to my mother, Ella Jeanne Colbert Oglesby.
From her lap, I heard my first story and read my first words.
She taught me to love all things.
She gave me life and she lives on within me.

Thank you, Mom.

Desert Brave

PROLOGUE

Abdul was in trouble. As vizier, it was hard enough to manage Caliph Amir's household on a calm day, but tonight was the caliph's birth-year feast and Abdul had to make sure everything went according to plan. Scurrying down the long corridor, he checked his scroll again. No mention of the strangers was on his list, but his informants told him even now they were approaching from the southeast. To make matters worse, no one recognized their tribal colors of turquoise, white, and gold. *This is a disaster! Are they friend or foe?* No one knew, but Abdul had to find the answer, or his life would be on the line.

This was not the first time Abdul had faced such a decision. Rising to his present position in the caliph's service had taken a lifetime of hard work. His was an enviable position, and he was constantly on guard for the jealous few who tried to usurp him. Ever vigilant, Abdul knew he could let no one find fault with his judgment, especially when it involved the safety of the caliph. He would have to bring it to the attention of the caliph.

He dreaded showing his ignorance, but he knew how easy it would be for an enemy to sneak inside unseen, especially with so many invited guests arriving all day long. Pausing at the tall, gilded doors leading to the caliph's private chambers, Abdul straightened his clothes. Assuming a mask of calm, he knocked twice and waited for the guards to answer. He was admitted at once. After passing through two more rooms, he found Caliph Amir lounging on a low couch, surrounded by several of his harem who were busy seeing to his needs, offering wine and fruit. Abdul bowed low and waited to be acknowledged.

Amir motioned him forward. "Abdul, how go the preparations for my celebration? Is all in readiness?"

"Yes, Exalted One, all is progressing well. It will be a wonderful feast and your wealth and style will impress all who attend," Abdul gushed.

Amir studied his vizier intently. "Abdul, why do you spread honey with your tongue when there is no bread present?"

"I speak only the truth, Majestic One, when I say that everyone is looking forward to the celebration tonight. No invitation was refused, and it has been the talk of the region. It truly will be an event to be written in history," he answered. When the caliph did not respond, Abdul tried not to squirm under his dark gaze as his mind raced to explain the uninvited strangers that were on their way. "In fact, everyone invited is already here, or will be shortly. I would not be surprised if a few uninvited guests show up to pay honor to the great and blessed Caliph Amir," he added hastily. As he spoke, Abdul looked about the room at everything but the caliph. The ensuing silence made him nervous, and he was forced to meet the piercing eyes of Amir.

"Abdul, what is it you're telling me by not telling me?" Amir said as he took a sip from his jeweled cup.

"Well, it seems there are six guests arriving from the southeast, and they are not on my list. I am sure it is my oversight and ask your forgiveness for my error," he humbly answered, bending his head to study his own jeweled slippers.

"Abdul, I have always relied on your efficiency and your ability to know everything going on in my palace, even things you should not know," said Amir.

Abdul paled, but wisely said nothing.

"Therefore, I can assume if you do not recognize these 'guests,' then neither will I." Abdul sat up to better consider the matter. "Hmmm, perhaps they are merely passing through on their way to another destination? Or they could even be lost," he speculated aloud while stroking his carefully groomed goatee.

"If I may be so bold, master," Abdul said, raising his head. "There are six men on horseback, leading one spare horse and two camels laden with supplies. As they are dressed in finery befitting a celebration, I would guess they are here to pay homage to the all-powerful caliph."

"Your instincts are usually good, my devoted one," Amir said. "I will allow them to approach and will offer my hospitality." He added a final command. "Tell Saif to send an escort to bring them into the stronghold. It is easier to avoid the cobra's bite when you keep him in plain sight. Now, I must make ready." He rose abruptly, scattering his harem like so many jeweled butterflies, and retired to his bedchamber.

"Yes, your Excellency." Abdul bowed low and hurried back to his duties. *Praise Allah for giving my caliph a generous nature.* He had done the right thing by bringing the matter to the caliph's attention and was relieved at not being held responsible for the unexpected visitors.

Hastening to the courtyard where the festivities were to be held, Abdul was pleased to see torches and potted palms placed at the entrance and giant oil-filled pots atop tall pedestals along the two stone walls flanking the open area. Low tables were set on each side, and at the far end was a raised circular dais inlaid with colorful mosaic tiles where Amir would sit upon an elaborately carved chair. The opening festivities were timed to begin when the rays of the setting sun would illuminate the dais. Following sunset, Amir and the leaders of each visiting band would retire to the feast hall to dine while the others remained outside for the informal celebration.

Abdul found Saif, the captain of the caliph's guards, assigning men to strategic points at the entrance, along the sides, and atop the walls of the courtyard. Relaying his message, Abdul listened as the captain ordered a dozen men to ride out and escort the strangers into the stronghold.

Satisfied, Abdul returned to inspect the feast hall. Tables were arranged in a U-shaped pattern and servants were busy setting out goblets, plumping pillows, and spreading rugs, while the musicians in one corner tuned their instruments. Tall vases around the room held huge palm fronds that would be used to fan the guests and to help ventilate the air that would become dense with the odors of hot food, sweaty bodies, and smoke from the hookah pipes. Seeing all was in order, Abdul returned to the kitchen, arriving just in time to stop the cook from carving more than the mutton. He broke up a squabble and was soon lost in the general chaos.

Abdul forgot about the mysterious strangers for the next two hours until he was summoned to the courtyard. Time was growing short, and he fairly flew down the corridors and outside to find Saif waiting by the dais. "What did you find out about the strangers?" Abdul asked.

"They are from the southern mountains," Saif said as they walked toward the entrance. "They said they are searching for new breeding stock for their herd." He paused to scan the placement of his men on the nearest wall.

Abdul digested this information. It was not unusual for strangers to come seeking breeding stock, as the caliph was known for his fine horses. "And what is your opinion of these men, Saif?"

Saif turned his eyes back to meet those of the vizier. "They are well armed, but that is as it should be when one travels the deep desert. Their manner is courteous and respectful, but their horses..." His voice trailed off as he gazed toward the pass leading into the stronghold.

"What about their horses?" Abdul asked, watching the captain's face closely. He could tell Saif was excited about what the scouts had seen.

"Their horses are magnificent," he exclaimed. "But that is nothing compared to the stallion!"

"Stallion? What kind of stallion?" Abdul's curiosity was piqued. The desert tribes valued their horses over all their possessions. Horses were considered a gift from Allah and represented great wealth, and the stallions were the backbone of a tribe's herd strength.

"There is only one kind of stallion, Abdul." Saif laughed, unable to resist teasing the feisty vizier. "But my men tell me this stallion has no equal in our lands. He is touched by the sun!" He could not hide his own impatience to confirm the scouts' report.

"Well, well, well." Abdul stroked his chin and mused aloud, "It seems our visitors grow more interesting by the minute. But everyone knows the caliph is always looking for good horses, and this may be just a ruse to gain entrance to his palace. What do you think? Are they a threat?"

"If I thought they were, their blood would even now be spilling into the sand," Saif scornfully replied. "There are only six of them, after all. Their numbers do not worry me, but they made one unusual request. They wish to be the last group presented to the caliph."

"Why is that so unusual?" Abdul asked as they turned to walk back towards the palace.

"Because…" Saif paused dramatically, "they wish to be presented on horseback!"

"On horseback? That *is* unusual." Abdul pondered this development, but upon seeing the first of the guests entering the arch, he knew time had run out. "Well, the caliph has granted their request, but commands you to send an escort. I will leave it to you. Now, I must change." He hurried off, his robes flapping around him.

• • •

As Amir ascended the dais, bathed with thick golden rays from the western sun, a flurry of drumbeats rang out and the tribes erupted with a cacophony of yells. Smiling, he signaled the first of the tribal leaders to come forward. A long procession followed as the leaders were announced and escorted to the dais, where they renewed their oaths to him. Just before sundown, a lone trumpet rang out, and the crowd fell silent, watching the caliph, who was watching the arched entrance with a rapt expression.

Before speculation could begin, the growing thunder of hoofbeats drew the crowd's attention to the entrance. The spectators were astonished when, with a burst of ferocious yells, six horsemen in robes of white, banded in gold and turquoise, galloped into the courtyard. At the last minute, they split formation, alternating left and right, until they formed a semi-circle in front of the dais. Sliding back on their haunches, six magnificent horses, three black and three white, reared in unison before coming to a stamping, snorting stop. The light from the setting sun shone from their strangely iridescent coats, creating glimmering halos around their flowing manes and tails. The crowd was stunned, and Amir rose from his chair at the spectacle.

What happened next was even more astonishing. The horses dropped to one knee and bowed before Amir. Sounds of amazement rolled in waves around the plaza, turning to awe, when a piercing neigh rang out and a bolt of shining gold charged through the arch. A shimmering golden stallion raced toward the caliph and slid to a halt before the dais, pawing and huffing. A silken mane adorned with beads of gold and turquoise flowed from its arched neck almost to the ground.

The crowd fell silent. Amir stepped forward, and when the horse's flashing dark eyes met his, he recognized an intelligence and spirit to match his own. Riderless, the horse remained in position while one stranger dismounted and approached.

"Your Eminence," the strapping dark-haired man spoke from bended knee. "My name is Tahar, and I bring greetings from my tribe. We have long heard of your power, and people know you as a fair and just leader of men. Your horses have an excellent reputation, and we have come seeking breeding mares, but were unaware of your celebration. We humbly apologize for arriving uninvited."

Amir could not help himself. Drawn to the great stallion, he made his way down the steps to the younger man's side and laid a hand on his shoulder. "Rise and introduce me to this animal."

Tahar stood and called to the stallion, who neighed in response and trotted forward. Amir marveled at the beauty of the animal and cautiously extended one hand, waiting patiently while the noble beast sniffed his palm. Their eyes met again, and Amir relaxed at the sign of acceptance he saw there.

Chuckling faintly, he moved closer and stroked the silken nose. Mesmerized by the color of its coat, he was even more fascinated by the texture. The iridescent hair was fine and sleek, as if nothing would stick to it, and was unlike anything he had ever seen or felt before. "What is his name?"

"Farid," Tahar said.

"Yes, you are well named, for you are indeed 'unique'," Amir said. Then he murmured under his breath, "And you are worth all the gold in my kingdom." He turned to Tahar, ready to bargain. "Just what would you ask for this miserable creature?"

Tahar's eyebrows shot upward at the slur, but he had played this game before. "Miserable creature?" he sputtered. "Why, this stallion is the best horse in the region! There is none faster!"

Amir walked around the stallion, noting the sturdy legs and deep chest. "You have certainly been too long in the desert, my friend," he jested with Tahar, thoroughly enjoying the exchange. "The only truth that you have told me is the obvious fact that he is a stallion."

"Well, I heard the caliph was an excellent judge of horses, but appears I was misinformed." Tahar shook his head ruefully. "Perhaps we should move on and find someone else willing to trade a few good mares for the chance to improve their herd."

Amir grinned and laughed. "Come, Tahar. Your men and horses are tired from their long travels. I would hate to have it said you were turned away from our gates, especially on such a day as today. I seem to recall I may have a few extra mares that would certainly improve your herd. From the looks of this poor beast, you are in great need. You must join my feast tonight, and tomorrow my captain, Saif, will introduce you to my herdmaster who will show you the mares I have to offer," he said, motioning for his captain.

"I would be honored to sit at your table," Tahar said with a bow. "But I must beg your indulgence once more. I wish to say farewell to Farid. It is hard to part with one of my treasures. Golden stallions are as rare as water in the desert."

"I will grant you time to see him safely settled," Amir said. As he was led away, the mighty stallion neighed one last time. The caliph, followed by the visiting leaders, retired to the feast hall, and soon music echoed from the rafters as the harem girls danced before the guests.

When Tahar returned, he was seated not far from the head table. The other guests found him to be polite but distant. The young man intrigued Amir, who watched him from the corner of his eye, noting he appeared to enjoy his meal, as well as the efforts of the dancing girls. Tahar smiled often, and Amir wondered at the younger man's flashing silver eyes. A rare color, he mused. But rarer still were Tahar's white robes banded in gold and turquoise—tribal colors Amir had never seen. He wanted to find out more about these visitors with their shimmering horses from the distant mountains.

As Tahar leaned forward to refill his cup, Amir glimpsed a large medallion suspended from a woven chain of gold around his neck. The medallion appeared to be made of beaten gold set with flashing yellow gems surrounded by turquoise stones in a strange random pattern. It was not an attractive piece, and he wondered at its significance, but before he could speculate further, a sudden increase in the tempo of the drums interrupted him. Ah, another wonderful gift has arrived, he thought as a whirling figure in crimson silks danced across the floor. The men howled their approval, and the lovely girl consumed all his thoughts for the rest of the evening.

Amir did not think about Tahar and his glorious horses until well after the sun had cleared the eastern peaks the next day. Abdul informed him the white-berobed men had departed at first light and Amir was slightly miffed but was confident his men could locate Tahar's tribe later. Dismissing further thought of the stranger, he hurried to the stable to admire his new golden stallion.

A few weeks passed before the caliph thought about his uninvited guests again. The men he sent to look for Tahar's mountain home found no trace of the strangers, and the few travelers they met had only heard of them through local legends. Discouraged and low on supplies, the men returned with tales of dreadful sandstorms, ferocious desert lions, and endless barren mountains.

Over time, the caliph's horses became known for their stamina, strength, and intelligence, but though he bred his new stallion to every color mare available, he never sired another golden stallion, only golden mares, and they were few. Amir puzzled over this mystery, and every few years, his desire for another golden stallion drove him to send more expeditions in search of the elusive tribe, but he never saw or heard from Tahar again.

Farid lived to a ripe old age, and upon his death, the caliph buried him in the courtyard where he first saw him. As the years passed, his people forgot the mysterious guests and their shimmery mounts, but the memory of the golden stallion lived on through the rare golden mares of the caliph's herd. The world marched onward, and empires rose and fell until, eventually, the relentless winds of the desert echoed through the crumbling ruins of the caliph's palace and the last evidence of the golden horses disappeared beneath the endless Arabian sands.

CHAPTER 1

The silver nose of the aircraft sliced through the desert sky that stretched toward the hazy, brown peaks of the far-off mountain range. Squinting against the harsh rays of sunshine reflecting off the wings and piercing the cabin window, Kira Fontaine settled deeper into the worn seat as she scanned the monotonous dunes below. With no clouds or point of reference, the plane appeared to be suspended over a sea of golden sand.

Turning her attention back to the interior of the plane, Kira glanced down the aisle at the few seats, their bent frames, speckled with rust, hosted cracked leather pads so depressed from previous use it was as if they still had ghostly backsides firmly planted in place. An odd assortment of bags and slatted crates were strapped to one another or to iron pull rings on the floor and contained an assortment of supplies and equipment.

Her father, Jon, searched the arid regions of the world, determined to locate life-giving waters to aid the growing population of mankind. Working with core samples and geological histories, he searched for underground sources of water. While the United States fought in the first world war, her father worked under the direction of the U.S. Government, and Kira finished her education. When the war ended, he returned to his search, and she worked by his side. His dream became her dream.

When her father announced he was heading to Arabia, she was thrilled. World War I was over, and the news was awash with stories of fantastic archeological finds in Egypt. She was eager to see them for herself. During their stopover in Cairo, while her father organized the next leg of their journey, Kira spent time at the local university to gain insights into Middle Eastern history, culture, and language. She was enjoying herself until the day they arrived at the airfield to board the cargo plane and she saw who was going with them. Kira had not counted on spending any time with Cassandra Miller.

Through half-closed eyes, Kira watched as the cause of her disappointment made her way down the aisle between seats.

"Wake up, honey. Would you like a drink of water, or maybe some milk?" Cassie asked in her best woman-to-little child voice.

Kira hid her irritation. She hated being treated like a child and answered with faux politeness, "No thank you, Miss Miller. And I wasn't sleeping. I was thinking about our next stop. I find it all very fascinating."

Cassie snorted. "Fascinating? What's so fascinating about sand, sand, and more sand? Nothing but sand and sun and barbaric nomads. Believe you me, you'll get tired of it, too. It's so dull." She didn't hide her scorn, and her tone sharpened. "We have four more hours of this boring ride before we reach the oasis—if it's even there. And you better stay away from that window. Your nose is already a mess of freckles." She wiggled away and the loud sounds of her laughter bounced behind her.

Silently fuming at the parting barb, Kira clenched her fists. *Why does everyone treat me like a child? I'm almost twenty-one. I may be slim, but I still look like a woman except for these darn freckles.* She sighed and tried to ignore the insults from her father's latest lover. Her mood ruined and unable to relax, Kira rose and went to see her father in the cockpit. Pushing the door open, she walked forward and tapped him on the shoulder.

Jon Fontaine glanced back at his daughter. White even teeth flashed in his tanned face as he spoke. "Not bored, are you?" Laughing, he added, "No, not you. You're just like your mother." His clear, blue eyes momentarily darkened with a flash of remembered pain. "Well, what do you think of this desert? Not quite as big as some you've seen, but I think you'll find it a lot more inhospitable."

Laughing in return, Kira smiled and gave him a light kiss on his forehead. "Of course, I find it exciting, as usual, but what makes this one so much more dangerous?"

"Oh, it's not just the desert," said Marco, always ready to supply answers to Kira's many questions. Marco was her father's longtime partner and co-pilot. Kira wasn't sure where her father had found him. Jon just showed up one day with Marco in tow. A jack of all trades, Marco soon became a valuable member in their expeditions. He was a fountain of information and could fix just about anything. "We're headed for the mountains of the northern Sinai. A dangerous place, Kira. These mountains have long been the stronghold of warring tribes who use them as a base for their raids in the surrounding areas. Not much is known about them except that they're fierce and bow to no one, and the only thing they value more than wealth are their horses. Men hold all the power and women are their slaves. Not a bad arrangement, some would say." Marco chuckled, knowing just how to push her buttons.

Kira's cheeks flushed with anger. "I think that's outrageous. I would never be a slave to a man. Why don't the women revolt?"

"Perhaps they enjoy their role. Besides, the young ones are sold to fill the sheiks' harems and are ensured an easy life. It is the only life they know. The older women expect nothing and spend their lives cooking and caring for their men." Marco turned back to his controls with a small smile, clearly waiting for the explosion that certainly would follow.

"Humph! They ARE barbarians!" Kira exclaimed with a shudder. Maybe Cassie was right, she thought, but Kira sure wouldn't admit that to Cassie.

"Now, now, girl, settle down and stow that temper. Enough questions. Why don't you fetch me something to drink? We still have a long trip ahead," her father said as he fiddled with the controls.

"Okay, Papa. Be right back." She kissed him on the cheek and hurried to comply. Returning to the hold, she found a metal cup and drew some water from one of the smaller cans stored in the back. When she stood up, she glanced out the nearest window, but the view had not changed, and she returned to the cockpit.

"Ah, relief has arrived." Jon released the controls to Marco and settled back to look at his only daughter. "Sit. Let's talk."

Kira sat down on the nearest thing she could find, his knee, and at once regretted doing something so childish. "I'm afraid I'm not the light-weight I used to be, Papa. Maybe I'd better move." She started to stand, but he stopped her.

"Nonsense, girl. You're slim as a reed and twice as light." He tugged gently on her long, golden hair. "When are you going to cut this mop?" he teased.

"Never! It's my one asset, and I'll never cut it. It's the only thing that keeps me from being completely plain."

"Plain, my foot," Jon exclaimed indignantly. "Why, you're the picture of beauty."

"Shush." She pressed her hand to his mouth. "You're just prejudiced. I might have been if I hadn't inherited your brains, your nose, and your height. No one wants a tall, smart girl with a big nose." She laughed.

"Well, at least you didn't inherit my feet." Jon winked at her, lifting one of his big boots, causing her to laugh harder.

Their lighthearted exchange was cut short by Cassie's arrival. "Well, how quaint, bouncing your little girl on your knee. And I thought she was too old for that." Kira jumped up, and Cassie wormed her way between them, leaning over to take the empty cup from Jon's hand, her pink silk top unbuttoned to display her "charms." "Darling, you should have told me you wanted a drink. I would have fetched you one," she admonished huskily. "You might have even talked me into sitting on your lap too, though I'm not quite as light as a child." Cassie cut her eyes to Kira, whose temper flared.

Marco came to Kira's rescue. "Indeed, Cassie. Kira needs to grow quite a bit to match your weight."

Cassie whirled around with a gasp. "Why you…"

"Now, Cassie," Marco said, enjoying himself. "Calm down, I was just kidding." He chuckled. Cassie turned and stomped out of the cockpit.

Kira struggled to hold back her amusement, at least until the door slammed. "Touché Marco! And thanks for coming to my rescue."

"Well, it is true," her father agreed with a chuckle. "Now, go sit down and keep your seat belt on." He turned his attention back to the controls.

Returning to her seat, Kira resigned herself to spending a few more hours with little to do except try to relax and catch a few winks. Watching Cassie in the aft section digging through the duffel bags, she knew Cassie was not happy to leave Cairo. Cassie had made it clear she did not enjoy field expeditions of any kind.

The true nature of Cassie's relationship with Kira's father did not escape her, and she hated her father had invited her along. Cassandra Miller, or Cassie, as she liked to be called, had been in the picture longer than any of his other "friends." She was also the youngest, not yet thirty years old. Kira's father had had a series of friends like Cassie ever since Kira's mother's death. Feeling a stab of pain from memories still fresh, Kira sighed and allowed her thoughts to drift back to her past.

Kira's mother had been fond of telling her about the day she met Jon, and Kira never tired of hearing the story. Her father, fresh out of an eastern college, was trekking through the deserts of Arizona when he stumbled upon the local Indian outpost. Kira was familiar with the outpost, having worked there herself when she was younger. It was owned and operated by her mother's tribe and served as a trading post, mail drop, and general meeting place.

According to her mother, it had changed little over the years. Long shelves were still piled high with every imaginable item, and low tables in the center of the room displayed blankets and clothing. Near the front door were rows of barrels, bristling with farming implements, including hoes, shovels, and picks. Painted pottery bowls filled with everything from hard candy to nails lined the counter, and a mammoth cash register perched like a bronzed gargoyle on one end. Intricately woven baskets of every color and shape, along with straw and felt hats, hung from the rafters.

Her mother claimed her father had the most beautiful sky-blue eyes and was the tallest man she had ever seen. Curiously, Jon was always showing up, needing unusual items that could only be found at the trading post. Jon would laugh when her mother told this part, admitting what Kira already figured out. He fell in love the minute he saw Tamara in her beaded shirt and deerskin skirt. When he met Tamara's mother, Grandmother Two Birds, for the first time, the old woman promptly pronounced him to be a "good man." Her father took that as a sign and wasted no time. They were married within the year.

Kira's grandmother was fond of reminding everyone how she knew about the baby before they did. By the following summer, Kira Fontaine had come into the world with bright blue-green eyes, golden hair, and skin the color of honey. The best of both worlds, Jon would say. Her parents celebrated by exchanging gifts. Tamara gave Jon a ring of silver, inlaid with turquoise, or sacred "sky stone" according to Zuni culture, and mother-of-pearl. He gave her a delicate filigree gold chain.

At the mission school, Kira excelled in her studies, especially science. She showed an affinity for languages, so she added English and Spanish to her repertoire. When she wasn't studying, she learned the ways of the Zuni, her mother's people, and Grandmother Two Birds was her favorite teacher. Soon, Kira could kill, skin, and cook everything from rabbit to elk, but never enjoyed it. What she enjoyed was weaving baskets and working at the trading post, where she fantasized about meeting her true love. But though she waited on many interesting young men who came to the Southwest intent on making their fortunes, no one really caught her eye.

When it was time to attend college, Kira threw herself into her studies, focusing on a degree in geology, but also signed up for courses in anthropology, archeology, and French. The first year would have been perfect except for the tragic loss of her mother. A freak train wreck claimed the life of Tamara when she was on her way to join Jon on one of his expeditions in the Northwest. Devastated, and unable to finish her second semester, Kira returned to the reservation and spent the next months in silent anguish, overcome with grief. Jon should have stayed with Kira and helped her through it, but he could not accept the loss of his wife and ran from reality, spending the next six months on a remote project in Alaska.

Missing him terribly, Kira felt like she had lost both her parents. It was Grandmother Two Birds who eventually broke through her lassitude, reminding her she must continue to follow her path in life. Kira' grandmother raised her with Zuni traditions, and Kira understood her grandmother's words, but she also accepted her Christian faith at a young age. In her heart, she knew that wallowing in grief without trusting in God was not acceptable. Praying to God for strength, Kira returned to her studies by the following spring.

Her instructors couldn't help noticing how she had changed, and her serious manner drove away the young men who wanted to get close. She spent her holidays with her grandmother and rarely saw her father, who never visited her at school. Eventually, she came to understand why—there were other women in his life now. But he never brought any home. Her grandmother would not allow it. Kira struggled to understand his need for the companionship of these mysterious women and felt the only way she could ever be close to him again would be to work by his side. It fueled her desire to earn her degree as soon as possible.

It all seemed so long ago now, she thought, and sighing, Kira pushed the old memories away and turned her thoughts to the journey ahead. Traveling in a land of little water, fuel, or airstrips was risky. Areas for landing were far apart, and fuel was hard to find. Most flights were spent meeting up with caravans and guides that could lead them by horse or camel into the more remote areas. They were heading towards such a place, and she hoped they would land soon.

Her father had purchased maps from the Museum of Antiquities in Cairo, but they were based on mostly verbal accounts. Luckily, he found a man in the marketplace who possessed a map showing all the existing oases in the area they were heading to, near the edge of extensive foothills of a mountain range running south from the Mediterranean Sea. When her father asked the man for help in securing a guide and supplies for the second leg of their journey, the old fellow promised they would find what they needed at the large oasis near the foothills. He was eager to help. Too eager, Kira thought.

They purchased the map and were about to leave when the man suddenly pulled out a bag and showed them a large gold medallion and gold chain that he swore had been found in the same region. He insisted the medallion was a priceless antiquity and had magical powers. Clearly fascinated by it, her father had to have it, which Kira thought odd, as he had never shown much interest in owning artifacts before. Her nose wrinkled in remembrance of the pungent odor of hashish that clung to the man's robes. She found his story of the medallion fantastical and decided he was definitely one camel shy of a caravan. She didn't trust the man, but her father made the deal.

Sighing heavily and praying she was wrong about the old man, she closed her eyes, lulled by the deep rumble of the engines, and allowed her mind to drift into a familiar daydream of snow-clad hills glistening in the morning sun. She could feel the crisp wind that sent small snow devils dancing between the tall pines' dark green skirts. Redbirds and blue jays flitted among the lower branches, and Kira could hear the swish, swish of her skis on the trail. Breathing in clear, cold air, she raced along, taking the small hummocks with practiced ease, barely feeling the light jarring of her skis reconnecting with the trail's hard packed surface.

Exhilarated, she raced faster and faster, until the rises and irregularities became more pronounced. Bump, jolt, and bump! Odd, she mused in dream- thought, it almost feels too real. Bump and bump again! Kira jolted back into reality as the slick mountain slopes faded and transformed into the smooth sides of the aircraft's belly.

Bucking and lurching, the plane shuddered and slid through the sky. Startled, she glanced out the window at the white nothingness, pressing her face to the hot glass, and looked down to see the desert floor alarmingly close. Hearing the sputtering engines, she knew their erratic flight was not because of air turbulence. Her first concern was her father. Releasing her seatbelt, she fought her way to the cockpit, threading between the shifting cargo.

Cassie's screamed, "What's happening?"

"Stay in your seat!" Kira cautioned in passing. "I'll see what's going on." When the plane dipped earthward in a gradual nosedive, she stumbled forward into the cockpit. "Papa! What's happening?" she shouted over the erratic roar of the prop engines as she grasped the back of the pilot's seat to keep from falling. Her father was fighting to control their descent when one engine exploded suddenly with a smoky bang, failing completely. Marco frantically flipped control switches to restart the engine, but to no avail.

Jon yelled out what reassurance he could. "Kira, help Cassie prepare for a crash landing and get back to your seat and strap in! I'm going to put her down!"

Her heart beating wildly, she staggered back to the hold. Cassie's eyes rolled, and her teeth were bared in a frozen grimace. Seeing she was in shock, Kira grabbed a bedroll and shoved it into the redhead's lap. "Here, take this and hug it tightly." Cassie's white-knuckled hands clutched the bedding desperately. "And keep your head down and bend over the roll!" Kira shouted as she grabbed an overstuffed duffel and assumed her own crash position.

The remaining engine sporadically rumbled, punctuated by explosive bangs, and the plane lurched sideways. Closing her eyes, Kira hugged the dusty duffel ever tighter and prayed. But she cried out when the second engine erupted with a final explosive bang. The sudden silence was more frightening than all the engines' malfunctions. The hold filled with the high-pitched scream of whistling wind as they rushed earthward. As the plane clipped the top of several dunes, Cassie screamed, but Kira was too terrified to make a sound.

When the plane lifted like it would once more gain the heavens, she watched in terror as her hair floated upward and the world became a topsy-turvy place as bags and boxes floated up and down. Overwhelmed by nausea and fear, Kira slipped into darkness when the plane slammed into an unyielding dune.

Her last sight was her mother's face. At first it was only a fuzzy image, but as it sharpened, Kira raised her arms and called to her. Her mother lifted one graceful finger to her lips in a shushing motion, and her warm brown eyes seemed to say, "It's all right. I'm here." Filled with contentment and feeling safe, Kira smiled. Her mother was here. Soon things would be set to right. She would sleep and not worry about the noises in the night. Embracing the descending darkness, she watched her mother's haunting image fade away.

CHAPTER 2

Kira woke to a world gone crazy. Struggling to clear her head, she knew immediately that she was hanging upside down from her seat. She was afraid to make any sudden moves, but before she could decide how best to proceed, the rotting fabric of the old seat belt gave way. Luckily, the ceiling, now the floor, was not far, and she fell on top of the duffel she had used for a crash cushion. Sputtering and sore, she clambered into a sitting position, stunned as she gazed at her surroundings.

Wails and whimpers rose from a pile of bags not far away, and she saw a very shaken Cassie struggling to rise. When Kira smelled the pungent odor of fuel, she knew the danger of explosion was imminent, but instead of escaping the plane, she hastened to the cockpit. Clawing her way over loose and broken cargo, she discovered several crates were blocking the door. Using hidden strength, she pulled them out of the way.

The scene in the cockpit would be forever engraved in Kira's memory. Her father and Marco hung suspended from their harnesses, wrapped in wreckage. The plane's windshield had shattered into a thousand pieces, piercing their bodies. Spilling in through the windshield, the creeping sand formed small dunes beneath them, and she watched in horror as drops of her father's blood fell upon the golden mounds, only to vanish like the precious water he had searched for all his life.

Kira broke the eerie silence with a low moan that rose to a heartrending cry and tried to reach her father's dangling arms. But when she stepped closer, she stumbled on the wreckage and fell forward. Shards of glass cut into her hands and knees and the sharp pain forced her to regain her feet. She grabbed his hand, but she couldn't detect a pulse. Overwhelmed with grief, she pressed his hand to her cheek, and tears coursed down her face as she leaned forward, calling to him and crying steadily.

The acrid smell of spilled fuel brought her back to her senses, and she brushed her tears away with a bloody hand, leaving red streaks across her face. Reaching over, she steeled herself to check Marco for a pulse, only to find that he, too, was dead. Battling for control, she bent her head, closed her eyes, and took a few deep breaths. When she opened them, her eyes were drawn to a glint of gold in the debris on the floor beneath her feet. *The medallion!* Reaching down, her fingers tightened around the medallion and chain that her father had been wearing. Wiping away the sand and blood clinging to it, she turned it over to study the oddly placed turquoise stones and bright yellow gems. The metal was still warm from her father's body, and she felt a strange sensation when she touched it. Shaking off the odd feeling, she placed the medallion around her neck, tucked it inside her shirt, and steeled herself for the onerous task of releasing Jon's body.

Startled by the screech of the cockpit door being wrenched farther open, Kira turned to see Cassie worming her way forward, just as Jon's body fell to the floor. A long scream broke the silence when Cassie saw her lover's ravaged face. Kira could not take the continuous high-pitched keening and slapped her hard across the cheek. Stunned, Cassie's hands flew to her face, and she ceased her incessant noise.

"Help me get him out of here," Kira growled at her as she tugged his big shoulders.

Averting her eyes, Cassie added her weak efforts to Kira's, and together they dragged his body into the aft area. The side door was loose, and when they pushed it out, they were assaulted by a flood of blinding heat. Because of the plane's position, it was a ten-foot drop to the sand below. Rigging a sling using a blanket and rope, Kira was able to lower his body and followed by shimmying down the rope. When she reached the ground, her legs crumpled, and she lay on the hot sand near her father, trying to catch her breath. She rested a few more minutes and briefly considered going back for Marco until the threat from the spilled fuel and Cassie's fearful whimpers from above forced her to reconsider. "Come on, Cassie! You've got to get out of there! There may be an explosion. You'll be killed!" she yelled.

"Noooo, noooo, I can't. It's too far!" Cassie wailed, gripping the doorframe tightly.

"Cassandra!" Kira shouted in exasperation. "Climb down now or you'll burn to death!"

Cassie tried to slide down the rope but lost her grip and fell with a thud. She roused enough to squirm weakly to Kira's side.

Kira hated leaving her father's body, but she had to be realistic. It was just too dangerous. Grabbing Cassie by the arm, she jerked her into a sitting position. "Get going. Over that dune." Together they crawled over the top of the nearest dune, and Kira cowered next to a trembling Cassie, waiting for the explosion from the spilled fuel that she was sure would ignite. Minutes passed, but the silence remained unbroken, save for the occasional hiss of the smoldering engines.

Fearfully, she eased over the dune to regard the wreckage, the sight weirdly distorted by the blistering heat rising in shimmering waves from the sand. She could see where the plane had slammed into the middle of one particularly large dune, with enough force to crumple the nose and flip it over and down the other side. Deep furrows from the plane's passage were already filling with the ever-shifting sand. Soon, there would be nothing to mark the skidding path of the plane to its final resting place. In time, Kira knew the plane itself would disappear beneath the sand.

Ironic, she thought sadly, as she lifted a handful of the golden sand, letting it dribble through her fingers. It was warm and yielding to the touch, making her forget its hidden strength. She knew it consisted of tiny particles of silicone, or glass, deceptively soft, but collectively it represented an intensely hard surface. *Cursed sand, cursed desert!* Her father's obsession to reclaim the arid regions of the world had robbed her of the most important thing in her life.

Angry, she threw the remaining grains aside and turned her attention back to the wreck. It would be dangerous to go near the plane before the fuel had evaporated, but exposure to the unrelenting heat beating down on her shoulders made her aware of another danger. Shading her eyes with one grimy hand, she searched for Cassie. The woman was curled up at the bottom of the dune, unmoving. Kira half slid, half crawled to her side.

"Get up, Cassie!" Kira nudged the still form. With the danger of dehydration, they would both be in trouble soon if they didn't get water and shade. Urging Cassie into a sitting position, Kira felt a small tinge of compassion when she saw the woman's vacant green eyes inflamed by tears and dust. "Oh, Cassie," she said. "We need to get you in the shade and see if you're hurt, but first, I need to make sure it's safe." She slid back down to the dune and cautiously surveyed the area near the wreckage for spilled fuel. One wing was missing, and the other wing dangled by pieces of twisted metal. The fuel had drained from the damaged tanks in the wings, and what had not evaporated was even now being absorbed by the sand. Satisfied the danger had passed, Kira helped Cassie back to the wreck, where they collapsed in the meager shade cast by the half-buried hull.

After resting a few minutes, Kira licked her dry lips, aware of her increasing thirst. Needing water, she steeled herself for the pain of more movement and searched for an easier entry point into the plane. She found it through a narrow split in the half-buried tail section.

Rummaging through the scattered cargo, she located the duffel bags she sought—hers, one of Cassie's, one of her father's, as well as Marco's. Belatedly, she thought of Marco still hanging in the wrecked cockpit, but she didn't have the strength to release him right now. Dragging the duffels outside, she returned to gather food and water. Most of the water containers had been damaged, but a few were intact, and she lugged them outside. When she paused to catch her breath, she noticed Cassie was missing.

Hearing muttered curses from over a nearby dune, Kira followed Cassie's tracks and discovered the reason for her disappearance. Cassie was furiously digging through Jon's bag. "Stop it," Kira yelled and started forward, only to be enveloped in a large khaki shirt tossed in her direction. Throwing the shirt aside, she bent down and grabbed Cassie by the arm. "What are you doing with my father's bag?"

"Money! I know he kept extra money in his bag. Where is it?" She jerked loose from Kira and continued her search.

To Kira's horror, she saw her father's money belt on the ground at Cassie's feet. Cassie had taken it from his body. "Give me that!" Kira reached for the belt.

Cassie was ready for her and grabbed the belt, clutching it to her chest. "No, it's mine, you stupid little half-breed! I earned it!" she screeched.

"Oh, I don't think so." Kira wasn't giving up without a fight and rushed forward.

Cassie turned to flee but stumbled and slid farther down the dune's sandy slope. Kira slid after her, seizing her by the arms, and both women tumbled, rolling and sputtering, to the base of the dune. When they pulled apart, Kira triumphantly held her father's belt, and hurriedly wound it around her waist. While Cassie sat and fumed, Kira gathered the items of her father's that Cassie had tossed aside and re-stuffed his duffel.

As much as she would have liked to walk away right then, Kira knew she couldn't do that, even to someone like Cassie. "We're going to have to stick together or neither of us is going to make it through this," she admonished the still glaring Cassie. "And right now, I need you to help me get Marco out of the plane."

"Me? Help you? I couldn't care less about Marco." She turned with a huff and crawled back over the dune, seeking the meager shade cast by the wreckage.

Lugging the duffel, Kira followed. She couldn't leave Marco hanging in inside the plane. He had been a good friend and deserved a decent burial, too. Knowing now she couldn't count on Cassie's help, she squared her shoulders and headed to the cockpit.

Freeing him from the webbing didn't take long. Not strong enough to lower his body, she was forced to push it out where it fell to the sand below. Grimacing at the crude methods she had used, she slid down the rope still attached by the door and pulled his body over by her father's. Exhausted from the heat and stress, she knew she was running out of steam but needed to bury both men before she could move ahead with any other plans. After a brief rest and a long drink of water, she began the heart-rending task of preparing her father and Marco for burial.

Re-entering the plane, she located a smashed crate of digging tools and gathered several useful items. Placing the tools and gear on top of a blanket, she dragged the lot back through the tear in the tail section. Seeing Cassie sitting with her knees drawn to her chest, Kira contemplated asking her for help again, but one look into those hard green eyes led her to discard that idea.

Digging was difficult. As soon as she scraped the sand away, more spilled into the hole. Frustrated, she had to accept that her father's final resting place would be different than what she planned. Easing him into the slight depression she had dug, she gently arranged his limbs and, swallowing thickly, removed the shards of glass from his body and cleaned his face as best she could.

Removing her father's silver ring from his left pinkie, she choked back a sob as she studied its banded turquoise face. It was the ring her mother had given him upon Kira's birth, and as she turned it back and forth, the inscription inside the band caught her attention. "Thank you for Kira. Love always. TF." She slipped it on her mother's filigree chain she wore around her neck. The ring joined the medallion, both touching her chest in rhythmic, heartbeat fashion with each movement of her continued, sorrowful task.

As she straightened his arms and legs, she suddenly remembered another personal item he always carried with him. She found what she sought in his trouser pocket. A small, round leather case containing a miniature compass. Stifling a sob, she remembered giving it to him after her mother died, with the words, "To help you find your way back to me." Gritting her teeth, she wiped the tears from her eyes, resolved to mourn another day. Stuffing the compass in her own pocket, she smoothed his hair, kissed his forehead, and laid a blanket over his body. As she covered him, she was struck by the cruel irony of how he had ended up like the precious water he sought, sinking beneath the sand. Remembering that deserts were full of predators and scavengers, she wasn't satisfied until she piled pieces of the plane's wreckage over the mound. She felt compelled to make a wooden cross with broken pieces from one crate and beat it into the ground by his grave.

Once she finished with her father, she directed her attention to Marco. After laying both men to rest, she was so tired that erecting the small tent she found was all she could do. Her last act was to retrieve the trail rations Marco had packed from the plane. The dried meat and day-old bread had no taste, but she was too exhausted to care. When Kira doled out a small portion to Cassie, the woman acted like she was about to say something but must have thought better of it after seeing the look in Kira's eyes. Cassie eagerly consumed her food and made quick work of the water.

Knowing now that she could not trust Cassie, Kira dragged her father's duffel into the tent. Using one of her father's bunched up shirts for a pillow, she curled on her side, breathing the faint but comforting scent of his cologne. Emotionally spent, she watched the glaring white light darken and become a golden glow before it faded into lavender, and listened to the faint hiss of the rising wind as it buffeted the musty canvas of the tent.

Remembering how cold the desert could be at night, she thought about Cassie, who was still sitting outside. Kira was still angry with her and considered letting her suffer, but her inherent kindness won out, and she called to her, "It's going to be dark soon and quite cold." After a few moments, Cassie crawled inside and settled down next to her. Neither of them spoke any words, and both gave in to the exhaustion of the long day.

CHAPTER 3

The next morning, Kira awoke to see faded tan canvas stretched over her head and, for a moment, didn't recognize her surroundings. When she tried to rise, she was assailed by a multitude of aches and pains and flooded with memories and emotions as she remembered the events of the previous day.

Clenching her eyes against the blinding light pouring through the tent opening, she forced her abused limbs to respond and crawled outside, pushing past the curled form of the still sleeping Cassie. Gazing about, her eyes fell upon the rude pyre she had constructed to protect her father's body, and she drew a steadying breath. He was dead, and so was Marco, and if she stayed here, she would be too.

Being so far from any known civilized habitation, it was unlikely the plane would ever be found, and their meager supplies wouldn't last long. Wiping her flushed face with the back of her sleeve, she had to choose some course of action, but she was afraid, until she remembered something else her grandmother told her—within everyone was a brave warrior waiting to be summoned. Resolved to find a way home, Kira reached deep and found hers.

Studying the hand-drawn map she found in her father's duffel, she easily located their point of departure from Cairo. Since their destination, the large oasis at the base of the foothills, was well marked, she could assume their general direction. Unfortunately, she didn't know the total distance between the two points. Her father had mentioned they would arrive before nightfall, so based on the time of the crash, she concluded they might have another seventy-five miles to go. Not that far for an airplane, but on foot, they would be lucky to reach the oasis in four days.

With this information, Kira took stock of their food and water. They had plenty of water, a good quantity of dried meat, and some crusty bread. The problem was how to carry it. They could only carry so much, and water was the most important item. Unfortunately, it was also the heaviest. Kira could barely lift even one of the heavy cans.

It was Marco's penchant for wine that led to the solution of their water transportation problem. In his duffel, she found the two waterskins full of wine he always magically produced, no matter where they were. These wonderful crescent-shaped bags, made of treated leather, were carried by braided shoulder straps. She emptied one waterskin, allowing the rich red liquid to drain into the sand, but Cassie knocked her off balance, almost making her drop the second one.

"What are you doing, you little savage? You're wasting perfectly good wine!" Cassie screeched, trying to wrench the waterskin from Kira's grasp.

Kira frowned at her words. Cassie was always quick to remind her of Kira's mixed Anglo-Native American heritage, although never within hearing of Jon. She obviously meant to insult Kira, but couldn't know it only strengthen Kira's pride. Kira had grown used to the slur on her ancestry during the time she spent at the "white man's" school and had long ago learned to deal with it. But now and then, it could still stir her temper, especially when it came from the likes of Cassie. With new determination, Kira yanked the waterskin free and stumbled away from Cassie. "Let go, you fool!"

They stood a few feet apart and eyed each other warily. Kira's eyes, normally the soft turquoise of tropical waters, darkened to the blue-green of glacial ice, and Cassie wisely backed away. Cassie picked up the first waterskin, squeezing it fitfully.

"Cassie, the nearest help is at least forty miles that way," Kira said, pointing toward the eastern horizon. "Just how long do you think you would last without water? We need some way of carrying it, at least three days' worth. These waterskins won't hold much, but if we're careful, and travel at night, they might be enough to get us to the oasis. Now, unless you're prepared to help, I suggest you stay the hell away from me."

Cassie dropped the waterskin in disgust, and with a final "harrumph," a sound that reminded Kira of a market-place camel, tossed her long red curls, and returned to the shade of the tail section where she reclined on a pile of folded canvas. "Little know-it-all," Cassie hissed as she fussed with the tarps, adjusting them for her maximum comfort. "See if I ever help her again." She closed her eyes and pulled the edge of one tarp over the top of her head to block out the incessant sun.

Ignoring Cassie, Kira focused on securing water for their travel. Once she figured out how to transfer the water from the large containers, she was able to fill both waterskins. It was not really enough, but with careful rationing, it might suffice. Setting them in the shade, she dug through the crates and bags to produce an assortment of other handy items: weatherproof matches, her father's knife in its leather sheath, another folding knife, a small hatchet, a length of thin climbing rope, and a first aid kit.

Next, she packed two knapsacks. Knowing Cassie's limitations, she filled Cassie's pack with dried food, matches, and one blanket, leaving some room for a few personal things. The pack she fixed for herself contained the rest of the items. She chose only a few pieces of clothing—a pair of socks, khaki pants, a short-sleeved shirt, one of her father's shirts, and a change of underclothes.

After she finished, she mentally prepared herself for the march ahead. It would be freezing at night, but that would be better than the deadly heat of the day, or so she thought. They each had a long "burnoose," the hooded robe favored by the natives of the region. Though simple in design, it was remarkably effective in creating temporary shade during the heat of the day and surprisingly warm at night.

The noon sun had long since fallen westward when Kira finished her preparations. Retreating to a shady spot by the plane to wait for nightfall, she sat with her back against her old duffel and helped herself to as much water as she could drink. Knowing they were leaving most of it behind, she filled a cooking pot and took a sponge bath. She removed her shirt and camisole along with the medallion and the necklace with her father's ring, and, using one of her bandannas, lavishly washed her upper body.

A noise from the tail section drew her attention, and she met Cassie's questioning glare. "Well, we can't take it with us, now can we!" Growing uncomfortable as Cassie continued to stare, Kira finished faster than she had originally planned. Cassie sported a classic hourglass figure men found highly attractive, and Kira figured her own boyish, slim-hipped figure was the cause of Cassie's derisive stare.

Before donning a clean camisole, Kira dumped the dirty, blood-stained water, refilled the pan, and leaned forward to rinse the sand and dirt from her long tresses. Using one of her father's voluminous shirts as a towel, she wrapped her head, slipped into a clean camisole, and placed the medallion and necklace around her neck. After washing the dirty camisole and spreading it over a nearby crate to dry, she relaxed in the shade and munched on some dried meat.

Cassie had evidently decided Kira had a good idea because she stalked over to borrow the pan and had her own version of a sponge bath. Kira watched her surreptitiously as Cassie stripped completely and slowly rinsed the grime from her pale skin with a smug expression. Taken aback by the casual display, Kira realized she shouldn't be. Cassie seemed to enjoy showing off her voluptuous body any chance she got. Rolling over on her side, Kira stretched out and drifted off to sleep, keeping one hand on the money belt wrapped around her waist and the other clasping her father's ring and medallion.

When she awoke later, the approaching darkness was painting long shadows between the dunes. Like lush folds of rich purple velvet, the shadows pooled and snaked around the feet of the mighty dunes as far as she could see. Kira rose with purpose now and glanced over at Cassie's still form. "It's time we were moving out," she called, donning her shirt and the burnoose before securing the knapsack on her back. Adjusting to the added weight, she took a few tentative steps to make sure she could manage it. *I can do this. I must!* She slipped the waterskin over her shoulder and turned to see Cassie struggling with her allotted load.

"What did you put in my pack?" Cassie complained as she fumbled with the straps.

"I assure you, Cassie, you have the lighter load." She helped adjust Cassie's bulging bag and placed the second waterskin on Cassie's shoulder, but noticed Cassie also carried a small bag.

She gave Cassie a questioning stare, but all Cassie would say was, "I need my personal things." With a huff and an attempt at a shrug, the effect of which was greatly diminished by the pack, Cassie spun around.

Kira watched in grim amusement as Cassie almost toppled over with the unaccustomed weight of the gear. "Oh, well, it's your back," Kira said. Trudging up the nearest dune, she allowed herself one backward glance at the upside-down plane and the remains of their supplies strewn about on the sand. Pity they had to leave the tent, but they couldn't manage even that much extra weight. Her gaze rested on the two mounds topped by the silvered pieces of the wreckage and marked by spindly crosses, all that remained of her family, left here in the lonely desert. *How long before anyone discovers the plane or even reports it missing?*

Feeling the cooling breeze skipping over the tops of the dunes, ruffling the sleeves of her burnoose, she was aware of the insidious movement of the golden sand. The desert never stayed still, and the landscape was always changing. She thought the name "marching dunes" had been well earned, and she knew the sand would have its way, swallowing the remains of her past.

"Well, Columbus, which way do we go?" Cassie whined, interrupting Kira's morbid thoughts.

Ignoring her, Kira turned her back on the wreckage, squared her shoulders, and walked southeast on what she hoped was their last known heading. Behind her, the sand continued its everlasting dance, spreading a golden blanket over everything in its path, and obliterated any sign of their passage.

CHAPTER 4

Kira was miserable. Exhausted, she trekked through the shifting sand, her legs protesting every step as she fought to maintain her balance. Her heavy pack weighed on her shoulders and dragged her backwards. She wanted to rest again, but the cold was intense, and she had to keep moving to stay warm.

When the full moon rose into the blue-black sky, it cast a silvery glow over the endless dunes. It was a cloudless night, and the stars were on full display. Kira felt reassured as she spotted familiar constellations like Leo, the largest one, and the Bear, which included the Big Dipper. Recognizing the three brilliant stars that adorned Orion's belt, she was able to navigate by using Polaris, the brightest star to the north, and Canopus, the one constant to the south.

When the moon set and the sand changed from silver to pearly gray in the pre-dawn light, Kira chose a place to wait out the day. She welcomed the return of the sun, until mid-morning, when it became scorching, and though they made rude tents from their robes, the heat sapped their strength, baked their skin, and dehydrated their bodies. The rest of the day was pure hell, and she longed for the return of night.

Shading her eyes with one hand while searching the far horizon for any sign of the elusive foothills, Kira lost confidence. *I was crazy to think I could lead us to the mountains.* The shimmering sand was hard on her eyes, as well as her mind. Colors faded, muted and bleached by the sun, which filled the sky with blinding whiteness. The dunes merged with the horizon, and she lost perspective and felt disconnected from reality. With no distinguishing landmarks, getting off course was easy, and she thanked God for her father's battered compass.

They had both already seen the infamous "mirages" they had heard about in Cairo. Once, Cassie looked out from under her robe and jumped up in excitement, claiming to see camels and riders headed their way. Her excitement turned to dismay when the wavering "camels" came no closer, changing shape to become a flock of tall, leggy, crane-like birds, before dissipating all together.

Kira was astounded to see a herd of racing horses with flying manes and tails, not unlike the ones she saw back home in America. How she loved to see them running wild and free, their coats the colors of the desert—black, tan, cream, red, gray, spotted and dappled. They thundered through the canyons and around the mesas, flowing like waves over the land. Now, she watched in awe until the herd shimmered and disappeared, becoming nothing more than undulating streams of super-hot air.

The only good thing about the first day was its effect on Cassie, who was so worn out she didn't share her usual complaints. For this, Kira was thankful. She had grown tired of listening to Cassie on the first night's march, whining constantly about her blistered skin, the horrible condition of her hair, and the state of her wardrobe. But she couldn't help feeling sorry for Cassie's woe-be-gone state. Cassie's milky-white skin, of which she was so proud, was extremely vulnerable, and the desert sun was strong enough to burn through the weave of their robes.

Thanks to her Zuni background, Kira's skin tanned easily, but even she experienced burns under these conditions. Her hair, normally a mix of golden hues, was being bleached silver by the sun. She kept her long tresses in a single braid, tucked inside her shirt with the hood of her burnoose pulled down almost to her nose.

The evening approached and, as the sun melted into the dunes, they set out once more. Kira plodded along silently. Seeing Cassie's face devoid of hope, Kira was again assailed by doubt. *Is this the right direction?* Wondering if she had miscalculated the distance to the hills, and the distance they could effectively cover, she also worried about their water supply. It was disappearing fast. Weary and discouraged, she strived to move at a steady pace and tried to ignore the painful blisters that had formed on her feet. Too weakened to talk, she exerted all her energy on walking.

Halfway through the night, they stopped for a brief respite. While Cassie managed a nap, Kira remained awake rather than take a chance of sleeping too long. While they were moving, she had not been as aware of her surroundings, too focused on their path. As she sat on top of a dune with her arms clasped around her knees, she looked up, gazing in wonder at the thousands of stars floating in a blanket of deep dark blue. It was a magnificent sight and the perfect setting for the luminous moon. Even the dunes were less daunting without the harsh light of the sun and were now clothed in muted tones of purple, black, and silver.

She watched in awe as a shooting star streaked across the sky and fell toward the far horizon. A warrior returning to earth, her grandmother would say. Her tribe believed when a warrior died in battle, his spirit would ascend to the heavens to become a star, providing light and direction for his earthbound brothers below. He would serve there until he was needed once again, and then he would descend in a blaze of glory to be reborn.

As she gazed across the dunes, the moonlight transformed the sand into a carpet of shimmering sparkles, and Kira imagined the dunes were made of millions of fallen stars, brave warriors waiting to be reborn. If she closed her eyes, she could almost believe she was back in the familiar desert of her birth. Fanciful nonsense, she thought. This is worse than mirages, she admonished herself. *This desert is nothing like the desert of home.* Here there were no familiar night sounds, only the eerie moan of the wind as it caressed the tops of the dunes. But thoughts of home continued to parade through her head, and for a little while, she forgot the dangers of the desert.

It was not long before Kira was shaking the reluctant Cassie, urging her to rise. Her ears were immune to Cassie's complaints, and Kira numbly stumbled onward. As they walked, the impatient sand filled their tracks, eliminating all signs of their passage. Time seemed to slow in the chilly quiet of early morning, and Kira was glad to see the first tinges of the dawn crawl over the eastern horizon. Pushing on until the sun cleared the dunes, she chose a spot where they could rest for another long, cruel day.

Kira shook her shrinking waterskin, feeling disheartened. Aching for just one sip, she removed the cap, but decided not to drink. Instead, she wet the corner of her bandanna and held it to her blistered lips. Resisting the temptation for more, she carefully placed the waterskin in the shade created by her pack. Curling on her side, she stretched her burnoose over her body to form a rude shelter to protect her from the deadly sun. Cassie was in a like position nearby, and Kira could hear her fitful snores. Closing her eyes, she succumbed to exhaustion.

The sun inched across the sky, and still they slept on. Had Kira awakened, she might have seen the dark shape soaring high above their heads. Riding the heated thermals, the King Vulture saw the two unmoving forms lying on the side of a large dune and, curious, drew its wings in slightly, angled its tail feathers, and slowly spiraled down for a closer look.

Puzzled by the lack of carrion scent, it squawked its displeasure and winged its way upward again to catch another spiraling thermal. The vulture would not venture too far into the deep desert and veered toward the southeast, where there was a better chance of finding tasty morsels closer to the foothills.

Kira would have been comforted if she had seen the direction of its flight, but she slept through the afternoon until the purple shadows oozed from the hollows between the dunes, flowing inexorably around each curve. As they grew, the cooling breeze woke her up, heralding the coming of night. She delayed rising for a few moments and was enjoying the delicious feel of the wind on her overheated skin when she saw Cassie hunched over in defeat and striving to sit up.

"I don't know if I can go on," Cassie whispered through cracked, bleeding lips.

Kira struggled to her feet and tried to sound optimistic. "Come on, Cassie, it can't be much farther. Maybe one more night, and then you can sleep all you want in the shade of the palms."

"Why can't we see the mountains yet," Cassie croaked in despair.

"I'm not sure, but I think we might be in a sort of valley, and the dunes along the edge are blocking our view," Kira said, praying her theory was right. "Come on, we must keep moving. We can't afford to waste one night of travel. Our water supply will not last." She reached down to offer a hand to the older woman. "Besides, we made it this far. We can't give up now." She knew if they stopped, they might lose any chance of reaching the oasis before they died of thirst.

She was relieved when Cassie finally raised her head, brushed the sweat drenched curls away from her sun-ravaged face, and reached for her outstretched hand. Once on her feet, Cassie stared toward the southeast, and Kira saw a new look of determination on her face. Together, they shouldered their packs and moved forward, but they moved much slower now. The strain of the past few days had taken its toll.

They concentrated on placing one foot in front of the other as the frigid night air became their enemy, cutting through their robes and numbing their faces. Once again, they longed for the return of the sun. The only sounds were their labored breathing and chattering teeth, and the ever-present wind slipping over and around the darkening mounds, singing a menacing song. Dulled by fatigue, they plodded onward to meet the dawn.

CHAPTER 5

A few miles to the east of Kira and Cassie's location, a group of berobed men crept silently and cautiously among the rocks on a hillside. These were dangerous men on a dangerous mission, and they proceeded with care. With Allah's help, they would soon return in triumph, bringing their master a grand prize.

Feeling confident, one lone man eased down a short slope and crawled on hands and knees around an enormous boulder. He craned his head around its edge to peer down the path and his brain barely registered the hoof that struck him in the forehead and flipped him on his back. It happened so fast no sound escaped his lips. The sound of another man approaching the same outcropping sent their prize hurrying away, and shouts rang out when the dead man was discovered. Now certain their prize knew of their intent, they lost all need for silence.

The berobed men leapt and scrambled down the rocky slopes, shouting as they tried to encircle their quarry. Catching glimpses of movement among the rocks, they knew they were close to success. Suddenly, one man screamed as a pounding mountain of gold appeared out of nowhere to knock him down and break free from their trap. The men saw the magnificent golden horse speeding away towards the dunes of the deep desert, and two gunshots rang out, signaling their watchman to bring their horses. When he appeared with their mounts, the men sprang into their saddles, and amid gunshots and whoops of excitement, they gave chase.

•   •   •

Hours later, the angry men reined in their stumbling, sweaty mounts. They were quiet, and their horses hung their heads in exhaustion, breathing heavily. "We can go no farther," growled Hashem, the captain of the men. He directed his words to the dark rider, who rode a huge black stallion.

Sheik Qadir wheeled his mount to glare at Hashem, causing the man to avert his eyes. "Then we will rest here. Hashem, you will take a man and bring me the golden she-devil. Do not harm her." Ordering the other men to relax, Qadir dismounted and checked his waterskin. It contained barely enough water for one day. They hadn't expected the horse escaping into the deep desert. He spat to clear the dust from his throat and angrily stomped over to the shade of a crude tent of blankets his men had erected for his comfort. Throwing himself down on the unyielding sand, he contemplated his latest attempt to catch the golden beauty.

Qadir believed he could breed a golden stallion if only he could find and capture the golden filly, but all his attempts had failed so far. The elusive creature appeared as if by magic and just as easily disappeared when pursued. Tales of her crafty ways circulated amongst his men who believed she was a spirit creature, but Qadir dismissed their superstitious conjecture with disgust. He knew she was real. In her veins flowed the same red blood as flowed in his black stallion, Shar, and Qadir would prove it once she was in his grasp.

For several years, Qadir had been searching for the rare golden horses. He even tried to steal one from his long-hated enemy, Sheik Akeem, whose tribe inhabited the hills to the west of his own kingdom. Akeem was the only one who had the prized creatures, though they were all mares. Qadir knew Akeem spent many years trying to breed for a golden stallion, but he was unsuccessful.

He still rejoiced in Akeem's death and wished he could get rid of Akeem's son, Jalil, just as easily. "Argh, that son of a camel Jalil," he exclaimed bitterly. Just thinking about the younger sheik caused Qadir's blood to boil. *Sheik Jalil and his silver Mirage.* Rumor was Jalil had found his silver stallion, hurt in the mountains. What Qadir wanted to know was how he tamed the wild horse and win his trust and devotion. All Qadir knew was burning jealousy, and he feared the pair would beat him at the next Tri-Annual Race.

With Akeem gone, Jalil was the only thing keeping Qadir from being the most powerful leader in the region. He swore he would kill Jalil, just like he had Jalil's father. Even now, years later, he felt a rush of pleasure in the memory of watching the old man bleed to death in the high mountain pass. Hashem had silenced the few men who knew how Qadir ambushed and murdered Akeem. Qadir trusted Hashem would always keep his dark secret safe. Hashem had been a member of his tribe for a long as could remember and was the keeper of many dark secrets.

Tired of waiting, Qadir rose, slapped the sand from his robes, and mounted his stallion. His thoughts strayed one last time to the filly in the desert. She could not survive without water and would have to return to the oasis soon. When she did, his men would be waiting. Fingering the coiled whip at his side, he grinned in anticipation. He knew how to inflict a great deal of pain without leaving marks. Excited by the thought of breaking her spirit, he snatched hard on the reins, causing Shar to snort in pain as the bit bruised his tender mouth. The stallion pranced sideways, unsettling Qadir, who merely chuckled at his horse's discomfort.

"You know who your master is, and if you do not behave, I will have to remind you again," he said coldly. Shar responded to the menace in his master's voice and eased his gait. Tired from the efforts of the past two days, Qadir cast one last look at the undulating dunes. Accepting defeat, for now, he headed for the comforts of his own kingdom. The thought of golden horses galloped away, replaced by a vision of golden eyes as he contemplated enjoying the delights of his favorite harem girl.

Settling deeper into his saddle, he waved to his men, and they followed him, disappearing into the hills.

•　　•　　•

That night, while Kira and Cassie made their way closer to the foothills, Hashem and his fellow tribesman, Nadim, continued to follow the lone horse into the desert. When they stopped for a brief rest, Hashem had a tough decision to make. The faint tracks of their prey were fading, and it was doubtful they would catch up with their quarry for some time. They could not continue at this pace into the heat of another day. It would be too much for their mounts, and they would not have enough water to return safely to the hills.

With mounting frustration, Hashem decided on a desperate course of action. Instructing Nadim to wait, Hashem urged his steed into a ground-eating canter, very grueling for any horse not bred to run in soft sand. When he glimpsed the golden horse moving in the distance, he pushed his mount harder. He was closing on the prize when his stallion caught the scent of the filly ahead and bugled a challenge. Cursing his stallion's lustiness, Hashem watched the filly look back and answer with a piercing neigh before bursting forward with new speed.

Realizing he was losing the race, and knowing the humiliation he would face upon his return, Hashem cursed aloud. Filled with uncontrollable rage, he pulled his rifle into firing position, steadied his sight on the fleeing form, and gently squeezed the trigger. The sharp report caused his horse to miss a stride, and he pulled the lunging horse to a restless standstill. There was no need to go any farther. He had seen the golden head jerk skyward and the shining body fall.

Wheeling about, he rode back to Nadim but when he saw the little man's eyes full of disbelief, Hashem demanded, "Swear to Allah, here and now, that you did not see that!" When Nadim hesitated, Hashem reached out and grabbed him by the throat, almost lifting him from his saddle. "Swear to me now, or I will leave your rotting corpse for the vultures," he yelled. The scared man could only nod as the pressure from the fingers around his neck prevented any reply. Hashem released him and turned back to the hills. "Come, we must hurry. I hope we do not pay dearly for our sheik's foolish desire." He whipped his horse, anxious to return to the safety of the oasis, and Nadim followed close behind.

As the two men rode off, they failed to see the filly try to rise and fall again. Her breathing slowed and the pale sand took on a rusty hue around her head, and the smell of blood wafted upward, carried high by the thermals into the afternoon sky. She still lay unmoving when the uncaring moon began its nightly passage and the cold wind wrapped around her like a shroud.

CHAPTER 6

The beauty of the first few moments of sunrise was lost on the two women the next day when the sun rapidly morphed into its usual blinding brightness. Kira longed to stop, but faced with dwindling water reserves, she knew they could not afford to. Cassie protested weakly, but finally gave up under Kira's angry insistence. As they pushed onward, they were so engrossed in their actions that they failed to see the dark shapes soaring on high.

It wasn't until later Kira was startled by a squawking noise. She stopped, cocked her head, and listened. After three days and nights of endless silence, except for the moaning and whistling of the night wind, she thought she imagined it. When she heard it again, she looked up to see familiar dark forms wheeling overhead. Half afraid the vultures were just another mirage, she hesitated, and then remembered mirages didn't make noises! With a harsh cry of excitement, she lurched forward.

Cassie had stopped to stare fearfully at the descending scavengers. "Ugh!" she croaked. "Are they coming for us?"

"Oh, aren't they wonderful!" Kira exclaimed as she scrambled up the next dune.

Cassie frowned. "Have you lost your mind?" But Kira didn't stop to answer her, so she called out, "Hey, slow down. What's so great about a bunch of vultures?"

Kira answered her from higher up. "Don't you see? They must have come from the foothills because they can't live in the deep desert any more than we can. They need water too!"

Curious about what she would find beneath the circling scavengers, Kira proceeded with more caution. Crawling laboriously to the top of the next dune, she looked down and, had it not been for the vultures' squawking presence overhead, would once again have thought she was seeing a mirage. She was stunned to see what she least expected. *A golden horse!* Kira could see red stains on the exposed side of its face and neck, and her heart tightened with concern. *There's so much blood! Is it dead?* She was about to go for a closer look when Cassie grabbed her arm.

"Can we eat it, do you think?" Cassie asked.

"Over my dead body!" Kira knocked Cassie's hand away and slid awkwardly down the dune toward the motionless animal. She kept a wary eye on the hungry vultures landing nearby. Notoriously aggressive, they were fearless and unpredictable when feeding. She crouched a few feet from the horse and watched it, relieved to see the slight rise and fall of its chest. Its eyes were closed and encrusted with sand and blood, as were its nostrils and mouth. Kira reached for her waterskin.

"Hey!" Cassie hissed, watching from a safe distance. "You're not going to waste water on that bag of bones! It's got one foot in the grave already. You'd better save that water for us!"

Kira ignored Cassie and eased forward within reach of the golden muzzle. Studying the situation, she wet the end of her bandanna and held it over the horse's mouth. A single drop of water fell on its lips, disappearing between them. Waiting another moment, she repeated the motion and was rewarded by a slight flickering of one eyelid. *Oh, thank God!*

As she watched anxiously, the crusted eyes opened slowly and, in a flash, rolled around, showing all white. Kira was familiar with this sign of fear in horses and remained still. The filly tried to raise its head, and it was enough to startle the encroaching scavengers. They milled about in chaos, squawking angrily, but came no closer.

Seeing the matted blood on the horse's cheek and neck, Kira was relieved the horse's movements did not generate any fresh flow. The source of all the blood seemed to be under the mane, high on its neck, but she needed to examine the area more closely, to be sure. The horse was agitated now, and when its dilated eyes locked with her own, Kira made soothing sounds until the filly calmed. Keeping up her singsong litany, she dribbled more water into the horse's mouth, smiling to see it so eagerly received.

Moistening the bandanna again, she carefully removed the crust from around one eye. As she worked, she studied the horse. Horses had been an integral part of her life, and what she saw before her was a superb specimen—a female with a deep chest and well-muscled legs. Even covered with dried sweat and gore, the coat was a glorious gold with an iridescence Kira had never seen before. The filly's beauty was marred by four long scars on its left flank, and Kira shivered wondering what had left that big of a mark. Both patient and nurse jumped when Cassie introduced herself.

"Leave that nasty creature alone and quit wasting our water. Can't you see it's dying!" She stumbled forward and made a weak grab for Kira's waterskin.

Frightened by the screeching creature that loomed over her injured head, the horse's nostrils flared, and it struggled to rise. Cassie stumbled back, and Kira rolled out of the way. Lurching to its feet, the horse stood on shaky limbs, eyes wide, huffing and snorting, but didn't move away. The impatient vultures hopped and waddled to a safer distance with a great deal of shrieking and fanning of wings, but they refused to leave.

Enraged, Kira rose and turned to Cassie. Trying to keep her voice low, not wishing to frighten the horse further, she ground out a warning to the redhead. "If you try that again, you'll be sorry. I'm going to help this poor animal whether you like it or not, and I will not allow you to harm her in any way." Her steely gaze went unchallenged, and she waited until Cassie backed away. When she turned back to the horse,

Kira noticed it was not looking at her, but was staring at Cassie. Maybe it was her imagination, but she felt animosity and disdain directed at the redhead and, out of the corner of her eye, watched Cassie move away.

Resuming her wordless crooning, Kira bowed her head and stretched her hand out until she could feel the steamy breath of the horse, snorting and sniffing in curiosity. The sound of flapping wings broke the silence and Kira hoped the vultures were finally leaving but resisted the urge to look. Her arm aching from the strain, Kira had almost given up when she felt the gentle touch of velvet lips on her upturned palm. Her heart leapt with joy, and she slowly lifted her head. Their eyes met and held, and she was humbled by the intense intelligence of the creature before her. It reminded her of when she had first seen the pyramids. Here was something grand and wonderful, something that defied explanation, something magical. She held her breath when the horse moved closer.

Kira trembled, half in fear, half in wonder, when she felt the horse's nose passing over and around her head, then down her arms and legs. Growing bold, Kira laid her hand on the filly's cheek, exploring the silky curves of its beautiful head, being careful to avoid the blood-caked areas. So intent were they on their mutual exploration that neither was aware Cassie had disappeared.

Kira looked around for her pack with the thought of sharing some food with the injured horse but was disoriented for a moment. Her pack wasn't where she had left it. And there was no sign of Cassie. Alarmed, she crawled up the dune behind her and cursed when saw her pack lying not far away, upended, its contents strewn about. Dismayed to find Cassie had stolen the last of the food, she was furious to discover her father's maps were missing, too. Cassie had always been self-centered, but this was cold-blooded!

Seeing the faint footsteps leading south, Kira considered following her, but could not bring herself to leave the injured horse, especially to run off in the wrong direction. Moaning in frustration, she hastened to re-stuff her pack with the items Cassie had discarded. Kira thanked God she still had her father's compass and money belt, and that the medallion and ring were safely around her neck.

Returning to find the horse licking the waterskin she had dropped, she gave it one more mouthful, this time using her hand as a cup. When Kira closed the waterskin and slung it over her shoulder, the filly nudged her, clearly wanting more, but Kira wasn't sure how far it was to the oasis and had to conserve what was left.

"I'm sorry, my beauty, but we can't afford to drink it all now," she said ruefully. "Maybe you would like to try a bit of my food, huh?" She offered a piece of the stale bread Cassie had either overlooked or disdained to steal. A quick sniff and the morsel disappeared. "Well, I'm glad to see you're not as choosy as my last travel companion. In fact, I think you are a distinct improvement." She smiled and caressed the soft face.

Collecting her thoughts and taking a deep breath, she shouldered her pack and adjusted her robe. "Come, my friend, we better get moving or our uninvited guests above will be returning for an extended visit." Her eyes followed the wheeling vultures who had taken to the air and apparently given up, at least for the moment. "I hate to disappoint them, but we're not on their menu today." Watching as they circled ever higher, she waited to see what direction they would take. Checking her compass, she determined they were heading eastward and knew they must be close to the foothills and, hopefully, water. She took a few steps before realizing the horse had not moved. "Are you coming?" she asked, pleased when the horse followed her without hesitation.

Together they walked with heads bent, and before long, Kira glanced up and gasped in disbelief when she saw the elusive foothills and, behind them, the low mountains. Looking behind, she realized her original theory was correct—the ground had been rising steadily, and the dunes had been blocking her view all along. What she had originally thought were distant foothills were, in fact, the tops of the mountain range. She spared a thought for Cassie, who was walking in the wrong direction, but promptly squelched her concern. Cassie had made a poor decision when she stole the provisions and the maps, leaving Kira without food and the means to find help. Kira would never forgive her for that.

A low whicker drew her attention, and Kira saw her new partner with her head raised high, testing the air. Kira recognized her cautious behavior and instinctively paused, allowing the horse to decide when to proceed. She could no longer refer to her as "it." When the horse swung her head back and forth and walked forward in a different direction, Kira hesitated but a second before following her guide on a more northerly route. The horrendous glare forced Kira to keep her eyes downcast, but when next she glanced up, she was relieved to see the rocky outcroppings of the foothills. Filled with new hope and imagining the welcoming shade and possibility of water, she decided she might make it after all.

Drained, she could barely keep up with the horse, but thankfully, the shifting sands had given way to hard packed grit, making it easier, if not more painful, to walk. When she looked up again and saw the outline of low palms ahead, she let out a cry of joy and hastened her pace. The blistered condition of her feet made her shambling gate worse, and Kira was left behind as the horse rushed to what was obviously a water-bearing oasis.

By the time Kira reached the cluster of palms and low-lying vegetation surrounding the oasis, she was frantic to find the water. Threading her way through the thickest cluster of scrubby bushes, she heard splashing and, with a final surge of energy, burst through to discover a large, tranquil pool.

Momentarily dazzled by the reflection of the sun's rays, she dropped her pack and money belt, discarded her burnoose, and fell forward into the shallows, reveling in the cool water. Lifting her head, she saw her new friend already knee deep by the far bank, drinking noisily. Flinging caution to the wind, Kira dragged herself farther into the water and, heedless of any silt or vegetation, gulped greedily from her cupped hands. It was heavenly nectar, but coming to her senses, she stopped, remembering it was dangerous to drink too much, too soon.

Seeing the horse watching her intently, Kira walked around to the far bank, coaxed her out of the water, and used the bandana to bathe her, beginning with her injured neck. Dark eyes watched Kira's every move, but the horse remained still while Kira gently rinsed away the dirt, sand, and caked blood. When Kira lifted the mane and saw the source of the blood, she recognized what could only be the result of a gunshot. Fighting to remain calm, she examined it closely, immensely relieved it was only an ugly furrow. When Kira finished her ministrations, the horse moved away from the water and laid down in the grass.

Satisfied she had done enough for her friend, Kira undressed completely and used the same bandanna to wipe away the grime from the last few days. Gathering her clothes, she rinsed them out, letting the dirty water run onto the ground so as not to contaminate the pool. After wringing out as much of the water as she could, she draped them on the trunks of nearby palms to dry. She wanted to wash her burnoose, but she needed it for the night ahead.

Wearing her father's shirt, which fell to her thighs, and with his money belt wrapped around her slim waist, she lay down close to the horse, feeling safer than she had since the wreck. Warmed by the memories of her father from the scent of his shirt, she snuggled deeper into the old burnoose, listening to the soft breathing of her new friend and guardian. Soon, they were enveloped in a profound silence, only broken by the breeze ruffling the fronds of the bending palms. The light grew dim, and they slept on, oblivious to the coming of night.

CHAPTER 7

Kira awoke surrounded by the sound of tiny chirps, reminding her of the sharp notes she had hit during her piano practice years ago. Listening intently, she enjoyed the little discordant tones. They belonged here in this land of contrasts. She opened her eyes to discover the source of the calls. Tiny fluttering birds darted in and out of the swaying palms. They were obviously feeding on something, and Kira's stomach rumbled with hunger.

Rolling over, she groaned in pain. The past few days had taken their toll on her body, and she rose unsteadily, her stiff sore muscles protesting and her feet aching. Remembering the horse, she looked about the clearing, dismayed to find herself alone. She thought maybe she had dreamed the whole affair. In her state of exhaustion and dehydration, it would have been possible. But upon closer inspection, she noticed a depression in the grass nearby. With a sigh of relief, she hastened to search for her four-legged friend.

The sound of pawing drew her to a clearing where she found several palms beset by a flock of the finch-like birds. The horse was feeding on small brown objects scattered around the base of the trunks, and she whinnied in welcome when Kira approached. Kira bent down and picked one up, delighted to find that it was a plump, juicy date, a fruit she had been introduced to in Cairo. Using her bandanna as a makeshift basket, she filled it with as many as she could carry, returning to the pool where she sat down to enjoy her feast. Surprisingly, she quickly felt satisfied, so she leaned back against her pack to study her surroundings in more detail.

It was a lovely place, quiet and undisturbed, but Kira suspected it was not the oasis her father had been headed for. It was too small, with no signs of any human visitations. Picturing her father's map, Kira did not remember this oasis being marked on it. As Kira thought back on how she had been led here, she concluded that only the horse and date birds knew of this place. All the better, she thought to herself. She welcomed the privacy, but she knew she could not stay here forever. Eventually, she would have to find a way back to civilization, wherever that was.

While she considered her choices, the horse suddenly appeared at the water's edge. Kira marveled at the silence of her friend's passage through the thickets and surmised this was indeed a creature used to living in the wild. When the horse waded forward to take long sips from the pool, Kira admired the rich golden hues of her glimmering hair and her long shimmering mane of silver gold. Back home in America, she might be called a palomino, but Kira had certainly never seen such a lovely specimen. The texture of her coat was unbelievable, and the iridescent color reminded her of the desert under the noonday sun and, yet, at the same time, made her think of the starlight on the dunes at night.

As if aware of Kira's scrutiny, the horse left the shallows and approached. Kira sat upright and could not resist offering a soft caress when the horse lowered her head, its silken mane sweeping forward to brush against Kira's shoulder. "My, but you are a pretty thing," Kira said as she stoked the underside of the horse's neck. The play of light on the golden coat reminded her of a piece of translucent amber her father had brought her from one of his trips. She had been mesmerized by the sun shining through its golden depths, causing it to glow as if filled with light. Inspired, she exclaimed aloud. "Amber! That's what I'll call you!"

Amber neighed and nodded her head, as if in confirmation, and her mane swept back, revealing the wound. Kira was glad to see it showed no sign of infection. The wound would leave a nasty scar, but luckily, it would be hidden by the filly's mane. Amber playfully nudged the exposed medallion hanging from Kira's neck, reminding Kira of her current state of undress. She had forgotten she was almost completely naked. "I'm getting as bad as Cassie," she said with a chuckle.

She gathered her dry garments, and once dressed, she leaned over the pool to splash water on her face, and seeing her reflection, she winced at the condition of her hair. After she tamed her long shining hair into one thick braid, her eyes were drawn to her father's medallion resting against her chest. Curious, she held it in her palm and studied the strange pattern of stones and gems more closely.

When a stray ray of sunlight pierced the palms above and set it aglow, she saw a faint pattern, one she hadn't noticed before. A band of horses had been inscribed around the edge. They seemed to move, and she shook her head at the fanciful thought, figuring she was suffering from desert sickness. She contemplated stashing the heavy medallion in her pack, but as she went to remove it, she felt a surprising warmth emanating from it, and tucked it back under her shirt. It felt right lying against her heart next to her father's ring.

Forgetting about the medallion for now, she filled her waterskin and returned to the clearing to collect a sizeable store of dates. Rolling them up in large leaves from a nearby plant, she carefully placed the green bundles in the very top of her pack. As she stood, trying to decide which direction to take, she felt a gentle push from Amber, who began walking toward the mountains. *Here we go again.* Shaking her head ruefully, and with a last look of regret at the lovely green oasis, Kira followed her through the thinning brush.

Once clear of the vegetation, Kira tried to turn back to the south, intending to follow the foothills, but Amber trotted in front of her and again pushed her back toward the mountains. Confused by Amber's behavior, but trusting her wild friend, she gave up and fell back in line. The path steepened, and soon it became more difficult to pick out the winding trail snaking in and around the rocks. *Where in God's name are we going?* As Kira climbed after the surefooted Amber, she scanned the path ahead. However, her view was limited to the craggy hillside that quickly transformed into a small mountain.

Several times, the path seemed to vanish, only to reappear miraculously just around another outcropping. The only time her guide broke her stride was when they passed under a natural arch of muddy-hued stone. Kira couldn't help but look upward. Desert born, she was aware of the places large predators used for ambush. Amber hesitated, then trotted faster, with her eyes looking upward until she had left the formation behind. Kira remembered the scars, possibly the marks of a lion attack, on Amber's flank, and she moved just as quickly as the horse.

After several hours of navigating the steep trail, Kira felt the effects of the last few days catching up with her and had to concentrate very hard to avoid falling on the slippery gravel and sand. A fall at this point could prove debilitating, if not fatal. So intent on keeping her balance on this treacherous stretch, she failed to notice Amber stop and nearly collided with her sizeable haunches. Panting, Kira saw why the horse halted so suddenly. A massive boulder sat in the middle of their path.

Sizing it up, Kira figured she could climb over it, but that would leave Amber stranded. Amber behaved like she had been this way before, but maybe she had not counted on the boulder. Perhaps it had been displaced by a recent rockslide. Puzzled, Kira watched Amber curiously, wondering what the horse would do now.

Expecting Amber would need room to turn around, Kira backed down the path, but stopped and watched in amazement as Amber lowered her head and walked into the shadowy edge between the rock and the hillside. It wasn't until she saw the last of Amber's shining tail disappearing behind the boulder that Kira thought to scramble forward. Pressing against the wall, she found an opening camouflaged by a bulge in the rock. The opening was tall enough Kira didn't have to stoop, but she understood why Amber kept her head lowered.

When she entered the cool dimness, she was astonished to find herself in a tunnel. Its sides and ceiling were remarkably straight and smooth, and it widened the deeper she delved. The light from the opening behind her faded, and she proceeded with extreme caution, keeping one hand on the wall and one hand raised to feel for any dips in the ceiling.

She hurried to keep up with Amber, who moved through the twisting tunnel with confidence. The light diminished entirely past the third turn, and the floor sloped downward, but Amber continued at a steady walk. Following closely, Kira lost all sense of time in the darkness and was very thankful to see the gradual return of light. Encouraged, they both picked up their pace and shortly arrived at the tunnel's exit.

The full glare of the noonday sun blinded her eyes when Kira stepped out of the tunnel. She blinked rapidly and, when her vision cleared, stared in disbelief. Spreading out before her was a long valley encircled by rocky cliffs. A path led down to a plateau bordered by low rolling hills, covered in pale green that paraded along the eastern edge. What made the sight so unbelievable was the slender stream winding its way through the hills. Groves of small, twisted trees lined its banks, and tall palms grew in clumps nearby. Overwhelmed, Kira failed to register the orderliness of the groves. It would be much later before she thought about this mystery again.

A hellish sound from the direction of the hills broke her silent reverie. Rising in challenge, the clear bugle that could only be from a wild horse pierced the air. Startled, she watched Amber burst forward, leaping down the path and breaking into a gallop, heading for the nearest hill. The challenge was repeated, this time closer, and Kira's eyes widened at the sight of a majestic golden stallion emerging from around the hill. Concern for Amber sent Kira rushing down the path, but she stumbled to a halt when she witnessed their meeting.

The two beautiful animals came together at breakneck speed, only to veer off at the last instant. Wheeling in tight circles, they slowed and pranced forward until their noses touched. They snorted and whickered, but when the stallion arched his neck and tried to sidle closer, Amber dashed back to Kira's side, leaving him in mid-neigh.

Kira held her ground but panicked when the huge stallion galloped toward her, until he slid to a stop before he reached her. Eyes rolling wildly, he screamed his challenge once more. Amber offered a calming nicker, but he ignored her. His displeasure was plain to see, and Kira figured he was agitated by the presence of a stranger in his valley. After much pawing and stamping, he let out a final warning, leapt down the path, and dashed back towards the hills. Kira understood clearly that she would not be harmed, but she also realized that she was not yet welcomed.

Amber watched the stallion's retreat and then nudged Kira down the path, and they followed the trail to the valley floor. Before them, the stream sank into the ground, creating a marshy area, but farther upstream Kira saw a grove of palms and short stubby trees. Finding a nice shady spot to camp, she dropped her pack at the base of a leaning palm and walked to where the stream widened even more. Clear and cool, it bubbled over flat rocks, and she could not resist the temptation to bathe her hot, blistered feet. While she sat cooling her toes, a wave of fresh sorrow swept over her. *Oh, if only Papa could have seen this.* He would have been so happy to find his theories were correct. Here was evidence of running water in the desert with a hidden source.

Off in the distance, she heard horses neighing. Probably the stallion's personal harem, she thought. Amber waited patiently while Kira enjoyed the cool spring water. But then she snorted and pawed the ground, casting her eyes towards the hills. Kira sensed her indecision and left the stream bank to stand beside her and stroke her silky neck. "Oh, go on. I'll be okay."

Amber seemed to understand and, after accepting a last caress, took off for the hills. Kira watched until she could no longer see the filly. Satisfied it was the right thing to have done, she set out to explore the immediate area. It yielded a surprising diversity of edible fruits and nuts. Besides dates, she found olive trees, lime bushes, pistachio trees, and almond trees. Thinking this must have been what Eden was like, she wouldn't have been surprised to come across an apple tree.

When she returned to the palm grove, she ate her fill of the ever-present dates and washed her sticky face and hands in the nearby stream. It was too late to build a shelter, so she built a fire instead and, wrapped in her burnoose, she fell into an uneasy sleep. She woke once in the night when Amber settled nearby, and feeling safer, she slept more soundly.

The next morning, she woke feeling refreshed, unconcerned that Amber was nowhere in sight, and focused on making a shelter. Armed with her father's knife and the small hatchet, she gathered lengths of fallen palm trunks and branches from the grove. Finding two trees growing close together set her plan in motion. She notched the top ends of two logs and secured them upright against the trunks, fitting a longer, thinner log horizontally between them to serve as a ridgepole. Leaning the remaining logs and longer branches against both sides of the ridgepole, she finished a rough frame resembling a wooden tent. A tree blocked one end, but the other end stopped just shy of the other tree, allowing her entrance. It looked rather rickety, but when she crawled inside to inspect the structure, she felt much more secure.

Drawing on her experience of Zuni basket weaving, she used the supple reeds from the marsh to secure palm fronds to the leaning logs by tying them in horizontal overlapping rows, creating a windproof screen that also provided shade from the harmful sun.

By sunset, Kira had successfully completed her new house but almost laughed aloud, imagining what Cassie would have said had she seen the crude lean-to. Still, she felt enormous pride at her accomplishment. After a meal of fruit and nuts, she stored her gear inside, and using her burnoose for bedding, she curled up and was soon fast asleep. Sometime during the night, she was awakened by a sound outside the shelter, but when she heard Amber's familiar whinny, her fears disappeared. Feeling safer, she drifted back to sleep.

The sun was climbing above the eastern ridge when Kira awoke to familiar piping in the palms and fingers of sunlight peeking through the woven sides of her shelter. Crawling out, she padded over to the stream to wash her face. The reeds caught Kira's attention, and their long stems stirred old memories. Seized by an idea, she collected several armfuls. Finding a shady spot to sit, she sorted the pliant strands by thickness and length and began weaving them into a primitive basket shape.

It had been many years since Kira had practiced making baskets, and she was ashamed of her first attempt, glad that her grandmother would never see it. It was a lopsided, comical affair that would undoubtedly unravel if she put so much as a date in it. Frustrated but persistent, she started over. This time, her efforts yielded a basket both symmetrical and tightly woven. It probably wouldn't hold water like Grandmother's creations, but it would hold dry items. By the time the sun had reached its zenith, she had completed one more basket, as well as a simple conical hat of palm fronds to help block the unrelenting sun. She chuckled when she tried it on, thinking perhaps she should change her name to Kira Crusoe.

She spent the rest of the afternoon collecting fruits from the groves nearby. As she worked, Kira pondered the existence of so many species of trees here in the hidden valley. From her studies of zoology and biology, she knew seeds could be distributed by wind and rain, and even through the digestive tracts of animals, such as birds, cows, and horses. Maybe that was the explanation, she thought. The date birds were everywhere, and there were horses. Undoubtedly, other life forms inhabited the area too. She was puzzled by the orderliness of the groves but did not question her good fortune for long and continued with her food collecting.

Back at camp, she stashed her food inside the lean-to and decided to brave the hills. A nearby branch provided her with a suitable walking stick/weapon, and thus armed, she followed the stream, hoping to get a glimpse of the horses she had heard. As she walked, she kept track of the sun's progress, wanting to be back at her camp before nightfall. Remaining alert, she kept a lookout for Amber and the stallion.

When the stream widened to form a substantial lake, she stopped, amazed to see so much water. Tall craggy cliffs loomed at its far end, and she realized she might be looking at the source of the water—either a natural spring or an underground river. If only her father could see this, she thought sadly, tears welling. This time she did not fight them, and they flowed like the waters of the hidden spring. She sank to her knees, racked by sobs, finally allowing the grief she had suppressed since the wreck to come forth.

Lost and alone, unsure of where she was and with no idea if she would ever find her way home again, Kira cried for the loss of her father, the death of Marco, and for all the fear and despair of her struggle through the desert. When she finally stopped crying, she realized she was holding her father's ring so tightly that it had imprinted a pattern on her palm. Unclenching her fists, she wiped her swollen eyes and sat until her breathing steadied. Sniffling still, she rose and walked to the lake, where she knelt to splash her face with the soothing water.

Kira had forgotten about Amber and the horses until she heard a noise like growing thunder coming from the far side of the lake. Rising, she grabbed her stick and searched wildly for a safe place to hide. Her options were few. The closest shelter she saw comprised several piles of rocks, and she ran to take cover behind them. As she peeked over the top, a herd of horses pounded through the groves and came to a sliding, splashing halt in the shallows. They milled about, squealing, and tossing their heads, drinking their fill. She thanked God the wind was in her favor and the herd did not detect her presence.

Astounded by their beauty, she stifled a laugh at the antics of the yearlings and newborns gamboling and frolicking in the water. She saw several golden mares, but no sign of Amber. Engrossed in her study of the herd, she jumped when a noise startled her from behind. "Why you little sneak!" she whispered furiously at her four-legged friend. "You scared me half to death."

Amber nickered softly, which Kira thought sounded suspiciously like a chuckle, and moved closer. Kira patted her nose. "I see now where you get your good looks." But in all the excitement, she forgot about hiding and found herself in full view of the horses. By now, many had noticed her and some of the younger members trotted a few steps in her direction.

One young stud crossed the shallow lake, water drops flashing like crystals on his black velvet hide. He trotted toward Amber, but before he could come any closer, an angry neigh rang out, and the herd parted as the golden stallion burst through. Clearing the water in great leaps, he bore down on the younger male.

The black stallion took a last look at Amber and turned to flee. He was quick, but the huge stallion was quicker. The younger male was no match for his senior and scrambled back to the herd with a bloody nip on his withers and dusty hoofprints on his ribs.

The victor trotted to Amber's side, his coat glowing with rich shades of gold and glints of silver, reminding Kira of the medallion with the flashing yellow gems set in gold. Gems set in gold. Set in "n-dee." Ndee was the Arabic word for gold. *That's it! I will call him Ndee!*

As if he heard her thoughts, Ndee turned his dark gaze in her direction. Kira worried about what he would do, but he seemed to forget her and turned his attention back to Amber. Kira thought Amber would submit to his strong advances, but strangely enough, Amber ignored him. Ndee appeared agitated by the filly's lack of interest but did not force himself on her. Instead, he kept a respectful distance. Tossing her head, Amber wheeled around to rejoin the herd. Rearing, Ndee followed with a loud bugle and began gathering his herd by snaking back and forth between them and the water's edge. He added a few sharp nips here and there and soon had them moving back through the groves. Kira watched until the last horse had vanished. *Well, at least he didn't attack me, and that's something.*

Now that the danger was past, she turned to examine the rocks she had hidden behind. Intrigued by what appeared to be a series of ancient crumbling walls crisscrossing the area, she felt tempted to explore them. However, being aware of the westering sun, she decided to return to her camp and focus on making another useful basket. Nibbling on dates and nuts, she worked until the lavender and pink of sunset faded to the indigo of night.

Later, when Kira crawled inside her lean-to and snuggled into her old burnoose, her last thought was of the silver flashes she had seen in the clear water of the nearby reed beds. She fell asleep dreaming of a fish dinner.

CHAPTER 8

Intent on saving her own skin, Cassie had left Kira with the dying horse, convinced she could make her way to safety without her. "It's just like that little know-it-all to think she could bring that nasty beast back to life," she groused aloud as she plodded along. *I'm not risking my life over a dead horse.* Delirious with the heat, she soon became lost. When she noticed the sun sinking into the desert behind her, she regretted striking out on her own.

Thick shadows snaked through the dunes, and she shivered as the cold evening breeze plucked at her hood, slipping chilly invisible fingers around her neck. Exhausted and at the end of her strength, she dropped to her knees. As she grabbed her waterskin, intending to only take a small sip, a sudden thirst overcame her, and she drained what was left. Angry and frustrated, she groaned harshly in the deepening gloom, cursing Kira for wasting their water on that dreadful horse.

When the stars emerged overhead, she roused herself to stumble onward, but moved slower and slower until she lost her balance while climbing one particularly large dune and tumbled down the far side. Succumbing to the cold and the lack of water, she slipped into unconsciousness.

By morning, Cassie's motionless body drew the attention of the vultures scouting the dunes near the foothills. They were circling down toward what appeared to be their breakfast when fate stepped in, causing them to break off at the last minute and beat a hasty retreat up into the sky. Cassie thought she was dreaming when she felt drops of water falling onto her dry and cracked lips. Desperate for more, she opened her mouth wider and moaned. She tried to open her eyes, but they were crusted shut. She struggled to rise until she felt a heavy hand pressing down on her shoulder and heard a harsh voice, a manly voice.

"Be still."

Cassie had no idea what he said because she had never bothered to learn Arabic, but the commanding tone was enough. She ceased struggling when she felt a wet cloth pressed over her face, sighing at the relief it brought. It helped to remove the caked sand and dust from her eyes. When she could finally open them, she saw the face of her rescuer leaning over her. Her vision was blurry, but she could see his dark leathery features and scraggly beard. His eyes were black as a moonless night, and when their eyes locked, his widened, and his thin lips curled in a cruel smile.

He said something and made a strange gesture with his hand, but she ignored him and reached for his waterskin. He brushed her hands away and gave her another sip. She managed a long swallow and then coughed weakly. When he lifted her to her feet, she didn't resist, and he carried her to the horse she saw standing nearby.

Groggy, Cassie did not know how long she had been unconscious. She remembered falling down the dune and then nothing. Now, she was at the mercy of a barbarian in the middle of nowhere, but she was not afraid. Wherever he was taking her had to be better than dying in the desert. He mounted the horse and hauled her up behind him. She swayed precariously, overcome by a wave of nausea, and would have fallen had he not reached back to grab her. He wrapped her arms around his waist and secured her wrists together in front of him with a cord. Slumping forward, she rested her cheek against his back.

The horse stumbled, unaccustomed to the extra weight, but settled into a steady walk when the man uttered a sharp command. Within minutes, they emerged from the dunes and were soon rounding the southern edge of the low-lying foothills. Cassie slipped into unconsciousness again, unaware of her surroundings, which was probably for the best—seeing how close she had come to the foothills would have sorely tested her temper.

It was growing dark when she was jolted awake by shouts and gunshots from berobed figures riding on both sides. Clinging to her captor, she bent her head and allowed her hood to hide her face from the crowd, but peeked around the man's shoulder, intrigued to see a building of tan stone with gilded doors directly ahead. The man stopped in front of the doors, cut the cord binding her wrists, and slid from the saddle, pulling her down to stand next to him.

A loud voice caused him to spin around and drop to one knee. He mumbled something in an apologetic tone and angrily jerked her down beside him. Pitching forward, Cassie caught herself with her hands and was trying to rise when a powerful hand grabbed her chin in a viselike grip and tilted her face upward. Her hood fell back, and she heard gasps from all around as she raised her eyes to meet the penetrating stare of the man holding her chin. Bottomless pools of pitch-black obsidian peered at her above a beaklike nose set in a face the color of polished walnut. He wore black from head to toe, except for a single blood-red cord fastened around his headwrap.

Furious at the way she was being treated, Cassie returned his stare with one of icy disdain, but as she continued to glare, growing disbelief replaced his stern look. "How dare you look upon me in such a manner," he growled, sending her flying with a painful backhanded slap. Pain exploded in her head, and with a cry, she fell sideways on the stones. Momentarily stunned, she lay whimpering in shock. *He spoke English!*

Before she could gather her wits, he shouted angrily at the men, and they dragged her inside the building. She was vaguely aware of passing over smooth tile floors and plush colorful rugs before she was hauled through tall ornate doors flanked by huge cloaked men bearing wickedly curved scimitars. Her head jerked back as someone pushed her forward, and she fell sprawling onto the hard floor. Tired of all the pushing and falling, she was filled with rage. Breathing heavily, she laboriously rose to her feet, turning to find the men were gone, and the doors shut. In their place stood a diminutive woman wrapped from head to toe in black silk, her unblinking beady eyes buried in wrinkles and peering from above a veil of darkness.

Something in the woman's glance made Cassie uneasy, and she tottered backwards until her heels caught on the edge of a rug. Stumbling, she turned to see a wide arched opening through which she spied a large pool surrounded by low tables and piles of vibrantly colored pillows. Long panels of creamy silk draped the walls, which were lined with stone pots of tall green-leafed plants.

The water was so inviting after the harshness of the desert, Cassie couldn't resist its pull. Stepping into the room, she paused when she heard soft laughter. A dozen girls, in various stages of undress, sat on stone benches or reclined on piles of silken pillows. A few floated lazily in the fragrant water, their lush, naked bodies on full display. Bright rays of sun streamed down from a natural skylight overhead, highlighting the steam that rose in scented clouds from the pool.

The black-berobed crone clapped her hands twice before disappearing back through the main double doors. Several girls advanced toward Cassie, and she raised her hands, prepared to defend herself, but their laughter disarmed her. Baffled, she allowed them to come closer. They pulled at her robe and stripped her of the remains of her tattered clothing. Never one to be self-conscious, she stood proudly before them, while the girls stared at her enviously, chattering back and forth.

Quick to grasp their intent, she allowed them to wash her body and but was curious why they appeared frightened when they saw her crimson hair. When they finished bathing her, they led her to the larger pool, where she eased into the warm water. Normally this would be heavenly, but her ravaged skin was very tender, and Cassie had to grit her teeth until she became accustomed to the temperature. Leaning back against the side of the pool, she relaxed with eyes half closed until she heard one of the side doors open and saw two servants appear carrying trays. They placed the trays on low tables nearby, and Cassie caught a whiff of something wonderful. *Food!*

Unconcerned by her nakedness, she abandoned the pool and staggered to the tables. Ravenous, she sank to her knees and began stuffing herself with the delicious fare. Besides slices of grilled spicy meat, the trays were heavily laden with bowls of dates, oranges, melon slices, almonds, honey, and round loaves of crusty bread. Two pitchers sat nearby—one held a sweet, thick coffee-like beverage she could not stomach, but the other held cool refreshing lemonade. Drinking greedily, she ate with gusto as the girls watched her with amused expressions. She ignored them, too hungry to care.

After a few minutes, she reached for the polished silver pitcher of fruit juice to refill her glass and almost dropped it when she saw her reflection. Her once pale complexion was angry red, marred by peeling skin, and already showing signs of freckling. Touching her cracked and bleeding lips, she felt like crying. Seeing her obvious distress, one girl took the pitcher from Cassie's hands and beckoned for Cassie to follow her to a stone bench draped in thick towels. Cassie understood what she wanted and laid down on her stomach. Like the proverbial cat, Cassie had landed on her feet, and she decided to take advantage of this situation. While the girl massaged her with warm oils, Cassie drifted off to sleep.

When the light changed to the rose and saffron shades of the approaching sunset, Cassie woke long enough to use what she hoped was a chamber pot and take a few sips from a pitcher of water left on a nearby table before returning to her silken bed, chased by the cool night air.

•   •   •

Meanwhile, in a room not far away, another woman also awakened. Disturbed by thoughts of the crimson-haired creature that had invaded the palace, the woman paced back and forth by the glow of a burning lamp. Her hand reached for a jeweled goblet sitting on a nearby table, and the light of the lamp was reflected by the faceted stones encrusting the rings that adorned her long, slim fingers.

She drank deeply, then set the cup down hard enough to send drops of the fermented wine leaping into the air. Curling her long-nailed fingers into a fist, she abruptly turned, flung off her voluminous purple robe, and buried herself in the piles of silk on a low bed. After a few muttered curses, silence returned to the room.

·   ·   ·

One other person was also having trouble sleeping. Outside, Hashem was awakened by disturbing dreams of red-haired demons. Rising, he stepped from his tent to relieve himself, and glanced at the sheik's palace, its shadowy walls sharpened by the light of the moon. For a moment, he imagined the pale-skinned prisoner he had brought to the sheik, spread out upon a silken bed, her soft limbs flung wide, and her crimson hair streaming over the pillows. The thoughts made him angry, and he fastened his trousers with a muffled curse and returned to his cold pallet. When he heard his horse, tethered beside his tent, utter a questioning snort, Hashem silenced him with a single command, and it was some time before he was able to fall asleep.

·   ·   ·

When Cassie woke the next morning, her first sensation was of delight, until she tried to stand. Every muscle hurt, and the skin on her face and arms was extremely sensitive. Hearing girlish laughter, she suddenly realized she was still in the bath chamber. Three naked girls lounged in the warm scented water, and another one in bright orange silk sat on the far side of the chamber, drying her long tresses. A fifth girl, this one in sheer yellow, was busy applying a reddish liquid to her nails. Cassie refused to react, wrapped herself in a silk sheet, and strolled to the poolside tables covered with trays of food.

Once again, she found an assortment of fruits and nuts, loaves of bread, and bowls of condiments. This time there was a pitcher of milk, but from what animal Cassie dared not guess, along with coffee and water. The fruit was delicious, and she enjoyed a healthy helping of bread spread with a sweet butter-like substance. She ignored the coffee and drank the water, not trusting the milk.

Sated, she settled on a pile of pillows, propping herself up to watch the harem girls. Several were quite attractive, but none stood out as exceptional. In fact, they looked very much alike to her, having the same brown skin, the same dark brown eyes, and the same long black hair. Judging by their reactions, Cassie figured she was the most exotic woman they had ever seen. She hoped to use that to her advantage. Unfortunately, her stint in the desert had left her not at her best, but she was confident that with a little time and a few more beauty treatments, she would restore her beauty. Then she could use all her charms to get out of this predicament.

Remembering the black eyes and powerful hands of the day before, Cassie seethed with questions. *Who is that arrogant man, and what is the extent of his power?* The size of the house and the number of harem girls showed he was certainly wealthy. *What is he going to do with me…or to me?* Whatever he had planned, she knew she would need all her cunning to make sure she came out on top.

Wanting answers, she realized she needed to learn to communicate with the girls and motioned for one of them to join her on the cushions. She couldn't believe her luck when she learned that Fatima, as the girl was called, understood English. Cassie immediately asked for her help.

Cassie wondered what lay beyond the other doors in the bath chamber and social room but was disappointed to learn that they only led to the harem bedchambers. She was more interested in the doors she had passed through when she first arrive. Fatima explained that the doors not only led to the front door but also to the sheik's quarters, the guest rooms, and the feast chamber, but they were always locked and guarded.

While Fatima brushed her hair, Cassie closed her eyes in contentment, only vaguely aware of movement at one of the side doors. A woman swathed in deep purple silk appeared in the doorway and scanned the room with her intense amber eyes. The harem girls fell silent and looked the other way. When Cassie raised her head, the woman ducked back behind the door and the girls resumed their conversations. Cassie was oblivious to the drama and failed to see the looks of worry and fear on the other girls' faces.

Later that day, the old woman in black showed up and, without so much as a word, gestured to one of the side doors. Cassie hesitated then remembered what Fatima had told her. According to Fatima, the creature was called First Wife and was the sheikha of the tribe. Sheikha was the title given to a sheik's favorite wife usually when she bore an heir. The sheikha was the ruling female and had great power. Cassie thought the woman was too old to be Qadir's wife and said so. Fatima laughed then explained First Wife was Qadir's mother and Qadir had yet to choose her replacement. Not in any position to refuse, Cassie warily followed the crone through the door.

About halfway down a long corridor, the woman unlocked and opened a door revealing a small bed chamber. But when Cassie stepped inside, she heard the door shut behind her with an audible click. "Damn!" she exclaimed aloud when she realized she was locked in.

She inspected the room and was disappointed to discover there was no other way out, except for a small window, covered with carved lattice. But it was too high to reach. Curious, she walked over to a leather-bound chest at the foot of the bed. Inside were layers of silk sheets and extra pillows. Closing the lid, she saw a tall cabinet against the wall and, opening it, found silk veils and robes in colors complementing her hair and skin color hanging on one side. Someone had put a lot of thought into this, she mused. At the bottom was a stack of folded tunics, along with two pairs of slippers, one plain leather and one gilded.

Next, Cassie investigated the jars and vials sitting upon a small vanity table and recognized the lotions and oils that were found in the bath chamber. Fatima had explained their uses. A serviceable oil lamp and a mirror stood on a larger table against one wall. Bored and having nothing else to do, she lay on the bed, testing the softness of the mattress. It was a nice bed, much better than the hard desert sand, she thought. Except for the locked doors everywhere, she decided things were looking up for Cassandra Miller.

Cassie settled into the daily routine of the harem. It began with morning meal served in their rooms, followed by beauty treatments in the bath chamber. Midday meal was served poolside, and afternoons were spent making new clothes, playing games, and gossiping.

On some days, unseen figures played music from behind mosaic screens on the east wall of the social room. Dancing to the rhythmic sounds, each girl expressed herself purely individually. It was like nothing Cassie had ever seen, but she was no longer surprised by the barbaric customs of these people. Sometimes Cassie joined in and though she found it somewhat diverting, she preferred spending more time learning Arabic from Fatima.

Two weeks passed before she could look at a mirrored surface without flinching. Her time in the desert had left its mark, or marks in this case, as freckles. She wasn't happy, but she knew they would fade in time. Other than that, she was pleased with the improvements to her skin and hair. But now and then, she would look up and see First Wife watching her. Cassie knew she was being groomed for something, and it wasn't long before she found out what.

One morning, First Wife showed up announcing that Qadir was planning a feast for the very next evening and that all the girls would dance for his entertainment. Everyone was excited except Fatima, who sat with an odd expression on her face. When Cassie asked Fatima what was wrong, she replied, "The sheik will probably choose someone for his pleasure. I have never been chosen and I never want to be."

"But don't you want a night of pleasure?" Cassie whispered, curious why she looked fearful. Fatima shook her head vigorously. Cassie couldn't understand a woman who did not enjoy being with a man. "Oh, honey, you don't know what you're missing."

"You do not understand. I have seen the others after they were chosen. The sheik is a violent man, cruel and sadistic," Fatima said with a shudder.

As Cassie contemplated Fatima's words, a sudden hush fell over the chamber. When she saw Fatima glance up, and then quickly back down, Cassie glanced over her shoulder to see a woman clothed in purple silk standing close by. The mysterious woman's delicate features were twisted in contempt, her full lips drawn back in a snarl, and her amber eyes were shooting daggers at Cassie.

Cassie rose and asked in a haughty voice, "Can I help you?"

The woman's eyes widened, and she answered in a scathing tone.

Cassie understood part of what the woman said, something about goats, but pretended ignorance. Her language skills had improved, but she didn't want the other girls to know of her ability to understand their language. That way, they would speak more freely around her, thinking she would not know what they were saying.

When Cassie remained silent, the woman struck her. Taken by surprise, Cassie failed to block the blow and the slap echoed through the room. Green fire shot from Cassie's eyes as she rubbed the red handprint blossoming on her pale cheek, but before she could retaliate, First Wife appeared out of nowhere and moved between them. First Wife said something to the purple-clad woman, causing her to lower her head and back away. But when First Wife turned to speak to her, Cassie pretended to listen while she watched her attacker stalk through the bath chamber and disappear through one of the smaller doors.

Fatima would not speak until First Wife had left the room, but then she told Cassie the story behind the woman in purple. Her name was Zahra, and she was the current favorite of the sheik. Cassie's lips curled as she thought about how she would repay Zahra when *she* became the favorite.

When Cassie learned that guards or other tribe members who had earned favor with the sheik were often given un-chosen girls as wives, allowing them to resume a normal life, it piqued her interest. Personally, Cassie did not plan to be there long enough to worry about that. Tomorrow night would be her debut, and she was going to make the most of it. Once she was the favorite, she would find a way out of this barbaric land.

With that thought in mind, Cassie rushed back to her room and tore through her clothes. She had worn all the robes at least once, and she pouted over the poor selection. The best robe was an emerald green, and she laid it out along with a matching veil. Oh, for some jewelry and nice shoes, she whined silently, as she glanced at her bare neck and feet. That evening, she went to bed early, wanting to be well-rested for the next evening's events, but she struggled to fall asleep.

The next morning, she was the first to the pool, where she spent an unusually long time soaking in the perfumed water. After toweling dry, she wrapped herself in a loose robe and sat down for a light breakfast of fruit and bread. She finished the morning with a long massage and began preparing her hair and body. First Wife visited the chamber to speak with Fatima, who informed Cassie she would be a special part of the evening's activities. Several girls were assigned to help Cassie, and they oiled every inch of her body and anointed every intimate part with perfume.

They washed and rinsed her hair with scented water and allowed it to dry in the afternoon sun streaming into the chamber from the skylight. While her hair was drying, they buffed and dyed her nails. She allowed them to work a few drops of fragrant oil into her hair, which they brushed into wild waves. Too nervous to eat lunch, she drank a little spiced wine and took a brief nap by the pool.

Just before sundown, she returned to her room to change into the emerald silk, but cried out in dismay when she discovered it was missing. Angry and unsure what to do, she was startled when First Wife and two servants suddenly appeared. The servants were bearing an inlaid box and packages wrapped in ivory silk. Stepping aside, Cassie watched as they laid out an exquisite outfit of sea green silk shot through with golden threads. She smiled in delight, but when she examined the garment, its design puzzled her. One piece looked like baggy pants, but the material was almost transparent.

Clearly, Cassie was confused and had to be assisted. The pantaloons sat well below her navel and clung snugly to her generous hips. The waistband had a sash with fringed ends attached to it, and they tied a clever knot that allowed it to hang just to her thighs. One girl held up a long piece of the delicate silk, and they made her hold her arms up while they deftly wrapped the silk once around her back and over one shoulder, barely covering her ample bosom. She lowered her arms and perched on her vanity chair while they brushed her hair until it shone with fire.

First Wife opened the box, and Cassie audibly gasped at the sight of the gold and emeralds lying on a bed of red silk. The servants wrapped Cassie's neck and waist with strands of gold chains and wove a delicate chain interspersed with flashing green gems in her hair. They applied dark lines around her eyes and red dye to her plump lips.

Cassie forced herself to stand still while First Wife inspected her, adjusting a chain here and a curl there before adding the final touch. From the bottom of the box, she lifted a fabulous headdress of filigree gold bearing an enormous emerald. She set it upon Cassie's head, and from the look in the servants' eyes, Cassie knew she was ready to meet the sheik.

As she was escorted through the bath chamber and social room, and into the main corridor, she walked slowly, with her head held high. Rhythmic desert music grew louder when she approached the tall double doors of the feast chamber, and she knew her moment had finally come. No matter what followed, she was committed to her plan and would find a way to get all she deserved. Many emotions filled her, but fear was not one of them. She had discovered a world revolving around one man, and she knew from experience not a man had been born who could resist her charms. Confident of the outcome, Cassie set her lips in a sultry smile, squared her shoulders, and prepared to enter the room.

CHAPTER 9

Cassie took another deep breath and waited for the doors to open. The musicians played a thumping rhythm meant to herald her entrance and, gathering the folds of the shimmering emerald silk shawl draped over her shoulders, she spun into the room with a series of twirls. Making sure the filmy material cloaked most of her form, she danced to the center of the room, halted, and bowed her head. The men fell silent, and she kept her eyes lowered until, with a sudden flourish, she raised the shawl high overhead and began weaving and twisting in an ever-widening circle, dancing with calculated abandon.

From the moment she looked up, she kept her eyes locked on the sheik. Even though she had only seen him the day she was dumped on his doorstep, she would recognize him anywhere. He reclined upon an ornately carved couch on a dais centered against the back wall, clothed in silk robes embroidered in patterns of black, blood-red, and gold. Light from the lanterns reflected off heavy gold bands encircling his wrists and split into colored beams as it shone through the fat rubies dangling from thick chains around his neck. Long, lean, and cruel, he was the epitome of a barbarian.

Panting slightly from her efforts, she parted her lips, moistening them with the tip of her tongue. Sheik Qadir, who watched the undulating movements of his latest acquisition, couldn't help but notice her alluring act. His lips curled in a sneering yet sensual smile.

The look in her brilliant green eyes clearly aroused him, and he glanced at his guests, smirking at their evident desire as they stared with rapt attention at the crimson-haired goddess dancing before them.

Gloating inwardly at their leering responses, Cassie timed her next move to the rising crescendo of the wild music and ended her dance by sliding toward Qadir with her body bent backward until her shoulders touched the floor. She threw her arms out to either side, thrusting her chest upward, and she kept her knees spread. Her filmy garment did little to hide her most intimate features, and she saw his eyes widen and recognized the lust in his gaze.

The music stopped, and silence hung heavy in the air until it was abruptly broken when the guests expressed their pleasure by pounding on the tables and roaring loudly. Qadir accepted the envious congratulations from his men and raised his hand, gesturing to the guards. They lifted Cassie up and escorted her forward to sit by his feet. She wisely kept her eyes lowered as she accepted a glass of wine from a servant. Being unfamiliar with their customs, she waited impatiently for Qadir's next move. However, when he ignored her for the duration of the feast, her pride was tweaked, and growing ire replaced her look of triumph.

By the time most of the guests were nodding or had slipped away with girls Qadir had supplied for their enjoyment, Cassie was in a full-blown temper. She stared at Qadir with undisguised fury. He merely smiled then suddenly rose and strode from the room. She stared in disbelief and stifled a curse. *He left without me!* She could not comprehend this insult and was about to voice her anger when two guards appeared and pulled her to her feet. *What now?* When she struggled to free her arms, a few of the more coherent men at nearby tables laughed, calling out rude comments that she barely deciphered but instinctively understood. Seething, she ceased to struggle and allowed the guards to lead her back down the long hall.

She thought she was being taken back to her room but was jerked off balance when her escorts turned in the opposite direction. Her cry was silenced when she realized she was being taken to the sheik's quarters. Following willingly now, she berated herself for falling for Qadir's childish deception, but her anger continued to smolder. *That bastard! He was planning to choose me all along!* Armed guards stood at attention outside his chambers and knocked twice as she approached. The door swung open, and a servant appeared to lead her inside.

Wary, Cassie stood with clenched fists, her breath coming in small gasps, and her heart pounding as she surveyed the front room with its ornate furniture and plush rugs decorated in complicated patterns of blood-red, black, and gold. Engraved oil lamps hung from the ceiling and her eyes alighted on a door to her right, but it was closed. An arched doorway directly in front of her drew her attention, and she quelled her anger, knowing her behavior would determine her fate. As she waited for instructions, the servant surprised her by pushing her toward the opening, then fleeing from the room.

Hesitantly, she approached the entrance and paused just inside the doorway, allowing her eyes time to adjust to the dim light. She barely spared a glance at the silk-covered walls and the tall armoires, their rich wood tones highlighted by the glow of oil lamps scattered on tables and suspended from the ceiling. Enormous ceramic pots with lush greenery filled the corners, and the air was thick with the pungent scent of burning hashish. After her exertions in the main hall, she felt dizzy breathing the intoxicating fumes.

A slight noise drew her attention, and her eyes widened when she saw a massive ebony bed with heavy panels of midnight-black and blood-red silk draped between towering carved bedposts. Reclining in the middle, Qadir rested upon sheets of shimmering gold, leaning against overstuffed tasseled pillows checkered in black and gold. His robe of black silk was loosely gathered at his waist, exposing a muscled chest of dark, wiry hair. The sight was enough to make Cassie's heart pound harder, and her suddenly dry lips parted in expectation. She had been too long without a man. Failing to notice his thin cruel smile, she took a tentative step toward the bed but came to an abrupt halt at his imperious command.

"Stop," Qadir barked. He appeared to be in no hurry and puffed lazily on his hookah pipe.

Waiting impatiently for his next command, she watched him leisurely study her body while tendrils of smoke rose and curled about his head like pale, writhing snakes. Reaching up, he pulled on a thick braided rope hanging in the folds of silk behind him. Cassie heard a faint chime and the low, throbbing tones of rhythmic music drifted through the wall of latticework to her right and filled the room.

Leaning back on his pillows, Qadir called out lowly, but firmly, "Remove your clothes."

Cassie was in familiar territory now and took her time, allowing each piece of silk to slide seductively down her body as she gradually revealed herself to him. Finally, she stood naked except for the golden chains and the jewels in her hair. She stepped away from the puddle of silk garments at her feet, intent on joining him on the bed.

Qadir ordered her to stop again. Puzzled, she complied and waited impatiently. For what seemed like an eternity, she stood before him, and her anger returned. Tired of waiting, she raised her eyes and glared at him.

"Dance for me," he growled.

Realizing he was playing with her, she swallowed her anger and swayed to the rhythmic beat of the muffled drums. Growing more confident, she twirled and spun around the room, moving with abandon, until her dance became more erotic, and she moved closer to the bed.

Cassie was so engrossed in her performance, she failed to see him move. A startled cry escaped her lips when he grabbed her hair and pulled her onto the bed. He laughed hoarsely at her cries of pain. Staring into his soulless eyes, she shuddered, reminded of a cobra she had seen in the market square of Cairo.

"Unhand me, you barbarian," Cassie ground through her clenched teeth, unaware of the effect her defiance was having on him.

His heavy-lidded eyes widened, and his hand lashed out, catching her on the cheek, bringing hot tears to her eyes. "I think we have had this conversation before, and I do hate having to repeat myself. It would seem you have yet to learn obedience to your master!" As he spat out the words, he grabbed her hands and secured them to the headboard.

"Wha…What are you going to do to me?" she stammered fearfully, as she tried to pull free.

"I am going to give you the first of many lessons," he answered harshly. As he spoke, he slid down and quickly secured her ankles to the bedposts.

While she watched, he discarded his robe, and she inhaled sharply—his desire was all too evident. When he retrieved a whip from a side table, a cry of dismay slipped from her as she realized his intent. He smiled cruelly and began the training.

Through gathering clouds of pain, Cassie had a fleeting thought of Kira, whom she had abandoned in the desert. She had a strange feeling of jealousy, thinking she would have been better off dying back there with the little half-breed and her miserable horse. Dimly aware of the other pains coming from her body as he fed his perverted passion, she finally succumbed and allowed herself to drift away. Overcome, Cassie sank into darkness.

It was a good deal later before Qadir discarded her body to seek his own rest. Cassie was carried back to her room, but she remained unconscious. When they placed her on her bed, she briefly awoke, wrapped herself in a blanket, and curled up in a tight ball. No one heard her call for help, or if they did, they ignored her. The evening breeze carried her moans of pain through the lattice and up into the uncaring sky.

CHAPTER 10

Cool indigo shadows hugged the lush banks of the slowly moving stream, and slender silver bodies flashed among the reed beds. The feeding fish darted from the shadows into the sunlit depths to snatch water bugs and floating flies, paying no heed to the woven basket suspended in the water. Kira remained motionless, her arms aching from holding the homemade weir. But patience was the key, as Grandmother had often explained. Become one with the water and the reeds, and the fish will forget you are there until it's too late.

Concentrating, Kira watched several fish dart out together and slid the basket behind them. Startled, they instinctively swam back to the safety of the bank and straight into her waiting trap. With a smooth scooping motion, she lifted the basket with its wiggling contents and returned to the shade of a nearby palm, where she cleaned the fish.

Wrapping the discarded bits in large leaves, she buried them some distance from her camp. She had yet to see any predators lurking in the valley, but she heard screams at night from beyond the cliffs, reminding her of the mountain lions of her childhood home. It was enough to make her cautious in disposing of anything that might attract them.

Cleaning her knife and rinsing her hands thoroughly, she used thin sticks to skewer the fillets and laid them over her small fire. Within minutes, the crispy morsels were ready, and she ate them directly from the sticks. Even without seasoning, they were delicious, a welcome change from the fruits and nuts that were her usual fare. The thought of how she must look, kneeling in the grass and eating her meal like a wild savage, inwardly amused her. If her college classmates could see her now, she thought with a chuckle. They had taunted her for her mixed heritage and for years it was the cause of many tears, but in the end, it only made her stronger. Kira was not ashamed of who she was. It was thanks to that very heritage she thrived in her new environment.

After her meal, she leaned over the pool and washed her face. Then she brushed her teeth with a toothbrush she had fashioned by flaying the ends of a thick reed stem, another tribal trick. As she rinsed her mouth, she studied her face. She had blossomed with good health from weeks of fresh air and food, not to mention the daily exercise of walking and swimming. Her skin had turned a golden tan, and her long hair was layered with shades of silver and gold.

Aware of the dangers of sun and wind on her hair and skin, she usually wore a long-sleeved shirt and trousers, avoiding the noonday sun and using the early morning and late afternoon for most of her tasks. Without conventional cosmetics, she used the natural oil found in the young palms as a salve for her skin and to condition her hair.

Her burnoose was becoming threadbare, and she used it only as a blanket now. However, her clothes were not much better, and she would be in trouble if she could not replace them soon. Later, as she lay in her crude shelter staring at the stars through the rough thatch walls, she contemplated how she might make some sort of clothing and remembered the looms her tribe used. Her head full of ideas, she soon fell asleep and dreamed of swaying palms and soft sandy beaches.

Time ceased to have meaning, and Kira lost track of how long she had been in the valley. When she stopped to think about it, it was like a story she'd read about something that happened to someone else. But at some deep and personal level, she knew she wasn't ready to face the past or make decisions about the future. Perhaps it was a natural reaction to the shock of her father's death, coupled with her harrowing experience in the desert. Her reality was survival in this secret place.

She spent much of her daily time gathering and preparing food, but she had a few hours each day with nothing to do. Initially, she kept close to her camp and ventured just far enough to find food. Amber visited her regularly and accompanied her on short walks. Ndee followed them occasionally, and Kira no longer feared him and felt safer when he was about. But eventually, her curiosity led her to investigate the mysterious walls she had hidden behind the day she first met Ndee and the herd.

Upon returning to the lake, she was astounded to discover a labyrinth of ancient ruins. An extensive system of walls surrounded the remains of several small one-room buildings clustered around a larger one. Small shards of pottery littered the site, and she admired their beautiful patterns and colors. She wasn't surprised to see a common theme—the figures of running horses. Fascinated, she returned to explore the site often.

One afternoon, she uncovered a bracelet of beaten silver and a simple gold ring, but they were nothing compared to her finds a few days later in and around the largest building. There she discovered tile floors and paved courtyards peeking through a light layer of sand. Though worn by time, their colors were still vibrant. She was intrigued by a system of basins, bordered with lovely turquoise and gold tile, and low stone benches eroded by wind and sand. Losing herself in flights of imagination, she tried to reconstruct the buildings in her mind and wondered what happened to the people who built it.

One morning, Kira was sitting on one of the benches when Amber interrupted her musing, looking for attention. Reaching up to scratch behind Amber's ear, she was careful to avoid the tender skin marking the old neck wound. When Amber nickered and moved closer, Kira stood up on the bench, leaned forward, and rested her arms on Amber's glossy back. Amber snorted and wriggled her ears but didn't move away. Many nights Kira had lain awake wondering if she could ride Amber, but she was hesitant to try, until now.

Gripping a fistful of mane, she eased one leg over Amber's back until she sat astride and for a moment, nothing happened. Then Amber's ears swiveled, and Kira detected a tremble in the silky skin under her legs. Amber turned her head to stare at Kira with a look of surprise but remained still, lulling Kira into thinking this was going to be easier than she thought. Alas, it was not to be. Amber's eyes rolled, and she moved forward in a stiff-legged walk. Kira held on tightly, ready to dismount at the first sign of rejection, but was unprepared for the speed and force of Amber's reaction and found herself deposited with great suddenness on the ground.

Dazed but unhurt, she saw Amber standing a few feet away, also dazed and unhurt. Kira burst out laughing at the baffled expression in the horse's eyes and rose unsteadily to her feet while rubbing her abused posterior. Snorting, Amber eyed her suspiciously, and Kira realized this was going to take as much time as it would with any untrained horse. Luckily, time was something she had plenty of.

Over the next few days, she placed a basket on Amber's back as they walked through the groves. After a few days, she added a second basket, joined to the first by a woven strap. Each day, she would add weight to the baskets, and after a few spills, Amber carried the loads without complaint. By the end of another week, Amber would let Kira sit on her back for a few moments at a time. Pleased with her progress, Kira longed to test Amber's gaits, but she forced herself to be patient.

Eventually, she got her wish. One morning, she eased up on Amber's back, rejoicing when Amber walked forward with no concern. A little urging was all it took, and Kira's heart soared when Amber broke into a canter, smooth as silk. Feeling the wind rushing through her hair, she squealed in delight when the horse broke into a gallop. Exhilarated, Kira held on tightly, fearing she might fall, but Amber seemed aware of her rider and transitioned carefully between her gaits. Before long, the two friends were dashing about the valley, causing Ndee no amount of trouble.

It was a turning point in their relationship. Amber had given Kira her trust, along with her heart, and Kira felt a bond with her that deepened daily. As they became more involved, Kira grew closer to Amber, who spent more time with her, hanging around the camp or in the ruins.

Blissfully happy, Kira made friends with the young colts and fillies, and they played chase with her in the shallows and enjoyed her scratching sticks too. The older horses remained aloof but grew to accept her. She was content to watch them and study the behavior of Ndee and his mares. Ndee still kept his distance from Kira, but she was thrilled when he accepted her presence and allowed her to mingle with his herd.

Perhaps she would have been content for longer if she hadn't found the chain. It began like any other day. The chirping of the date birds awakened her at sunrise, and after a quick meal of fruit and nuts, she spent the morning digging in a part of the ruins marked by a greater abundance of the gold and blue tile work.

Using crude tools she fashioned from natural materials, Kira painstakingly revealed intricate tile inlays surrounding a broken dais. By the base of the wall behind the dais, she found bits and pieces of woven cloth buried beneath the rubble. The turquoise color of the material had faded, but the designs were still fresh. She suspected that the metallic threads used in their creation were made of gold, since they appeared impervious to decay.

Using a brush of frayed reeds, she cleared away the larger pebbles and bits of stone until she could pry one corner of the material from the ground. Startled to see a brighter glint of gold beneath the ancient fabric, she grabbed her waterskin and dribbled a bit of water on it. With a pounding heart and nervous fingers, she worked the metal free of its earthly grasp. Bit by bit, she uncovered a heavy rope chain, and when the last of the dirt broke loose, she beheld a large gold disc hanging from the chain. She carried it to the lake's edge, dipped it in the water, and gasped in disbelief at the familiar pattern of turquoise stones and yellow gems.

Attracted by Kira's obvious agitation, Amber stepped closer, but was unprepared when Kira ran over and leapt up on her back. Snorting, Amber hesitated, but Kira urged her into a canter that became a fast gallop as they headed back to camp. Throwing herself off before Amber came to a complete stop, Kira scrambled into her rude shelter.

Seconds later, she crawled out, clutching her father's old shirt. She laid the ancient medallion carefully on the ground, and with trembling hands, unwrapped her father's shirt, exposing his gold medallion. She had quit wearing it every day and stashed it in her pack along with her mother's chain and father's ring for safekeeping.

Tears dripped down her face as the memories came rushing back. She could smell the acrid smoke from the burnt engines, feel the pain of the glass shards cutting her palms, and see the horror of her father's dead body. Her ears filled with buzzing, and she swallowed thickly as she stared at the twin disks. The only difference was the chains.

The chain that belonged to her father was made of finely crafted gold links, while the chain from the valley was a rope made of twisted gold strands. Otherwise, they were identical. But how was that possible, unless, maybe, there was a connection? Shame filled her heart when she remembered suggesting her father was talking nonsense when he insisted there was something special about the medallion. Here was proof he had been onto something, and she cried harder at the thought that she was the only one who knew that now.

Unaware of how long she cried, she was roused by gentle nudges from her confused horse. Sniffing loudly and wiping her face with her father's shirt, Kira placed her father's medallion around her neck once more. At first it lay cold and heavy on her heart, but when it warmed from the heat of her skin, it suddenly felt right, as if it belonged. Slipping her mother's chain with her father's ring over her head, she felt the strength of both items. She wrapped the medallion and chain from the ruins in the shirt and stuffed it in her pack. Emotionally exhausted, she leaned back against the trunk of a palm, deep in thought, and stared at the far cliffs with one hand pressed against the medallion that warmed her chest.

As the shock faded, Kira felt a gentle breeze caress her cheek, and she blinked in surprise when she heard her grandmother's voice whisper in her ear.

"Kira, it is time." The breeze tickled her neck.

"Grandmother, is that you?" She sat up and looked wildly about.

"Yes, Kira, and you must follow your path." The voice was fading.

"Grandmother?" Kira called out, but the voice was gone, and the breeze had vanished. Sighing, she never doubted for a minute she heard her grandmother. She knew her grandmother was right—she could no longer hide away in the valley, pretending she was lost, and ignoring all that had happened. Her father was dead, and with him his dreams, unless she could return to civilization and share them with the world.

Fortified with new resolve, she rode Amber back to the lake, choosing a shady spot next to the ruins where she could watch the herd and think and plan. Transporting food would not be a problem but keeping it fresh would. Transporting water would be the real issue, but she had the waterskin, and she knew where at least one oasis was, thanks to Amber. And based on her father's original map, she knew a bigger oasis existed somewhere to the south.

While she shifted through ideas in her head, a sad thought struck her—she would be leaving the herd behind. With misty eyes, she watched the colts and fillies frolicking nearby and realized this might be the last time she would see them.

Ndee stood guard close to where she sat, and Kira admired his glorious golden coat in the noonday sun. She had come to rely on his presence, feeling safe whenever he was near. As if sensing her regard, the stallion trained his dark gaze toward her. Smiling at his intense look, she raised a hand in a half salute. Puzzlement settled on his regal features for a split second, then snorting and pawing, he turned his attention back to his wards, as if to hide his interest in the insignificant human.

She smiled at his transparency until she felt a stab of sadness through her heart, knowing that tomorrow she would have to say goodbye to her secret valley of gold. But she was comforted knowing she'd carry the memory of this place deep in her heart forever, next to her father's face and her mother's smile. Resolved, she stood and sent Ndee a heart-felt mental farewell.

Kira had never been one to waste time debating with herself. Once she had made up her mind, she usually acted quickly, some had said recklessly, to put her plans into action. Now was no different. Returning to her camp, she sorted through her worldly possessions, choosing only what she would need. For food, she chose mostly green fruit that would ripen as she traveled and added the inevitable dates and nuts. Satisfied she had as much as she could carry, she looked with regret at the baskets she would leave behind. Perhaps a future archaeologist would find their remains and wonder how Native American designs ended up halfway around the world.

Shaking her head, she prepared her last supper under the date palms. Anticipating she would have a limited supply of food and water in the desert, she cooked double her usual share of fish and ate as much as she could manage. As the sun slid behind the craggy cliff tops, she buried the last of the fish bones and lay by her small fire to gaze up at the sky. Pale blue faded to lavender, which was soon replaced with the deep purple-red and gold of sunset. She always found it amazing how the ruddy hues melted into midnight-blues. God's color wheel in motion, she thought dreamily as she drifted into slumber.

The next morning, Kira rose with the sun and looked out over the marsh, relieved Amber was nowhere in sight. As she stood, saying a silent farewell, tears threatened until she felt the medallion under her shirt growing hot. Without thinking, she pulled the ancient one from her pack and stared at it, amazed yet again at how similar it was to her father's. At that moment, Ndee galloped up and slid to a stop with a half-rear. When he stomped once and gazed at her intently, she suddenly knew what she had to do.

A few minutes later, she dusted off her hands, gathered her pack, and with a last look at her crude home, turned to follow the trail up the hillside to the tunnel. Afraid to face her friend and say goodbye, Kira hoped to reach the tunnel before Amber showed up for their morning ride. Amber belonged safe in the valley, just like the ancient medallion now buried beneath the palms by her camp. Unfortunately, before she reached the top of the path, a familiar neigh rang out, and with a thundering of hooves, Amber caught up with her. Kira could not help crying as she stroked Amber's forehead while the horse playfully nuzzled her hair.

"Oh, go on, Amber," Kira cried, striving to regain her composure as she pushed Amber back down the path. "I've got to go back and find my people, and you must stay here with Ndee and the herd. You will be safe here." Choking back a sob, she spun and ran to the tunnel entrance. Behind her, Amber whinnied, but Kira refused to look back, knowing it would break her determination. Engulfed by the cool darkness, she stumbled forward, blinded by her tears, pausing only once to rub her head, which she bumped painfully when she forgot to duck.

Passing the last tight corner, she saw the far entrance looming ahead and hastened toward the light. Intent upon getting out of the tunnel, she didn't hear pursuit until she fell forward into the blinding light. Dazed and crying, she stopped to lean against the steep sides of the enormous boulder blocking the entrance when she heard hoofbeats echoing behind her. Whirling around, she glared angrily at the emerging horse, waved her arms frantically, and shouted, "Go back! You can't leave the valley! You'll be captured… or killed!"

Amber simply trotted closer and stood calmly, apparently unconcerned by Kira's agitated manner. Kira tried unsuccessfully to turn the horse, but no amount of shouting or arm waving helped. With a cry of frustration, she attempted another tactic and moved as fast as she dared down the path, believing the horse would not follow. But she was disappointed when Amber not only caught up with her but also pushed her aside to take the lead. "Hey," Kira yelled as she stumbled after her, "wait up! Would you just stop a minute?"

Amber refused to stop, and Kira lost control of her temper and chased the horse down the treacherous path. By the time she reached level ground, Kira's anger had dissolved, and she arrived exhausted from her exertions to find Amber waiting patiently. Overwhelmed with relief at not having to say goodbye, she hugged Amber's silky neck, whispering her thanks. Amber merely snorted at her foolish antics. Feeling stronger with her friend by her side, Kira forged ahead, determined to reach the oasis by nightfall. Amber was content to follow and together they left the valley behind.

Kira's spirits continued to rise, and by the time they reached the first scrubby bushes on the outskirts of the oasis, she felt like her old confident self. The small pool appeared to be undisturbed, and the travelers settled in for the night. Kira ate some of her rations and took a quick dip before turning in. She lay floating in the shallows, watching the approaching sunset and feeling the cool fingers of the evening breeze as it ripped the surface of the water and traced the contours of her body. Shivering slightly, she left the pool, slipped into her clothes, and wrapped herself in her old burnoose. Using her pack for a headrest, she made a bed on the grassy bank. Amber stood guard nearby and Kira, feeling safe, fell asleep almost at once.

The evening passed without incident, and they both woke refreshed early the next morning. Kira ate a quick breakfast, washed down with water from the pool, before gathering fresh dates while Amber finished a meal of grass. Unsure as to the exact direction to take, Kira walked toward the south, trying to stay near the foothills. Amber walked by her side, keeping a watchful eye on the horizon. By noon, Kira was feeling the effects of the relentless sun and found a shady spot near a large outcropping where they could stop and rest.

When the sun passed its zenith, they returned to the trail and continued their journey. Amber took the lead now, and Kira followed, thinking Amber knew where she was going. By the time the sun approached the western horizon, patches of scrubby grass appeared near their path, and looking ahead, Kira was excited to see the familiar silhouette of nodding palms. She would have walked straight into the oasis had not Amber stopped near the first line of low bushes. Kira paused to see what she would do next.

Amber was on the alert, swinging her head back and forth, testing the air. After a few minutes, she walked forward, stopping every few feet to sniff the air. Kira followed silently. When they emerged from the brush, Kira saw the shining water under a thick cluster of palms, but

Amber paused one last time. After another moment, she appeared to relax and trotted to the large pool to drink her fill.

Kira joined her for a long, satisfying drink before dipping her bandana in the cool water to wash her sweaty face and arms. Behind several palms, she found a good place to sleep. Curling up in her burnoose, she looked up to see Amber standing at attention nearby. She noticed the farther Amber got from the valley, the more alert she became, and Kira realized Amber would not be sleeping that night. Worried about her friend, Kira watched her for a few more minutes. Amber lifted her head and huffed, sniffing the night air, and her ears twitched at the sound of a distant howl. Hearing the far-off predator, Kira shivered, thankful Amber was on guard. When no more sounds echoed from the hills, Kira drifted to sleep thinking about what might lie ahead.

CHAPTER 11

The next morning, Kira was awakened by the mournful sound of the dying breeze blowing through the rocky landscape. Shaking the sleep from her head, she grew alarmed when she saw Amber was nowhere in sight. Without Amber to guide her, she didn't know where to go. Fighting back despair, she shouted, "Amber! Amber, where are you?" Silence. *Where is she?* Kira panicked. She knew she couldn't turn back. Even if she could find the valley again, it would only be a temporary haven. When Amber didn't appear, she calmed her fears, and began walking, praying Amber had chosen this path for a reason. She knew the horse would find her if she wanted to.

While she travelled along the outskirts of the foothills, her mind searched for a plan. If she could bargain for transportation and get to a major town, she could at least send word to her grandmother back home. Remembering her father's money belt, she wondered just how much money it contained as she had never counted it.

Seeking the shade of a rocky outcropping, she removed the heavy band of leather and emptied its contents on the ground, surprised to find several hundred dollars in local currency, greenbacks, and gold pieces. The sight of the gold was reassuring—her father had known the value of this universal currency. Satisfied with the tidy sum, she stuffed everything back into the belt and secured it about her waist.

As she readjusted her clothing, she untangled her mother's chain that was wrapped around the medallion hanging around her neck. Removing the medallion, she studied the disc with renewed interest. Running her fingertip over the irregular turquoise stones embedded in its surface, she pondered their meaning. Kira knew from her studies that turquoise was actually quite rare and could only be found in a few places. Egypt and Persia were the closest sources to this region. Archaeologists had found turquoise in the tombs of the pharaohs. Its value was based on depth of color and degree of hardness. The stones in the medallion were threaded with silver, which spoke to their rarity and worth. The medallion was worth a lot, but she knew she would never part with it.

When the midday sun reflected from the tiny sparkling jewels embedded around the long stone set in the middle, she was reminded of yellow topaz, although these gems were much too brilliant. The thought of yellow diamonds never entered her mind. As she studied the disk, the size and placement of the turquoise stones tugged at another memory. *I've seen this pattern before, but where?*

Engrossed in her thoughts, she failed to notice the shadow that drifted over a rock nearby. As she leaned over to get a better look at the medallion, something lightly bounced off her shoulder. She glanced over to see it was only a small pebble, and she returned her attention to the disk. When she felt a series of bumps on her head and back and saw more bits of stone bouncing down around her, she inhaled sharply and, trusting her instincts, dove sideways, twisting around to look at the ledge above. Her swift reaction saved her life, but it was not enough to prevent the injury that followed. Her thigh exploded in pain, and she screamed and rolled back against the hillside. When she raised her tearful eyes, she looked directly into a pair of blazing yellow ones. Before her crouched a huge tawny lion, spitting and growling in fury.

Shocked, she froze, her mind in a panic. She couldn't tear her eyes from the snarling predator crouching a few feet away. Near her hand was the stout walking stick she had brought from the valley. Returning to her senses, she grabbed it. The lion made a swipe with one meaty paw at the paltry weapon, nearly knocking it from her hands. She brandished the stick, even though she realized what a pitiful defense it was.

Thoughts of a horrible death almost overwhelmed her, but she refused to succumb to her fears. Trembling, she tried to scoot backwards, closer to the cliff side, but the flaring pain from her leg stopped her. A brief glance downward weakened her resolve. Her pant leg hung in tatters, exposing four bloody furrows. When the lion crept closer, she could not take her eyes away from the menacing figure. *Oh God, please don't let me die like this!* She gripped the staff tighter and waved it at the lion. Suddenly, she felt a surge of power, as if her warrior ancestor rose inside her. Struggling up on one knee, she screamed at the lion, "Aieyaa! Aieyaa!"

Growling and lashing its tail erratically, the lion paused but must have decided she was no threat because Kira could see it was about to spring. She saw the look in its eyes and recognized the mind of a fearless predator. Gulping nervously, she steeled herself for the inevitable pounce, but what happened next was so sudden, she yelled aloud. Amber's ear-splitting scream filled the air, along with the thunder of her hooves.

The lion barely had time to turn and defend itself from the churning golden fury descending on it. One hoof, as hard as a desert mountain, lashed out, catching the lion on the shoulder. The blow sent it rolling, and it howled with rage. When it tried to regain its feet, Amber jumped forward, both front legs extended. The lion squealed in pain as it took the blow on its side, and Kira swore she could hear its ribs breaking.

Amber turned to deliver a powerful kick, but her hooves met thin air as the lion rolled away, squalling. It wasted no time and spun around, streaking toward the rocks, howling with each awkward jump as it climbed higher to safety. Stomping the ground, Amber screamed her challenge, as if half-hoping it would return to fight, but the lion never stopped and disappeared in the rocks above.

Kira cried out, and Amber cantered back to her side, where she lowered her head and gently nudged her. "Oh, Amber!" Kira sobbed as she reached to hug the silken neck of her friend. "You didn't leave me. You saved my life!" She buried her head in the soft curve of Amber's neck. "But you could have been killed," she admonished, hugging her tighter, as she tried to ignore the increasing pain in her leg. Amber snorted as if in disbelief. "Well, you could have been seriously hurt," Kira continued and looked up at her beautiful face. Amber merely nickered, as if to say she was never in any real danger. Feeling faint, Kira released her hold and sank to the ground.

Amber sniffed Kira's thigh, blowing warm breaths on the wound, and when their eyes met, Kira could see her concern. "Yes, yes, I know I have a big problem, but really, it's going to be okay," she said, more to reassure herself than her friend. Kira knew she had to act fast to stop the bleeding. She tried to reach her pack and Amber helped by nudging it closer.

With shaking hands, Kira pulled out her knife and cut a long strip from the old burnoose and wound it around her thigh just above the wound, tying the ends in a loose knot. Slipping the hatchet handle under the loop, she gingerly twisted. The pain was excruciating, and she feared she would pass out, but a slow numbing in her calf let her know it was working. With her other hand, she fumbled with the waterskin and poured water over the ravaged area. The blood and dirt washed away, but the increase in pain took her breath away. Gasping, she fell backward, eyes clenched tightly, fighting to remain conscious.

When she looked down again and saw her ripped flesh, she blanched, but was relieved to see the bleeding had slowed. Mindful not to leave the tourniquet too tight, she released the pressure. She saw the medallion on the ground beside her and, wanting to keep it safe, she wrapped it in her father's shirt and pushed it into the bottom of her pack.

Feeling fainter by the moment, she tucked herself behind a small rock ledge. Exhausted, she lay in the meager shade and drifted in and out of consciousness, plagued by nightmares of giant lions leaping from high hilltops. Once during the night, she cried out in pain, and her eyes rolled fearfully as she looked for the ghostly beasts. Amber stood like a silvery statue in the moonlight, and when Kira saw her, a calm washed over her. She slipped back into fevered dreams, but now her charging golden guardian chased away the lions. Even in her sleep, she was aware Amber was watching over her. But when she woke again, she gasped weakly in alarm when she saw her guardian had disappeared. Softly crying, she hoped she hadn't been abandoned and prayed that Amber had gone for help before falling back into complete darkness.

CHAPTER 12

The boy brushed the silky brown bangs that escaped his headwrap away from his eyes and surveyed the nearby hills, bored as young boys often are when assigned a task that involves constant silence and minimal movement. When his family had stopped to make camp, his adoptive father, Saad, suggested that he, Jabari, take the first watch. So he scampered up the slope until he found his present perch, where he could watch for approaching travelers or wild beasts.

After an hour in the scorching sun, Jabari was contemplating finding another lookout point, preferably in the shade. He sighed in frustration. So far, their annual trading trip had been uneventful. They had encountered no other travelers between their stops, and wild lions or hyenas hadn't bothered them, either. But he still kept the rifle by his side.

Wanting to be the first to offer much-needed goods to the isolated hill tribes, Jabari's father, Saad, had assembled a small caravan of camels and, along with his family, and started the trip two weeks earlier than normal. They planned to end this year's journey on the high plateau where the Tri-Annual Race would take place. The final trading stops were always Sheik Jalil's and Sheik Ehsaan's kingdoms in the high mountains—they were the friendliest tribes and, more importantly, the wealthiest.

They had made good time that day and were not too far from their first trading stop. Jabari was glad for the rest but eager to continue the journey, even though it would be weeks before they reached Sheik Jalil's, where he would see the fabled golden horses. Maybe this year he could talk Jalil into letting him ride one. Jabari liked nothing better than riding horses. When he was astride a desert mount, he could imagine he was more than just an adopted son of a simple trader.

While fidgeting atop his rock and lost in fanciful thoughts—mostly involving silk robes and a golden horse—Jabari was startled when he heard a noise behind him. He cautiously turned his head until he could see the westward trail out of the corner of his eye. The last thing he expected to see was a golden horse poised for flight, and he stifled a yell of surprise. It looked ready to run, and he knew he must not startle it.

When he saw it relax, he slid down from the boulder until he stood on firm ground and gazed in wonder at the filly. *I must be dreaming. This cannot be happening to me.* His mind raced feverishly, trying to think about what to do. Then he remembered the sweet dates he had stuffed in his pocket. An energetic boy, Jabari often carried snacks to enjoy between the rest stops. He pulled out the warm, sticky fruit, extended his hand palm up toward the horse, and stood still, afraid any movement would scare the creature into flight.

As minutes passed, his arm trembled while sweat dripped down his cheeks, but he found his patience was rewarded when she slowly approached. The world seemed to stop, and Jabari closed his eyes in anticipation, listening to the beating of his heart. He imagined he could hear her mighty heart pounding in matching rhythm. He nearly jumped out of his sandals when he felt her warm, moist breath on his palm. Peeking out of one eye, he watched her lips hover over the dates, and she sniffed his hand and arm several times before plucking them from his palm.

When he raised his eyes to meet hers, he recognized the intelligence shining within their depths. Mesmerized, he forgot his previous caution and reached out to touch her velvety nose. She stood still, allowing him the opportunity to touch her cheek as well. Convinced he was dreaming, he eased forward but stopped when she took a step back. Waiting, he was relieved she did not bolt, and he reached out again. This time, she lowered her head and allowed him to caress her neck. Flooded with joy, he continued his soft stroking, his fear forgotten.

Jabari's eyes traveled over her magnificent body, noting that she bore no harness, nor were any marks to be found of bridle or saddle. His eyes widened in shock, seeing the scars on her flank. He had seen similar marks on wounded camels—the marks of the desert lion! She had been very lucky to escape such a powerful beast.

Admiring her long silky mane, his hand traveled underneath it, and she shook her head. Attuned to her response and curious, he lifted the silvery golden mass and revealed an uglier scar—one he distinctly recognized. He had seen what bullets did to predators that his father had to shoot while they journeyed through the isolated foothills, and a surge of anger engulfed him. *Who would shoot such a horse?* Jabari knew of many men who would give all they had to own one of the mythical golden creatures, but to kill a horse, any horse was unheard of. Horses were a gift from Allah.

Clucking in sympathy, Jabari talked out loud, as was his wont around horses. "You have been through great dangers and have suffered many hurts, my friend, and yet here you stand, still proud and free... and so beautiful!" At the sound of his voice, she rubbed her head against his shoulder and nudged him one last time before walking back up the trail.

Surprised, Jabari called out, "Where are you going? Please stop!" She looked back at him, shook her head, and stomped her foot. Jabari had a gift for reading animals and communicating with them as well. He sensed what she wanted and hastened to follow, but then paused. "I can't go off into the hills with you! I can't leave without letting my father know." Flustered, he thought hard.

Jabari knew he should tell his father, but how could explain he had met a golden "spirit" horse and that the horse wanted him to follow her? *He will think I have desert fever, or I am making it up!* Jabari had a reputation for telling elaborate stories, and he knew it would be difficult to convince his father. His mind in a whirl, he had an idea. Collecting several stones, he laid them out in a simple design. With his hand, he smoothed a spot of ground and, using the tip of a small, jeweled dagger he kept hidden in his robe, he etched a series of symbols next to his design.

"Hold on, my beauty," he reassured the horse, who paced back and forth. "I must finish this, or my father will not know what has happened." Stepping back, he surveyed his handiwork. It was roughly done, but his father could read it. Satisfied, he advanced to the horse's side. "Lead on, oh golden one."

The horse trotted back in the direction from which she had come, and Jabari was hard pressed to keep up. "Hey! Slow down. I only have two legs to your four!" he cried out as he stumbled along. When he glanced up and found he'd lost sight of her, he panicked. *Oh, merciful Allah, please don't let it disappear now!* The trail became twisted and narrow, and he pushed ahead and almost collided with her rear when he rounded a tight turn. Gasping for breath, he bent over. "You have led me on a wild chase, my friend."

Straightening, he wondered why she had stopped next to a low shelf of rock by a sheer vertical wall. He saw nothing unusual until she lowered her head and nudged something behind the shelf, and he caught sight of a small, booted foot. *What in Allah's name have we here?* This was a day of many surprises, he thought as he peered over the rock shelf, then nearly tumbled forward in shock when he saw a young woman lying on the ground. *A foreigner!* He inhaled sharply at the sight of her pale face and long silvery braid, but gasped louder at the sight of her ravaged, bloody leg.

The horse whickered and continued to nudge the injured woman, and Jabari's heart fell. "You may be wild and free, my beauty, but you have given your heart to someone," he said sadly. When he had first seen the golden horse, he had thought that he might claim her as his own, but she obviously belonged to the woman. He shook his head ruefully and knelt to help the woman. Alarms flared in his head when he inspected the blood-encrusted wound. He recognized the marks.

"Merciful Allah," he exclaimed out loud. He laid his hand on her neck and detected a faint pulse. "Well, your friend is still alive, and that is certainly a miracle," he said to the horse.

The woman must have great courage to have survived the attack and still have the sense to treat her wound, he thought, as he studied the crude tourniquet wrapped around her thigh. But it was obvious she was unwell. The high color in her cheeks suggested fever, and her failure to wake was not a good sign.

Needing room to maneuver, Jabari urged the horse to move back. She complied with a neigh of frustration and the sound was sharp against the rocky landscape. When the woman stirred fitfully, Jabari took heart, having feared he'd arrived too late. And it would be too late if she didn't receive medical attention immediately. He needed to get her back to camp. His mother, Samira, would know what to do.

Trying to lift the woman, Jabari found he didn't have the strength and considered leaving her while he sought help. The problem was he doubted his ability to find the way back and was worried the lion might return. As he eased her back to the ground, she moaned louder, and when her eyes flew open, he was stunned. He had never seen eyes as blue-green as the still shallows of an oasis pool. When she struggled to rise, he grew alarmed.

"Amber," she cried out.

Amazed at her strength, Jabari helped her into a sitting position as she continued to call out the word "Amber." Her speech reminded him of the foreigners he had heard in the coastal marketplaces. He had learned a few words during his rare visits, but he did not understand this one. When the horse rushed to her side, he made the connection. *So, she calls her Amber.*

"What is your name?" he asked the woman in broken English, but she did not appear to hear him. Her failure to acknowledge his presence was worrying, and he tried again to lift her. "You must try to stand," Jabari yelled in Arabic. "Get up now!" He wasn't sure if she understood his language, but she must have heard the urgency in his voice because she struggled to stand. Leaning her against the cliff, he let go long enough to reach for the horse. He coaxed her forward until she was parallel to the shelf and her back was level with the woman's chest.

Jabari helped the woman onto Amber's back and held his breath, afraid she would slip off. But she only slumped forward with a groan and draped her arms around the horse's neck. After sending a prayer to Allah, he shouldered her pack and turned to speak to Amber. "My friend, you must help me take her to safety. You must go with great care and walk smoothly," he explained as he stroked her cheek, hoping she would understand.

Amber's ears twitched back and forth, and she stepped forward. Jabari walked close by her side, holding the woman in place, and together they began the slow journey back to camp. Jabari felt his spirits lift, and he whispered words of encouragement and prayed they would reach safety before the sun set.

CHAPTER 13

"Samira, my flower, how are you coming with our midday meal?" Saad called out. His stomach was reminding him, as it usually did, that evening was approaching.

"It won't be long now," the cheery voice of his adored wife floated over the backs of the resting camels. "Perhaps you should call for Jabari?"

Having helped his brother, Amal, finish mending a harness for one of the camels, Saad stood, rubbing the small of his back, and nodded his head in silent agreement. Lumbering to the lookout area where he had left Jabari earlier, he chuckled to himself. *I am sure my son is tired from his first watch.* His son. Jabari was not really his son, but in Saad's heart, and the heart of his wife, he was. He smiled at the memory of finding the boy long ago. It was certainly the hand of Allah that led him to the oasis that fateful night.

The oasis was along the old northern route, one they no longer travelled. It was in an area far from their present camp on the southern route. His family had stopped for the evening and were setting up their tents when one of their camels wandered off. When they found it, it was drinking from a small, hidden pool of water. They were shocked to discover the bodies of four dead men all dressed in black nearby, but even more so to find a tiny infant wrapped in black rags lying among the bodies.

Covered in blood, the baby boy cried fitfully, but Samira quickly determined he was weak but unhurt. One look into his silver eyes and he became hers. She took charge with the fierceness of a mother lion. When she removed the rags to wrap the baby boy in clean cloth, a small object fell at her feet. Saad picked it up and discovered a sheathed dagger made of gold and encrusted with turquoise stones and yellow gems. It was of obvious worth, and Saad tucked it away in his shoulder pack and continued his investigation of the area.

A great struggle had taken place, but why everyone was dead, except the baby, was a mystery to him. He thanked Allah the vultures had yet to descend, or the baby would have suffered the same fate. The men appeared to have died recently, maybe within the last two days, and Saad was fearful their scent would attract hyenas or lions. With the help of his brother, Amal, he dragged the bodies away from the oasis and buried them in the sand.

Samira fretted over the baby and tried to coax it to eat, but it was too young for solid foods. Forced to use the only source of milk available, her camel, she filled her waterskin and coaxed the tip into the infant's mouth, offering her thanks to Allah when the baby accepted the substitute without protest.

Saad had never questioned her about what would happen to the infant. As far as he was concerned, the law of the desert and the will of Allah had spared the baby's life, and he knew they had been chosen to find him.

"Oh, my brave little boy," Samira crooned. "I will call you Jabari."

Saad exchanged a warm look with his young bride. As usual, they were in complete agreement. By the next morning, they were confident he was going to be fine, and they had packed up and resumed their travels. The secret of Jabari's birth remained buried in the sand with the unknown dead.

The following years were good to Saad, who credited his growing fortunes to the rescue of the baby that fateful night. Jabari was a joy to his new family. With his caramel hair and silver eyes, he grew into a handsome fellow. Quick and intelligent, he was unusually mature as well. When Jabari was old enough to understand, Saad presented him with the dagger and told him how he had come into their lives. Jabari was saddened to discover they were not his real parents, but Saad assured him they were his mother and father in every sense of the word, and they loved him as their true son.

Lost in his memories, Saad suddenly realized he was near the rock where he had left Jabari to stand guard, but he was nowhere in sight. Concerned, he searched the immediate area, but to no avail. "Jabari, Jabari!" he shouted. Only the wind answered his calls. Desperate, he tried calling once more. "Jabari, where are you?" His concern blossomed into fear. *Where did he go? What made him leave the safety of the camp?*

Hampered by his ample girth, he climbed laboriously over the tumbled rocks, puffing from his exertions. Searching near the slopes, he soon discovered Jabari's rough marker, stones placed in the shape of an arrow pointing west. The crude symbols scratched in the dirt read, "follow me." He wanted to rush in the direction indicated but he had to stop and think.

He knew he shouldn't leave Samira and Amal without a word, but he was torn between his desire to find Jabari or to return to camp for more help. Fortunately, he didn't have to make a choice when a golden horse appeared on the trail ahead. "Allah, save us!" he exclaimed aloud, so startled to see the mythical creature that he fell backwards against the rocks. The horse didn't look surprised and stopped not far away. That's when he saw Jabari standing by its side.

Jabari rushed into his father's welcoming arms. "Father, Father, you must help her! She has been injured!"

Saad stared at the horse. "What have you found, my son?" he questioned as he cautiously approached. "Father of fathers," he whispered when he saw the pale complexion and silver blond braid of the woman slumped upon its back. "A foreigner!" He stood staring in disbelief until Jabari's pleading voice roused him from his shock.

"Father, we must get her to camp. Her injury is very grave!"

"Calm down, my son. We will take care of her," Saad reassured the boy. Dazed by the sudden turn of events, he pondered to himself. *Allah, what have you brought me this time? Another orphan in the desert?* Shaking his head, he started walking toward camp, and Jabari and the horse followed.

The tired group finally came upon the welcoming sight of Samira bending over the fire, stirring her pot. Looking up, she paused in her cooking, and her jaw dropped at the strange sight that met her eyes. Before she could utter a word, Jabari rushed to her side.

"Mother, Mother, please, you must help," he cried and tried to pull her closer to the horse.

Samira gasped seeing the fresh blood trickling down from the woman's leg and staining the golden hide of the horse. "Jabari, get your uncle Amal and clear a space by the fire," she directed. "Saad, bring her to me." No one questioned Samira when she was in control, and everyone rushed to comply.

In a matter of minutes, they had the woman stretched out on a clean rug by the fire.

"Why she is a foreigner!" Samira gasped. "And she is so young."

"Yes, my sweet," Saad agreed as he watched Samira work. Her small brown hands gently lifted the torn trouser away from the wounded area, and her eyes widened at the sight of the mangled flesh. She hurriedly checked for other injuries, then placed a pot of water on the coals while Saad tore strips of cloth to use as bandages. She flushed the area with warm water, then frowned.

"Saad, I must clean deeper. I will need your help."

Saad and Amal restrained the wounded girl while Samira performed the difficult task of reopening each tear to flush out any hidden dirt. The woman moaned, and the horse became agitated and moved closer, blowing and snorting.

"Jabari, watch the horse," Saad warned.

"Yes, Father." Jabari calmed the horse with a litany of soothing talk, smiling when she responded and settled down long enough for him to stroke her neck and withers. "We will not hurt your friend," he crooned near her silky ear. Saad handed him a long silken cord to place on her head, but Jabari refused it with a slight wave of his hand. "No, Father, we cannot tie her up. She will not run away as long as her friend is here."

Ever amazed at his son's insight, Saad quietly backed away and continued to watch Samira work on her patient.

•   •   •

Samira was relieved to see the cuts were not as deep as she had first feared and flushed the area once more with water. Mixing herbs and pieces of molded bread with warm water, she formed a doughy paste. If Kira had been awake, she would have recognized a concoction familiar to many cultures as a prevention of infection. When the bleeding slowed, Samira applied the herbal mixture in liberal amounts before wrapping bandages around the entire thigh.

Samira washed the woman's flushed face, and her gentle motions and soothing tones must have pierced the woman's fever-clouded mind. The woman's eyes fluttered open, and she stared into Samira's soft brown ones. "Mama?" she whispered hoarsely.

Samira paused, not understanding the word, but she understood the look in the pain-filled, blue-green eyes. This young woman believed Samira was a loved one. Tears welled in her own eyes, and her heart ached with sympathy. "Hush, Hush my little flower." Samira wasn't sure if the woman understood her language but was thankful when the woman closed her eyes and fell asleep with a hint of a smile on her lips.

Laying a cooling cloth on the woman's forehead, Samira began to worry. Dehydration was a real danger now, but she decided to let her rest a little longer before attempting to get her to drink. Covering her with a light blanket, Samira disposed of the bloody rags and soiled water. Once she had the woman settled, Samira sat down with the family to partake of their overdue meal.

After everyone finished eating, Saad and Amal checked on the camels, and Jabari helped her clean up. When the men returned, they joined Samira and Jabari by the fire to discuss the day's events. Darkness descended, and the fire cast a warming light on their faces.

"Now, tell me. Where did you find her?" Samira glanced at Saad and Jabari.

Jabari spoke first. "I did not find her, Mother. She found me, or Amber did."

"Amber? Who is that?" Samira was confused.

"Her horse. She calls her Amber."

"And how do you know that?" She looked hard at Jabari, and he told his story in detail, astonishing the family.

"I wonder how she got here," Amal said as he stirred the fire, which responded with a snap, sending a swirl of sparks spiraling skyward. "She is obviously a foreigner. Look at her hair and those eyes…"

"What I want to know is where the horse…uh, Amber…came from," Saad countered. "I have never seen such a splendid animal. Even Sheik Jalil does not have one such as her."

"She is magnificent," Jabari responded dreamily. "Except for the scars on her flank and neck, she is perfect."

"I saw the ones on her flank, but where is the one on her neck?" Saad asked, glancing Amber, who had eased closer to the woman. The dancing flames reflected in her deep brown eyes, and her amazing coat shimmered in the firelight. She seemed to move even when standing still.

"It is under her mane near her left ear. It is the mark of a bullet." Jabari's voice was harsh with contempt.

"A bullet? You mean someone shot her?" Amal's eyes widened in shock. "Who would be so stupid to kill such a glorious creature?"

"This is becoming more mysterious by the minute," Samira whispered, looking over at Amber. But Jabari's gasp caught her attention. A large gold medallion suspended from a thick chain of gold dangled from the boy's hand, spinning slowly, capturing and reflecting the firelight. Samira shivered. She had the same feeling she had the night they found Jabari in the desert. She broke the ensuing silence. "Jabari, where did you get that?"

"It was in her bag."

"Well, put it back! You must not handle it." She tried to grab it from him.

"But, Mother, do you think it belongs to her?" He traced the patterns with his fingertip.

"Let me see that." Saad reached for the medallion. Jabari reluctantly released it to his father, who bent closer to the firelight to study it. "I've never seen it's like," Saad murmured.

"I'm telling you both, put it back," Samira said sharply. "It must be important to her."

"Calm down, dearest one. We are only curious. No harm done," Saad said, handing it back to his son, who wrapped it and placed it back in the woman's bag.

"I wish she could talk to us," Jabari said.

"Soon enough, my son," Samira said and rose to check on her patient.

Amal also rose. "I think it would be wise to keep an eye out tonight. Whatever attacked the young woman may return. I will take the first watch." He gathered his staff and saber along with a spare rug.

"Good idea, my brother," Saad agreed. "Wake me when you are tired."

"Can I help, Father?" Jabari asked.

"No, enough has happened on your watch today."

"Oh, all right," Jabari groused, "but at least let me stay by the fire."

"Very well, but do not bother the creature," Saad said, gesturing to Amber.

Jabari hastened to gather his sleeping rug and place it near Amber. Samira checked on her patient before joining Saad in their tent.

Harsh cries woke the entire family during the night, and Samira rushed outside, alarmed to see the woman trying to rise. She held her gently by the shoulders, calming her with soft words and a cooling cloth upon her forehead. Samira was able to get her to swallow a few sips of cool water infused with pain-killing herbs.

Wiping the woman's fevered brow, she crooned a quiet lullaby and smiled when the horse sidled nearer. Amber had obviously been alarmed by the woman's distress. Such loyalty could only come from great love, Samira thought, and she wondered how this young woman had won the heart of such a noble beast. Seeing that her patient was finally sleeping soundly, Samira checked her bandages. The bleeding had stopped, but the long gouges were swollen and inflamed. It looked painful and would take time to heal, but Samira knew that with care and vigilance, the woman would recover—she was young and seemed strong, with a powerful spirit.

Feeling more confident, Samira removed the soiled bandages, applied a fresh coat of her special poultice, and re-wrapped the leg with clean bandages. Pulling the blanket back over the sleeping woman, she returned to her own tent and was soon asleep. The camp was quiet except for the whistling of the night breeze among the rocks and the occasional crackle of the fire. Much later, when the moon slipped below the horizon, only Amber heard the far-off roar of an extremely frustrated lion.

CHAPTER 14

If Amber had been closer to Qadir's holdings, she might have heard the painful howls from a very different creature, one as frustrated as the lion. Cassie was awake and recovering from another night of satisfying Qadir's warped cravings. Bruised and aching, she made her way sluggishly to the bath chamber, intending to scrub every inch of her abused body. Lately, she waited until the other women were gone, hoping for a little privacy. She did not care for their all-knowing stares when she disrobed, her body showing the marks of the sheik's passions.

Easing into the steamy water, she sighed in frustration as her mind slowly awakened to contemplate her current situation. Things were not going as she had originally planned. True, she had become Qadir's favorite, but the price was proving too high. Moving to the side of the pool, she availed herself of the cooling lemonade and fruit that was always placed within reach. Thoughts and plans took shape in her crafty mind while she finished her breakfast. *I must find a way to gain control over that man. He is going to kill me if I'm not careful.* Feelings of despair washed over her. She was already dreading the coming night, and it was with great effort she banished them. *I will survive this. I will get out of this hellhole if it's the last thing I do!*

Moving to lie on a cushion-covered bench, she looked up when Fatima entered the room bearing a tray of oils. The woman paused at Cassie's presence and turned away, but Cassie called out to her, "Wait, don't go." Hating to see the pity in Fatima's eyes but needing to talk to her, she motioned Fatima over to the bench.

Fatima hesitated, but her eyes widened at the bruises Cassie couldn't hide. "May I offer you a massage?"

"Yes, please. I would like that," Cassie replied honestly.

As Fatima massaged soothing oils into her skin, Cassie closed her eyes and relaxed, and asked with an innocent air, "Does Qadir ever go anywhere?"

"Oh, yes, he often goes to trade for horses with other sheiks, and this year he will attend the Tri-Annual Race where all the tribes compete for the best of the herds."

"Does he take any women with him?"

"Only those he wishes to trade or sell," Fatima said casually.

"You mean he can sell us, like animals?!" Cassie's eyes flew open with indignation.

"Why, of course. We are his possessions. Women are only valued for their ability to give pleasure, produce sons, and prepare food."

"Barbaric," muttered Cassie. "What will happen to me when Qadir tires of me?"

"It will be as it has always been. If he still wishes to have you now and then, you would be like Zahra and live in the palace. If not, you will end up pleasuring one of his men, or he will sell you or gift you to someone. "

Learning that she could become the property of a tribal member turned Cassie's stomach when she remembered the leering faces at the evening feasts, in particular, that of Hashem. Ending up with Hashem would be as bad as Qadir's if the gossip was to be believed. The thought of his dirty, pawing hands and crooked yellow teeth made her shiver. *I cannot let that happen! But what can I do?* She rolled over to look up at Fatima. "Are those the only options?"

Fatima moved to work on her thighs and calves. "Unless you get pregnant."

Cassie could not suppress a small groan when Fatima touched a particularly sore spot on her thigh. "What would happen if I had his child?"

"It would depend on whether you bore him a son or a daughter. A daughter is of no consequence. The sheik needs a son for his heir. Once a woman bears an heir, she is granted much power and becomes First Wife and sheikha." Fatima moved to work on Cassie's arms.

"And what would happen to the current First Wife?"

"She would be allowed to stay in the house, but the new sheikha would be in charge," Fatima said, wiping her hands on a nearby towel.

Cassie's mind was spinning with possibilities. Now she understood why First Wife had the keys to every door and came and went at her leisure. "So, Qadir has no heir, but does he have any daughters?"

"Alas, he has no children at all, even though he has tried for many years with many women. No one knows why this is so, but you must never ask him about it. He almost killed the last person who did," Fatima warned, then added, "There are some that refer to him as the 'Royal Gelding,' but not to his face, of course. He is easily enraged and even more so regarding this issue."

"Hmm." Cassie considered this latest, and maybe most valuable, bit of information. "Then he would place a great value on the woman who could give him an heir."

"I do not think it is possible…with any woman." Fatima refilled their cups and lowered her voice to a whisper. "Many of his former women have children now, by other men. I think he cannot have one."

"Well, you never know," Cassie mused as she sipped the honeyed tea. "I have known many men who tried hard in their youth only to be rewarded with age."

When Fatima shrugged, Cassie could tell she wasn't comfortable discussing the sheik's impotence, so she questioned Fatima more about the harem and the main house, hoping to learn some new detail that might come in handy later. A plan was forming in her scheming mind, but she needed time to sort it out. She returned to her room early, needing to rest before the evening, in case Qadir called for her again.

As she removed her robe, she grimaced in pain, but her recent conversation with Fatima strengthened her resolve. She must appear willing and find a way to keep Qadir interested. It might provide her the only chance of escape.

Unfortunately, Qadir sent for her again that evening. Later, when Cassie was assisted back to her bed, after having been badly used, she saw that First Wife had left the usual cup of wine on her table. For a minute she wondered why First Wife was being kind to her. She knew there had to be a reason, but she was too tired to think about it. As she contemplated the ruby liquid, Cassie knew it contained more than just wine, but she didn't care. It soothed her nerves, dulled the pain, and allowed her to sleep without dreams. The dreams were confusing and terrifying, and she often awoke crying in the night.

Angrily, she ripped off the soiled remains of her outfit, leaving them in pieces on the floor and reached for the goblet. Craving its effects, she drank greedily. The potion took effect sooner each time, which was both welcoming and disturbing—she suspected First Wife was making it stronger. Shortly, Cassie passed out on her bed, but the potent drink ensured there would be no screaming tonight.

CHAPTER 15

The early morning sun was partially hidden behind the eastern foothills when Kira awoke. Breathing deeply, she filled her lungs with the familiar sharp scents of the desert. Puffs of warm air bathed her face, and she opened her eyes and tried to focus on the large object hovering over her face. Recognizing Amber, she smiled and tentatively reached up to caress the horse's cheek, but she froze when she heard voices and the clank of metal.

Confused, she cut her eyes toward the noise and was astonished to see people sitting around a small brazier perched over several flat stones. They were speaking in low tones and busy preparing a meal. Since they had not noticed her yet, she took advantage of the moment to study them. She realized this was some sort of family unit. Two men were studying a piece of leather harness, and a woman was ladling something into a bowl, which she handed to a young boy. Their clothing was rustic, and she saw several camels kneeling beside two tents.

When Amber's nicker drew the attention of the people around the fire, Kira was relieved to see no animosity in their looks, only kindness and concern. She struggled to rise, and the woman rushed to her side and helped her sit up. Smiling, the woman held a cup to her lips, and Kira took a small sip of warm liquid. *Boy, that's good.* She glanced at the men and the boy who watched from the fireside. When she smiled shyly, their looks of concern turned to ones of relief.

The boy spoke to one man and Kira recognized the Arabic word for father. She tried to speak, but the woman made hushing sounds while offering her more of the delicious brew. After Kira gulped down the rest, the woman eased her back down, but when she turned away, Kira grabbed her sleeve. "Shukran," Kira whispered in Arabic.

The older woman's face brightened at being thanked. "Afwan!" she offered in return, which translated to "you are welcome" or "think nothing of it."

Kira, exhausted by the effort it had taken to sit up, closed her eyes and drifted back into a fitful slumber.

During the next few days, Kira despaired over her wounds, but the woman who she learned was called Samira, put her fears of infection to rest, and her careful tending hastened the healing process. The first chance she got, she rummaged through her bag to verify she still had all her belongings. Not that she didn't trust the family, but she had to be sure. She was happy to see everything was still there, including the money belt, the compass, and the medallion. Not wanting to draw attention to the medallion, she decided not to wear it for now, but continued to wear her mother's chain with her father's ring around her neck.

Over the following weeks, the soothing oils Samira had given her appeared to lessen the scarring. Unfortunately, she would always bear the marks of her encounter with the desert predator, just like Amber. But instead of considering them a disfigurement, Kira came to regard them as a reminder of God's grace and was thankful to be alive and to have made such wonderful friends.

Kira discovered that Saad's family had a good working knowledge of English from having traded in the cities along the coast. And with her increasing knowledge of Arabic, she found it easy to converse. One night around the fire, Jabari asked her about the medallion. Startled, she couldn't respond at first. *How did he know about the medallion?*

Samira apparently noticed. "Kira, Jabari meant no harm. We were trying to find out where you came from, so we looked in your bag. I apologize for invading your privacy." She cast a stern look at her son.

"I am sorry, Kira. I should not have looked." Jabari's face filled with chagrin.

Kira surmised they had done only what most people would have in the same situation. She forgave them at once. "It is not a problem, Jabari. I understand."

Jabari's eyes brightened at her words, and he asked eagerly, "Where did you get it?"

Samira tried to hush him, but Kira waved her concern away. "It's all right, Samira. The medallion belonged to my father." She smiled sadly and pulled her father's ring from the neck of her robe, holding it up for Jabari to see. "As did this."

Jabari studied the silver ring with the Zuni sun face depicted in turquoise and mother-of-pearl and his eyes narrowed at the unfamiliar design. "What does it mean?"

"It is the symbol for my people's greatest spirit—the sacred Sun Father."

"You do not believe in Allah?" Jabari asked with a serious expression.

"Jabari! You know better than to ask someone a question like that. What Kira believes is her personal business," Samira admonished.

"No, it's all right. I don't mind," Kira said. "Jabari, it's complicated, but I'll try to explain. I am the child of two peoples. My father believed in one God. My mother also believed in one God, but not at first. Her people believe in many spirits and the Sun Father is the most powerful." Kira glanced down at her ring fondly. "I was raised in both cultures, but I too came to believe in the one God."

"So, we are not so different after all." Jabari grinned.

Kira laughed softly, but considered his words as she tucked the ring back inside her robe. "Perhaps not." She relaxed and contemplated the fire, and the family fell silent, each absorbed in their own thoughts.

As the weeks passed, she grew to love Saad and his family. Adventure and companionship filled her days, and dreamless sleep filled her nights. Feeling stronger, both in body and spirit, she spent countless hours walking and riding between the stops they made along the way.

Ever curious and having time on her hands, Kira concentrated on building her knowledge of the people who had befriended her. They were as independent and resourceful as her grandmother's people. Many of the things they did were similar, such as finding and preparing food, mending clothing, caring for livestock, not to mention understanding how to survive in their environment. Whatever they couldn't make, they bartered for. It was easy for Kira to slip into their lifestyle, and as she had as a child, she flourished.

Wanting to pay them back for having saved her life, Kira worked hard to contribute to the family and enjoyed helping Samira with meals and even taking her turn at night watch. What she did not enjoy, though, was having to remain hidden at every trading stop along the way. She understood Saad when he explained the danger of her being seen. He worried constantly whenever they approached a new encampment, explaining that blond hair and pale skin were as rare as water in the desert, and as valuable.

Thankfully, the traditional clothing for women was very concealing. Women wore full robes with headwraps and veils, and Samira kept Kira covered from head to toe. To hide her paleness, Kira learned how to darken her skin with a dye provided by Samira. Whatever she used was effective, but she hated having to apply it every other day. It was hard for Kira to remember to hide her eyes. Her eye color was uncommon, and Samira cautioned her to avoid eye contact and keep her head bent with eyes downcast whenever they chanced upon strangers. So far, her luck had held.

Saad also insisted she remain hidden at each stop until they were ready to move on. Frustrated, Kira would sit in her darkened tent, listening to the people and animals, wishing she could see them, speak to them, and experience the market scene. After a few stops, she came up with the idea to cut a small slit into the side of her tent where she could peek out and watch the surrounding activities. Unfortunately, Saad discovered her looking out and tried to put a stop to it. A rousing argument ensued after they left the next day, with Kira emerging victorious. He would allow the peep hole but placed the tents farther from the main areas and surrounded hers with his resting camels. Kira wasn't amused. She missed watching the people, but she missed watching Saad and Jabari do their magic shows even more.

It was only days after the lion's attack when Kira first witnessed Jabari practicing tricks and sleight-of-hand. His best trick was to produce a bird, which she learned later was called a speckled pigeon, seemingly out of thin air. Saad taught him most of the tricks, but Jabari was so skillful that he surpassed his father in the mastery of the mystic. Sometimes after dinner, Saad and Jabari would work together to produce a show, one she found extremely entertaining.

As for Amber, she had to be hidden as well. Saad gave Kira a dark compound to rub into the horse's coat that effectively changed the brilliant gold and silver to dull brown and tan. Amber's superior confirmation was difficult to hide, but draping her in an old blanket and covering her with assorted bundles of trade goods helped. Kira was sure Amber was not happy about it, and frankly, neither was she. Amber continued to keep her distance from the other members of the family but grew to trust Jabari and accepted treats from his hand.

Each evening when they were on the road, the family told stories around the fire, and Kira listened avidly. They rarely asked her questions until one night. She had seen Saad staring at Amber who stood not far away and could see he wrestled with something. She wasn't surprised when he turned to her and spoke, "Kira, we know little of your past. Would you mind sharing some of it with us?"

Kira thought about it, but she had learned to trust them, so she decided they deserved to know her story. "I will tell you what I can," she said. She told them about the plane wreck, how she found Amber injured in the desert, and the lion attack, but didn't mention the valley. That seemed to satisfy the family.

"Well, that explains how you won the heart of Amber," Saad said. "She is a rare creature, but we have seen other golden horses, as will you, when we visit Sheik Jalil's kingdom. He has several, but only females."

"He does not have a stallion?"

"Oh, no. Golden stallions are mythical. No one has ever found one and only a few people have ever seen one."

Kira hid her smile, thinking of Ndee. The golden stallion was not mythical, but she vowed to never reveal the knowledge of the secret valley. Instead, she nodded in pretended ignorance and asked him to tell her more about the mythical beasts. While she listened to his stories, she wondered why Sheik Jalil could breed only females, and then she thought of the valley herd. She had seen no golden colts there either, only fillies. Maybe it took a very special pairing to breed a golden stallion.

Jabari asked the most questions about the golden horses. When he confessed his dream that one day he would ride one, Kira figured she could make his dream come true, for a price. She offered him a chance to ride Amber in exchange for magic lessons, and he couldn't say no.

Surprisingly, Amber allowed him to climb up on her back, and at first, she trembled and snorted, dancing in place. But she settled when he talked to her in his most calming manner. It was as if she understood what he was saying, Kira thought. Holding tight to her mane, never attempting to take control, he gave her his complete trust, and before long, the two were dashing around the camp and became a familiar sight.

When Saad expressed concern for Jabari's safety, Kira listened as wise Samira put his fears to rest by reminding him how special Jabari was. Unaware of Jabari's origin, Kira assumed Samira was referring to her child as every mother does. Saad merely nodded and smiled indulgently. But he didn't have to worry. The horse and boy rode as one.

The days passed, and when they were close to Jalil's kingdom, they encountered two of his men who were returning from delivering invitations for the pre-race meeting. Hosted this year by Jalil's tribe, attendance was mandatory if a tribe wished to take part in that year's Tri-Annual Race. Luckily, Kira was in the tent when the messengers appeared, but she listened to the exchange with interest. According to Saad, they would be at Jalil's during the meeting.

Around their fire that night, Saad could speak of nothing else but the prospect of more customers, saying it could well turn out to be the best year he had had for a long time. Later, Jabari confided to Kira his excitement about the upcoming gathering. Not only would he get a chance to see the magnificent stallions that would be entered in the race, but he might get to perform his magic as well.

Kira could only think it would just be another boring stay in the confines of a stuffy tent. But out of gratitude for Saad's family and what they had done for her, she kept her thoughts to herself. At least it sounded like a large gathering, and she was hopeful Saad would locate them closer to the center of activities. Perhaps she could hear what was going on and, just maybe, sneak out at night or in the early morning and get a look not only at Jalil's famous herd, but maybe even Jalil himself. Storing that thought to consider later, she decided she needed to learn more Arabic. Jabari found her to be an apt pupil, and she was becoming more fluent.

Besides sharpening her language skills, Kira learned the intricate dances that Samira taught her around the fire at night. Uncle Amal would produce a small drum, and Saad played his flute, and Kira would weave and spin, following in Samira's footsteps. Jabari kept time with his enthusiastic clapping while Amber watched from the shadows. The dancing obviously made her nervous and her ears swiveled back and forth as she listened for predators that might be attracted by the noise. Luckily, the result was just the opposite. The music and laughter only drove away any curious creatures.

By the time they approached the pass to Jalil's kingdom, Kira felt a new confidence in her and Amber's ability to remain hidden. Her knowledge of Arabic had increased, so even if she was stuck in the tent, she could at least understand what she heard. The entire family was excited, but Jabari most of all. He talked of nothing but Jalil's herd.

The only one clearly not excited was Amber. She was skittish and easily startled. Despite the bond that existed between her and Amber, Kira was oblivious to Amber's awareness of the path ahead and her strange stirrings, not of excitement but trepidation. Amber's desert-born instincts warned her of hidden danger, and she remained on high alert as they drew closer to the entry to Jalil's stronghold.

CHAPTER 16

Cassie had always welcomed her monthly cycle, but never so much as now. It had started early that morning and First Wife had brought her the pads and wrappings the harem girls used, but tired of trying to understand the old woman's jabbering, Cassie ignored her. She'd figure it out on her own.

By midday, she was assailed by cramps, but she welcomed them, too. They were terrible, but anything was preferable to having Qadir's brat. At least she had something to help with the pain, she thought as she sipped on yet another goblet of the drugged wine that was frequently placed in her room. But she was bored and had nothing to do except ponder her current situation.

Qadir hadn't succumbed to her charms like she'd planned, and she was tired of the pain he inflicted on her. Lately, she felt like giving up, but then her innate sense of survival, along with her complete self-centeredness, would lift her up and she'd keep going.

Suddenly seized by a long cramp, she curled on her side, sniffing and wiping her eyes. *Oh, why did this happen to me? I'm a nice person. I don't deserve to be here. How am I going to escape?* They always locked her in her room, and the only time she could go out was for visits to the bath chamber, Qadir's bedchamber, and, once a week, the private confines of an inner courtyard. The only way out of the house, as far as she knew, was through the door leading from the social chamber to the feast hall and beyond.

In the hopes she might escape, Cassie was squirreling away anything of value that she could use as currency, such as loose gems she found in the social room from broken jewelry or goblets. She even broke one of her own decorative hair pins and removed a nice little emerald. Luckily, no one seemed to notice. Once she found a silver coin and added it to the stash, which she kept in a leather bag buried in the bottom of her chest.

Hoping to gain more information, Cassie pretended to ignore the harem girls while she listened to their conversations. Despite her patchy Arabic, Cassie managed to learn that there were distant coastal cities where foreigners could be found. She was sure she could arrange passage back to some civilized country if she could just get to one of those.

When her cramps finally subsided, she took another sip of the sickly sweet brew. Clearing her mind of her chaotic thoughts, she succumbed to the potion and fell asleep, dreaming of sailing ships and calm seas.

The next morning, she woke with one thought on her mind. She needed more answers, and there was only one person who would help her. Calling for a servant by ringing a small bell by her door, she was shortly on her way to the bath chamber. Bypassing the pool, and under the watchful stares of the other girls, she made her way into the social room to look for Fatima. Predictably, the girl was in her usual place, mending a garment.

"Sabah al khayr," Cassie spoke quietly, wishing her a good morning in Arabic.

Startled, Fatima looked up at her. "Sabah al noor," she replied. And a good morning to you.

Cassie settled cross-legged on a cushion close by and looked about the room casually to make sure no curious ears were nearby. Fatima kept stitching, and Cassie picked up a bit of needlework to play along. "Fatima, I need your help."

Fatima continued to stitch but cocked her head slightly in Cassie's direction.

"Tell me more about the palace. Are there any other ways out?" Cassie whispered.

Fatima pretended to scrutinize Cassie's mending. "Hmm, I think you are doing much better. Some of your stitches are still crooked. You should concentrate and try harder. But overall, you are doing better." She returned to her own work, her brow furrowed.

When Fatima remained silent, Cassie grew impatient and reached over as if to compare her work to the other girl's work and whispered, "Well?"

Before answering, Fatima added another bit of incense to the little burner nearby. Usually so gentle, Fatima now turned a fierce gaze on her but kept her voice low and neutral. "Don't you just love this perfume? It is one of my favorites. I believe Hashem bought it at the market by the sea," she said, looking hard at Cassie.

Cassie paused, puzzling over Fatima's cryptic reply and tried a different tactic. "Tell me about the city by the sea. Is it far from here? Does Qadir ever go there?" She kept her eyes downcast, pretending to be absorbed in her work.

"Oh, it is far to the south, or so I've been told. We are not allowed to leave this house, and I have never been beyond this kingdom, but I heard tales of the white-skinned foreigners that come in their big ships. It is a place I really have never wanted to see." Fatima stopped to change her thread. "Hashem travels there to conduct business for the sheik. There are rumors he may be planning another trip soon." Fatima glanced briefly at Cassie but appeared agitated.

Is she telling me Hashem could help me get to the coast? Cassie was still confused and was startled when Fatima began putting her things away and collecting her fabrics.

"Oh, it is later than I thought, and I must prepare for the meal. Perhaps I will see you in the pool. Ma salama," Fatima said as she left the room. Peace be with you.

"Allah hafes," Cassie responded with the standard reply, almost without thinking. *May God be with you.* Feeling it might be wiser to remain working on her own piece for a little longer after Fatima left, she sat quietly, but grew angry at Fatima's words. Cassie was sure Fatima knew more about the palace, but the woman was too scared to tell her. *Damn these heathens and their petty games!* Sighing in frustration, she furiously picked at the silk fabric, but it wasn't long before she tired of the pretense and returned to her chamber.

•   •   •

After Cassie left the room, First Wife left her hiding place behind the scrollwork. Although both women thought they had been more than circumspect in their quiet conversation, First Wife heard their words. She hadn't maintained her position of command all these years without learning all she could about her charges. She knew all the secrets, and she held all the power, as long as her son, and no other, ruled. Now she added new information to her cache of secrets. Knowledge was power, but only if one knew when, how, and to whom, to reveal it. Mind seething with plans, she hurried back to her chambers.

When she heard Qadir's voice, she sidled closer to the secret door that joined their chambers and listened, always on the lookout for more information that she could twist to her evil purposes. What she heard next confirmed what she already knew. Her son was an idiot, and his plan would surely fail.

•   •   •

"Is it true that your special one is in her dawra cycle?" Hashem was bold to ask. Qadir looked furious, and for a minute, Hashem thought he might have made a fatal mistake speaking of Cassie's monthly cycle. It would only remind Qadir of his continuing failure to produce an heir.

"You must be more careful, Hashem. You trespass where you should not!" Qadir shouted, piercing him with an angry look.

Hashem wondered if Qadir was angry because he wouldn't be enjoying Cassie's company that night or because Hashem had broached such a sensitive subject. He paused, noticing the sheik's hand stray toward the dagger he kept hidden in his robes, and he quickly apologized. "Forgive me, my sheik. I was just hoping for good news. I am sure it will not be long before this one bears you a son." He wisely lowered his eyes and held his breath.

"Indeed. It is but a matter of time. I too am sure she will prove to be a good breeder." Qadir relaxed and raised his goblet to sip the warm honeyed tea.

"Yes, yes, my sheik. Indeed, Allah will bless you," Hashem said as he refilled his own cup. "And what news of the meeting?" As winner of the previous Tri-Annual Race, Sheik Jalil was required to host the pre-race meeting for the next race, and Hashem was looking forward to the opportunity to learn more of the younger sheik's current strengths and weaknesses.

Qadir and his immediate guard would attend, along with his stallion, Shar. This would be Shar's first time to compete. The stallion had been too young for the last race, but at five years old, he was now ready. Qadir had ridden his old stallion, Ubaid, during the last two races, both won by Akeem. Hashem wondered why Akeem had not taken Qadir's stallion either time, as was his right. Sometimes a stallion wasn't taken if he belonged to an ally of the winner, or if he was considered of poor quality. Ubaid was a fine horse but never a great one, and since Qadir had never been Akeem's ally, everyone knew Akeem considered Ubaid not worth taking. It was an insult.

Qadir strode about the room as he talked. "I have been thinking, and I have decided to take the foreign woman to the meeting."

"Are you not afraid someone will steal her?" Hashem was worried. Jalil wouldn't be supplying any women for the men's pleasure—he was notorious for his disdain of slavery. Having Cassie in the encampment might prove too enticing for anyone looking for a night's pleasure.

"Ha! Let them try." Qadir laughed confidently. "We will certainly be on the lookout for trouble, but I have no fear of that. Besides, I am thinking she will captivate Jalil, and I want him to want her. Then we can use her to help us defeat him."

"How? What is your plan?" Hashem was all ears. He had a hidden interest in Cassie, and it was critical to know what might happen to her. "Surely you will not sell her?"

"Oh, you will learn in time what I have planned." Qadir removed his robe, signaling Hashem that he must leave.

"I remain your servant." Hashem tried to sound sincere as he backed from the room. Once clear of Qadir's chambers, he all but ran outside. Frustrated that Qadir had not told him his plans, Hashem would make some of his own—ones that would involve Cassie.

•   •   •

Thanks to her cycle, Cassie was left to her own devices for a while. So she threw herself into making sure she would look her best when Qadir next sent for her by taking advantage of the many beauty treatments that were available. She even avoided drinking the nightly potion, intent on sharpening her mind for the days ahead.

When Cassie learned she was to accompany Qadir to the much talked about pre-race meeting, she was ecstatic. All the important sheiks would be there, including the mysterious Jalil. Cassie was curious about him, having heard he was well-liked, wealthy, and reportedly very handsome. That Qadir absolutely hated him made her want to meet him even more.

First Wife had informed her she would have to dance for the visiting tribes at the feast, so Cassie practiced her most sultry moves and experimented with exotic materials and makeup. This was her chance to gain the attention of someone other than the monster who had captured her.

While parading around the harem, Cassie boasted of her upcoming trip, but became puzzled when the girls showed no signs of jealousy. In fact, Fatima acted happy at being left behind, and in her selfish way, Cassie did not bother to ask her why. No one had explained to her that some girls might not come back, as they could be sold or given as gifts to Qadir's allies.

Finally, the big day arrived, and the caravan was assembled. The harem girls were clothed in dark robes and veils, placed on camels, and tied to their saddles. Cassie found the whole affair boring and felt quite annoyed when she discovered herself tied to a smelly, ugly camel, far away from Qadir's side. By the time the entire group was moving out of the main pass, she was already burning up in her thick robe. Feeling nauseous from the awful smell and swaying movement of her camel, she fought to hold her temper. Praying it would be a brief trip, she was already looking forward to their first stop and swore that if she survived this, she would find a way to escape.

CHAPTER 17

The sun was but a promise on the horizon when Sheik Jalil stopped by the heavily guarded stable building. A thundering neigh echoed from within, and Jalil smiled. His mighty silver stallion, Mirage, was impatient for their morning ride, and so was Jalil. He quickly saddled him, and together they raced across the far pastures. It was the day before the pre-race meeting and invited sheiks and their entourages would arrive shortly. His kingdom was about to be overrun with strangers, many of whom coveted Jalil's golden mares. Jalil needed to check on the safety of his herd.

As he rode, Jalil marveled at the beauty of his land. Breathing deeply, he savored the scents carried by the early morning air—a wisp of charcoal from the fire pits, a hint of new growth from the reed beds bordering the creek, and the subtle smell of sand. Bare headed, his dark brown hair shone with caramel highlights in the rising sun, his long muscular legs gripped his mount firmly, and his hands were gentle but commanding on the reins. Mirage responded to his subtle signals, and together, they made a formidable pair.

When he saw the first of his posted guards, he waved and rode on, threading his way through the herd, pleased to see the newborn fillies and colts appearing healthy and active. He saw a few bays with their dark red coats and black stockings, several chestnuts, a couple of duns with their camouflaging tan coats, and even a solid black. Several exhibited the rare iridescence his horses were famous for. A sudden flash of golden brilliance from behind some nearby bushes drew his attention. *Perhaps it has finally happened?* But when a tiny golden foal ambled up, followed by her cloud-white mother, Jalil was only slightly disappointed to see that it was a filly. He was always happy to see another golden horse, even if it wasn't a stallion. *Maybe someday.*

When a silver colt ran by, he recognized one of Mirage's own, and his good humor was restored. Perhaps that one would be as good as his sire. One day, Jalil knew he would have to replace Mirage, but he quickly put that thought from his mind, unable to conceive of losing his closest friend.

Having verified his herd was safe, he headed back to the compound, but instead of returning Mirage to the stable, he took him to the special stalls built inside the back of his palace. They were more secure and heavily guarded. Racing stallions were always at risk, and Jalil could not afford for anything to happen to Mirage.

Not happy to be confined inside, Mirage snorted his displeasure and glared at Jalil.

"Calm down, my friend. It will only be for a few days." Jalil hid a chuckle as he stepped from the stall. Mirage stomped angrily and turned away to sulk in private.

Jalil rushed to the main hall, where he was scheduled to meet with Fahad, his captain and right-hand man. He found a light meal and beverages laid out on the long table and was pouring his second cup of tea when Fahad strode into the chamber.

"Welcome, Fahad. Join me." Jalil gestured to the chair across from him.

"Thank you, my sheik." Fahad took a seat and waited patiently.

"Are you hungry?"

"No, my sheik. I have already eaten. But I will have some tea," the older man said as he poured a cup.

"Fahad, please call me Jalil. At least when we are alone." Jalil had known Fahad all his life—he had served as his father's advisor and was family as far as Jalil was concerned.

"Very well…Jalil." Fahad smiled, obviously pleased. "So, how is the herd?"

"Safe. And I've already moved Mirage inside."

"Excellent. My scouts reported the first of our guests are even now approaching the pass. I expect it will be a very busy day," Fahad said, taking a sip.

Jalil glanced at the list of invited sheiks. "Any word yet of Qadir?"

"No, but he will be here. He cannot afford to miss this race. My spies tell me his herd is in poor shape, and rumors are circulating of unrest in his kingdom."

"I am not surprised. He is a cruel and ignorant leader. But I am afraid he has little chance of winning this year's race." Jalil smirked.

"I wouldn't be too sure about that," Fahad said seriously. "His stallion, Shar, has been rumored to possess great speed."

"It will take more than speed to beat my Mirage," Jalil said confidently. "But we will see him tomorrow." Jalil was referring to the stallion viewing that would be held early the next morning. Everyone would be able to see all the competing riders and their mounts on display.

"I will not argue with you. Mirage has the heart of a desert lion."

"Of that, there can be no doubt. And with Allah's help, we will surely win," Jalil said fervently.

Fahad nodded. "So, will you take Shar from Qadir?" He was speaking of the losers' penalties.

Jalil leaned back, his eyes narrowed in thought. Every sheik entering a stallion was bound by the rules. The losers might have to give up not only their stallion but also up to five mares, winner's choice, from their herds. Such losses could cripple a tribe, but the winner could grant immunity to a tribe and spare their stallion or mares. This move strengthened many alliances. If Jalil won, he would have the power to deal Qadir a devastating blow.

"I do not know yet. Shar might prove his worth, and then again, he might not finish the race."

"There is that chance. It is extremely demanding…and dangerous," Fahad agreed. "But so is the pre-race meeting."

"Are you ready? Do you need more guards?" Jalil was justifiably concerned. The event consisted of three parts, all of which would take place the next day. The registration meeting would be held after the stallion viewing, and the sheiks would review the course rules, approve the course layout, and sign their oaths. The day would end with the traditional feast and celebration. For the next three days, his kingdom would be host to a great number of strangers, some of whom coveted his golden mares and would not mind inflicting damage on his herd or his family.

"I am confident we can handle the visitors," Fahad said reassuringly. "It is not as if we don't have the experience. Our tribe has played this role before, many times. Everything should be fine, but I hope they are bringing their own women."

"As do I. I do not condone slavery and will never provide girls for anyone's entertainment. I am glad our tribe allows women to keep their freedom. I know most of the other men think they are silly and deceitful creatures, only good for cooking, providing pleasure, and producing heirs, but not I."

"I agree. But speaking of women, has your mother found you a suitable wife yet?"

Jalil choked briefly on his tea. "What? Are you serious? I have no time for a woman. I still have so much to do. Besides, I have yet to meet a woman that is worthy of being the next sheikha of our tribe."

Most men of his age and position would have had several wives by now, but Jalil had never found a woman whom he wanted to share his life with. Since his father's death, Jalil's life revolved around taking care of his family, his tribe, and his herd. A kind and generous lover, he enjoyed the company of women, at least physically, but he had no time for them. And he didn't want any young princes or princesses yet.

Perhaps he would be lucky enough to find a woman like his mother, one who would challenge him but also support him to the death. *Not likely.* That kind of woman was as rare as a golden stallion in his mind.

He dismissed such conjecture because it was distracting him from his real purpose that morning, which was to prepare for the next day.

"Well, if I know our current sheikha, she will not give up." Fahad laughed heartily. He had known Jalil's mother, Nasira, since the day she wed Akeem.

"Unfortunately, you are right. But come, let us go over this list one more time. You know most of these sheiks and their stallions, and I must be ready for tomorrow."

Fahad was quick to comply, and together they reviewed the contestants, highlighting their strengths and weaknesses.

After Fahad left, Jalil remained at the table, deep in thought. He remembered Fahad's earlier comment about the dangers of the race. It involved long distances and rough terrain. To have any chance of winning, each tribe had to have their best stallion, but even the best could experience tragedy as riders and horses might get injured. The race was a profound example of the culture in which it had been conceived. Only the hardiest, strongest, and smartest would survive.

Jalil's father, Akeem, had been the winner three years past, and three years before that, thanks to Rayham, their senior stallion. But Rayham and Akeem were killed in the mountain pass north of his kingdom not long after the last race.

If it wasn't for the miracle of Mirage, Jalil wouldn't have been able to compete in the upcoming race. He thanked Allah every day that he was the one to find the injured stallion in the mountains five years ago. Healing the young stallion and earning his trust took a long time, but in the end, they had bonded and become inseparable.

Mirage was one of the main reasons for his tribe's continued breeding success, siring wonderful horses with iridescent coats in all colors. He was also responsible for the rare golden ones, but only females so far. This was a constant source of frustration for Jalil. It was his dream to have a golden stallion, such as the ones that were spoken of in their myths and legends, but alas, it had never happened.

The distant sound of two gunshots interrupted his musings, and he immediately stood up, recognizing the signal that the first of the guests were arriving. But before he left the chamber, he paused to glance at the far wall with its floor to ceiling mural. Just as he had been as a child, Jalil was captivated by the picture of his kingdom from ages past. The long-dead artist had captured the rich tones of the desert world, and Jalil could almost feel the warmth of the sun reflected off the palace walls. It was magical, and men and women clothed in robes of turquoise, white, and gold appeared to move across the wall as they went about their daily affairs.

But what really drew his attention was the sight of the herd running through the rolling hills, led by a shimmering golden stallion. In his heart, Jalil knew that somewhere a golden stallion existed—the proof was on his wall—and with Allah's help, he would find one someday.

Someday, he thought, but he put all thoughts of the golden stallion from his mind as strode from the chamber. He had more important things to deal with now.

CHAPTER 18

Kira sat just inside the entrance of her tent, watching Samira and Jabari sitting outside by the fire. It was the morning before the pre-race meeting, and Saad had chosen to arrive at sunset the day before to avoid bringing attention to Amber or Kira. He reminded the family events like these attracted a certain element and one had to hold tight to their purse, their belongings, and especially their women.

Watching Jabari, she smiled at his evident excitement. He appeared as mesmerized as she was by the cacophony surrounding their camp—camels were groaning, horses were neighing, goats were bleating, and men were shouting. She shook her head, remembering his questions from the night before. He had voiced his disappointment when he learned he wouldn't be able to see Jalil's golden horses. Saad explained why Jalil had hidden the herd, and Jabari seemed to understand but professed how sad he was that he couldn't even ride Amber. If any recognized the golden horse under the brown dye, it would be disastrous, and they all hated to think what might happen if she were discovered.

Kira had to remain hidden as well. Her unique beauty made her as desirable as Amber. The only thing that put a smile back on Jabari's face was hearing about the feast following the formal meeting the next day. Jabari had confided in Kira that Saad had agreed to ask Sheik Jalil if Jabari could perform his magic show for the gathered guests.

When Kira saw Saad and Amal leave to conduct business, she knew it would not be long before Jabari made his escape as well. She envied him and his freedom to roam about and take in the spectacle. And just as she expected, he begged Samira, who gave him permission to seek Saad but cautioned him to stay out of trouble. He bowed and thanked her profusely, and Kira laughed out loud as she watched him dash away, weaving and dodging through the incoming caravans.

"You must be quiet, Kira. It is important that you remain hidden until we leave this place," Samira chastised gently from her place by the fire.

Tired of having to sit in the hot, dark tent, fully dressed, even though no one could see inside, Kira whispered loudly, "Samira, why can't we go to the feast tomorrow night?"

Samira sighed. "Kira, only the men are invited. And you cannot imagine what evil could befall if you drew their attention," she said while continuing to work the needle through the roughly woven robe she was mending.

"But Jabari said there would be women there, too."

"Only enslaved women."

"I thought you said Jalil was different and didn't enslave women?" Kira stretched out on her stomach, propping her chin on her hands.

"He doesn't," Samira said, setting her mending aside to pour a fresh cup of tea.

"But why is he so different? What is he really like?" Kira was burning up with curiosity over the infamous sheik.

Samira fixed a second cup of tea for Kira and moved to sit cross-legged on a soft tasseled pillow by the entrance of the tent. Her face took on a pensive expression. "Well, I cannot tell you much about him. He is certainly different, but then, so was his father. It is said Jalil does not keep a harem and doesn't like women," she said, and then paused to correct her last statement before Kira could interrupt. "Maybe it is not so much that he dislikes them, as he appears to have no use for them."

Kira's eyes widened. "Maybe he likes men?" She suspected there were men like that back in her days at the university but had never asked anyone—it was a taboo subject.

"What?" Samira appeared shocked by the question. "Kira, you must not speak of such things!"

Evidently it was taboo here too, Kira thought as she considered her next words. "Well, maybe he just hasn't met the right one, a woman, I mean," she whispered, feeling very decadent about having this discussion.

Samira choked back a laugh. "From what I understand, he has plenty of opportunity. His mother has been trying to get him to take a wife. It is important he produce an heir, especially now that his father is dead."

"What happened to his father?"

"He was murdered," Samira said sadly.

"Murdered? How awful for Jalil. Do they know who did it?" Kira listened intently now.

"No. His throat had been cut. I heard it was Jalil who found him." Samira shook her head with a sorrowful look.

For once Kira had nothing to say. She knew first-hand what it was like to see the death of a beloved one, and she understood the agony, the feeling of helplessness. Her eyes filled with tears at the remembered pain, and her heart went out to the young sheik.

Seeing Kira's tears, Samira said, "Yes, he has suffered like you. It is all very sad though. Jalil's family has known such great tragedies, first losing Jalil's little brother, and then his father. Ah, so much death, so many mysteries."

Normally Kira would have paid more attention to the mention of death and mysteries, but she was remembering her father. Overwhelmed, she laid back down and remained silent, and Samira returned to her mending.

Late in the afternoon, Kira roused when Saad, Amal, and Jabari returned from a long day of trading. Kira busied herself around the entrance of her tent where she could listen and watch. She heard Saad telling Samira how they had disposed of almost all the original goods they had brought with them. He said he was blessed, indeed, and now he could concentrate on trading the items he had bartered for along the way.

When Kira first joined Saad's family, he had told her how he had perfected his route over the years. He knew the tribes' needs early on their route, so he brought along the items they needed. He also knew which items he could get from them that would be desired by the tribes farther along the route. From what Kira understood, Saad was a savvy trader and usually did well.

When Saad finished storing his trade goods in the tent next to Kira's, he approached Samira by the fire. "Well, my love, we are done, and we are hungry."

"You are always hungry, Saad," she affectionately replied. "Come, rest. I will fix you all something to fill your bellies, but then you will need to go to sleep early. Tomorrow will be a big day." She scanned the area, then made eye contact with Kira, gesturing for her to join them by the fire.

Saad settled down on a soft cushion, and turning to his wife, "Will you be all right when Amal and I go to the feast tomorrow night?"

"Certainly. I can defend our camp," she said fiercely. "Besides, Jabari can help."

"I do not doubt your abilities. But Jabari may be tied up for part of the time." He told her of Jabari's request.

"What? You wish to perform for the great Sheik Jalil?" Samira's eyebrows rose as she looked at Jabari.

"Oh, yes! I know he will be impressed, and maybe then he will allow me to see his golden horses." Jabari tore a piece of the warm flat bread his mother had laid out for them, and his eyes danced with excitement as he chewed.

"Well, I do not know, my son," she said, adding more stew to a plate for Amal, "but this is a serious event, and perhaps Sheik Jalil should not be bothered by the distractions of a young boy."

"Oh, Mother, of course he will want to see my show. He will be amazed and entertained, and that is what tomorrow night is all about. He will be ready for a distraction by then." Jabari gulped his stew, talking with his mouth full.

"Swallow first, my son. You look like our oldest camel," Saad said, laughing out loud.

Kira chuckled, but only half-listened. She was thinking about Jabari. *Men and boys. They can go about as they please.* Then she lifted her head. *That's it!* She stared straight at Jabari, mentally calculating his size, and a plan began to take shape in her mind.

Jabari looked at her curiously, but she shook her head slightly and cut her eyes to his tent. He looked back at his family. "I think I will practice my magic. Thank you for dinner, Mother." Jabari helped his mother clean up, as he always did, before asking, "Can Kira help me practice?"

"Yes, that will be fine, but stay inside and keep your voices down."

Kira waited impatiently for Jabari to retrieve his bag and join her in the tent she shared with Samira. Once he was seated, Kira leaned over and whispered, "Jabari, I am thinking about sneaking out tomorrow night. I want to see the feast."

Jabari hissed in alarm, "You cannot go out at night! They do not allow women at the feast. No, it is too dangerous, and besides, someone would see you."

"Who said anything about a woman?" she whispered with a grin.

"I am confused. You are a woman. How can you not be a woman?" Jabari asked, leaning back on his heels.

"Well, what if I was a boy?"

"A boy? You are not a boy. Look at you." He blushed. "You are definitely not a boy."

"But I could be, if you would lend me some clothes," Kira happily explained. "We are almost the same size, and if I had some pants and a shirt like yours, I think it would work."

"Oh Allah, save me," Jabari whispered loudly. "You cannot be thinking of doing this. If you are discovered, well, I hate to think of what could happen to you. And if I help you, I hate to think of what will happen to me."

"Don't be silly, Jabari. I'll be very careful. I can hide my hair under a wrap, and no one will see my eyes in the dark," Kira pleaded.

"I will have to think about it." He fumbled with his bag of magic items. "But right now, I need to practice if I am to perform for the sheiks at the feast."

"Of course," Kira agreed. "We can talk about it later." She let it rest for the evening. Having planted the seed, she would water it some more in the morning.

Together, they practiced what tricks they could within the confines of the tent. Keeping Jabari distracted was easy, and Kira let him think she had forgotten about sneaking out, but she would look through his clothes tomorrow while he was at the stallion viewing and see if any fit. She would have to be extra careful to keep Samira from seeing what she was up to. Samira was smart and, like any good mother, seemed to have a sixth sense about knowing when someone was up to no good.

After they finished practicing and Jabari returned to his tent, Kira settled in for the night. Her last thoughts were of imagining what would happen tomorrow, and she fell asleep, content with the thought she might get to see Sheik Jalil after all.

CHAPTER 19

As darkness descended upon Jalil's kingdom, so did Qadir. Most of the participants clustered around their tents, eating their evening meals, and left the areas between the individual camps open. It was easy for him to bring in his camels and equipment and set up his own camp by the ample light from the many campfires. It also made it easier for him to deploy his spies, who would gather information about current tribal alliances—who supported whom, which ones were still in place, and any new ones that had been formed.

He had Hashem secure a campsite far removed from the informal market area formed by the smaller tribes, giving his tribe more room and a great deal more privacy. Qadir had five tents erected, facing a central fire pit, with the largest one for himself. It was bedecked in privacy curtains, and quite opulent with thick rugs, low tables sporting small oil lamps, and dozens of large cushions. He even had a bed.

The second tent was for the harem girls he planned to sell or give as gifts. A third tent was for the storage of supplies and provided a temporary sleeping spot for off-duty guards. The fourth tent was for his personal servants. The last was for Shar. Unlike the other sheiks, Qadir did not like to share his tent with his stallion.

As he lounged by the fire, watching his men and servants getting the camp in order, Qadir fingered the knotted leather whip he always carried on his side as he thought of Jalil. Anticipation filled him as he thought of seeing the son of his arch enemy again. This was the year of Qadir's revenge, and he had been planning for some time how he would ensure that he, Qadir, would be the winner of this year's race.

It had been three years since his last defeat, and he still burned with humiliation. Sheik Akeem and his precious Rayham had won the last race and stolen Qadir's chance to get the golden mares. And though he had rid himself of Akeem and Rayham, it did little to aid his cause in the end. Now Jalil was sheik and Qadir hated him even more. *Curse Jalil and his family to the end of time!* This year Jalil would pay.

His mood improved when he remembered killing Akeem, Akeem, and his stallion, Rayham, two years ago. He still felt a zing of pleasure from slashing Akeem's throat and seeing the pain and disbelief in Akeem's eyes as he died choking on the blood bubbling from his neck. Luring Akeem out with the false story of a golden stallion had been easy, and Qadir was just lucky he showed up alone in the mountain pass. Hashem was the only living witness, and Qadir made sure he knew what would happen to him if he ever revealed what he knew.

Lately, Qadir was considering getting rid of Hashem. He suspected the man was up to no good, but so far, his spies had failed to produce anything to support his suspicions. It didn't help that Hashem lost the golden filly in the desert, but at least he had brought him the crimson-haired beauty.

Qadir enjoyed having to tame Cassie every time they came together, but lately, he noticed a certain sullenness and reluctance during their sessions. Perhaps he would give her a chance to rest. It might lull her into thinking she'd lost favor, and he knew she wanted to be the queen of the harem. Like all women, Cassie was deceitful and narcissistic. *Yes, I will let her stew in her own juices until she understands who is in control.* And if he tired of her or she failed to produce an heir, he could always sell her to the highest bidder.

He was distracted when his herdmaster approached.

"My sheik, I moved Shar into his tent," the man said as he bowed low.

"Very good, but I noticed he is not as lively as usual. Is something wrong with him?" Qadir was oblivious to the fact that the last three years under his training had stolen some of the horse's natural spirit. Shar had learned too well the bite of Qadir's whip.

"No, my sheik. He is just tired from the journey and unsettled by the presence of so many other stallions. He appears to have settled down," the herdmaster said, but he didn't make eye contact.

Clueless as usual, Qadir accepted his answer and dismissed the man, who quickly fled.

A servant approached and announced his tent was ready and Qadir moved inside, where he could rest in more comfort. Another servant delivered his evening meal, and he was just sitting down to eat when Hashem showed up.

"My sheik, do you have everything you need?" Hashem said.

"Yes, for now." Qadir casually speared a meaty slice of lamb and dipped it into a nearby bowl of spicy sauce. "Have you sent my spies out yet?"

"Yes, my sheik."

"What about the girls?" Qadir swallowed and reached for his goblet of wine.

"They are safe in their tent and under guard."

"Good. Make sure you post extra guards around Shar's tent. That is all," Qadir said with a dismissive gesture.

When he saw Hashem hesitate, he asked, "Is there something else?"

"My sheik, will you want Cassie brought to your tent tonight?"

"No, I want Cassie to be well-rested. She will perform at the feast. And I believe one of my allies is sending me a special gift later." He smiled cruelly at the thought of breaking a new girl.

"I see. Then if it is all right, I will be out this evening, gathering what information I can," Hashem said, his face tense and his eyes unblinking as he waited for Qadir's response.

"Very good, Hashem, you may go." Qadir said, with a wave of his hand, but as he watched Hashem step out of the tent, he wondered at the strange look he had seen on the man's face. Before he could decide if it was anticipation or excitement, his thoughts were interrupted by a servant bringing more wine. He forgot about Hashem and returned to his meal, already contemplating the girl he would use for his pleasure that night.

•   •   •

Hashem was feeling both anticipation and excitement when he left Qadir's tent. It was what he had hoped for. Hashem was obsessed with the crimson-haired woman, and now he could finally take what he wanted. He had developed a reciprocal relationship with First Wife. She had asked him to get Cassie pregnant in exchange for keeping some of his secrets. He had agreed, but she didn't know that he had much greater plans, some of which involved Cassie.

Unfortunately, there was no way he could speak to Cassie—they were never alone together. He thought he might send her a note, but even though he had learned to speak the language of the foreigners he dealt with in the coastal cities, he had not learned to write it.

His plan was to lure her with the promise of helping her escape. Of course, he had no intention of letting her escape. He could use her as he desired until she became pregnant with his child, following First Wife's instructions. *Stupid old woman.* She thought Hashem only knew half of her secret, that Qadir was impotent. She wasn't aware Hashem knew the other half—who Qadir's real father was. But Hashem had a greater secret. The joke would be on First Wife in the end, Hashem thought, grinning evilly as he made his way to the back of Cassie's tent.

Lifting the edge of her tent, he slithered inside on his belly, and raised his hand to cover her mouth and crawled on top of her, effectively pinning her within the confines of her blanket. Cassie awoke immediately and struggled to throw off her attacker.

"Stop," Hashem whispered in English, his lips right next to her ear, and Cassie froze. "I'm warning you, my sweet, you will only suffer if we are found together. Be still and listen." His guttural whispers seemed loud in the tent's stillness, and he saw her glance toward the dividing curtain behind which the other girls slept. "They cannot hear us. They will not wake. I made sure of that."

Her eyes widened in alarm, and feeling her cringing, he chuckled, his tongue darting out to taste the delicate curve of her ear. "Come, we need to talk somewhere private." Rearing back to look in her eyes to gauge her reaction, he added more bait. "Don't you want to get out of here?" Seeing the alarm vanish from her eyes, he eased his hand away from her mouth.

Cassie looked deep into his dark eyes, her own narrowing. "How do you know my language?"

"I will explain everything, but not here." He did not wait for her response and turned and lifted the side of the tent, holding it for her so she could slip through. "Keep down and keep quiet." She hesitated for a second, then hastened to join him outside. "Wait," he cautioned when she rose. Pulling a lightweight black garment from inside his own robe, he cast it over her head, and grabbed her hands, tying them together with a cord. She gave him a questioning look, but he motioned her to silence and led her past the camels, who were undisturbed by his familiar smell.

Moving as fast as he dared, he all but dragged her beyond the boundary of the encampment. The moon was dim. It would not be full until the night of the coming race, so they proceeded carefully. When Hashem passed a row of bushes, he jerked her down on the hard ground beside him.

Cassie impatiently said, "What is your plan? Can you get me away from Qadir and take me to a coastal city? And why am I tied?" She shifted back to glare at him.

"Too many questions, always with you, too many questions. I had to tie you to look like a slave girl in case someone saw us. I will help you, but first, you will help me." He pushed her down on her back and deftly held her bound hands above her head while she lay helpless on the ground. He parted her legs and lay fully against her with his lean and hungry body.

Cassie clearly realized what was going on and tried to kick him off. Preparing to scream, she choked when he stuffed a rag into her mouth, effectively silencing her. She continued to struggle, even though she was no match for his strength.

"I can see why Qadir enjoys you so much." He laughed and leaned in to lick along her jaw and bite hard on her earlobe. She squealed in pain, and he found himself more aroused than he had ever been. He nipped through her robe, biting at her soft, full breasts through her thin tunic while he reached down to loosen his own robe. Her robe had fallen open when he forced her legs apart and he pulled the fragile silk away from her body.

When she stopped struggling and moaned softly against her gag, he looked down, expecting to see terror on her face, but instead he was surprised to discover lust. He was glad she had stopped fighting him and was undulating beneath him. With a groan, he looked into her flashing eyes and at her moist full lips, parted not in agony but in pleasure. *By all that is holy, she's enjoying it! Is she this way with Qadir, or is it only I that can satisfy her?*

When he was finished, Hashem rolled off and lay on his side, watching her as she relaxed. "Well, my pet, that was unexpected. I am already looking to enjoy that again." And in fact, surprisingly, he was feeling a renewal of passion.

When he released her hands, she pulled her gag out of her mouth. "I'm glad you had a good time. Don't get used to it," she replied coldly and tried to rise.

"Oh, I don't think you understand," he said. "I will be getting very used to it, and so will you." He laughed and pinned her hands, pushed the gag back in her mouth, and had his way with her again.

After he finished with her the second time, he hauled her back to camp, slipped the bindings from her wrists, and stuffed her back into her tent with a whispered warning. "Keep quiet about this. Qadir would punish me, but he would kill you if he knew."

As he walked away, he saw one guard look at him and smirk, probably thinking Hashem had gotten lucky with one of the harem girls. Hashem knew the guard would not tell on him; after all, this kind of thing was not uncommon. Satisfied, he slipped into the supply tent, lay down, and fell asleep, still feeling the pleasurable effects of his time with Cassie.

•   •   •

Cassie was finding it difficult to sleep. She sat motionless in shock, trying to make sense of what had happened. Shivering, she came to her senses, kicking herself mentally for losing control and letting that monster give her pleasure. *God knows I deserve it.* She couldn't remember the last time she had felt the satisfaction of her own release. Qadir was too rough, and his ways too painful, but Hashem was just rough enough. *Why did it have to be him?* He was a nasty creature with his yellowed teeth and muddy eyes, and she was mad at herself for letting him see her pleasure, worried that he would find some way to use that against her.

Fidgeting with her sleeping robe, she noticed how soiled it was and realized she needed to hide the evidence of her night's encounter. She stripped off the offending garment, wadded it up, and stuffed it in the bottom of her bag to dispose of later. Using water from a pitcher on the table, she made haste to wash away the proof of his pleasure. Shaking from the aftereffects of their encounter, she dumped the water at the edge of the tent. Not once did she think about the fact that she just had unprotected sex during a critical time of her cycle.

Still smelling him on her body, Cassie rubbed scented oils over her thighs and arms to mask the odor. Slipping on a fresh set of silks, she rolled up in a blanket and tried to relax. Dawn was close now, and tomorrow was the big day, but at least she would not be summoned until the feast. Knowing she would have plenty of time before the celebration to get ready, she finally relaxed enough to drift off to sleep.

Back at Qadir's house, First Wife was having trouble falling asleep as she thought about the risk she was taking using Hashem to bring her plan to fruition. Pacing back and forth in her chamber, she remembered all the plotting and scheming she'd done over the many years to ensure her power. Her only chance to keep her power rested on the foreign she-devil. The problem was Qadir couldn't sire a child, and she'd hoped it was the fault of the many women he had taken, but as time passed, she accepted the truth, even if he would not.

First Wife had been much younger when she realized the same truth about her late husband, the old sheik, but she was so much smarter than his other women. The old sheik had lived out his days, thinking he had fathered a true heir, and Qadir's real father never knew either. Once the pregnancy was confirmed, she made sure her lover didn't survive.

Years later, when Hashem revealed he knew Qadir was impotent, they came to a mutual agreement. But she still kept an eye on Hashem, knowing there would come a time when he would outlive his usefulness. When she finally fell asleep, she was praying Hashem would succeed where Qadir had failed.

CHAPTER 20

The whole encampment was stirring early the next morning, preparing for the stallion viewing. It was always a tricky affair because of the volatile nature of the male horses, so each pair of horse and rider would enter the courtyard separately, one after the other. The whole affair was carefully organized by Jalil and his men, with each pair being allowed about ten minutes due to the numerous entries and tight schedule.

As each pair rode in front of the viewers, they were evaluated on the rider's skill, the rider's control, the spirit of the stallion, and the stallion's style and confirmation. And it was expected that the audience would try to test the rider's control of the horse by making noises or sudden movements. Once a pair completed a circuit of the courtyard, the stallion would be removed to its camp and the rider would return to the viewing. Only then would the next pair enter. In this manner, everyone saw every horse and rider. It was important for each sheik to see the competition because once he signed the race register, at the formal meeting that followed, he was bound by the rules and must race or forfeit.

As the event progressed, Jalil watched without too much concern. So far, he wasn't impressed. There were only three more pairs to see, including him. He was pleased to see Sheik Ehsaan, his longtime friend and ally, ride in on his chestnut-red Mukhtar, a beautiful and well-trained stallion. Mukhtar had finished in the top three for the past two races, and though he was older, Jalil knew he would be the one to watch.

Qadir was the next to last to enter and showed his disdain for procedure by riding in on Shar before Ehsaan had barely cleared the courtyard on his way out. Jalil noticed Shar showing signs of extreme nervousness—his eyes rolled, and white flecks of saliva flew from his gaping mouth. Qadir jerked the reins, causing Shar to dance left and right. When Shar fought the bit, Qadir made a great show of bringing him under control. Most of the spectators fell silent, perhaps in sympathy for the horse. Qadir seemed to ignore them and raised his head haughtily, as if to say he had already won, while giving them all a look of derision. When he finished his circuit, he dismounted by the entrance and let his handlers take the agitated horse away.

Of course, Jalil saved Mirage for the last. Now the audience would see a real matched pair, he thought with pride. Mirage, his silver coat shining in the midday sun, pranced into the courtyard, carrying Jalil dressed in flowing, white robes banded in his signature turquoise and gold. The stallion paid close attention to the subtle signals from his master. A light touch on the reins and a gentle pressure from one leg were enough to direct Mirage into a slow, tight canter. Jalil sat relaxed in his saddle, enjoying his mount's smooth gait.

When one of Qadir's men jumped up suddenly, yelling and waving his hands at a non-existent fly, while stomping in a circle in a blatant attempt to unsettle Mirage, the great stallion seemed to cast a hard look in his direction, but never broke his steady pace. Jalil ignored the man completely. The audience laughed in appreciation, and Mirage obligingly neighed in response. Exiting amid sounds of approval, Jalil missed seeing Qadir slap his man across the back of his head.

But Jalil did see a boy hiding behind a large planter, watching him with rapt attention. From the description Jalil had been given, it was likely the son of Saad. Earlier, he had given permission to Saad for his son, Jabari, to perform at the feast. He smiled to himself. At least part of the evening would be enjoyable.

Once the stallions were secured in their respective tents, the sheiks and their chosen riders, along with two of their men, met in the main hall. While the competitors and their men filed into the hall, he watched carefully for any sign of trouble. Servants brought pitchers of drink and trays of simple food for the hungry and thirsty men once everyone was seated. When everyone was settled, Jalil rose and thanked all who had come. Then he began with a reading of the rules, which rarely changed, and this year was no exception.

Next, he presented the layout of the course, and when he finished, he opened the floor for discussion. One sheik requested a course change, and Jalil listened as Sheik Amit, a loathsome fellow and longtime ally of Qadir, asked that a section of the course from previous races be replaced. This was not entirely unusual, but the section he proposed be added was very rough and diverted the racers through an old mountain pass. Jalil's father had ridden that part of the course on Rayham, and Jalil felt confident that Mirage could handle it as well. After all, his stallion could handle the soft sands of the desert, the slippery scrabble of the foothills, and certainly the harder stone of mountain paths.

Jalil was curious, though, when Qadir joined in to agree with Amit, and Jalil exchanged a look with Fahad, who was watching Qadir closely. Fahad shrugged slightly, but Jalil could see this turn of events bothered him. When Jalil looked over at his ally, Ehsaan, the older sheik was frowning and looked puzzled too. Another sheik voiced his concern that the pass had been a source of danger in years past because of the wild lions, but Qadir laughed scornfully at the sheik, insinuating that he was a coward. Tempers flared as the sheiks argued, and Qadir chuckled quietly while he stared at Jalil.

Jalil knew he was being tested, and it made him miss Akeem even more. After he restored order, he allowed a few more men to voice their opinions, but Qadir's slur had the expected result. None of the dissenters could tolerate being accused of cowardice, and when the vote was called, the altered course was accepted. When Amit smiled at

Qadir, Jalil noted the exchange. *What are they up to?* He would have to speak with Ehsaan after the meeting.

The last part of the meeting was always tedious, but it was the most critical. Twenty sheiks would have to take the oath and sign the official race registration. In this way, they were legally obligated to abide by the rules and the results of the race. If they lost or failed to take part in the race, they forfeited as outlined in the rules. It was a serious commitment.

As soon as the last sheik made his mark, Jalil closed the meeting by thanking the participants and reminding them of the forthcoming feast and entertainment being held in the courtyard. The men filed out. Some of them headed back to their campsites for a brief respite before the feast, but some were already packed and prepared to depart, having finished the required part of the event. Smaller tribal groups often left early to return to their own holdings, where only a skeleton crew of men had been left to guard their home and herd. Once the room was clear, Jalil hurried to check on Mirage and asked Fahad to accompany him so they could discuss the recent development.

•   •   •

While the sheiks attended the registration meeting, Cassie was hard at work getting ready for the evening ahead. It was critical that she look her best. She was sick of Qadir and hoped she might attract the attention of another sheik who might help her escape.

Thankfully, her latest ensemble, with its accompanying accessories, was in order. She would wear black and scarlet silks with glittery gold embellishments. She had altered her veil to expose her emerald eyes, which she outlined with black and highlighted with golden dust. Additionally, she dyed her lips and intimate areas crimson.

Her pantaloons were of a heavier silk, and because they were not as revealing as she liked, she had altered them by adding gossamer panels of black silk on the inside of both legs to reveal more of her intimate assets at strategic times during her dance. She knew that Qadir would be incensed, and the thought of how he might retaliate filler her with a slight tremor of fear, because she was sure he would retaliate. But she would risk it—she was prepared to do just about anything to escape this nightmare of an existence.

The excited chatter of the other girls as they waited to be summoned drove her crazy. She was tired of having to share her tent with the silly bunch of idiots. The only thing affording her any privacy was the curtain suspended between her sleeping area and theirs. She wondered about the divider when she first arrived, but after last night's adventure with Hashem, she knew who had set it up. Feeling the pressure now, but declining to associate with the other girls, Cassie remained on her side of the tent, where she went over her dance routine in her head and waited anxiously for the night to begin.

CHAPTER 21

Across the encampment, Jabari was busy getting ready for the feast. Sheik Jalil had granted his wish to perform, and he was beyond happy. But he still did not understand why his father said Jabari had to leave immediately after his show, so he asked him again. "Father, why can I not stay longer at the feast?"

"Because. That is my final word." Saad said firmly. "Now hurry, we are almost ready to go."

Frustrated and thinking he could get more information from his mother, Jabari stopped by the fire to speak to her. "Mother, do you know why I cannot stay longer at the feast?"

Samira was busy preparing a simple meal for her and Kira and stopped to answer him. "What did your father tell you?"

"He did not explain."

"Jabari, you are much too young for that kind of entertainment," she said cryptically. "Besides, I need you to protect me, guard the camp, and watch over Kira and Amber."

Jabari realized he would get no further with her, either. "All right, I will do as you say, but I wish I could stay and see the dancing," Jabari grumbled convincingly. He was already planning a little excursion later when his mother would be occupied watching the camp. And he was confident she was safe here in Jalil's holding and would not need his help.

Avoiding his mother's eyes, he finished packing his magic gear. He was worrying about Kira's plan to sneak out until he was distracted by his mother watching him intently. He sighed with relief when she was distracted by Kira's soft voice from the woman's tent. His mother made him very nervous. She always knew when he was up to no good, and he wondered if all mothers had this strange power. He pulled on his voluminous and brightly colored robe with an outrageously tall turban. The costume concealed his gear and also helped him look the part of a mystic. When he was ready, he joined his father and Amal, following them to the same courtyard where the stallion viewing had been held.

The courtyard had been transformed by colorful tribal banners, tall flame-topped torches, and long, low tables. The central area, paved with flagstones, was open and swept clean. Guests clustered in their tribal groups on both sides, sitting or reclining at their respective tables, and a small band of musicians played near the entrance. Servants in robes of pale turquoise loaded the tables with pitchers and platters of assorted beverages and food.

Jalil and his men were sitting on a raised area at the far end of the courtyard, and Jabari admired his robes of brilliant turquoise and white, tied with golden cords. Jabari spied Qadir lounging halfway down on one side, his black and scarlet robes reflecting the light of the fires and blending with the night shadows. The older sheik's hand fingered a thin coil of leather hanging from his waist and now and then he would turn his head slightly to listen to whatever the sinister-looking man behind him was saying. Jabari chuckled, recognizing the man from the viewing, and wondered if his head was still sore, but his laughter died when he saw Qadir's face. Jabari had heard many stories of the cruel sheik and gave him a wide berth as he made his way toward Jalil's table.

As Jabari approached in his outlandish costume, Jalil looked up and smiled. "Ah, our mystic has arrived," he teased lightly but kindly. Standing, he waved his hand to silence the musicians. One drummer responded with a flourish of loud beats, and Jalil now had everyone's attention. "Behold, my fellow sheiks and honored guests. We have been blessed with a visit from a great traveling mystic known around the world as Jabari the Magnificent. He has offered to give us a display of his powers and magical skills." There was laughter, clapping, and table pounding.

Fearless as always, Jabari was quite the sight in his swirling robes and elaborate head piece, and he was enjoying himself immensely. "Thank you, oh mighty Sheik Jalil. You honor me as well to grant me the opportunity to entertain your esteemed guests," his clear youthful voice rang out. "I will now show you wonders and magic like you have never seen. You will be amazed, but there is no need to be afraid. Before I finish, I will put everything back in order." The guests fell silent at this announcement, clearly intrigued. "My servant Saad will assist me now," he explained, motioning for his father to bring a tall table and a colorful bag into the courtyard. Saad hurried to set the items by the boy's side. Placing a small oil lamp on the table, he lit it and returned to join Amal near the entrance.

"I will now use all the skills I have spent many, many, many years perfecting to amaze you with my magic," Jabari declared with a flourish. This was the cause of much laughter, as his age was all too evident. But Jabari was not offended. He was in his element and having fun. "Behold, oh great and mighty sheiks," he yelled, and with a dramatic swirl of his hands, he proceeded to work his magic on the crowd.

His true skill was in knowing how to treat the leaders, and he made some of the sheiks' personal items disappear before their eyes, only to have them reappear in another guest's pocket. When he ended his act by producing a pigeon from out of thin air, the men were thoroughly entertained and showed their appreciation by banging their tables, throwing him small coins and gems. Gathering the offerings, Jabari bowed to all sides and especially to Jalil, whom he thanked profusely and sincerely for allowing his "humble" self to perform for such honored guests.

Jalil laughed heartily. "You are welcome, O Great Jabari. We will look forward to having you share more of your magic someday. Inshallah." He flipped the boy a large gold coin.

Jabari caught it with one hand, then flipped it into the air, where it promptly disappeared. Winking at Jalil, he bowed and marched from the courtyard to the sound of more applause.

Saad fetched the table and bag and met him just outside the entrance. "I am so proud of you, my son." He hugged him tightly.

"Thank you, Father. I had so much fun. It was wonderful," he replied with shining silver eyes. "But I guess I'd better get back to the camp."

"Yes indeed," his father said. "I will help you get everything back to our tent."

Leaving Amal at the feast, Saad and Jabari returned to find Samira tending the fire, and Jabari rushed into her arms. "Oh, Mother," he exclaimed, "it was wonderful, and look!" He tossed the handful of coins and small gems he had received onto the rug by her side.

"Jabari! Where did you get these?" She looked up with a fearful expression.

"The sheiks gave them to me. Jalil himself gave me the gold coin." He plopped down to study the pile in more detail.

Samira was speechless. Grabbing him by the shoulders to still his chatter, she forced him to look into her eyes. "My son, I am so proud of you. You have earned every one of these gifts with your hard practice." She hugged him fiercely.

Taken aback at the strength of her hug and her heartfelt words, Jabari felt like crying. *I will not cry. I am too old to cry. Men do not cry.* Well, maybe just a little, he thought as he sniffed and snuggled deeper into her warm embrace.

•   •   •

Kira sat nearby, enjoying the tale of his success and was sad she hadn't seen his show. Someday, she promised herself. For now, she was eager to get on with her evening plans. She had pestered Jabari all day about her desire to sneak out that night, and he had finally agreed. With most of the sheiks and their key men at the celebration, and the many that were in the process of departing early, it would be a good time to practice her subterfuge.

After Saad left to return to the feast, Kira feigned tiredness and retired to her tent. It was easy to make it look like she was wrapped up in her sleeping rug—a few pillows and bundled garments became a slender form in the darkness of the tent. Donning the clothing she had stolen from Jabari, she hid her braided hair under a headwrap and covered herself in an old traveling robe and waited impatiently for the signal from Jabari.

With the men away, Kira knew Samira would stay close to the fire where she could keep watch. When Kira had asked Saad why he was so comfortable letting his wife take a watch while they traveled, he told her he had no qualms about leaving Samira in charge. She was resourceful and was no stranger to a scimitar. He himself had trained her in its use. Desert born, she was tough when she needed to be, and she would defend her family to the death.

Waiting anxiously, Kira peeked out of her tent and watched Jabari yawn loudly as per their plan. He then told Samira that he was exhausted from his performance and would retire to his tent. Samira merely nodded and continued to work on her mending. After some time had passed, Kira heard their prearranged signal when he scratched lightly on the back of her tent, and she slipped out to join him.

Standing up, she froze when Amber whickered softly. Rushing to Amber's side, Kira calmed her with a whispered word before melting into the night beside her fellow conspirator. Amber watched them leave, but she remained beside the sleeping camels as commanded.

Kira was so excited to be free of the confines of her tent, Jabari had to keep a hand on her arm to prevent her from breaking into a run.

"Slow down, Kira," he said. "You must not run. It will only draw attention. Control yourself. It is not far to go."

Understanding the wisdom of his words, she struggled to contain her enthusiasm. Glancing right and left, she saw several of the camps while making their way to the courtyard. "Where are the stallions?"

"The sheiks keep them inside their tents."

"Will we get to see the golden horses?"

"No, silly girl. Jalil will not take any risks and will keep all his horses hidden until everyone has gone."

"Oh, that is a shame," Kira complained quietly, but brightened when she saw the lights and heard the music spilling from the courtyard.

"I hope to see them tomorrow. Father will trade with Jalil's men, and I think mother has been invited to meet with Jalil's mother and sisters," Jabari said.

"Perhaps I can come with you."

"I will have to think about it. But hush now. We must be silent and keep out of sight, but I think we will get close enough to see the dancing girls." He seemed excited by the thought and hurried along.

Kira was just happy to be out of her tent and followed him closely. They crept down the outside of the courtyard and ducked behind a row of low, decorative plants. Once they were in place, they watched, enthralled by the splendor of the scene.

From their vantage point, Jabari pointed out the infamous Qadir and his men sitting across the courtyard. Kira shuddered. The sheik would have been almost handsome except for the hardness of his face and the coldness of his eyes. But the man who stood behind him was even scarier looking, his face leathery and scarred. Many other fascinating men sat around the courtyard, but it was the head table that drew her eyes.

"Is… is that him? Is that Jalil?" Kira stared at the young sheik in his glorious robes. His white teeth flashed when he laughed out loud at something one of his men said, and his long fingers held a jeweled goblet from which he sipped. *Oh my.* She felt breathless and didn't know why.

"Yes, that is him. He is truly a great sheik, just like his father was before him." Jabari looked at him with admiration. "He will be the one to ride Mirage, and I am certain he will win this year."

Kira had no comment. She was busy studying Jalil's handsome face and broad shoulders and unconsciously tried to move closer to get a better look.

"Where do you think you are going?" Jabari hissed, pulling her back beside him.

"Oh, I'm sorry. I, I was just, well, just trying to, you know...," she stuttered in confusion.

"No, I do not know. I only know that you had better stay put and keep quiet. It won't be long now." As if Jabari had given the command himself, women danced into the center of the courtyard, moving with intricate steps and vigorous leaps as they performed for the guests. Kira fell silent, shocked by their display, and the men responded by pounding the tables and shouting encouragements.

•   •   •

Sitting at the head table, Jalil pretended to smile. He didn't approve of enslaving women and was hoping someday more tribes would free theirs, but for now, he would enjoy the show. After all, he was a man, and the girls Qadir had brought were lovely enough to keep his attention, though not enough to stir his desires. Frankly, he couldn't wait for the whole thing to be over and was thinking about how great it would be when everyone left tomorrow, until he noticed Qadir's sudden interest.

All evening, the arrogant sheik had remained aloof, acting bored, and casting disdainful glares at the other guests. Qadir had not even paid attention to the young boy's magic show. Now the man was leaning forward, staring at the entrance, while fingering the ever-present whip at his side. The girls came to a sudden halt and knelt with heads bowed and arms outstretched.

When the musicians began a slow eerie tune, the notes wavering, rising, and falling, a lone woman completely covered in shining black silk walked slowly into the courtyard, stopping in front of Qadir's table with her head bent. The musicians began playing faster, and Qadir clapped his hands once. The woman sprang into action, circling the courtyard, the silken material covering her body floating higher and higher. Suddenly she flung the material away, revealing her scarlet and black silks, her pale, white skin, and long, shining, crimson hair.

The crowd was shocked to silence, and astonished, Jalil was surprised by her appearance and didn't notice the look that passed between the woman and Qadir. He also failed to see Qadir's sinister smile.

She danced, whirling and twisting, flaunting her lush body for everyone's enjoyment. Her wanton movements were designed to entice, and she smiled at Jalil as she made her way around the courtyard. She kept her brilliant eyes locked on him and he could see the lust in their emerald depths.

Jalil studied the woman who tried to get his attention. This was not new. As a sheik with no harem or wife, he had become accustomed to women seeking his favor. When the sultry redhead finished her show by sliding forward with knees bent and spread, he hid his disgust and feigned enjoyment, clapping his hands along with the others. Evidently, he was convincing because she flashed him an inviting smile.

•   •   •

Qadir, watching from the sidelines, became enraged when he saw her attraction to his enemy. Surprised at the intensity of the jealousy he felt, he tamped his anger, knowing he couldn't afford to let petty emotions impede his plans, plans that he had spent years making. Once he had eliminated all of Akeem's issue, there would be nothing to stop him from taking Jalil's herd and kingdom. He fought to maintain control, but now it wasn't anger he tried to suppress. Seeing her stoke the lust of all the men in the room, he found himself aroused by the modifications to her outfit that allowed glimpses between her lush thighs.

Qadir watched Jalil closely while Cassie danced and thought he knew what he was thinking. It was obvious to him the younger sheik wanted Cassie, and Qadir was feeling quite happy with the success of this part of his plan. Soon, he would figure out a way to use her to ruin Jalil. Ordering two men to escort Cassie back to her tent, he continued to finger his whip, anticipating his next session with her.

•   •   •

As Kira walked quickly back to their camp, she was astounded by what she had seen. *Cassie! Cassie is alive!* There was no mistaking that pale skin, that red hair, and that figure. *How could she be alive? How did she get here? Why is she performing dances for those men?* Jabari was by her side, but she was so busy thinking about Cassie, she wasn't paying attention and was walking way too fast.

"What is wrong with you?" Jabari hissed, tugging at her sleeve.

Kira didn't answer, but she slowed her pace and concentrated on making her way in the dark, avoiding tripping over sleeping men and camels. Thankfully, they were both able to slip back into their respective tents unseen by Samira, who was still keeping watch by the fire, waiting for the return of Saad and Amal.

Pulling off her boy's clothes, Kira buried them in her personal pack before donning her sleeping tunic. Consumed with thoughts about Cassie, she shivered as she lay wrapped in her blanket, head spinning and heart pounding. Tomorrow she would find answers. Maybe she could find a way to talk to Cassie.

Almost forgetting, she dug in her pack for her father's ring, and was satisfied to find the medallion was still safely wrapped in the old shirt. Slipping her mother's chain over her head, she tucked it inside her tunic and, with one hand clasping her father's ring, fell into an uneasy sleep.

CHAPTER 22

The family was awake at first light, preparing for their day of trading with Jalil's tribe. Samira cautioned Kira to stay inside as a few tribes had yet to depart. But she promised once they left, she would consider letting her sit outside as long as she remained fully veiled and did not leave the camp.

When Jalil's mother, Nasira, sent word inviting Samira to join her for the midday meal, Samira sorted out the items she had secured along their route she knew would interest Nasira. Soft leather hides for slippers and belts, finely made chains and bracelets, and exotic herbs and spices were a just of the things they might want. The women of Jalil's tribe were known far and wide for their skilled weaving, and Samira was excited to trade for the beautiful cloth and the ready-made garments they might have. She hoped to purchase a new set of robes for each of her family members as well.

She could trade much of what she brought, only saving a little for their next and final stop at Sheik Ehsaan's kingdom. Qadir's kingdom was located beyond Ehsaan's, but they would not be stopping there. They hadn't attempted to barter with his tribe for many years because his men were surly, and the women weren't allowed to see the goods. Trading with Qadir's tribe had never been profitable.

With the race still almost two weeks away, they had plenty of time to take a few extra days with Jalil's tribe if they wanted, and at Ehsaan's too, time they could spend relaxing and enjoying the last days of their travels, as well as make plans for the future.

For some time, Amal had been talking about settling down and becoming a permanent member of a tribe. He wanted a home and a family, so he was searching for a wife, but it was difficult to do that on the road. Samira also desired a permanent home, but more than that, she desperately longed for another child, one that she could call her own. She often pondered why they hadn't been blessed with one yet. Her husband hoped for this as well. He said he wouldn't mind another son but would be just as happy with a daughter. Samira dreamed of a daughter. Saad had Amal and Jabari, both good companions, but both men. Samira longed for a woman she could talk to.

After preparing a light meal of honeyed tea, warm bread, and some soft cheese she had traded for with a servant from a neighboring camp, Samira hurried to get the men fed. Saad and Amal were meeting with Jalil's men this morning, and she knew Jabari would be off to the stables, hoping to see Mirage and the famous golden mares.

Shaking her head, Samira was ever puzzled by her son's obsession with horses. To her, they were just another stock animal, albeit worth a lot more. She understood the importance of stallions and their use in breeding better stock, and she also knew that they held even greater value if they could be raced. But to Jabari, horses seemed to be special. He claimed to be able to communicate with them, which had always seemed rather fanciful to her, until she had seen first-hand the relationship Kira had with Amber. There was no doubt in her mind now that some horses were much more than just another ignorant but useful animal.

She had wondered many other things about Jabari over the years. He was a mystery with his caramel hair and bright silver eyes, and even now, she shivered when she remembered the feeling she had when she first held him as a baby. Yes, there was something special about Jabari. Eager to get on with her day, she put all thoughts of Jabari from her head. She needed to concentrate on her upcoming meeting with Sheikha Nasira.

•   •   •

Kira waited until the men departed before joining Samira by the fire. "Sabah al noor, Samira."

"Good morning, Kira. Join me." She motioned for Kira to sit beside her.

"Is it safe?" Nervous, Kira glanced about. But the encampment was almost empty except for a large group loading their camels as a few men stood nearby, holding their horses. One figure, obviously a woman because she was completely covered in dark robes, had her hands tied together and was being held by a man. *Cassie?* Kira quickly looked away.

Samira raised her eyebrows at Kira's reaction but merely said, "Come, sit."

Approaching the fire, Kira knelt gracefully and accepted a cup of tea. She paused between sips to take a deep breath of fresh air, inhaling all the strange and wonderful smells she had grown to love. Exotic spices from her drink, dusty leather from the camel harnesses, and a faint whiff of the camels themselves, all wrapped up in the dry sharp scent of sand warming in the rising sun.

"Tell me, Kira. What do you think of Jalil's kingdom so far?" Samira said.

"Well, I haven't been able to see much." Kira tried not to sound ungrateful.

"I am sure it is difficult, but I expect you have been sneaking a few looks, hmm?" Samira was busy tending the fire and missed Kira's startled expression. Kira choked at the mention of "sneaking."

"Are you all right?" Samira patted her on the back.

"Oh, oh...yes. I just swallowed a bit too fast," Kira said, hiding her guilty face for a moment and blotting her lips while thinking if only Samira knew just how much "sneaking" she had done.

When Samira handed her a piece of the warm bread slathered in soft cheese and drizzled in honey, Kira munched on the delicious morsel and considered her next words. Though she had told her new family most of her story, she had left out a few minor details. Like Cassie. Being duped by the callous woman was embarrassing, and it was easier to assume she had perished in the desert, especially when she remembered the woman's cruelty when Cassie stole her things and abandoned her after they found Amber. Perhaps now was the time to come clean.

Having recognized Cassie at the celebration and learning she was with Qadir, Kira knew she needed to share the complete story with her new friends so there would be no surprises. Now that more people knew about Cassie, it would only be a matter of time before someone discovered her connection with Kira. Finishing her bread, Kira took one more swallow of tea and set the cup down nearby. *I might as well get it over with.* "Samira, I have to tell you something."

Samira must have heard the seriousness in her voice because she knelt beside her, clasped her hands together, and waited with a patient expression.

"Well, I didn't completely tell you the truth about the day my father was killed," Kira said to Samira, watching her closely. Samira's warm brown eyes showed nothing but encouragement, so Kira told her the real story, this time filling her in on Cassie and the betrayal. Agitated, she relived the trauma of the crash and the harrowing days that followed, and when she finished, she bowed her head, exhausted by her own emotional tale.

"Kira, Kira." Samira pulled her into a warm hug. "Everything will be all right. You are with friends now, and we will look after you." She comforted her and offered her more tea. "What made you decide to share this now?"

Kira glanced toward the last long line of departing camels, with Qadir on a black stallion in the lead, and caught a final glimpse of the dark-robed woman bound to a camel. It had to be Cassie. But not wanting to confess to her late-night adventure, Kira carefully considered her answer. "Well, I heard…well Jabari heard some gossip in the camp about a foreign woman with red hair, and I thought it could be Cassie."

"Do you want to find her?"

"No, uh no, not really. I don't think she would welcome my help." Kira fumbled with the cords securing her robe, praying Samira wouldn't ask her anymore about Cassie. Thinking about Cassie imprisoned by the cruel Qadir, Kira felt a stab of guilt until she remembered that fateful day when Cassie abandoned her.

"Perhaps you are right. I think that woman, wherever she is, will surely find her own way in the world." Samira paused in her speaking.

The air was heavy with implication, but when she said no more, Kira knew Samira didn't approve of Cassie's behavior.

Shaking her head as if to ward off the uncomfortable topic of Cassie, Samira asked, "Well then, what do you really want, Kira?"

"I want to get word to my family," she said softly. Seeing Samira's nod of understanding, Kira added, "But I don't know how or where to start."

"Kira, we will have plenty of time to talk about this once we are on the road to Ehsaan's. Saad will know what to do. For now, I need to finish getting ready to meet with Nasira. The men will be tied up all day with trading and who knows when Jabari will return." Samira touched Kira's arm. "I am sorry, but you will have to remain hidden in the tent until I get back. I know it is a disappointment."

"Of course, you are right," she said, bringing a smile of surprise to Samira's face. "I need to be careful. I will stay here and work on my sewing."

Rising to help Samira, Kira's mind was already spinning with plans. With everyone gone, it would be easy to slip away for a few hours, dressed as a boy. She might get to see the golden horses and maybe even Jalil himself. Ever since seeing him at the feast, she could not stop thinking about him.

Just as Samira started to leave the camp, Kira stopped her. "Thank you, Samira, for all you have done for me. You saved my life, and I will always be grateful." She hugged her and hurried back to her tent and didn't hear Samira's parting words.

Wiping her eyes at sudden tears, Samira watched her go and said softly, "Someday, somehow, I will help her find a way home. But oh, how I will miss her. She is like a daughter to me."

CHAPTER 23

Jabari dashed out of camp as soon as his father and uncle left. He wanted to avoid Kira before she could corner him, knowing she would try to talk him into taking her with him. That girl was becoming more trouble by the day, he thought, remembering their adventure the previous night. It had been both exciting and terrifying, and if they had been caught, it would have been a disaster.

Thanking Allah again for protecting him, Jabari made his way directly to the stable area. As he neared the corral, he saw Jalil working with Mirage and approached slowly, not wanting to startle them. When Mirage stopped prancing to stare at him, snorting and pawing the ground, Jabari was entranced. He momentarily forgot about Jalil.

Jalil chuckled. "Come here, boy," he said, motioning Jabari closer. "I see you are a fellow lover of horses."

Slipping under the fence line, Jabari stepped nearer to Mirage. "Oh, yes, my sheik. May I touch him?"

"Certainly. He won't bite, at least not unless I tell him to," Jalil joked as he patted Mirage's silky neck.

Jabari took another cautious step forward, keeping his arms by his sides and his eyes downcast. Mirage came forward to meet him and lowered his head to sniff him from head to toe. Feeling like he was in a dream, Jabari jumped back when Mirage blew hard on his face.

Jalil laughed out loud at both of their expressions. Still laughing, he lightly smacked Mirage on the shoulder. "My friend, be easy on the boy. I think you scared him."

Mirage tossed his head and neighed loudly. Stunned, Jabari stood still, waiting to see what the horse would do next. Before he knew it, Mirage moved closer and allowed Jabari to pet his chest and neck.

"Oh, Allah, I have died and gone to heaven. Mirage, you are glorious," Jabari praised the horse while continuing to stroke him, marveling at the silkiness of his coat and mane, so much like Amber's. Then Mirage allowed him to move around him, and under him, even letting Jabari to pick up his hooves.

Eyes wide in surprise, Jalil mumbled to himself, "Never has Mirage responded to anyone like this." Then he spoke louder. "You evidently know something about horses. So, Jabari, what do you think of Mirage?" He looked at him, a curious expression on his face.

Jabari paused in his study of the horse to stare at Jalil. "You remembered my name?"

Jalil laughed. "Well, who could forget Jabari the Magnificent? Of course, I remember who you are. Now, tell me, what do you think of this fine animal?"

Studying the handsome face of the young sheik, Jabari thought Jalil was making fun of him, but seeing the sincerity in his green-gold eyes, he took a moment to formulate his answer. "Well, I think he must be about five years old. There is an odd scar on his right rear leg, perhaps an old injury. He looks to be in excellent condition, but his left front hoof should be checked. He may have picked up a stone. I have not checked his teeth, but his eyes are clear, and his balance is good."

Jalil's eyes widened in wonder, and he strode forward and picked up Mirage's front foot. Peering inside the hoof, he reached into his robe, pulled out a bit of twisted metal that served as a hoof pick, and carefully removed a small pebble he found lodged there. Setting the hoof down, he rubbed Mirage's leg before moving back beside Jabari.

When he felt a large hand on his shoulder, Jabari looked up to see Jalil staring intently at his silver eyes, so intently that Jabari squirmed, suddenly afraid he had angered the sheik.

Jalil relaxed his gaze. "Jabari, I apologize if I made you uncomfortable. My friend, you have very sharp eyes indeed. You are correct on every point. And thank you for noticing the stone. It was small and probably would have fallen loose, but it could have caused damage all the same," he said with a nod.

Shocked but recovering quickly, Jabari bowed. "You are welcome, my sheik. I am but the son of a simple trader. I hope I have not offended. But I would ask one favor of you."

Jalil waited, stroking Mirage's face. "What would the son of a simple trader request of his sheik?"

Jabari squared his shoulders and took a deep breath. This was the moment he had dreamed of.

"Would you let me see your golden mares?"

Jalil seemed to consider the request. "You know, my golden mares are my most prized possession next to Mirage. Few men outside my tribe are allowed to see them." Jabari frowned, but Jalil smiled and added, "Do not fear. I cannot say no to those eyes of yours. My herd is even now being moved here, and if you are willing to wait, you will have your wish."

Jabari's face split into a huge smile, and Jalil smiled in return. "I tell you what, my magical friend, why don't you join me for a tour of the stables. I have a few new foals too small to turn out. I might value your opinion of them. Come." With a final pat on Mirage's flank, he turned to walk inside the larger stable building.

Jabari didn't hesitate. After wishing Mirage a good day, he moved fast to catch up to the long strides of the sheik. *Wait until I tell Kira about this!*

•   •   •

If Jabari had waited but a few minutes more, he could have told her face-to-face. Kira was even then crouching behind some bushes at the far end of Mirage's corral. Dressed in her boy's outfit, with her head covered and her skin still stained a dark brown, Kira was confident she wouldn't be recognized.

Stealing away from camp had been easy. Once everyone was gone, Kira dressed in the boy's clothes, donned her headwrap and a light robe. By taking her time and acting like she had every right to be walking through the compound, no one glanced twice at her. When she arrived at the corral, she hid behind the bushes where she could watch Jabari interact with the silver stallion and the tall, handsome sheik.

The horse was impressive, but it was the man standing by his side that was truly magnificent. Close enough to get a good look, she was fascinated by Jalil. His rich laughter tugged at something deep inside her, and she stared wide-eyed at his flashing white teeth, watching his lips when he spoke to Jabari. Kira touched her own lips without thinking, wondering what his lips would feel like on hers. The blood rushed to her face when she realized the direction of her thoughts.

As it had last night, her heart began to beat faster, and she squirmed, her body coming alive in the oddest places. *What is happening to me?* Confused by new feelings and wild longings, she tore her gaze from Jalil and back to Mirage. When Jabari and Jalil moved away toward one of the stables, she breathed deeply to calm herself and waited for them to disappear into the building before cautiously approaching the corral.

Mirage swung his head around, and she watched as he paused and sniffed. Apparently, he sensed no danger because he calmly walked forward until he was close enough to touch. Looking into his dark, liquid eyes, Kira held out one hand, palm up, and waited. He reached out his long neck and sniffed her hand. Tickling his lower lip, she laughed when he responded in typical horse fashion by moving his upper lip back and forth rapidly.

Emboldened, she rubbed a spot between his eyes before reaching around to stroke his cheek. *Oh, Mirage, you are truly magnificent!* It was as if he heard her compliment, and he arched his powerful neck. *Oh, yes, you know how handsome you are, don't you.* He neighed as if in agreement. So intent was she in petting him, she almost failed to see the two figures headed her way. Forgetting to keep her head down, she turned to stare at them. *Oh, no! Jalil and Jabari!*

Jalil strode forward furiously with fists clenched, but stopped abruptly when Kira's bright blue-green eyes met his.

Kira froze, momentarily stunned by his ferocious stare, but then panicked, backed away from Mirage, and ran from the corral.

"Wait!" Jalil's voice rang out.

Overcome with fear, she raced through the bushes and trees peppering the landscape, slipping under another fence line. Twisting and turning, she risked a backwards glance, relieved the stables were no longer in sight. The land was sloping downward, and soon she came to the stream that ran through Jalil's kingdom. Not knowing where to go, she scrambled over a rocky outcropping and found a deep split in the rocks near the water. Tucking herself inside, she prayed no snakes or scorpions were hiding in the shady spot.

•   •   •

When Jalil broke into a run, Jabari hesitated, already aware of who Jalil was chasing. He recognized his old trousers peeking from the ratty robe, as well as the headwrap Kira used to cover her golden hair. Knowing he had to do something quick, he threw himself on the ground, rolled on his back and began yelling as if in pain while holding his leg.

Hearing Jabari's cries, Jalil halted and looked back to see him on the ground, obviously hurt. With a last glance in the direction the stranger had run, he looked back at Jabari. Sighing, he returned to the boy's side, picked him up carefully, and carried him toward the stable, while calling for help. A man rushed out of the building, and Jalil explained the situation, sending him to gather others to search for the intruder. Setting Jabari on top of a rough table, Jalil took time to check the boy to determine the nature of his injuries. "Where does it hurt, Jabari?"

"I think it is my ankle." Jabari grimaced convincingly, holding his leg up. When Jalil felt his ankle and eased it back and forth, Jabari was quick to play his part. "Ow! That hurts!"

"Well, it is not broken," Jalil said. "It is probably only a sprain, but you must not walk on it. I will wrap it, and then I will take you back to your tent." Jalil reached for a roll of cloth they used when bandaging the horses, and in no time at all, he had the ankle properly wrapped and bound.

"Thank you, my sheik. It is already feeling much better." Jabari moved to sit on the edge of the table. "I beg of you, could I not rest here for a bit, maybe outside where I could see the herd when it returns?" He pleaded with Jalil.

"I guess that would be all right," Jalil said. "But I must find the stranger that was with Mirage. He may have been trying to hurt him."

Jabari knew Jalil's fears were real. Rival tribes had been known to injure a competitor's stallion before the race. He had to think fast again. "But that was no stranger. That was just my cousin, Bassam."

"Your cousin? What was he doing with my horse?"

"Oh, I am sure he meant no harm. His parents were killed by bandits last year, and he now lives with us. He is quite harmless, and he also loves horses, just like me." Jabari fussed with his bandage, keeping his eyes averted, afraid that Jalil would see through his lies. "You could see that Mirage was not afraid." He hoped he wasn't trying too hard with Jalil.

Jalil considered for a moment before responding. "I lost my father in the same manner and understand how painful that can be. But tell Bassam that if he wants to see my horses, he should come with you."

A lean man in dusty robes interrupted them. Jalil was quick to make the introductions. "Jabari, this is my herdmaster, Sakhr. Sakhr, this is Jabari."

"Ah, yes. I have heard of you," Sakhr said with a small smile. "You are Jabari the Magnificent, are you not?"

"Oh, well, yes Sakhr. That would be me." Jabari was inordinately pleased to be recognized.

"Yes, Sakhr. We are blessed to have such a famous person in our kingdom. That said, Jabari has suffered a slight injury. Please take him and find a safe place where he can watch the herd. And please have someone find his father, the man known as Saad, to tell him of the accident. Inform him we will bring the boy back to his tent." Jalil turned to depart but spoke once more. "I am sorry you that got hurt, Jabari. Now I must go and call off the search for Bassam."

"Thank you for helping me, my sheik, and also for the honor of seeing your splendid horses. I never meant to cause you such trouble," Jabari said, ashamed of having lied to Jalil.

Jalil reached out and rubbed the boy's head, chuckling. "Do not worry, my little friend. It was not such a bad thing. Besides, you saved Mirage from further injury by finding that stone."

Jabari smiled, knowing the stone was not all that serious. "You are welcome, my sheik. I will be available to advise you whenever you need."

Jalil roared with laughter as he left the stable.

Sakhr helped Jabari find a suitable spot from which to view the herd. "Young Jabari," he said, "you are good for the sheik."

"What do you mean?" Jabari asked, his brow furrowed with puzzlement.

"The sheik has not laughed this much in a very long time. Anger at his father's murder and sadness for his mother's pain have been his constant companions for the last few years. He has a lightness of spirit around you, something we have all dearly missed."

"I am glad I could help him," Jabari said sincerely. He was about to ask a Sakhr a question about the herd when he heard shouting and felt the thunder of hoofbeats rumbling in his chest. Filled with excitement, he watched in awe as a flood of horses came running, like a wave of color, shot through with threads of gold. He was certain he was in heaven, thinking it was a shame that Kira missed seeing the herd, but prayed she had made it back to the tent without being discovered.

·　　·　　·

Unfortunately, Kira had not made it back yet. After hiding in the rocky hole, she finally slipped out, anxious to return to camp. If she didn't get back before Samira, she would be in big trouble. She climbed up a sharp rise and peered over the top, relieved there was no one in sight, but she had no idea where she was. Praying Jalil had given up the chase, she trudged along, hot and tired, in what she hoped was the right direction.

God must have smiled down on her, she thought when she finally spied her camp. Samira had not yet returned. Amber neighed loudly when she approached, and Kira rushed to her side to quiet her. She waited as Amber smelled her all over, chuckling when Amber snorted as if in anger. *She must smell Mirage.*

"Oh, calm down, Amber. It was just Mirage, and he is not half the horse you are. It's you I love, not him," she whispered fiercely.

Amber snorted again, as if reminding her stallions were nothing but trouble, and Kira hugged her neck, assuring her she was indeed the holder of Kira's heart. When Amber calmed down, Kira ducked inside her tent and changed back into her tunic and robe. Stuffing Jabari's clothes in her bag, she lay down to rest from her adventure and shortly fell asleep.

The sound of men talking outside the tent awakened her. Groggy, she rose, straightened her clothes, and looked outside to see Samira directing two strangers who were setting large bundles down by the fire. Samira had returned triumphant and hurried into the tent, excited to show Kira the things she had bought or traded for.

When she saw Kira's rumpled robes and messy hair, she grew alarmed. "What happened to you? Are you sick?" She rushed over to feel her forehead. "You are hot! You need to drink something now. Let me get you some water." Darting back outside, she returned almost at once with a waterskin and a cup.

After drinking two cups, Kira assured her she was fine, and Samira seemed convinced. Wishing to distract her, Kira asked about her meeting with Nasira, and soon they were busy admiring the items Samira had obtained.

They were deep in conversation when they heard a commotion outside the tent. Samira rushed to investigate, and Kira peeked out to see a man carrying Jabari, his ankle swathed in bandages.

"Oh, Allah! What has happened? Jabari, are you hurt? What did you do?" Samira was distraught. She tried to pry Jabari from the arms of the man, who wisely set him down quickly and gently.

"Do not be alarmed," the man said as he backed away, letting Samira fuss with the boy. "The sheik himself tended to his leg."

"The sheik?" Samira looked down at Jabari and then back at the servant with utter confusion written on her face. Kira winced, worried about what might be revealed. *Is he really hurt? Or did he save me with a distraction?* She leaned closer to the opening to catch every word.

"Yes. The boy was with Mirage," the man said.

"Mirage?" Samira's voice was rising in anger.

The man tried to explain again. "Yes. The boy hurt himself while chasing his cousin."

"HIS COUSIN?" Samira glared at Jabari. Kira had to stifle a gasp, knowing she had put Jabari in a difficult position. She could see that Samira was so upset she was having trouble forming a complete sentence.

The man, having executed his sheik's orders and seeing Samira becoming more agitated, took advantage of her distraction and left at once.

Samira was still staring at Jabari, but he was looking everywhere but at her. Finally, he met her eyes and opened his mouth as if to speak.

Kira had seen enough. "Jabari, wait!" Easing out of her tent, she walked over and placed a hand on Jabari's shoulder, but looked at Samira when she said, "It is all my fault."

Looking back and forth between the guilty eyes of her son and the resigned ones of her friend, Samira's posture relaxed. With a sigh, she took a minute to fix a kettle of tea before sitting down in front of them with a determined stare. "Well then. Please explain how my son got injured, why the sheik got involved, how we suddenly have a cousin, and how you knew all about it." She poured three cups and waited.

Even though her questions were directed at Kira, Jabari was the first to speak up. After telling the tale of his visit to Mirage and how he had been invited on the stable tour, Jabari was interrupted by Kira when he got to the point where Jalil saw the stranger with Mirage.

"That is enough, Jabari. The rest of the story is mine to tell." Kira took a sip of her own tea and explained. "You see, I snuck out of my tent and went to see Mirage." When Samira tried to speak, Kira held up her hand. "I was dressed like a boy, and no one knew I was a woman. Everything was fine until Jalil came out of the stable while I was petting Mirage." Seeing Samira's eyes widen, she added, "Don't worry, he was not close enough to see me. But I panicked and ran. I hid down by the stream, but he never showed up."

Jabari hurried to explain further. "Yes, yes, you were running, and Jalil ran after you, and all I could think of was how to keep him from catching you, so I fell and pretended to hurt my ankle." Seeing the look in his mother's eyes, he dropped his head in shame.

"So, you lied to the sheik?" Samira stared intently at her son.

"Well, yes, sort of. I did hurt my ankle… a little." He squirmed under her hard look. "But he was still insisting someone find her, so I told him the stranger he saw was my cousin."

"Ah. And just what is your cousin's name?" Samira's voice was deceptively calm.

"Bassam," Jabari said, smiling tentatively.

"Well, I am glad to know that you have a cousin. I did not know. And just where did Bassam come from?"

"Umm, well, umm, I told the sheik how Bassam's parents were killed by bandits and how he came to live with us some time ago. Oh, and he loves horses too." Jabari smiled bigger. "It worked too, I…" He stopped abruptly, and his smile disappeared at the stern rebuke written on his mother's face.

"Well, well, well. I am sure your father will be glad to hear of your meeting with Sheik Jalil and also that we now have a cousin named Bassam who lives with us." Samira smiled tightly, looking at them with unblinking eyes. "I think both of you should return to your tents and spend some time thinking about how you are going to explain this to Saad."

Kira felt horrible about the mess she had created. She and Jabari rose together, and Kira reached out to help Jabari. He cast her a sheepish look and walked back to his tent without a limp. She had forgotten it wasn't a real injury.

•   •   •

Half angry and half amused, Samira watched them disappear into their tents and shook her head. Allah must have been watching over them. She still couldn't believe what they had done that day. While she sat by the fire, preparing a light meal for her family, she thought about how complicated her life had become since Kira joined their family. She never dreamed she would meet someone like Kira, much less grow to love her like she was her own daughter. It was like Kira was meant to become a part of her family. It was destiny. It was kismet. Shivering as the evening cooled, she stoked the fire and settled closer.

Before she could think much more about it, Saad and Amal returned, leading a heavily loaded camel. "What have you done, husband? I thought we were trying to get rid of our supplies." She smiled, though, remembering all the new bundles in her tent.

Saad returned her smile with one of his own. "Ah, my lovely, such bargains we found today! We could not pass them up."

Amal laughed at their teasing, and Samira's strange mood vanished like a drop of water in the sand, as she hurried to finish getting their meal ready. Seeing Saad in such a good mood, she decided not to tell him about Jabari's adventure yet. There would be plenty of time to discuss it tomorrow as they travelled to Ehsaan's, the last trading stop before the race.

CHAPTER 24

The next day, the family rose early to get a good start on their journey to Ehsaan's kingdom. Kira packed her things, checked her skin to make sure it was property dyed, and donned the new traveling robe Samira had got from Nasira. Jabari had new pants and tunics to go along with his robes, and Kira made sure he gave her his castoffs. She was finishing her packing when she heard Jabari run up outside. He had been to see Jalil's herd for a last look at the fabled golden mares. Kira wished she could have seen them too, but after the previous day's adventure, she knew it would not happen.

Once all was ready, they mounted up and started their four-day journey. They were not in a hurry, and Kira looked forward to a leisurely ride. She hated having to ride a camel but understood it was the smart thing to do, at least until they were well away from Jalil's.

Glancing over at Amber who walked between her and Jabari, she was glad to see the horse's camouflage was holding up. Kira thought she could see some of her original shine trying to peek through and would have to reapply the hateful brown liquid when they stopped for the evening.

As she rocked along on the back of her camel, she thought about the wild events of the day before. Thank God Jalil had not discovered her. She laughed again at Jabari's fantastical tale of his orphaned cousin, Bassam. *Cousin indeed. Only Jabari could have thought that up. I wish I was his cousin. Then maybe I wouldn't have to leave.* Surprised at herself, she sat up a little straighter. *Do I want to leave? Do I want to go back to America and finish my schooling? What about grandmother? Surely, I need to return and take care of her, right?* Confused, she tried to sort through her thoughts and emotions.

While contemplating her future choices, a vision of deep green-gold eyes flashed in her mind. *Jalil.* Lately, Kira found she could not stop thinking about him. Ever since she locked eyes with him in the corral, she would see his face and hear his laugh in the middle of the most mundane activity. It was becoming most irritating, and she needed to forget him somehow.

The next few days were idyllic as they traveled slowly but steadily. The paths they took were empty of other travelers, but they posted regular watches each evening, though no danger presented itself.

The evening meals were leisurely affairs, and Samira continued teaching her how to prepare some of their favorite dishes. Kira enjoyed learning about the many exotic spices they used—ones she had heard of but never tasted. Garlic, cinnamon, paprika, and red chili pepper were all familiar, but cardamom, saffron, and coriander were new. When Kira described the peppers she cooked with back in America, like cayenne, hatch and jalapeno, Samira said perhaps those might be too much for her.

At night, they heard the far-off, jarring laughter of the striped hyenas and the howling of sand cats, a small species of feline found in the foothills. Jabari explained the little cats could live without water, easily run on shifting sand, and detect prey beneath the sand. They sounded like fascinating creatures, and Kira would have liked to have seen one, but they were too elusive. Luckily, the lions were scarce. Kira saw a herd of gazelle and Jabari told her there were also red foxes hiding in the foothills. It reminded her of the desert back home, and she felt a wave of homesickness.

As they neared Sheik Ehsaan's, Kira was enjoying their daily routine so much she was sorry to leave the road. She had grown closer to Samira, as they shared their dreams and stories of their youth. Kira told

Samira about her parents and more about the cultures she had been raised in. It helped Samira understand why Kira knew how to survive in the wild and why she was so knowledgeable about the world. In turn, Kira learned about Samira's childhood, how she met and fell in love with Saad, their struggle to have children, and the miracle of finding Jabari.

When Samira spoke to her about being able to sit outside of the tent while they were at Ehsaan's, Kira was ecstatic. She brightened at the thought of being able to help her with meals and keep an eye on Amber. But her enthusiasm was dampened when Samira reminded her she would have to continue wearing the full veil and applying the hateful brown dye to both her and Amber.

During the course of their journey, Samira told Saad about the fiasco at Jalil's, and he gave Kira and Jabari a stern lecture. But Kira noticed that Saad found it amusing too, and the family started making Cousin Bassam a standing joke. Vowing to be on her best behavior, Kira promised she would not stray beyond the confines of their camp. Of course, she would never tell Samira about her adventure with Jabari the night of the dance. Kira would go to her grave before revealing that.

When they approached the pass to Ehsaan's kingdom, several riders greeted them at the entrance and escorted them into the compound. The riders directed them to a shady spot near the stables, where they could erect their tents and secure their camels. Saad sent his thanks to Sheik Ehsaan and agreed to report to the main house in the morning to discuss their business.

Curious, as always, Jabari watched the tribe members and evaluated their horses. He confided in Kira that the horses looked to be of excellent stock, but he would withhold final judgment until he could examine them more closely. "I'll have to speak to the sheik about that," he told her.

"Well, I see you have become more confident since your encounter with Jalil." Kira said, a twinkle in her eye that Jabari missed.

"Yes, Jalil appreciated my advice. I image Ehsaan would welcome it too."

"Perhaps you have grown too big for your pants, Jabari." Kira stifled a giggle.

"My pants fit just fine," said Jabari, slightly miffed. "Kira, you say the strangest things."

Kira just laughed.

Ehsaan's servant brought them a nice leg of lamb, along with some round loaves of fresh-baked khubz, a bread that could be eaten anytime. That evening, they sat around the fire, enjoying a platter of kabsa, made with lamb and spicy rice, accompanied by the versatile pita bread that was a staple of their meals. Afterwards, they shared sweetened dates, pistachios, and almonds. While they ate, Kira listened as Saad discussed their plans for the next few days. When the wind rose, running its cooling fingers through her hair and lifting the edges of her robes, she retired to her tent where she was soon fast asleep.

In the early morning, the sweet smell of warm chubab—a small, sweet, crepe-like bread—lured Kira from her dreams. *Yum!* It was one of her favorites, especially with yogurt and date filling. Throwing on her robe, wrap and a full veil, she hurried outside, knowing she would miss out if Jabari was already up.

As she expected, he was already standing by the fire with a chubab in hand, although it appeared he had forgotten about it entirely. He seemed transfixed by the musical laughter of a young girl who sat next to Samira. Dressed in a finely made tan robe with a delicate veil of pale-yellow silk and matching slippers, the girl's hands fluttered as she spoke.

Kira tapped him on the shoulder. "Jabari? Are you all right?"

"Huh?"

"I said, are you all right?" Kira poked him harder.

"Um, yes, um, why certainly." His trance interrupted, he turned to look at her. "Why would you ask?"

"Well, I don't know, but perhaps you should finish your breakfast, which you are now wearing." She smothered a laugh, pointing to the filling dripping down his leg.

Jabari glanced down, then up quickly to see the young girl watching him and smiling behind her veil. Blushing, he handed what was left of the chubab to Kira and grabbed a rag from his pocket. Rubbing furiously at his pant leg, he mumbled and scowled, darting glances at Kira and the girl.

Samira smiled but withheld her laughter. Instead, she directed the young girl's attention to Kira. "Adara, this is Kira, my adopted daughter. Kira, this is Adara, daughter of Sheik Ehsaan."

Kira's heart warmed at hearing Samira publicly announce she was part of the family. Holding back happy tears, she returned her attentions to their guest. "Hello, Adara. It is a pleasure to meet you."

"The pleasure is mine, Kira. I have already heard so much about you this morning."

Kira gave Samira a questioning glance. *What did she tell her?*

"Yes, Kira, I told Adara about your losing your parents and how you came to live with us."

"Oh Kira, I am so sorry to hear of your loss. It is so sad." Adara was obviously sincere in offering her condolences.

"Thank you, Adara. It has been difficult, but I am happy to be part of this family now." She smiled warmly at the girl but wondered which story Samira had told.

"It must be nice to have a sister." Adara directed this to Jabari.

Jabari smiled broadly, and his chest puffed out. He was clearly smitten by the beautiful creature speaking to him. "Yes, indeed, it is. Do you not have a sister or a brother?"

"No, sadly, I am the only one. I know sometimes my father is sad that he has no son, but he tells me I am just as good."

Kira could hear the confidence and truth in what she said.

"I am sure he is right," Jabari said, dazzled by her smile.

"Yes, he even taught me to ride and to fight, although I am not so good at fighting yet. But I am very good at riding."

"Me too. It is my favorite thing. Why, just yesterday, I was riding Amb..." Jabari stumbled when Kira bumped into him.

"Oh, I am sorry, Jabari, please forgive me. I am so clumsy," Kira said, squeezing his arm hard, hoping he would get the message before he said too much about Amber.

"It is not a problem, Kira." Jabari cringed but changed the subject. "I was going to say that I was invited to see Sheik Jalil's herd just recently, and I even got to meet his stallion, Mirage. He is truly marvelous."

Adara was easily diverted and jumped to defend her father's stallion. "Yes, I have seen Mirage, too, and he is a very nice horse, but I think Mukhtar is just as good."

"Oh, maybe so, but I have yet to examine Mukhtar, so I cannot say." Jabari explained with a nonchalant air.

Kira had to look away, afraid she would burst out laughing.

"Well, we must see that you have the chance. I will ask father to let you see Mukhtar and our herd. I am sure he will agree."

"If Sheik Ehsaan agrees, I will be honored to see your father's horses," Jabari said, bowing low.

Adara abruptly stood, obviously quite taken with Jabari. "I will go right now and find him. He is practicing for the race and is likely to be at the stables." She turned to Samira. "Thank you, Samira, for sharing your fire with me. I have enjoyed meeting you and Kira, and I hope we can spend more time together while you are here."

"It is I that should thank you, Adara. It has been a pleasure. Your father and mother have a lovely daughter." Samira thanked her graciously.

Seeing Adara about to leave, Kira asked, "Adara, may I come with Jabari to see your herd?"

"I do not think that will be a problem. Do you like horses too?"

"Oh, yes, very much indeed."

"Well, I will be sure to include you as well. Goodbye for now, my new friends." Adara waved as she walked away.

Kira and Jabari exchanged pleased looks, but Samira shook her head. "If, and that is a very big 'if,' you get invited, you two must be on your best behavior. Kira, you are taking a risk and will need to keep your eyes hidden. And Jabari, you must not bother the sheik with too many questions." She fixed them with a stern look.

"Yes, Mother." Jabari agreed at once. He finished what was left of his chubab and reached for another.

"Of course, Samira. I just hope we get to go." Kira was quick to agree.

Samira seemed to be satisfied. "Well, until we hear from the sheik, you both need to make yourselves useful. Jabari, one of the camels' harnesses needs to be repaired." Jabari nodded and went to get the leather tools from inside the men's tent. "Kira, will you help me clean up? Then we can sort through the items I plan to show the sheikha."

Kira forgot about Ehsaan's herd for a while. But once, she glanced outside to see Jabari mending the harness, and it was obvious he had not. He appeared to be distracted and kept looking toward the stables. Poor Jabari, she thought, and prayed Ehsaan would grant his wish.

CHAPTER 25

The morning passed without incident, and without an answer from Ehsaan. Jabari repaired the harness and then retired to his tent to practice his magic. Kira helped Samira make gursan—a hearty stew of vegetables and beef with thin pieces of bread placed on top. With the extra lamb provided by Ehsaan the previous day, she also taught Kira how to make harees. A combination of coarsely ground wheat and lamb marinated in a mixture of butter, water, and spices, the harees would need to soak overnight and would be perfect for the next day's midday meal.

The two women were busy preparing the food and did not see the attractive young man approach their camp until they heard him clearing his throat. Kira avoided eye contact, and Samira set her bowl down as they waited for him to speak.

"Greetings. My name is Baqir. I am the herdmaster, and I bring you greetings from Sheik Ehsaan. He has sent an invitation for your son and daughter to visit the stables, should they so desire."

"Thank you for your message, Baqir. I am sure my children would indeed love to do just that." Samira turned to call for Jabari, but he was already dashing from his tent.

"Is it a message from the sheik?" He looked at the man, his voice filled with hope.

Baqir smiled at the look of excitement on the boy's face. "Yes, my young one. If you and your sister wish to see our horses, you must come with me."

"Of course we do. Thank you. Come, Kira." Jabara grabbed her by the arm, and it was all Kira could do to keep up with him. Together, they followed Baqir to the stables, and while they walked, Jabari talked non-stop. She worried Baqir would be offended, but he answered Jabari's questions and shared his expertise with ease. Kira was just as interested in what he had to say and listened closely.

After they toured the stable buildings, they entered the pasture where the horses were grazing. Mukhtar came charging up to investigate any possible threats to his herd and Baqir's eyes registered surprise that neither Kira nor Jabari showed any fear. They remained motionless, awaiting the stallion's arrival. When Mukhtar stopped, Baqir reached out to stroke his face. "Hello, my friend. I have brought some new friends who wish to meet you."

Mukhtar sniffed Jabari first, then allowed him to stroke his neck. "Yes, Mukhtar, you are a very fine stallion, and I can see that you have some very fine children as well."

"I am impressed by your skill in handling the stallion, young man," Baqir said.

Jabari bowed slightly and said, "Thank you. Horses and I have an understanding."

When Jabari stepped back, Kira held out her hand, and it was the same story. Before long, they were talking and petting the stallion, admiring his deep chest and glossy chestnut coat. Kira laughed when she saw Mukhtar showing off. The stallion knew he was good looking, and he enjoyed being the center of attention. But she and Jabari were both startled when Mukhtar suddenly tossed his head and neighed loudly. Looking behind her, she saw Sheik Ehsaan walking toward them, and they both stepped away from the horse.

The sheik stopped in front of them, and Baqir made the introductions. "My sheik, these are the children of Saad, the trader. Jabari and his sister, Kira."

"Welcome, Jabari and Kira." Ehsaan nodded formally.

"It is an honor, Sheik Ehsaan, to meet you and to see your fine horses, especially the great Mukhtar," Jabari said, bowing with one hand over his heart.

Kira bowed but kept silent, knowing it was not always correct for a woman to speak, especially to a sheik.

Ehsaan waved a hand as if to say, "it is nothing." "I am glad to meet you too, Jabari the Magnificent."

At Baqir's puzzled expression, Ehsaan chuckled, "Baqir, I will explain later. For now, it is enough to know that we have been honored by his visit." Jabari looked both sheepish and pleased. Ehsaan said, "I understand you have a way with horses?"

It was a question, and Jabari honestly replied, "Yes, yes, I do. I love horses."

"I can see that. My Mukhtar is not usually fond of strangers, but he has accepted you."

"Thank you, Sheik Ehsaan. I am honored by your observation." Jabari grinned, his silver eyes flashing.

"You also have a way with people. Sheik Jalil must have been charmed by you if he allowed you to visit Mirage. Perhaps it is one of your magical powers," Ehsaan said with a small smile, but then his eyes focused on Jabari's face. "May I ask you, do I know you? Have we met before?"

Jabari looked baffled. "Not that I know of. I do not remember meeting you on our past visits, but it is an honor to meet you now."

"Hmm, interesting," the sheik said. "You appear familiar to me, but I cannot place my finger on why." His eyes narrowed as he stared harder at Jabari, who fidgeted under the sheik's scrutiny. As if realizing he was making the boy uncomfortable, Ehsaan turned his attention to Kira. "Well, daughter of Saad, it appears you also have a way with horses."

Kira paused, unsure of how to respond. But, seeing he waited for her answer, she responded. "Yes, Sheik Ehsaan. I dearly love horses. They are one of God's greatest gifts." She reached to pet Mukhtar again.

"We believe horses are the greatest gift," Ehsaan said seriously, but for a minute he hesitated, gazing intently at her. Kira kept her eyes on Mukhtar, realizing too late that she had said God, not Allah. Luckily, Mukhtar neighed as if in agreement and nudged Kira's shoulder, distracting the sheik.

Ehsaan chuckled and said, "Well, Mukhtar likes you too, Kira. I guess if my stallion approves of you, you can be trusted." Everyone laughed when Mukhtar shook his head up and down. "It is unusual to find a woman consumed by all things horse, but I know of another, and I believe she is about to join us."

Kira saw Ehsaan looking past her, and she glanced behind her to see a young girl running toward them. *Adara.* Suddenly, Mukhtar whirled around and charged toward Adara. When he appeared to not be slowing, Kira instinctively made to run after him.

Ehsaan stopped her by saying, "Stay, Kira, she will be all right."

Anxious, Kira watched as the mighty stallion ran up to Adara, stopping just in time, and she smiled with relief when Adara threw her arms around his neck and hugged him tightly.

Ehsaan chuckled. "She won his heart a long time ago, but thank you, Kira, for caring enough to run after her."

Kira bowed her head, not really knowing what to say. When she raised her head, she found the sheik looking directly at her face. Her eyes wide, she paused, and then remembered to avert her gaze, hoping he had not seen through the veil.

When Ehsaan hesitated and stared at her just a second longer, Kira had a sinking feeling he had noticed her eyes. Before she could speculate further, they were joined by Mukhtar, who put an end to their silent exchange by rushing back to Ehsaan.

"Well, for a minute, I thought you had forgotten me," Ehsaan teased his horse, tugging at his silky forelock. Mukhtar nickered and nudged Ehsaan in the chest. "Yes, Mukhtar, I forgive you. Now be off with you. You need to check on your harem," Ehsaan said and, with a final caress, sent the horse charging off before addressing his daughter. "Well, my little sand cat, it seems Mukhtar likes your new friends, but somehow, I knew that would be the way it would go."

Adara looked up at him adoringly. "Yes, my sheik, we are going to be the best of friends. I've come to give you a message from the sheikha. She asked if you could come by the house before you take Mukhtar for his ride."

"I will certainly do that. Tell her I will be by shortly."

"Thank you, Father. Oh, and she also sends a message to Kira and her mother. She would like to invite them to the house later today for a visit." Adara looked expectantly at Kira.

"Why, that would be lovely, Adara. Please tell the sheikha that we would be honored," Kira said.

"Oh, that is wonderful. We can get to know each other, and you can tell me about your travels. We will send someone to escort you later today. Thank you, Kira. Goodbye, Jabari. It was nice to see you again. Bye, Father. Bye, Baqir. Bye, Mukhtar." She spun and dashed off, leaving everyone smiling.

Jabari looked stunned, and Ehsaan laughed out loud. "Well, it seems that we have all been given our orders today." Now everyone joined in the laughter. Hearing a strident neigh coming from inside one of the nearby buildings, Ehsaan turned to his herdmaster. "Baqir, would you check on the white mare that foaled last night?"

Baqir, too, was alerted to the sound and responded. "Yes, my sheik. At once." Bowing, he left with a parting farewell. "Goodbye, Jabari. Goodbye, Kira. I hope you enjoy your visit." They thanked him and waved him on his way.

Kira realized she needed to deliver the sheikha's message and quickly said her goodbyes.

"Thank you, Sheik Ehsaan, for allowing me to see Mukhtar, but I must return to help my mother now." She bowed but hesitated, waiting for Jabari.

"You are welcome, daughter of Samira. May Allah go with you on your journey." Ehsaan nodded gravely.

Jabari frowned and started to say goodbye too until Ehsaan stopped him with his next words. "Come, my little friend, perhaps you can tell me what you think of my Mukhtar."

Looking up, his silver eyes shining, Jabari replied in typical Jabari fashion, "Well, there are those who say that I have sharp eyes, and I would be glad to tell you what I think about your great stallion."

Again, Ehsaan studied the boy's face for a minute before saying, "Then come. We shall walk and talk for a little while, but then I must go see my sheikha, who will tell me what I must do next." They all laughed, and Ehsaan and Jabari began examining Mukhtar and discussing his finer points.

As Kira left, she glanced back once, smiling as she saw the two walking around Mukhtar. *That boy.* She was sure Samira would not mind that he was with the sheik, and she hurried back to camp, eager to tell her about the sheikha's invitation.

It was midafternoon when a guard came to escort them to the house. He helped carry the bags into a private sitting chamber where Sheikha Issa and Adara rose to greet them. Kira was astonished when a bundle of fur dashed between her legs and wove around her ankles.

"Oh Kira, I am sorry if she has bothered you. Adara, you must learn to control your sand cat," Issa said.

"Do not be afraid, Kira. She will not hurt you," Adara said. "I have had her since she was a kitten. Hyenas killed her mother and littermates, and she was the only one left."

Kira reached down to stroke the beautiful black and gray striped cat, whose loud purring filled the room. "Aww, poor little orphan. What is her name?"

"We call her Gigi because she thinks she 'rules the world.' I will put her away. If she stays, she will never leave us alone. I will be right back." Adara giggled as she picked up the little sand cat and carried her from the room.

For the next few hours, the women had a delightful time sharing stories and trading goods. Issa served cooling lemonade and an assortment of candied fruit, nuts, and bread. Kira felt so comfortable, almost too comfortable, and she had to remind herself she needed to continue to play the role of Samira's adopted daughter. She caught Issa looking at her once or twice with a puzzled expression, but luckily, Samira diverted her attention whenever it happened.

Kira learned Issa and Ehsaan were good friends and allies of Jalil and his family. She also found out Adara was an only child, but that Issa longed for more, having lost a baby boy at birth.

"That must have been very hard," Kira said with compassion.

"Yes, it was. I did so want more children. But at least I know what happened to my baby, unlike Jalil's mother, Sheikha Nasira," Issa said.

"I remember hearing something about that years ago, but never heard exactly what happened," Samira said.

Kira perked up at the mention of Jalil's name. "Sheikha, did her baby die?"

"No one knows. He was kidnapped and lost forever." Her eyes were filled with sadness.

"What!" Both Kira and Samira exclaimed together.

Their raised voices drew the attention of Adara, who was sorting through some bracelets. "Oh, I heard all about that, too. The baby was Jalil's little brother and was taken from the house," she said.

"Adara, you were not even born when that happened. Who told you that?" Issa fixed her daughter with a stern look.

"Uh, oh, well, I am not sure, Mother. I think I heard the servants tell of it." Adara was looking decidedly uncomfortable.

"In the future, please talk to me if you hear things of that nature before telling others." Nasira waited for Adara to acknowledge her. Properly chastised, Adara nodded and then cleverly diverted the conversation by asking Samira about her travels on the southern trade route.

The incident was forgotten by all except Kira. The thought that Jalil had lost his little brother so tragically saddened her. As an only child, she could not imagine losing a sibling. It must have been devastating. But her mood passed, thanks to Adara. Kira found her irrepressible and so much fun. She sang a song for Kira and even did a little dance while the women clapped along, enjoying her antics.

Being an only child like Adara, Kira found it easy to connect with her. They shared a love for horses, a subject Adara could talk about all day if allowed. Adara had very strong opinions about their care and breeding, and admitted she wanted to ride in the Tri-Annual Race someday. Most people would have laughed to hear such talk from a twelve-year-old girl, but Kira understood her dream. She, too, would jump at the opportunity to take part.

Kira was telling Adara what she could about the pre-race meeting, but Issa interrupted her when she mentioned Qadir's name.

"Did you say Qadir? Now there is a man I prefer we did not talk about. I wish he would not race this year."

"But, Mother, of course he will race. He has Shar, a truly great horse, although not as great as Mukhtar or Mirage. Shar would be so much better if he belonged to someone else," Adara said.

"I do not know enough about his horse to say one way or the other, but I do know that I do not like that sheik. He is not an honorable man," Issa said.

"What makes you say that?" Samira asked.

"He beats his women." Issa's voice had hardened.

"Then I would have to agree." Samira's eyes reflected her feelings.

"He beats his horses, too," Adara said sharply.

"Adara!" Issa face reflected her shock. "How do you know that?"

"Baqir found one of his horses. It was very sad. She was covered in whip marks and half starved." Adara's face reflected her anger as she spoke.

"Oh, how horrible! No horse deserves to be whipped." Kira agreed vehemently.

"Do you see him often? I understand he lives close to here," Samira asked as she poured another glass of lemonade.

"He is not invited to our home, though he is indeed a very close neighbor. Our lands adjoin his," Issa said. "But enough of Qadir. He is not worth our words." She turned to Kira. "You have a strange accent, Kira. Where were you born?"

Before Kira could panic, Samira launched into her fabricated story of Kira's childhood. She explained that Kira was raised near a coastal city and had been orphaned at a young age. Issa clucked in sympathy and looked kindly at Kira, who tried to avoid eye contact. Samira's story was quite the tale, Kira thought. She laughed silently, thinking that Jabari had learned from the best.

Adara listened spellbound. Watching Adara, Kira knew there might be questions later, and she paid very close attention to the details of Samira's story so she would have the "facts" memorized.

It was late in the afternoon when Kira and Samira bid their hostess farewell. They returned to their camp where the men were playing tawilat alzahr, or backgammon, a centuries old game that originated in the area. While Jabari watched Amal try to beat Saad, Kira helped Samira put away the items they had bartered for, and then both women began the evening meal preparations.

After they had eaten, the family sat around the fire, enjoying the night sounds of Ehsaan's peaceful compound and discussing plans for the next day. They decided to stay one more day before heading to the race grounds. Kira spent some time with Amber until the moon climbed into the sky, and the family adjourned to their respective tents for the night.

Unable to fall asleep, Kira lay awake, her mind awash with the memories of the past few weeks. As she listened to Samira's soft breathing, she wondered how she could leave her newfound family behind. For the first time since her mother's death, Kira felt like she had a real home, and though she missed her grandmother every day, even her grandmother's home had never felt like this. It was like she belonged here, she thought, as a parade of images rolled through her mind—Saad and Samira working together by the fire, mischievous Jabari with his shining silver eyes performing a trick, Amber grazing in the sun, Adara dancing and singing with joy, and last, a pair of intense green-gold eyes. Lost in her memories, she finally fell asleep, only to dream of Jalil.

CHAPTER 26

Jalil awoke early, consumed with thoughts of the race that was fast approaching. But as he dressed, his mind briefly drifted elsewhere. He had spotted Jabari and his family when they had left the previous day, headed for Ehsaan's. He couldn't help smiling at the memory of Jabari's magic show and his way with horses. The boy intrigued him, and Jabari's silver eyes nagged at Jalil's memory, but he didn't know why.

And he had noticed something else—the horse with Jabari's family. Covered in a travel rug and carrying two cross-tied bundles, it looked like a packhorse. But Jalil had a sixth sense when it came to horseflesh, and even from a distance, he could see something was different about that horse. Once again, he couldn't put his finger on what.

Shaking his head to clear his thoughts, he concentrated on his most important concern—the race. His head had to be in it. Too much was riding on the outcome and much still needed to be done.

His herdmaster, Sakhr, was traveling with him this year and was handling the preparations for the care of the many horses and camels that would be required to transport his men and equipment to the racecourse. At least they would not have to worry about water. A few small oases marked the route they would travel, and a large one by the racecourse would handle the needs of the participating tribes.

It was Jalil's trusted adviser, Fahad, who was probably more overworked than anyone at the moment. He worked on the organization of the caravan and the sheik's personal entourage to ensure enough equipment and security would be present. He would not be traveling with Jalil but would remain behind to guard Jalil's family, the compound, and the herd, thus freeing Jalil to concentrate wholly on the race. It was Jalil's first, as well as Mirage's, and would require all their stamina and heart.

While Jalil made his way to the stables, he thought back over the results of the meeting. The last-minute change by Amit added a treacherous section of mountain trail, one which had proven dangerous in past races, and Jalil wished his father were here now. Akeem would have remembered it and been able to share information that would help Jalil navigate the area. And having his father at the race, knowing he would have been waiting for him at the finish line, would have increased his courage and peace of mind. But whoever took Akeem's life had robbed Jalil of that. Jalil swore yet again he would find who was responsible and make sure justice was served. *Oh, Father. I wish you were here today. I could use your words of wisdom.*

Wearing his father's medallion during the race, as per tribal tradition, would have also provided comfort, but he had been cheated of that honor as well. Akeem's gold medallion, which he had worn every day since Jalil could remember, disappeared the day his father was murdered.

The events of that day were still a great mystery. Fahad and his network of spies made numerous attempts to find the man who delivered the message about the golden stallion sighting, but that man was never seen again. It was the message that sent Akeem rushing off, alone, to search the remote mountain pass.

Personally, Jalil suspected Qadir had something to do with Akeem's death. Fahad's men had discovered one of Qadir's men near the pass after they found Akeem. The man claimed he was delivering important messages to Sheik Amit, a longtime ally of Qadir's, and apparently it was convincing enough to throw off his men, but Jalil had his doubts.

It was common knowledge Qadir hated Jalil and his family and would love to see Jalil ruined. Jalil knew Qadir coveted his golden mares and his kingdom. Qadir had few allies, and they were just as nefarious and untrustworthy in their dealings as he was. Most men had a "price," one they would sell their loyalty for, and Qadir surrounded himself with such men, along with a collection of greedy sheiks intent on causing trouble for the more stable tribes. Jalil could not understand having allies without mutual trust.

Akeem had known Qadir for a very long time and advised Jalil to never trust him. Fahad also warned him—reports of Qadir's behavior had led Fahad to consider him slightly less dangerous than a king cobra.

Memories of finding his father that day invaded his thoughts, made more horrible by seeing Akeem's beloved stallion, Rayham, dead by his side. Akeem lay on his back, his unseeing eyes staring up at the sky, his life's blood staining his robes and the surrounding stones. It was a gruesome sight, and Jalil suffered nightmares for a long time after. But it was worse for his mother.

He didn't think about the medallion until his father's body was brought back to the house.

Nasira had been waiting. Somehow, she already knew disaster had struck and rushed to kneel by the body, tears rolling down her cheeks. When she reached to open the neck of her husband's blood-stained robe, Fahad tried to intervene and she shot him a fierce look as if to say, "How dare you."

"It is not there, sheikha," Fahad said sorrowfully.

"What?"

"It was not with him when Jalil found him."

"Are you sure?" She looked up at Jalil with a desperate look.

Their passionate exchange had puzzled Jalil until he realized they were talking about the medallion that Akeem always wore. His future, Akeem had said. "I did not see it." Jalil looked at Fahad. "Did you search the area?"

"Yes, my sheik." By calling him "my sheik," Fahad was the first to acknowledge him that day as Akeem's successor. "I also did not find his dagger," he said, looking back at Nasira.

Jalil remembered his father's ornate gold dagger. Akeem inherited it from his father. It was an ancient family heirloom. Like the medallion, it would have been Jalil's someday.

He watched as his mother, her face blank, kissed Akeem's cold lips, and then rise slowly as if she suddenly aged. With bowed head and arms hanging at her side, she left the room. It would be a long time before she regained any sense of her former zest for life.

Jalil and Fahad shared a look that day. No words were spoken—none were needed. They would search until the end of time for whoever was responsible for this crime.

Shaking off the gloomy memories, Jalil entered the stables where he found Mirage enjoying an early morning meal of grain mixed with dates and camel milk. The horse whinnied in welcome but did not stop eating. Jalil laughed and reached over to rub his forehead. "Do not let me interrupt, oh mighty Mirage."

Sakhr chose that moment to walk up. "My sheik, I was looking for you. I wanted to see if you would like to take a ride through the north pass today. It would take a few hours, but the terrain is like the new course addition, at least so I've been told by Sheik Ehsaan's man."

"Yes, that is a very good idea, and tomorrow we can practice in the deeper sand. But I do not want to ride Mirage the day before we depart. He will need to be well-rested for what is to come."

"Excellent, my sheik. I would like to accompany you if that is acceptable… so that I may observe Mirage."

"So, I am to be treated like a child yet again," Jalil teased in return. When he was a boy, Fahad had been sent many times to chase him down and stop him from riding his horses to places he was not supposed to. This time, though, Jalil suspected Fahad had said something to Sakhr, and Sakhr's next words proved him correct.

"I apologize, my sheik. I only mean to see to your safety." Sakhr smiled sheepishly.

"Oh, it is not a problem, my friend. You have not offended me in the least. It is wise advice from someone whose advice I will always try to heed." Jalil slapped the man on the shoulder. "Come, let us give

Mirage some time to recover from his feasting, and then we will give him a chance to work off that big meal. You are welcome to come…if you think you can keep up."

Laughing, they went to assemble Jalil's gear. They understood the importance of practicing with all the gear that Jalil and Mirage would be wearing in the race. This included a heavy robe, a loaded rifle, a sword, and a dagger, as well as two waterskins and a bag of grain. Before they left, Jalil informed Fahad of their plans, and Fahad insisted a few armed men accompany them. Jalil knew better than to argue.

The final days flew by, and Jalil finally found himself on the road to the race. Maintaining a steady pace, they arrived on the fourth day and Jalil remained outside the entrance, having already decided he wanted to be the last one to enter to avoid the noise and crush of the other tribes and spectators.

When the signal was given, Jalil started toward the entry gates and as he rode forward, he smiled as he saw the shadow of his father on his beloved Rayham riding by his side. He vowed he would make his father proud.

CHAPTER 27

Qadir was not worried about anything other than his plan to ruin Jalil. He spent the last days before the race working out the details with Hashem to ensure Shar won and Jalil never finished.

Having Sheik Amit propose the course change had been a stroke of genius, but Qadir did not share his real reason with Amit for wanting the dangerous section added back in. He couldn't risk anyone knowing his plan to kill Jalil. So, he told Amit the story of how Jalil had found Mirage and convinced Amit that Mirage had a fear of mountain passes. Pleased with the success of his plan so far, Qadir spent most of his time thinking about what he would do with Jalil's prized Mirage, his golden mares, and his women.

Amit had been easy to manipulate. He didn't have an entry in the race, and Qadir agreed to supply him with some new brood mares to rebuild his dwindling herd. Amit had never had much success with his breeding program and spent more time trying to acquire wealth by other, faster methods, such as bargaining with the likes of Qadir and attacking smaller tribes. That mentality played right into Qadir's hands.

Actually, it was Hashem who came up with the original idea of the course change, and he was already on his way to the treacherous pass where he would remain hidden until Jalil and Mirage made their passage. As Qadir's kingdom adjoined the racecourse, it had been easy for Hashem to slip away unseen.

Qadir had spent many years waiting for the fruition of his plans, and soon it would all be his. He was pleased with his success so far, but his only disappointment was that Akeem was not wearing the medallion the day he was killed. It was the one thing Qadir really wanted. He had heard stories about the medallion. It supposedly held a secret, but he never found out why it was so important to Akeem.

At least he had Akeem's dagger. Unfortunately, he could not wear it, not yet, because Jalil would recognize it. But if all went well, he would soon get rid of Jalil, then he would have it all. Once he was in Jalil's house, he would find that medallion.

Thank Allah, Akeem had no other heirs. Jalil's younger brother would have been the next sheik if something happened to Jalil, but Qadir eliminated him a long time ago. Qadir would add Jalil's sisters to his harem, and the eldest, Akilah, would be the first he would use. She was young and perhaps would bear him a son.

The subject of an heir was a constant source of irritation. When First Wife informed him Cassie was late in her monthly cycle, Qadir was cautiously hopeful. But if Cassie was pregnant, he would need to be very careful with her because he could not risk damaging his unborn child. He would have to avail himself of one of the other girls. There were several he had not sampled, and Zahra was always an option. He had not been with her in a long time. *Yes, she will be of use tonight.*

Satisfied, and patting himself on the back for being so smart, Qadir sent for a servant to deliver a message to First Wife to bring Zahra to his chambers after the evening meal. He smiled, thinking how angry Cassie would be when she learned Zahra was in his bed. Somehow, he knew Zahra would make sure she was told.

•   •   •

Of course, Cassie was angry, but not because of Zahra's news. Cassie's period was late. *What am I going to do with some desert brat? They don't even have a real doctor around here.* She knew Qadir could not be the father, not with his track record, and figured it had to be Hashem's. Cassie had grown to hate him even more than Qadir, and not just because he took her with almost as much force, but because she always enjoyed it in the end, a fact that she could not hide from him. Her only consolation was that at least he did not beat her.

She was also angry at the fact that he could sneak her outside the house whenever he wanted. A servant would escort her through a hidden door in the storeroom near her quarters and take her to Hashem's tent, where he would have his way with her. No doubt Hashem had the help of someone on the inside, and she knew it had to be First Wife. Only First Wife knew when Qadir didn't summon Cassie. She hated that the old woman now had leverage over her by knowing about her assignations with Hashem. *Well, two can play that game!*

Now that Cassie was coming to grips with the fact she could be pregnant, she needed to make new plans. Thankfully, Qadir was leaving her alone, as was Hashem, so she had more time to consider her options. Hashem was still promising to get her to safety, but Cassie knew deep down he was lying. He had blackmailed her into becoming his plaything by keeping her plans to escape a secret, and either way, he would continue to have her.

The problem was, if she had a baby, she would need to pass it off as Qadir's if she was to remain in the harem and gain power. Of course, that meant she would also have to eliminate First Wife. If the evil woman told Qadir the truth, then Cassie would find herself kicked out of the harem. And if he didn't kill her outright, he would probably give her to Hashem. *Hashem would love that.* But even if Qadir accepted the baby, and she got rid of First Wife, Hashem would always be able to control her because he also knew the truth. In every scenario, Hashem was a winner. Unless, with First Wife out of the way, Cassie could gain enough power that she could get rid of Hashem too. It was food for thought, but for now, she would play the part of being pregnant and hoped her period, if it did return, would be after the race.

If she had heard correctly, she would not have to attend. Qadir would not take a chance of endangering his heir. The good news was Hashem would also go to the race. He had let slip something about a special task he needed to take care of for Qadir. Perhaps she could find out more about that before they departed. Otherwise, she would concentrate on keeping her strength up and finding a creative way to hide her period if it returned, because she had no doubt First Wife was watching her like a hawk. And if she was lucky, she might even find a way of escape.

•   •   •

The "hawk" was indeed watching Cassie closely. First Wife was already going through several plans in her mind on how she was going to handle Cassie and Hashem. Before bringing Hashem into her web of deceit, she considered making sure Cassie never had a baby by adding certain herbs to her evening wine, but First Wife still wanted her son to have his heir. If Cassie bore him a son, she would get rid of both Cassie and Hashem. It would not be easy, but it was doable. It had worked once before, a long time ago, and she knew what to do. With them out of the way, she would have absolute control over the heir-to-be. For now, she would consider her options while she waited to see if indeed the woman was really pregnant.

•   •   •

Hashem gave little thought to either woman while he packed for his journey to the infamous mountain pass added to the racecourse. Leaving two days before Qadir would give him time to search for the location that would offer the best opportunity to strike. He was planning to take his old partner-in-crime, Nadim, the same man who had been with him the day Hashem shot the golden filly, but he was having second thoughts. Nadim had asked him why they were leaving a few days early and where they were going, and Hashem just said it was the sheik's business, thinking Nadim was not bright enough to figure it out. When the little man hinted he needed something more to keep him from remembering all the other times he had helped Hashem do Qadir's dirty work, Hashem told him they could discuss it when they returned.

The more he thought about it, the more likely Nadim would never return. This might be the perfect time for Hashem to remove more than one problem, and he was looking forward to the days ahead. Qadir enjoyed inflicting pain, but for Hashem, it was all about the kill.

CHAPTER 28

Kira often thought of herself as a real woman of the world until that day. She had seen the steamy streets of New Orleans, the bustling avenues of New York, the grandeur of Buckingham Palace, and the towering pyramids along the Nile, but nothing could hold a candle to the sight of the tribes arriving at the racecourse. This was no stately parade. This was a rousing tumultuous display of wealth and power.

She and Jabari stood by their tents near the wide pathway leading to the section set apart for the competitors. They watched as sheiks passed by in flowing robes, fully armed with swords, spears, and rifles, leading stallions draped in silk. Each leader was accompanied by his best and strongest warriors, who were shouting and yelling, waving swords, or shooting their rifles, their horses prancing and rearing. It was all swirling colors and thunderous noise. Kira loved it. Jabari was spellbound. He pointed out each of the tribes and gave her his opinion on their stallions. Kira was delighted when Sheik Ehsaan rode by, accompanied by Baqir leading a green silk-draped Mukhtar, but there was only one sheik she wanted to see.

Jalil was one of the last to enter. The westering sun cast a golden light upon him. The scene reminded her of a renaissance painting she had seen in Paris, a work by an old master, with deep rich colors and exquisite details. Jalil, like an avenging angel dressed entirely in shining white, rode a glimmering white mare.

Sakhr, riding behind him, led Mirage, who was covered with a flowing blanket of silver silk. Jalil's men also carried swords, spears, and rifles, but they rode sedately in tight formation. Their horses were some of the best Kira had seen that day. Unable to take her eyes from Jalil's regal figure, Kira watched until he disappeared into the crowd. He seemed to take the light with him, and the sun seemed to lose some of its shine, and the colors faded. Sighing, she followed Jabari back to their camp.

While helping Samira prepare their evening meal, Kira asked her if any sheikhas would be there, and Samira explained that the race was a rowdy event, and it was dangerous for sheikhas, and even more so for their children. The only women were servants and harem girls brought for sale or trade. Hearing this, she understood now why Saad was so adamant she stay by the tent and not go wandering off for any reason.

Later, by the fire, Saad shared the details of the race with Kira. It was a two-day event, starting the next day with the formal check where competitors would meet in front of the race council—a group of older sheiks chosen from those not racing that year. The competitors would present their stallion for inspection, and the race council would give each rider a marker to wear around their neck. The marker had to be shown at the beginning and the end of the race. After the markers were distributed, the competitors were free to rest and relax until the second day—race day.

According to Saad, on the morning of the race, each stallion would also have a mark etched into one hoof. Until then, the council kept the nature of the mark, and its placement, a secret. The riders would assemble at the starting line, where the council would explain the course for everyone to hear. Then the stallions would be presented, and the mark inscribed on the chosen hoof. Riders would mount up and try to maneuver their horses in a straight line across the track, keeping them under tight rein until they approached the posts that marked the starting line.

It was always difficult, and the stallions would inevitably challenge each other, making it dangerous for both horse and rider, as well as any spectator standing too close to the track. The riders were encouraged to increase their speed while maintaining the line, so that by the time they reached the posts, most of the horses would be busy running instead of fighting. A gun would be fired when the first horse passed the posts, announcing the race had officially begun.

After that, for the next twenty-four hours, the racers would face a grueling course, encompassing many types of terrain, from soft shifting sand to hard mountain stone. To complete the course would require everything the horse and rider had to give. Food and water were optional and at the discretion of the rider, as were any rest stops. While she listened to Saad, Kira worried about the horses. *Why would anyone put their horse through this? How can they survive?*

Kira waited with excitement mixed with trepidation for the next two days to unfold. She held a whispered conversation with Jabari about the various horses and their riders. But she paid particular attention to his assessment of Mirage's chances. She hoped his glowing opinion was correct.

•   •   •

What Kira did not know was that for centuries, the Arabian horse had evolved to dominate this environment. Their elongated nasal cavities and enlarged nostrils allowed for better breathing, their deep chests and large lung capacity could process increased oxygen intake and blood circulation, and their delicate legs were as strong as steel, making them fast and agile.

Their endurance was legendary, but what made them the perfect companion of the desert people was their extreme intelligence and loyalty. They were tough, resilient, and brave, the same qualities that were embodied by the men who rode them. When paired correctly, the horse and rider became one, a truly winning combination.

It would take all of these traits to get each pair across the finish line because not only did they have to deal with natural dangers, but also the threat of man-made dangers. That was what Jalil was worried about now that the day of the race was almost upon him. He knew Mirage could handle the course. He was more concerned with the unknown traps which may have been set to target him. No doubt, as the winner of the last two races, Jalil's tribe was envied by some and resented by others, and such resentment often led to nasty, underhanded, sometimes fatal "accidents."

The outcome of this race was critical to the power and wealth of a tribe, so much so that many had resorted to desperate acts. Injuries because of slips and falls were not uncommon. Because of this, the council would have men posted along the course at strategic points to monitor the racers and to provide medical and rescue help. Once in a rare while, an injury resulted in the death of a horse or rider. Anything could happen and often did, and not just during the race. As a result, the stallions were watched carefully in the hours before the race, and each sheik kept his stallion in his personal tent under guard.

In order to protect Mirage, Jalil's tent was the first to be erected in his camp. Jalil then remained in his tent, mostly to settle his horse, while the rest of the camp was put in order. Sakhr made sure plenty of fresh water and grain were available for Mirage. The food was guarded and Sakhr himself sampled the water before giving it to Mirage. While Jalil groomed Mirage, he remembered how his father had added to their herd and brought prestige and wealth in past races.

When he won the last race, Akeem didn't choose any stallions from the losers. When Jalil asked him why, Akeem said that Mukhtar was the only stallion of any value, and he would not rob Ehsaan of his best stud. That was the year Akeem retired Rayham, who was past his prime. The chances of him winning again were not good, and he would not risk losing him to another tribe. That was also the year that Akeem was murdered in the north pass.

Since he had no other stallion old enough to race, Jalil knew it would be another six years before he would have the chance to ride in another Tri-Annual Race. And he had accepted that, but then he found Mirage. It was truly a miracle that he discovered the two-year-old silver stallion wounded in the high mountain pass to the north of their holdings. Every day, he thanked Allah for Mirage, yet as he stood brushing his stallion's lustrous coat, he was filled with sadness. He would give anything for his father to see him ride Mirage in his first race. Jalil swallowed hard and felt a strange new strength fill his heart. It was now all up to him, and with Allah's help, he would not let his tribe down.

When he finished grooming the stallion, Jalil called for Sakhr so they could check over his equipment. Later, he planned to call on Ehsaan for a brief visit before retiring for the night. In the morning, he wanted to register early in order to have time for a quick ride before the midday meal. It was a risk, but both he and Mirage were feeling the tensions of all those around them, and a morning gallop would take off the edge and keep his horse limber. Seeing Sakhr approaching, he waved the young man in.

Together, they went through a checklist, examined each piece of equipment and weaponry, and made sure everything was in good working order. Tired from his journey, Jalil was already looking forward to a good night's sleep.

CHAPTER 29

Kira woke early, in time to see Jabari leaving to explore. Frustrated, she felt somewhat better she could sit by the fire as long as she wore a full veil and did not draw attention to herself. Wanting to see more of the stallions, she kept an eye out, hoping to catch a glimpse of any that were being exercised, but Shar was the only one she saw, and only briefly. He looked distressed, and Kira remembered seeing how Qadir handled him when he arrived the day before. The sheik had flicked him with his whip often, as he did now, and she cringed along with the horse.

She poked angrily at the fire, inwardly cursing Qadir. *That man does not deserve that horse. In fact, he does not deserve any horse. He is cruel and demanding.* She prayed that if Jalil won, he would take Shar away from Qadir. Even if Jalil could never race him, Shar would still be a good stud. She could see his excellent confirmation. *But what if Qadir won?* Horrified, she couldn't imagine Mirage or any of Jalil's golden mares being given to him. The very thought made her nauseous, and she hoped that if Jalil didn't win, Ehsaan would. But having seen Mukhtar up close, she didn't think he could. Mukhtar would probably finish because he was experienced and more than fit, but he was older, and she doubted that he had the speed to win.

Kira, worried for her new friends, human and horse, wished the race was already over, and yet, she hated to see it end because then she would be forced to make a decision. Saad and Samira had promised to take her to the nearest coastal city, where she could contact someone from her country who could help her get home. *But what will happen to Amber if I leave?* She knew Jabari was the logical choice to care for her, and he would love nothing more, but would Amber be safe with him, always on the road and forever having to hide her true nature? She wondered if she should reveal Amber to Jalil. He would cherish her, she would be safe in his kingdom, and Jabari could visit her when they stopped on their annual route. Maybe it might be better for Amber to return to the hidden valley where she could live out her life in safety as part of Ndee's herd. But how would she get her there?

Questions spun in her head, but then sadness struck her as she realized that if she left, she would never see Amber again. The thought broke her heart. Kira missed her grandmother terribly, but she realized now she would miss Amber and her new family more. Confused and frustrated, she spent the rest of the day watching and listening to the amazing people and animals surrounding their camp, knowing she might never see the likes of this again as well.

When Jabari returned for the evening meal, and finished cleaning up, he settled by the fire to regale them with what he had learned on his trek around the encampment. Since this was one of the few times the tribes were all together, it was the best place to catch up on news and gossip from the region. Jabari reported that more foreigners had been seen farther inland, and new weapons were being introduced into the area.

He mentioned rumors of war waged in far-off lands. Only Kira knew firsthand how serious that could be. She had lived through one already. The tribes ignored this news because they were too isolated to care, except when embargos affected the supply of weapons or items they relied on from outside their country. According to Jabari, they were more interested in new heirs being born, which tribes were forging alliances, and which ones were no longer supporting each other. Listening as her adopted family talked about their world, Kira found it easy to forget hers. Here the most important thing was family, and of course, horses.

When Jabari mentioned he had stopped by Jalil's camp, she perked up. "How is Mirage?" she asked innocently. She honestly wanted to know about the stallion, but she was hoping to hear about Jalil.

"I did not get to see him, but I am sure he is fine," Jabari said as he refilled his tea. "I also stopped by Ehsaan's camp. The sheik was gone, but Baqir spoke with me. We talked about the racecourse," he said, as if he had conversations like this every day.

"I expect they are both worried about Qadir and Shar," Kira probed, still hoping to hear more about Jalil.

"I do not think they are worried about Shar. He is a strong stallion, but I fear he has not the training or the rider to prove a threat in this race. I think they should be worried about Qadir, though." He sipped his tea and studied the fire with a solemn look on his face.

"Why do you say that?" Saad was quick to ask.

"I spent some time near Amit's camp. He was not there, but from what I could hear, his men were very excited about something." Jabari frowned as if he was still trying to figure out what it could be.

"Hmm. I never trusted that sheik. He is as unscrupulous as Qadir, and it is well known that he has no love for Jalil either, but I think it goes beyond that. Didn't he propose adding the old mountain pass back to the course?" Saad leaned forward now, waiting to hear his son's answer.

"Yes, Father, they say he did, and I think it was voted in. We will certainly know when they announce the course before the race."

"So, did you also go to Qadir's camp?" Kira was worried about Shar.

"I did, but I heard nothing interesting. Though now that I think about it, someone said Hashem was not here, and that is odd, because Qadir goes nowhere without him." Jabari stared at his father.

"Yes, that is strange, very strange indeed," Saad said, looking thoughtful as he reclined back to gaze at the stars. Samira continued to sit quietly, but her face reflected her husband's somber mood.

When no one offered any further information on Jalil, Kira tuned them out as she stared moodily at the dying flames.

Having depleted his store of tidbits, Jabari decided to practice his magic. "Kira, would you like to help me with a new trick?"

"All right, but only for a little while. I am feeling more tired than usual and will probably go to sleep soon," she said as she rose to join him in the tent.

After an hour of working with Jabari, Kira excused herself to retire for the night. Saad had promised her she could attend the start of the race, and she was eagerly looking forward to the event. Bidding Jabari goodnight, she went to check on Amber one last time.

Her mood mirrored Amber's agitation. All the talk of intrigue had left Kira with a strange restlessness tinged with foreboding. Something was going to happen. She could sense it. Trying to shake off the feeling, she stopped by the fire to say goodnight to Saad and Samira before seeking the comfort of her tent. Settling under her cover, she cleared her mind and said a quick prayer for Jalil and Mirage. Sleep was long in coming, but eventually she was breathing deeply, lost in dreams of blue-green water and soft golden sand.

CHAPTER 30

There was no sleeping in on the morning of the race. Every camp was astir, and as the sun peeked over the eastern horizon, the sound of men and horses grew at an alarming rate. Amal and Saad hurriedly fed and watered the animals while Samira stoked the fire. Kira helped prepare the morning meal, and they made fresh pita to use in scooping up a savory, spicy yogurt sauce and added fresh fruit to go with the usual assortment of nuts.

Straining at the bit, Jabari could not wait to hear the course layout and see the start of the race. Kira was just as excited, if not more so, knowing she might leave them soon. If this was her only chance to see the infamous race, she didn't want to miss a second. Samira would stay back and wait for their return, having witnessed it years ago, but she was concerned for her children. Saad assured her he and Amal would stay close to Jabari and Kira and bring them back immediately after the start.

When they heard the horns signaling the racers to assemble for the reading of the course and the marking of the stallions, they hustled off, following the throngs of other spectators headed for the starting line.

Saad found the ideal place where they could see all the action. Kira went unnoticed as everyone's attention was focused on the sheiks of the race council. It wasn't long before another blast from the horns signaled the stallions were to be brought to the track. The horses, covered in flowing silks representing the colors of their tribes, were led into the area behind the starting posts, prancing and lunging. A group of men marked the left front hoof of each stallion, previously inspected and registered, with a secret symbol chosen by the council. It was just another way to ensure the integrity of the race against false entries. It was rare, but not unknown, for someone to substitute a horse either before the race or close to the end.

When the last stallion was marked, the signal was given, and the riders wearing their tribal colors leapt into their saddles, brandishing rifles and swords, while the stallions danced and reared. The riders maneuvered their stallions, forming a roughly horizontal line across the track. Kira loved seeing the shining black sheen of Shar but cringed at the sight of his cruel rider clothed in solid black. Near him was the flaming red-chestnut of Mukhtar bearing a cool and calm Ehsaan clothed in green, but her eyes were drawn to the man in turquoise and gold, who rode on a stallion with a coat that shone like polished silver. *Jalil!* Her heart pounded, and she prayed God would keep him safe.

The entire line moved forward, and Mirage strained toward the starting line, as if he knew exactly what was coming. Highly agitated, Shar seemed unfocused, and flecks of foam already dotted his mighty chest. Ehsaan had positioned himself between Qadir and Jalil, and Mukhtar appeared to ignore the stallions on either side and stared straight ahead—a sign of a horse that knew what was coming.

As the racers picked up speed, Kira inhaled sharply when one horse broke the line and bolted into the spectators. Another whirled around and temporarily ran away from the starting line before his rider regained control and turned him back. The officials could not stop because the stallions were moving too fast. When the first horse reached the starting posts, the gun was fired, and they were off!

Kira watched several stallions leap to the front with impressive speed, but she knew they couldn't hold that pace for the twenty-four hours it would take to complete the course. Shar was in the lead, and she saw the fierce expression on Qadir's face. Both Jalil and Ehsaan took off at a controlled gallop, and a few others were also being cautious and kept close behind.

Jabari yelled, "Mirage! Mirage! Jalil!" Kira forgot Saad's warnings and yelled even louder than Jabari, "Jalil! Mirage! But she doubted Jalil could hear her voice over the yelling and the gunfire. It was absolute madness, and her heart was racing as fast as the stallions. The thunder of their hooves traveled up her legs, and she watched breathlessly until the last horse disappeared into the distance.

After the cacophony of the start, the ensuing silence seemed louder as the spectators wandered back to their campsites. Kira stared off into the distance, imagining she could still see the dwindling racers, but realized it was only a mirage. With a deep sigh, she followed Saad and Amal, who urged them back to camp where they would have to wait and wonder and worry until sunup the next day.

The starting line was also the finish line, and officials were stationed almost two miles away on the final stretch. They would signal when the first rider approached in the morning, but Kira wanted to be at the finish line as soon as Saad would allow. She and Jabari wanted to see who would be first, but more importantly, who would even finish. For now, they settled in to wait through what would be a very long day and night.

•   •   •

As for the Jalil, the drama had just begun. After several hours, he was keeping a steady pace, a mixture of trotting, cantering, and a slow gallop. A few riders had passed him not long before, and Shar was nowhere in sight, but most of the riders were still behind him, including Ehsaan.

As the day progressed and the sun grew hotter, he slowed Mirage to a fast walk. By late afternoon, he decided it was time for a break. They would face the worst part of the sandy track during the cooler evening hours, so now was a good time to rest.

Finding a shady spot by a rocky outcropping, he dismounted and loosened the girth strap. Walking around Mirage, he stroked him and praised him greatly as he looked for any sign of injury. He gave him a few mouthfuls of water and fed him a few dates as well. Munching on one himself, he took the time to lift each hoof to check for lodged stones and bruising but found none. Satisfied, he tightened the girth and climbed back into the saddle and was about to leave when Ehsaan appeared.

"It is good to see you, my friend. How is Mirage holding up?" Ehsaan asked as he slid off his horse and loosened the girth.

"So far, so good. We have had a little water and a little rest, but I need to move on. Will you be all right?"

"Absolutely. Old Mukhtar is still in good shape, and he has the heart of a lion. He will finish the race, of that you can be certain." Ehsaan gave his stallion a loving pat and his expression grew serious. "Jalil, I feel like we will not see each other after this stop. You must go forward quicker than I. This is not a race I can win. I rode for only one reason—to keep an eye on the son of my best friend. But I must warn you, I have heard some things that are very concerning to me. I believe they proposed the course change for a very specific reason. It has something to do with you. I just know it. I fear for your safety and that of your horse. Humor an old man and pay close attention when you enter the pass. Be on the lookout for anything unusual and trust your instincts and those of Mirage. He will protect you." Ehsaan reached for his waterskin, preparing to offer a sip to Mukhtar.

"You are not an old man, Ehsaan, and I will heed your advice, as you are a trusted friend and ally of my family. You honored my father, and I will never forget that." Jalil put his hand to his heart and bowed his head. "And you are right, I must go. Allah be with you, Sheik Ehsaan." As he rode off, he glanced back once and saw Ehsaan bow his head, no doubt sending a prayer to Allah on his behalf. Unsure of what lay ahead, he smiled grimly. With a final wave, he signaled Mirage to a full gallop, unaware that, to Ehsaan, he was the image of Akeem astride Rayham.

The sun was melting into the western horizon when Jalil approached a long stretch of soft sand. It would be slow going until they cleared the dunes and reached the foothills, which meant, unfortunately, it would also be dark when they entered the old pass. The last few races had veered around this area, following the foothills—a safer route. Now he and Mirage would have to climb the steep stony pass, and once on the other side, they would have a slippery descent before they reached the final stretch. It was a shorter route, but it would take more time because of the dangerous nature of the terrain.

As Jalil and Mirage labored through the soft sand in the growing dark, they passed horses whose riders had ridden them too fast for too long. One was limping and being led by his rider. Jalil called out to offer water, but the rider waved him on, saying he would be fine. Another was lying on its side, his rider kneeling by his head. Jalil's heart broke at the sight and prayed it might survive. The rider took the water he offered, and Jalil said he would send help when he could. The rider bowed with respect and gratitude.

He passed two more horses that were struggling but were still pushing onward. The last horse was walking with its head bent, and his rider was whipping him. Without breaking stride, Jalil rode up to the rider and grabbed the whip from his hand. He left the man cursing him, but he did not look back. Because there were few rules in this race, he did not fear repercussion—it would be his word against the rider's. The bloody marks on the man's horse would tell a tale that would not sit well with the race council if the horse survived.

Together, Jalil and Mirage pushed ever onward. Jalil talked to his stallion and could tell he was listening. Mirage did everything Jalil asked of him. He knew Mirage was tired, but he knew his stallion had the heart and strength to carry on.

The moon was riding high when they finally reached the entrance to the dangerous pass. Jalil pulled up and stopped to survey the area. Seeing Mirage was calm, but breathing a little hard, Jalil took a few minutes to let his courageous horse catch his breath. He knew Mirage was tiring, and frankly, so was he. Dismounting, he loosened the girth and leaned close to his stallion, wrapping one arm around his neck, enjoying the warmth against his side. He could feel the steady beat of Mirage's mighty heart and the rise and fall of his chest as his stallion gulped deep breaths of air. Wisps of pale gray steam curled wildly around his head as the cold desert wind stole the heat from their bodies.

Now that he was experiencing his first race, Jalil was stunned as he remembered his father's. *How did he do this? And so many times?* His father had been an amazing man, and Jalil's pride in his accomplishments doubled when he thought of how his father had endured the races for his tribe and family. Jalil knew he could not fail.

The only horse ahead of him now was Shar, and he could hardly believe the black stallion had done so well, considering how Qadir treated him. Perhaps he had misjudged the young stallion. He might be as powerful as Mirage. But then, disgusted at doubting his stallion, he put all thoughts of failure from his mind. He needed to get on with the race, but first he had to check Mirage.

As he stepped back to begin his examination, he paused, awed by the sight of Mirage bathed in the light of the full moon. His silvery mane cascaded done his arched neck, and his coat glowed and shimmered. With chills running down his back, Jalil saw him live up to his name. *Mirage.* When Mirage turned to look at him, Jalil looked deep into his eyes and felt like he could read his soul. His unearthly beauty struck Jalil, reminding him that he had never solved the mystery of his stallion's origin.

When Mirage snorted, as if to say, "Let us go," Jalil felt a sudden urge to hurry. He tightened the girth strap and jumped back into the saddle. "Come, my beautiful friend. We must go. But be prepared for anything," he warned his horse, not feeling silly in the least for having spoken out loud. He knew Mirage understood him.

The footing became treacherous when they entered the pass. Loose gravel covered the steep trail on top of slick stone, forcing them to slow. But Mirage showed his inborn skill. Surefooted, he carefully picked his way and kept a steady pace. Not once did he stumble, and Jalil gave him a loose rein, wise enough to let him take charge. At one point, the trail leveled off, and for a time, the going was easier. However, Jalil was not fooled. Around the next bend, the trail dropped steeply, and now Mirage needed all his skill to proceed without injury.

Just as they neared a final outcropping, Mirage stopped abruptly, and Jalil was immediately on the alert when he felt Mirage's muscles bunching under his legs. A shiver ran down the Mirage's neck, and his ears swiveled backward and forward, as if trying to follow a sound. Huffing, Mirage tensed, and Jalil held on tight.

Feeling the hair rise on his neck, Jalil strained to see or hear what had triggered his stallion's response. It was fortunate he was holding on so tight because Mirage chose that moment to leap forward. Jalil heard a gunshot and felt a burning pain in his arm. Shocked, he held on and prayed for deliverance while the echoes of the blast careened around them, making it impossible to know from where the shot had originated.

The next few minutes were a blur as Mirage slid down a trail so steep that he was almost sitting down on his haunches. Leaning back in the saddle to keep from pitching forward over Mirage's head, Jalil was aware of the pain in his arm but dismissed it because he was too busy trying to stay in the saddle. Another shot rang out, the blast echoing off the surrounding rocks, and he heard the whine of the bullet as it passed by his head.

Mirage screamed in pain but never hesitated. Time seemed to slow, and Jalil knew this was a moment he would never forget—if he lived through it. All his senses were tuned to the sound of Mirage's labored breathing, the slam of his hooves against the stone, the rattle of the pebbles and rocks that cascaded down the path, and the echoes of yet another gunshot.

Jalil wasn't aware of leaving the pass until Mirage broke into a wild gallop, almost leaving him behind. Grabbing a handful of mane, he held on for his life. It was difficult to take control again—one arm was not responding, and the pain was tremendous. When Jalil finally managed to convey to Mirage he needed to slow down, the horse faltered, slowed to a canter, then eased into a stiff-legged walk. Glancing back, Jalil saw nothing following them.

As the sun began to light fires along the distant mountain tops, Jalil could see bright red blood staining the sleeve of his robe and dripping down his side. Suddenly remembering Mirage's scream of pain, he urged him to stop.

Sliding awkwardly to the ground, he gasped in pain and held tight to one stirrup to catch his breath. When the growing light revealed a long bloody furrow down the side of Mirage's neck, Jalil was overwhelmed with relief. The wound was bleeding sluggishly, but, thankfully, did not look too deep. When Jalil carefully probed it, Mirage nickered as if to say, "It is not that bad." He touched his forehead against Mirage's and said a quick prayer. Leaning back, he looked into his soulful eyes and felt a lightness in his heart, and when Mirage snorted and tossed his head impatiently, Jalil understood. It was time to press on, or it would all be for nothing. Worried that whoever had shot at them was going to catch up and finish the job, he pulled himself back into the saddle and urged Mirage forward. They were running out of time.

They were some distance from the pass when Jalil remembered he had seen no men posted at the entrance or the exit of the pass. That would interest the race officials. *Where are the lookouts? And come to think of it, where is Shar?* They had passed every racer except one—Qadir. Jalil's heart stuttered at the thought that Qadir might just win the race. Desperate now, he gave Mirage his head. As he rode, he scanned the ground but didn't see any tracks showing a horse had passed through here. Strange, he thought. Shar should be ahead of him, but where were his tracks?

He was deep in thought when Mirage's ears swiveled suddenly and Jalil heard the pounding of hooves. He risked a look over his shoulder and saw the powerful black stallion galloping toward them, which explained the mystery of Shar.

Mirage didn't hesitate and took off like a shot, breaking at once into a full gallop. Even Jalil was taken aback by Mirage's speed. He was running like he had never run before, and Jalil once again held on for dear life. He could not hear much over the thundering hooves of his own stallion, but Mirage's ears once again alerted him to trouble. Shar was pulling up on his left, and Jalil glanced over to see Qadir glaring at him with hateful eyes, his lips stretched in a snarl. Looking ahead, Jalil could just make out the hordes of spectators lining the track in the distance and shots rang out, alerting the officials that the first horses had been sighted.

It was a race that only happened once in a lifetime. Both stallions were well matched in size, and strength, and it seemed like it could go either way, but Mirage was racing for love and loyalty, something Shar did not have. As Mirage pulled ahead, Qadir did the unforgiveable. He pulled out his whip and began beating Shar, urging him to go even faster.

Horrified, Jalil saw the pain in the beautiful black face of the young stallion, and his heart went out to him. Shar tried to go faster, and perhaps he could have won had Mirage not felt his master's legs asking him for more speed. He could not let Jalil down and surged ahead, now leading Shar by a nose, then a neck, and then a shoulder. As they barreled toward the screaming crowds, he pulled even farther ahead and flew over the finish line, almost a full length in front of Shar.

Amid wild shouts and gunfire, Mirage, covered in sweat and breathing heavily, slowed from a gallop to a canter before he could slow to a trot. Concerned for his horse, Jalil half fell from the saddle, eager to relieve Mirage of the extra weight. Holding on to the stirrup with his good arm, he pleaded with Mirage to slow down. "Mirage! You must slow down! Please!"

His master's voice finally registered, and Mirage realized he was dragging Jalil down the track. As Mirage slowed to a walk, Jalil tried to release the girth strap, but he could not manage with his horse still moving. Taking a risk, he drew his dagger and sliced through the sweat soaked leather, letting the saddle fall to the ground.

Sakhr reached him first. "I saw the blood, my sheik, on you and Mirage. Your arm is injured…what happened? Jalil couldn't answer and Sakhr caught him before he fell to the ground.

Alarm spreading over his face, Sakhr put Jalil's arm around his neck but could not manage both Mirage and Jalil. Jalil, feeling the effects of blood loss and fighting to stay conscious, handed the reins to the boy who ran up behind Sakhr. Jalil saw the boy's eyes widen and smiled through his pain. "Take care of him, Jabari. He trusts you, and so do I."

As they turned to head back to the finish line, Jalil heard the screams of a horse in pain and looked up to see the heartbreaking scene unfolding before him. Qadir had jerked Shar to a standstill and leapt from the saddle. Holding tight to the reins, he was beating the horse with powerful strokes. Shar, too exhausted to pull free, jerked and twisted, but could not escape the cruel bite of the whip. Shar's mouth grew bloody from the bite of the bit and blood ran freely from the slashes, and he screamed in pain.

Shocked and horrified, Jalil tried to pull away from Sakhr, but before he could advance even one step toward the tortured horse, a small, berobed figure dashed by, veil streaming and voice yelling in rage, "Stop! Stop it! Leave him alone!"

Jalil watched in disbelief as a woman grabbed Qadir's whip arm. The sheik's anger grew, and he kept whipping the poor stallion, while the woman who was attached swung in the air, dangling from his arm. Qadir couldn't continue and stopped to dislodge her. When she fell back, he grinned and turned to strike the horse once again until she savagely yanked the whip from his hand and threw it across the track.

He lunged toward her, but she deftly dodged past him, turned to the rearing horse, and held up her hands. She crooned to Shar, but the crowd was too loud, and the horse could not hear her.

At any moment, Jalil expected her to be pounded into the ground by the stallion's sharp hooves and was sure she was about to die. He could not let that happen, and feeling a new strength, he yelled at Sakhr to get Mirage and Jabari to safety and lurched toward the woman.

Somehow, her soothing tones must have reached Shar's ears because he stopped rearing, although he still shook, and his eyes rolled wildly as he fought to regain control. The woman continued to weave a calm melody with her sing-song voice until, finally, he hung his head, gulping air as he trembled with exhaustion.

Jalil stopped not far behind the woman and watched, amazed, to see the crazed stallion become docile and allow her to step close enough to lay a small hand on his bloody neck. Shar was still struggling to breathe, and Jalil realized the horse needed to be walked until he cooled down, or he would be in danger of foundering.

But when Jalil took a step closer, Shar threw up his head with a snort of fear. Seeing that something had spooked the horse, the woman turned and froze. Jalil also froze. Her veil had dropped, and he felt himself falling into a pair of soft, blue-green eyes, rimmed in red and wet with tears. She stared back into his green-gold eyes. Both were staring into each other's eyes when Qadir struck.

When the whip sliced through the air and landed across the shoulders of the lovely woman still staring up at him, the force of the blow knocked her to her knees. Jalil jumped forward to catch her as she fell, and together, they hit the ground. He almost passed out from the pain as he cushioned her fall with his own body.

Saad rushed forward when Qadir raised his whip again and plowed into him, using his substantial girth to pin the spitting, cursing sheik to the ground.

"Get off me, you unworthy son of a hyena. I will have you shot for this!" Qadir struggled in earnest. "Let me up! How dare you interfere with a sheik and the discipline of his horse!"

"You will not touch her again!" Saad yelled. He refused to budge and continued to hold him down until the sheiks of the race council and some of Jalil's guards joined him.

"Release him," one elderly sheik commanded.

Saad stood up, dusted his robes off, and stepped back. Qadir scrambled around on the ground until he could stand and then he lunged toward Shar.

"Stop, Sheik Qadir," another sheik commanded. "You are in violation of the rules, and you must not damage the stallion."

"That is my stallion, and I will do as I wish." Qadir stopped with clenched fists and glared at the man, but wisely stood still. Several guns were pointed in his direction, mostly by Jalil's men.

"No, Sheik Qadir," another elder sheik intoned with a gleam of what looked suspiciously like satisfaction in his milky eyes. "You are a loser, and your stallion is forfeit, pending the decision of the winner."

Jalil could see Qadir was struggling. The sheik was vibrating with anger, his swarthy face flushed a dark red, and his eyes narrowed. Jalil could not believe his ears when Qadir spat out his reply, "Fine! There is no need to wait. Jalil can have him. This worthless horse is only good for hyena meat!" With that final scathing remark, Qadir turned and stomped off, leaving Shar in the middle of the track, bleeding, and in danger of foundering.

The council sheiks looked at each other, clearly trying to decide what to do. When Saad's brother, Amal, spoke up, Jalil was surprised.

"I will take him to my tent and await your decision. He will be safe, and I will care for him, but first he needs to cool down," Amal said, bowing to the sheiks.

The sheiks shared another look and then nodded in unison. Jalil watched as Amal cautiously approached Shar, who stood trembling and blowing hard, obviously in shock. Crooning a low melody, Amal spoke softly, "Easy, easy, my friend. I am going to help you now, and soon you will be far away from all of this."

Amal exuded such confidence that Shar allowed him to come nearer. Jalil was relieved when Amal ignored the reins and untied the hateful bridle, its bit covered in blood, and dropped it on the track with a look of disgust. Still speaking soft words of encouragement, he took the soft cord from his own robe and slipped it around Shar's neck. Before he tried to lead him away, he undid the girth strap and dropped the saddle in the sand. Now that Shar was free of any equipment, Amal led him slowly down the track, away from the crowd. The horse seemed to have given up, and Jalil was afraid Qadir may have finally broken his spirit.

Jalil fought to stay conscious as he lay on the ground, still cradling the woman in his arms. She moaned once and lifted her head, but stilled, when their eyes locked. "Who... who are you?" he asked.

She remained silent, then reached a hand toward his brow, but before she could complete the motion, Saad lifted her up and carried her away. Still reeling from seeing her unusual eyes, Jalil barely noticed as his men picked him up and carried him back to his tent. Straining for another glimpse of the mysterious woman, he tried to protest, but could only gasp weakly before sliding into oblivion.

CHAPTER 31

The race was history making, and the crowds went berserk. All the spectators witnessed Qadir's shameful and unforgiveable display by Qadir when he abused his stallion, and much laughter followed when a mere woman stopped him. But when everyone discovered that the winning rider and his stallion were both wounded during the race, outrage spread all over the camp. This would be a tale long told, and everyone agreed it was a race that they wouldn't soon forget.

Jalil was barely conscious when he was carried to his tent. One of his servants removed his blood-stained garments and an elderly woman carefully cleaned his wound. He dozed off, but when he woke, his first thought was of Mirage. "Mirage," he groaned, but when he tried to rise, a pair of strong hands gently restrained him.

"Easy, my sheik. Mirage is fine," Sakhr said and helped him to sit up, placing soft cushions behind his back.

Mirage had heard his master's call and neighed loudly from behind his curtain. Relieved, Jalil slumped back against the pillows and glanced wearily up at Sakhr. "Thank you, Sakhr."

"My sheik." Sakhr bowed.

"How long was I unconscious?"

"Not long. It is but midday."

Jalil closed his eyes briefly. Taking a few deep breaths, he was about to ask more questions when they were interrupted by Jalil's healer, Maryam. She bustled into the tent, holding a large goblet.

Jalil eyed it suspiciously. "Is that what I think it is?"

"Yes, my sheik. And you need to drink it. It will help you heal and will relieve your pain."

Jalil reluctantly took the goblet and took a cautious sip. Maryam waited until he took another before disappearing around the curtain to help Sakhr with Mirage. Placing the cup on the table by the bed, he sighed. But before he could relax, one of his guards entered the tent. "My sheik, you have a visitor."

Before the man could make a proper announcement, the tent flap opened to reveal Sheik Ehsaan, his face etched with worry and his eyes full of fire. His robes were covered in dust, and it was obvious he had just finished the race. Jalil, seeing his old friend, called out faintly, "Ehsaan! You made it!"

Ehsaan's relief was apparent at finding Jalil awake and aware. "Ah, Jalil, as I told you many times, Mukhtar may be old, but he will always finish his race. I am happy to say that once again, we managed to be the third pair to cross the line."

"Oh, so always the harem girl, never the First Wife," Jalil joked weakly.

Ehsaan laughed out loud. "Yes, my friend, sad but true. But come, do not overexert yourself. When I heard you were hurt, I came at once." Ehsaan moved closer to see the extent of the damage.

"It is not as bad as we feared, Sheik Ehsaan," Maryam said, bustling back from behind the curtain. "It is a gunshot wound, but the bullet passed through the arm and missed the bone. I stopped the bleeding, but I need to change the dressing, if it is allowed."

Seeing Ehsaan's eyebrows rise at the mention of a bullet, Jalil motioned for him to remain silent. He knew Ehsaan wanted the details of what happened, but Jalil wasn't ready to share them with just anyone. He would wait until he and Ehsaan were alone to discuss his suspicions.

"Of course, Maryam. You always know what to do, and it is rare that one of your patients does not survive." Jalil smiled as he teased her.

"My sheik can rest comfortably knowing that he will not be one of those," she teased back as she repacked the wound with a smelly concoction before binding it with clean strips of cloth.

"Now Ehsaan, I want to hear about your race. Please, sit, sit. Tell me what happened." Jalil pointed toward a low table where a servant placed an ornately carved chair for the older sheik.

"Are you sure, Jalil? You have been sorely wounded. Should you not rest?" Ehsaan hesitated.

"Ehsaan, I will be fine. Maryam has said it will be so."

Maryam chuckled. "I am done, my sheik. Call me if the pain worsens, but yes, you should be fine. As long as you rest, and the sooner the better," she said, casting a stern look at Ehsaan.

"Do not worry, Maryam, I will not take too much of your sheik's time." Ehsaan nodded as he settled into the chair.

"Humph," the old woman snorted, gathered her things, and bowed as she left the tent.

Jalil chuckled. "She is a treasure, make no mistake. And she does know her business," he said, feeling his arm gingerly. Glancing around to make sure they were alone, he motioned for Ehsaan to move his chair closer. "Now, tell me, what of Mukhtar?"

"He is tired, but he is fine, as am I. I am just as glad it is over. It will be our last race. We are too old to play these games."

"Nonsense!" Jalil was quick to protest. "You are still able to challenge the best of us."

"Thank you, Jalil, for your kind words, but I fear you may be suffering from a fever brought on by your wound." He smiled, and so did Jalil. "But truly, our ride was uneventful, although I see yours was not, even after you crossed the finish line. Now, you must tell me, how is Mirage?"

"See for yourself." Jalil gestured to the gold silk curtain behind which Ehsaan could hear loud munching. Listening, Ehsaan nodded his head. "That does not sound like a stallion in pain."

"No, but he is tired and very sore. The wound on his neck is painful, I am sure, and it will leave a mark. But he will make a full recovery. He is, without a doubt, the bravest and strongest stallion I have ever ridden. Even after he was shot, he never gave up."

"Shot? Mirage too? I was not told that. Where did this happen? Did you see who did it? You must tell me everything. I suspected there would be trouble." Ehsaan was now sitting upright, his fists clenched.

"It all happened in the mountain pass, just as you feared. We were so busy trying to get down that dangerous slope that I could see nothing except the path. The moon was high, but the shadows were deep. I was shot right after we had started our descent. I could not tell where it came from, but evidently from somewhere above. It was the second shot that hit Mirage, and it, too, came from above. I thought I heard a third shot, but I'm not sure now. I was too busy trying not to fall off. Thank Allah, Mirage knew what to do."

"So, you passed Qadir on the trail. Was that before the pass?" Ehsaan leaned forward, intent on hearing the answer.

"Well, no. Wait… what do you mean?" Jalil was confused, but his eyes widened as he suddenly remembered something he had forgotten. "I should have passed him because when I hit the final stretch, he came up behind me." Jalil stared at the ceiling of his tent, trying to sort through his jumbled thoughts, but exhausted from his ordeals, he could not make sense of it. Puzzled, he glanced at Ehsaan. "How can that be?"

Ehsaan sat back in his chair, considering this information, and Jalil could see that he too was baffled. A servant interrupted them and brought a small tray with a pitcher of tea and two ornate glass cups. Jalil struggled to sit up, and the servant tucked an extra pillow behind his back. After the servant left, Ehsaan and Jalil sipped their tea, and considered Jalil's last question.

Jalil was startled when, suddenly, Ehsaan looked up then slammed his cup down so hard it shattered. "He did not use the pass!"

"What? How can that be? Unless…you mean…?" Jalil's eyes widened as he realized what Qadir had done.

Ehsaan responded before Jalil could speak. "Yes, he cheated! He must have followed the old course through the foothills. He was ahead of you and did not have to hurry, knowing you would not make it through and that I was too far back to be a threat. He probably thought he had plenty of time to finish the race. And with you dead, no one could tell of his deceit."

"And when I came out of the pass, he was coming around the old path and saw me. That is when he broke into a gallop."

"We must tell the council of this treachery!" Outraged, Ehsaan scrambled to his feet.

"Sit down, Ehsaan," Jalil said firmly.

"But Jalil, the truth must be told."

"And just who will they believe? I have no evidence, and it is my word against Qadir's. I know I have many friends and supporters who will back me up, but Qadir has his allies as well. Let's not forget who proposed the course change in the first place."

"But wait, what of the lookouts posted at the pass? Surely, they can verify the facts."

"I did not see any lookouts. Odd. But the truth will come out, eventually. It doesn't matter now. I won. That is all that I care about." Jalil slumped back, suddenly feeling exhausted.

Ehsaan relented and sat back down. "Well, for now, I will keep my peace. But from this point forward, I will do everything I can to expose Qadir for the criminal that he is. Mark my words, Jalil. Now that your tribe has defeated him once again, and a woman has humiliated him in front of everyone, he will seek revenge. Qadir is like the cobra that hides in the sand—you will not see it until it is too late. You must kill it before it kills you."

Jalil heard the absolute seriousness in Ehsaan's voice, and he had to agree. "You are right. I am going to keep an eye on him from now on."

"I heard what happened at the finish line," Ehsaan said, his voice laced with anger.

For a minute, Jalil was lost in the memory of the morning's drama, remembering the woman who had attacked Qadir and calmed Shar, and her beautiful blue-green eyes, like still water in a cool oasis. *Wait!* He had seen eyes like that before... but where?

When Ehsaan cleared his throat, Jalil looked up and tried to concentrate. "Yes, I shall never forget the look on Qadir's face when he realized he had lost once again. But what he did to Shar was unforgiveable. Thank Allah for that woman. But who is she and what happened to her?"

"Baqir said that our friend Saad, the trader, carried her away."

Jalil nodded. "Yes, I think I remember that now. But what happened to Shar?"

"Saad's brother, Amal, is caring for the horse and keeping him safe. The council agreed. I sent my men to set up a tent for him and one of my guards to watch over him." Ehsaan sat back and smiled, sipping on his tea.

"Thank you for that, Ehsaan. I will send my men to relieve yours," Jalil said, holding out his cup so Ehsaan could pour him more tea. Lying back, he once more adjusted his arm. "Well, this will provide entertainment around the fire for many years to come. I only wish my father could have seen me cross the finish line." He shook his head sadly.

"Yes, I know Akeem would have been so proud of you, Jalil. You are the son any sheik would be proud to claim," Ehsaan declared with all sincerity.

Jalil smiled, sat his cup down beside the bed and reached out with his good arm, which Ehsaan was quick to grasp. "Thank you, Ehsaan. You have been, and always will be, an honored friend."

They shared a look that spoke of many years of friendship, but Jalil was fading.

Ehsaan appeared to notice and stood up. "Jalil, I must attend to Mukhtar. He probably thinks I have abandoned him. And you must rest. There will be much to do tomorrow. Let me know if you need any help, otherwise I will see you at the selection meeting."

"I will certainly let you know," Jalil murmured drowsily as Maryam's potion began to take effect. "Oh, and Ehsaan?"

"Yes, Jalil?" Ehsaan paused.

"It was a good race, was it not?"

"Yes, Jalil, it certainly was. Good night," Ehsaan bowed and left the tent.

Jalil settled back into his bedding and tried to get comfortable. His arm throbbed, but he was so tired he knew it would not keep him awake tonight. Closing his eyes, he drifted away with visions of blue-green eyes floating in clouds of gold.

CHAPTER 32

Across the camp, someone else was finding it hard to fall asleep. Kira tossed and turned, her back aching from Qadir's blow. The entire afternoon seemed like a bad dream filled with images of blood and the sound of whips and screaming horses. She could hardly believe what she had done. But when she heard Shar's screams and saw the monster whipping him, she knew he had to be stopped.

When Jabari had returned earlier, he pestered Kira with questions. "Why is Shar here? What is Amal doing with him? Where did that tent come from? And who is that?!" He pointed to the guard that was standing by an unfamiliar tent.

Kira signaled for him to lower his voice. "Please don't startle Shar. Amal just got him settled and is treating his wounds. Go and speak with your father, Jabari. He will explain."

While Jabari went to search for Saad, Kira had peeked into Shar's tent to watch Amal carefully clean Shar's cuts and dress them with Samira's ointments. Amal assured Kira the wounds would heal, but there might be some scarring.

Shar was a mess, and her heart hurt as she thought about the abuse he had endured, both mentally and physically. He seemed unaware of her and, in fact, seemed unaware of anything. Remembering the look of despair and fear in the stallion's eyes, Kira wondered if he would recover from the race and the beating without his spirit being broken.

Even now, she felt nauseous just thinking about it, but she took some comfort in knowing he was safe in his tent and was being cared for by Amal.

But Kira was worried about Amber, too. She had been acting odd since they arrived and was further agitated when Shar showed up with Amal. Though Shar ignored her, Amber refused to settle completely, and Kira had a hard time calming her down. She had a bad feeling and wondered if Amber could sense that Kira was planning to leave.

Later, as she listened to the muted sounds from the surrounding camps and the quiet breathing of Samira, who lay nearby, Kira forgot about Shar and Amber. She was remembering the feel of Jalil's strong arms when he held her close, shielding her from Qadir's whip. Her body filled with strange desires and her breathing quickened as she thought about his lips, and she longed to touch his face. Flushed with heat, she threw off her sleeping rug, struggling to get him out of her mind. Her racing thoughts and the pain from Qadir's blow only made it worse.

After the day's fiasco, she knew she needed to get away, but she was more conflicted than ever. Jalil had seen her face, and maybe even Qadir had as well. Although Saad hadn't given her a hard time about the attack on Qadir, she knew what she'd done was dangerous and there might be repercussions. She didn't regret it, though, especially when she thought about the damage to poor Shar.

Earlier, when Kira asked what would happen to Shar, Saad explained Jalil would make his decision in the morning at the selection. Kira wanted to see the ceremony, but she knew they wouldn't allow her to go, not after what she had done to Qadir. As frustrating as it was to be a woman in America, it was even more so in Arabia, and she missed her freedom now more than ever. Feeling desperate, she considered sneaking away during the night but could not bring herself to leave before hearing the results of the race and seeing Jalil one more time.

Sighing, she fussed with her cover, seeking its warmth again now that the evening breeze had cooled her body. Her father's medallion was safely hidden in her pack, but she still wore her his ring around her neck. She idly stroked it as she thought of her adopted family and newfound friends. Could she leave them? And what about Jalil and

Amber—Amber, whom she knew so well, and Jalil, whom she wanted to know better? *What would life be like without them?*

"Kira, what is wrong, my daughter?" Samira's low voice interrupted her fidgeting.

"Oh, Samira, I don't know what to do anymore," she whispered.

"Well, you have a hard decision to make, and you will have to make it soon. Tomorrow we will be back on the road. I would like to have left today, but now we must wait for a decision about Shar."

"You don't think Jalil will refuse to take him, do you? You saw what Qadir did to him." Kira rose on one elbow, clearly upset.

"Calm yourself, Kira. And lower your voice. Personally, I do not believe Jalil will give him back. Jalil has a kind heart, and he loves horses as much as you," she spoke with confidence.

"Oh, I pray it will be so. But I wonder if Shar will ever truly recover," Kira said, feeling calmer, but still worried.

"It is in Allah's hands. Now, you must try to sleep. We cannot make any decisions tonight, and tomorrow we will be very busy. Once it is determined what will happen to Shar, we will decide where we go from here." Samira rolled over, effectively ending their conversation.

"Thank you, Samira." Kira paused, then whispered quietly, "I love you, Samira."

There was a second of silence, and then Samira softly replied, "And I love you, Kira."

It was the first time Kira had heard her say those words, and her heart filled with anguish, and her mind with chaos. *What will happen to Amber? How do I say goodbye to my family? My family.* Startled by her thoughts, she realized they were indeed her family now and she didn't know if she could leave them. But she had to decide tomorrow.

A fleeting memory of Jalil astride Mirage, his robes glowing in the morning light, danced through her head, only adding to her pain. Fighting back tears, she finally drifted off, her last thought a prayer. *God, please show me the way.*

CHAPTER 33

Jalil woke with the sun, acutely aware of his throbbing, swollen arm but feeling better for having slept through the night. He was relieved when Maryam stopped by to change the dressing and pronounced him fit to attend the Selection Ceremony but only if he agreed to behave himself and avoid using the arm. Thanking her, he agreed he would be careful and chuckled when she rolled her eyes as she left.

Before sitting down for a light meal, he spent a few minutes with Mirage, wishing his arm was not so sore. Unable to brush him, Jalil had to be content with feeding him treats and telling him, again, how wonderful he was. Mirage nickered as if in agreement and pushed his head against his master's chest.

Jalil saw that Sakhr had prepared Mirage by wiping him down with a cool damp cloth, combing his tail until it looked like silk, and braiding his mane with long turquoise ribbons and delicate chains of silver. Jalil was pleased that Sakhr left Mirage's wound exposed. It was, after all, evidence of treachery, as well as a badge of honor.

One of Jalil's servants helped him dress in a white tunic, white pants, and polished black boots. He wore an outer ceremonial robe that was also white, but it had sleeves adorned with bands of gold and turquoise. A wide band of turquoise silk, embellished with running horses embroidered in gold thread, circled the bottom edge. Instead of an ornate turban, Jalil wore a simple white headwrap secured with a twisted cord of gold and silver. Satisfied with his outfit, the only thing missing was his father's medallion, he thought ruefully.

Jalil was bursting with pride when he saw Mirage. His bridle and saddle, dyed a pale gray to match Mirage's coat, were also embellished with flashing bits of silverwork. Mirage shone with a silver luster, and the ribbons of silk and the silver chains woven into his mane danced in the breeze. His tail flowed like rippling water, and even his hooves flashed in the sun—Sakhr had polished them until they shone.

Jalil leaned forward to whisper in his ear. "Are we not both a sight, my friend?" He laughed when Mirage neighed loudly. When he prepared to mount up, Sakhr stepped forward to assist, but Jalil waved him off. Even with his injured arm, he was strong enough to climb up into the saddle one-handed. Picking up the reins, he signaled Mirage forward through the camp toward the area where the council had assembled. The crowds parted, allowing him to move in front of a raised dais, where he stopped when he faced the seated men, and waited for them to begin.

The eldest sheik stood and clapped his hands, and the crowd fell silent. He cleared his throat and, with grand style, announced the results of the race, ending with the proclamation of Jalil as the winner. The crowd cheered, and Jalil saw a boy bouncing up and down between Sakhr and Baqir. He recognized Jabari and acknowledged him with a wave. Jabari stopped bouncing. His silver eyes widened, and he bowed low.

Jalil smiled, amused and pleased at the boy's response. *That boy. What is it about that boy?* The sharp report of a gunshot broke his reverie, and he looked up to see the sheik holding a pistol by his side.

The crowd fell silent again, and the sheik cast his eyes left and right, studying the losing sheiks, each standing with his stallion, lined up on both sides of the circle. Seeing that he had everyone's attention, he repeated the rules before announcing it was time for the selection.

Jalil gazed at the surrounding faces. Most of the losing sheiks looked on with stoic expressions, but a few scowled, and one was openly angry. Ehsaan looked proud and unafraid. Qadir stood at the end of one line, without his stallion, a sneer on his face. He glared at Jalil and turned to spit upon the ground. The sheiks closest to Qadir edged away, casting him looks of disdain. Jalil ignored Qadir's insult for now. It was time for him to make his selections.

Sitting astride Mirage in the winner's circle, Jalil remembered the day his father had decided Jalil could train Mirage and ride him in the next Tri-Annual Race. Jalil had been ecstatic and could barely contain his joy. He had asked his father what to do if he won. Rather than tell Jalil what he wanted him to do, Akeem asked Jalil what he thought he should do.

Thinking hard, Jalil told his father that since it would be the third consecutive race that his tribe had won, it would be hard for the other tribes to pay the price. Jalil's family had profited greatly from the last two. Jalil stated that if he won, he would take none of the competitors' stallions and maybe only a few mares from each of the tribes that could afford to lose them. Akeem nodded, smiling at the wise words from his heir, and agreed his son had chosen a good plan.

Today, Jalil would follow his plan except for one change. Facing the council, he made his proclamation. "I will not take any stallions this day… except one." Jalil saw the losing sheiks' stony expressions replaced with hope. Qadir merely sneered and looked bored. He looked directly at Qadir and said, "I choose Shar." The crowd cheered, and Jalil smiled to see the relief on Jabari's face, but Qadir's face twisted with a look of such animosity even Jalil was taken aback.

The old sheik had to fire his gun once again to restore order and then made the announcement, saying, "So let it be written. Sheik Qadir, from this day forward, the stallion known as Shar, belongs to Sheik Jalil. You must give him all breeding records and the title of ownership."

Qadir spat again and stomped off, yelling back over his shoulder. "That horse is worthless. Good riddance!"

The eldest sheik ignored him and turned his attention to Jalil. "And now, Sheik Jalil, what is your wish for mares?"

"I have decided to take two mares from the tribes of Sheik Ehsaan, Sheik Ahmed, Sheik Sayyid, and Sheik Malek. I will send my herdmaster to each of you over the next few weeks to make the selections."

The losing sheiks all bowed in relief, and the sheiks whose mares had been selected were pleased. Mares were chosen from tribes who had the best breeding stock, so it was an honor. The council rose and bowed to Jalil, signaling their agreement.

Every losing sheik advanced, one by one, to offer thanks for Jalil's mercy, and he acknowledged each one with a nod of his head, pleased to see most were sincere, and some even smiled when they spoke. It left him with a positive feeling about the future. The region had been rife with unrest over the past few years. Perhaps this would help bring them all together again.

Ehsaan was the last to approach. Leaving Mukhtar standing with Baqir, he walked forward to speak with Jalil. "Thank you, Sheik Jalil, for sparing my stallion."

"Sheik Ehsaan, I would never have separated two friends." He bowed his head as did Ehsaan. The older man turned to walk away, but Jalil called to him, "I would speak with you, Sheik Ehsaan before we leave camp. May I visit your tent?"

"Certainly, Sheik Jalil. I will go there now and await your arrival."

"Thank you. I will see you before midday." Jalil watched him as he walked away, looking forward to what he was about to share with him.

As Jalil rode from the circle, he knew this day would stay ingrained in his mind and heart forever. But now that the race was done and over, he needed to get his people and his stallion home to their families. Returning to his tent, he changed into comfortable traveling clothes, and after posting extra guards with Mirage, he asked Sakhr to accompany him to Ehsaan's camp.

When Jalil entered the tent, Ehsaan rose to greet him. "I hope you are not here because you have changed your mind about Mukhtar?"

"I think we already established that Mukhtar could have only one master." Jalil laughed as he sat in the chair provided for him.

"Well, that is a relief. But if you are not here to deprive me of my best friend, then what is it you wish to discuss?" Ehsaan also sat and reached for fresh grapes.

Jalil helped himself to a bit of bread, which he dipped in a sauce of ground chickpeas and creamy yogurt. As he chewed, he was smiling inside. He enjoyed drawing out the suspense and knew Ehsaan would be pleased to hear what he had to say. "I have come to ask a favor of you."

Ehsaan looked up with a curious expression. "Anything, Jalil."

"It seems I have an extra stallion now, and I do not think Mirage likes him. Unfortunately, this stallion is not in the best of shape, but with the right care and training, he might prove to be a most excellent stud. I was wondering what I could do with him." He sipped his own drink, watching the play of emotions on his friend's face.

Ehsaan's brow furrowed in confusion. "Jalil, I am not sure how I can help. Are you speaking of Shar?"

"Yes, as a matter of fact, I am. I thought perhaps he would be a fine gift for the right person."

"A gift? You are thinking of giving him away?"

"Yes, and I would like to gift him to you, Ehsaan. I think he will prove to be a very fine stallion, especially in your care. Would you take him off my hands, old friend?"

Ehsaan's stunned expression said it all—he was flabbergasted. Jalil already knew he had planned to retire Mukhtar. The great stallion's racing days were over. And without another trained stallion in his herd of Mukhtar's caliber, Ehsaan's tribe would not be able to race again for many years. Shar might never race again, but he would be invaluable as a stud. Jalil knew what he was offering might change Ehsaan's future.

"Ehsaan, say something." Seeing Ehsaan staring at him, without a sign of emotion, his eyes wide and unblinking, Jalil was afraid he had offended the man, until he saw the older man's eyes shine with hope.

"Jalil! You cannot give me such a gift! Shar is an outstanding horse. It is too much!"

"No, Ehsaan, nothing is worth as much as our friendship. Shar is yours." He held out his good arm.

Ehsaan held back but for a second and then clasped his arm tightly. "I accept, Jalil, but only if you accept one of his firstborn in return."

"So let it be written. Now, let us go and get your new stallion." Jalil rose, and together with Sakhr and Baqir, they made their way to Saad's camp.

CHAPTER 34

Kira was sitting by the fire, warming some fresh bread when she looked up and saw Jabari standing completely still with lamb filling dripping down his leg. "Jabari, watch what you are doing. What is wrong with you?" She chuckled, shaking her head. *What is it with this boy and food?*

Jabari said nothing and continued to stare at something over her shoulder. She saw Samira scramble to her feet, almost dropping her tea in the fire. Kira turned to see what they were both looking at and froze when she saw Jalil and Ehsaan approaching. Motionless, she jerked in surprise when Samira grabbed her by the arm.

"Kira, you must hide, now!" Samira hissed.

Kira needed no urging, hurried into her tent, and sat down close to the entrance where she could watch and listen.

Jabari still stood as if in shock and Samira laid a hand on his shoulder. "Jabari, go help your father."

For once, Jabari asked no questions. "Yes, Mother," he said as he reluctantly walked around the tent.

"Saaaadd!" Samira called out. Her husband was behind the tent checking on the camels, and Amal was tending to Shar.

Saad poked his head from around the corner. "Yes, my flower?"

She gestured wildly towards the approaching men.

"Oh, I see Sheik Jalil has come to claim his stallion," he said, as if it was just another day.

Kira almost laughed at the expression on Samira's face, who looked decidedly frustrated and was frantically wiping her hands.

Samira grabbed cups and a tray, preparing to offer them something to drink. Saad joined her and they waited as the two sheiks and their herdmasters approached.

"Greetings, Saad. Samira." Jalil said.

"Greetings, Sheik Jalil, Sheik Ehsaan." Saad bowed low and Samira bowed silently.

"Greetings, Saad. Samira." Ehsaan responded.

Saad gestured toward his fire. "May I offer you something to drink?"

"Thank you, Saad, but not today," Jalil declined politely. "We have come for Shar."

"Yes, my sheik, he is ready to go. My brother Amal has dressed his wounds with the help of my Samira." At this, Samira bowed, but again said nothing.

"Then undoubtedly he has received the best of care." Jalil smiled at Samira, who blushed. "But there has been a development. Shar now belongs to Sheik Ehsaan," Jalil said. Kira was listening intently and almost gasped aloud. She saw everyone smiling, and her grin was just as big. Her eyes filled with tears of joy for Shar.

"This is indeed good news," Jabari piped up. Evidently, he couldn't wait any longer to see the sheiks and rushed to their side.

Everyone laughed at his excitement, and Ehsaan was the first to speak. "Yes, Jabari. I have been given a most wonderful gift. Would you please ask Amal to bring out Shar?"

"Yes, Sheik Ehsaan. I will have him brought forth," Jabari said with great aplomb. He hurried to summon Amal, but it was unnecessary. Evidently, Amal had heard their conversation and was prepared, and he led the big stallion from the tent.

Baqir was the first to make a sound. He gasped at the sight of the whip marks crisscrossing the stallion's neck, shoulders, and face. Shock filled Sakhr's face, leaving him speechless. Jalil and Ehsaan moved together, approaching slowly, both of their faces suffused with angry disbelief. Shar didn't react and seemed to not even care that they were there.

Ehsaan made the first contact, as was his right, and moved closer to the horse's head. It was a critical moment and Kira was relieved to see Ehsaan stop and wait with one hand outstretched. When Shar finally reached out to sniff his hand, Ehsaan let out an audible sigh of relief. But when he reached for the lead rope, Shar flung his head back. Startled, Ehsaan stepped back. Amal spoke softly to the stallion, who calmed and lowered his head.

"Amal," Ehsaan said, "it appears you have gained his trust, but I need to take Shar back to my kingdom. Would you be able to accompany us and take charge of him for now?"

Before answering, Amal looked at Saad. The family had discussed their future travel plans and had decided they would take Kira somewhere so she could send word to her family. Kira knew Saad was counting on Amal for his support and help to get them there safely, but she could see the conflict on Amal's face.

Samira and Saad smiled at each other, and Kira smiled, too. She understood what an opportunity this might be for Amal, who had been looking for a home and a wife for a long time. But she also knew that it would be hard for Saad to lose his trading partner and wondered what he would say. It didn't come as a surprise to her when Saad nodded at Amal.

Amal's face brightened, and he looked at Ehsaan and answered with joy, "Yes, my sheik," acknowledging his allegiance. "I will be honored to help you take Shar home."

"Excellent, Amal. You have great skill, and once we are home, I would welcome you into my tribe if you wish to stay. We could use a man with your talents."

Amal grinned and bowed low, blinking rapidly to hide his emotions. Saad smiled even bigger, but Kira could see the sadness in his eyes. Samira remained silent, and her shoulders slumped. Kira was filled with worry for her family. *How will they manage on the road without Amal?*

Though she had been concentrating on the drama between Samira and Saad, she kept glancing toward Jalil standing tall in the sun. She had not seen him since the debacle at the finish line when he held her in his arms. Her eyes lingered on his smiling face and her heart pounded, so loud she actually thought they might hear it. *Silly me.* Jabari's sudden words startled her, as she had momentarily forgotten anyone else existed.

"Congratulations, Uncle! This is wonderful news." Jabari was quick to let his opinion be known, causing everyone to laugh and helping to dissolve the tension.

Kira knew he was genuinely happy for Amal and for Shar, but she detected a little jealousy, too. Amal now had a permanent home, if he wanted it, and a chance to work with Ehsaan's herd. Though Jabari often dreamed of the far horizons, Kira sensed he also dreamed of a home and a herd. Perhaps he would attempt to convince his parents to stay too.

Shar was becoming restless, and Amal suggested they move him soon. Ehsaan nodded in agreement. Both sheiks offered their thanks to Saad and left with their herdmasters, followed by Amal leading Shar. Saad and Samira watched them go, their faces filled with conflicting emotions.

Kira sat back on her heels and wondered if this would be the last time she saw Jalil. After hearing Amal's decision, she needed to speak to her adoptive parents. The time had come. Once they were out of sight, she adjusted her veil and stepped outside. Approaching Samira by the fire, she said, "We need to talk."

Samira looked up and nodded. "Yes, my daughter, we do. Come and sit. Jabari, please check on the horse and camels," she said, clearing a space for Kira. Saad sat nearby and waited for the women to get settled. Jabari grudgingly left to tend to the animals.

Once Jabari was occupied with the stock, Saad opened the discussion. "My brother has chosen to help Ehsaan, and I think he made the right decision. It is time for him to have what he needs, and he cannot do that with us always on the road."

"You are right, my husband," Samira added, "Ehsaan's tribe is a good choice and I know for a fact that there are several eligible women who have not been spoken for."

Kira was quick to agree. "They were all so nice to us, and I could see how much they value their herd. Amal is lucky to become a part of Ehsaan's tribe."

Saad nodded. "Yes, he is lucky indeed, but this means we must change our plans, at least for now," he said, looking seriously at Kira. "We cannot leave here and take the long road to the coast without Amal's help. It would be too dangerous, and I would need help with the stock, more than Jabari can give. For us to make that trip safely, we must join a larger caravan, and I know of none that are making that trip right now."

"So, what will we do, Saad?" Kira asked hesitantly, feeling like she already knew the answer.

Saad looked at Samira and then back at her before answering. "The smart thing to do would be to follow Amal back to Ehsaan's. It is but two days' travel, and I could find some work to do for Ehsaan's tribe until we could locate a caravan heading south."

Samira still had not spoken, but reached over and took hold of Kira's hand. Kira glanced down at her hand, clasped in Samira's, noticing how much lighter her skin was—the brown stain was fading. She was so tired of having to hide, and now it seemed she would have to keep applying the hateful dye on herself, as well as Amber. She could not help but sigh aloud.

Samira now spoke. "Kira, maybe while we are at Ehsaan's, Saad could talk to the sheik. He is an honorable man, and perhaps if he knew your story, he could help you. Then you might not have to keep coloring your skin."

Kira momentarily brightened at the thought, but her worry returned. "What about Amber? She also needs to be free. This is no life for one such as her." Kira looked at Saad, hoping he would know what to do.

Absently stirring the fire, he seemed to consider her words. "You know, Kira, Ehsaan has an exceptional herd. You have seen it," he said. "Fine horses, indeed. You said so yourself. And now he has a new stallion, one of unquestionable abilities. Yes, Shar may not race again, but he will certainly increase and improve the herd, and Amber would be highly prized. Just think, Ehsaan would have a golden mare. He would treasure her and provide her with love and care." He looked at her with tenderness. "You know you cannot take her if we go south. She will always be a target. Men will want her, and nothing will keep them from trying to take her and use her for their own gain."

Kira sniffed and swallowed hard, knowing he was right. She had always known she would have to leave Amber behind, but she had never faced it until now. It was becoming all too real, and a tear slipped from her eye.

Samira sought to ease her pain. "Saad, should we not speak to Ehsaan first? He might not want us to come to his kingdom."

"Samira, I will certainly speak to Ehsaan. In fact, I am hoping to see him today. But I know, in my heart, he will not object to our family visiting his home, at least until Amal has decided whether to join his tribe." He then looked at Kira and placed his hand upon her shoulder. "I care greatly for your happiness. You are like a daughter to me. But I think this is the only thing we can do right now."

Kira studied his kind eyes and then glanced at Samira, who was watching her intently. For a moment, she briefly considered that maybe she and Amber could run away and return to the valley. Then she sighed again. It was too far away, and it would be too dangerous. Though part of her was secretly glad to postpone what was going to be a very painful parting, she also knew it would have to be done... eventually. Resigned for now, she agreed with Saad. "Of course, you are right."

"Then I must go and speak to Ehsaan. I expect he will be leaving soon and if he agrees, we must be ready to travel. And Samira is right, too. I believe, Kira, we can confide in Ehsaan. In fact, I feel we must and see no reason to delay. We cannot lie to him, and we must trust someone if we are ever going to get help. Will you to go with me to tell him your story?"

Closing her eyes and trying to control her fears, she asked, "Do we have to tell him about Amber yet?"

Samira boldly interjected. "Saad, would it not be best to keep Amber a secret for the time being?"

"Yes, Samira. It is not wise for others to know that we have a rare golden filly traveling with us. It would be difficult to explain and dangerous as well. I do not think we should let anyone see her true color yet. Kira, can you keep her disguised until we reach Ehsaan's?"

"Yes, Saad," Kira answered. Amber was not going to like it one bit, Kira thought. It was obvious she hated the smelly stain as much as Kira did.

"Very well. I will send Jabari to request a meeting."

Kira merely nodded and returned to her tent where she sat near the entrance, finding a piece of mending to keep her mind distracted. As she worked on the garment, she listened to Saad and Samira continue their conversations.

"Oh, Saad, I know how disappointed she is, but I am so glad she will not be leaving us yet."

Saad took her hands in his. "My flower, what do you mean?"

"How can I explain? All these years of traveling with you and Amal, with no woman to visit with? Of course, I love Jabari as my own, but he is, after all, just a boy and soon to be a man. And I always wanted a daughter."

Kira's heart fluttered in her chest. She felt the same kinship.

"Samira, Samira, love of my life. I know you want more children, as do I. Merciful Allah, I never understood why we were not blessed, but I always hoped for it. Maybe it is time for us to stop traveling and build a home, a place where children can be born," Saad said.

Kira felt tears threaten as she watched Saad raise Samira's hands to his lips and kiss each one lovingly.

"Oh, Saad!" Samira was gazing at him with longing. "If only we could."

"Samira, I will make it so. This must be a sign from Allah. Amal has finally found a home, and now we might have as well."

They were still sitting by the fire, holding hands, when Kira saw Jabari returning. He stopped when he saw his parents and almost turned away, his face flushed, until his father called to him.

"Jabari! Wait! Do not go. I need you to do something for me."

"What is it you need me to do?"

"I need you to go to Sheik Ehsaan and ask him if he would grant me a meeting in his tent today, before the sun has set. Tell him I need to discuss a matter of great importance and need his advice. And while you are there, you can check on Amal, too, but you must return with the sheik's answer as soon as you can."

Kira saw Jabari square his shoulder, looking more like a man than he ever had. He promptly responded, "I will do as you ask, Father. I will go at once."

Jabari took off so fast Saad had to laugh, and Kira smiled. *That boy.* Shaking her head, she approached Samira and offered to help Samira pack. Without Amal's help, she knew they needed to get started right away. Samira agreed and engaged her help, and soon the two of them were hard at work, each absorbed in their own thoughts.

CHAPTER 35

Jalil wanted to leave as soon as possible, longing to return home. Stopping by Ehsaan's, he proposed they join their caravans for the trip. Ehsaan agreed, almost at once. As they sat discussing the details, a servant brought refreshments, and while Ehsaan filled his goblet, Jalil traced a finger along the carving on the arm of his chair, thinking about the events from the day before.

His preoccupation obvious, Ehsaan asked, "What is on your mind, Jalil? Are you well? Does the arm hurt?"

Jalil looked up and smiled. "No, no. I am fine. I was just wondering what happened to the woman, the woman who defended Shar. Do you know?" Jalil leaned forward, eager to hear the answer. He didn't understand why he was so obsessed with her. He had never worried about a woman before, but now found he couldn't stop thinking about her.

"I heard Saad took her away, but no one has seen her since, and no one knows who she is," Ehsaan said. "You should ask Saad. Perhaps he can tell you more."

Jalil considered his words as he helped himself to some fruit. "Will you see him before we leave?"

"Yes. I was thinking Saad might want to journey with us as well. Without Amal, it will be difficult for him to travel, with only one boy and two women to help," Ehsaan said as he refilled their cups.

"What about the other boy?"

"What other boy?" Ehsaan look confused.

"Jabari's cousin, Bassam."

"I know of no cousin, and I met the whole family when they stopped to trade with us. Jabari questioned Baqir about the herd, and Samira and her daughter spent time with Issa and Adara," Ehsaan said, reaching for more fruit.

Jalil was intrigued. "When they were at my home, I saw a boy petting Mirage, but he ran off when I tried to talk to him. Jabari said it was his cousin, Bassam, and that Saad had adopted him after bandits had killed the boy's parents." Jalil leaned back in his chair. "But I never saw a daughter."

Ehsaan raised his eyebrows. "And I never saw another boy, but I met the daughter. Of course, she's not his actual daughter. Her parents were also killed by raiders, and Saad's family took her in. She is a delightful girl. My Adara has already declared her to be a friend for life." He chuckled. "And Mukhtar has agreed. She certainly has a way with horses. But a boy? I saw no boy except Jabari. Maybe the other boy is wary of strangers? He could have stayed in his tent at their camp, and I would not have known."

Perplexed, both men stared at each other. Ehsaan continued, "It appears we have a mystery. Perhaps we need to find out more about Saad's extended family."

Jalil considered this information while he drank his tea. But it was not Saad's family that consumed his thoughts. It was the woman with the blue-green eyes. He glanced at the turquoise stones set in the gold armband he often wore. It had been a gift from his mother years ago. Seeing the vibrant and varied colors of blue and green, he wondered if that was why her eyes were so familiar. *Who is she? Maybe she is enslaved? Or worse, some man's wife.*

For some reason, the thought that she might belong to another made him angry. He could not stop thinking about her and wanted to know more about the woman who had attacked Qadir. Perhaps he could find out tomorrow. If Saad was accompanying them to Ehsaan's kingdom, he would have time to ask him about her then. With that happy thought, he agreed with Ehsaan that Saad's family should join their caravan.

Once they decided that, the two men continued discussing their plans for the return trip. They were deep in conversation when they heard a slight disturbance near the entrance to the tent.

"Whoa, boy, stop! Where are you going?" Ehsaan's guard cried out.

Alarmed, Ehsaan and Jalil strode to the flap and peered outside to see his Ehsaan's guard holding Jabari.

Jabari ceased struggling and shook off the guard's hands. He took a step back and straighten his tunic and headwrap. "I am on urgent business, and I must see Sheik Ehsaan."

The guard smothered his smile as he listened to his formal request. "And what is the name of the visitor who seeks an audience with my sheik?"

Jalil listened intently, curious what the boy would say next. He struggled not to laugh at Jabari's serious response.

"I am Jabari the Magnificent. He will know me by that name."

The guard stifled a laugh. "Can I trust Jabari the Magnificent to wait here by the fire until I can speak to my sheik?" The other guards posted nearby were leaning in to listen, and Jalil could see them trying hard not to smile.

"Of course, I will be glad to wait here for his summons," Jabari answered calmly, standing with his hands on his hips.

Jalil waited for the guard's response, ready to intervene if the guard turned Jabari away.

The guard stared hard at Jabari for another minute before he answered. "Wait here until I return," he said, and ducked inside the tent, barely avoiding the two sheiks standing just inside.

Ehsaan and Jalil returned to their chairs and Ehsaan gestured to the guard, who turned and held the tent flap open. "Well, Jabari the Magnificent, it appears that you are well known to Sheik Ehsaan. He has granted you an audience. Surrender your weapons and you may enter."

"Thank you. I do not have any weapons, and I will see the sheik now." Jabari smiled broadly and entered the tent. When he saw Sheik Jalil sitting across from Ehsaan, he paused with his eyes wide.

"Jabari! Come in, my trusted friend. Come in," Ehsaan said as both men struggled not to laugh at the expression of surprise on the boy's face.

Jabari recovered almost at once. "Greetings, Sheik Ehsaan. Thank you for granting me an audience." He bowed low. "But I see you have an important guest, even more important than Jabari the Magnificent." He bowed again, embracing his role. "I apologize for the interruption and will be glad to wait until it is more convenient for you," he said, turning as if to leave.

Jalil chuckled, enjoying the boy's clever talk.

Ehsaan maintained a serious expression. "No, Jabari, you are not interrupting. Please, stay and tell me what is on your mind. I am sure Sheik Jalil, whom you also know well, will not mind. As long as you do not mind sharing what you have to say in front of him."

Jalil gave Jabari an encouraging grin. "No, I do not mind at all. Jabari may speak freely, unless he would prefer I leave?"

"Oh, no, no, Sheik Jalil. It is only a simple message I bring. I am here to make a request to Sheik Ehsaan on behalf of my father, Saad. He begs a few minutes of your time today to ask your advice regarding a matter of some urgency." Jabari spoke so formally and with such seriousness that both men now paid closer attention.

Ehsaan exchanged a quick look with Jalil. "Jabari, I will be glad to speak with Saad. You can tell him he may call on me before the sun sets today."

"Thank you, Sheik Ehsaan. I would be honored to deliver your answer."

When Jabari hesitated, Ehsaan spoke again. "Jabari, was there something else on your mind?"

"Yes, sheik. I was wondering if I might speak to my Uncle Amal?"

"Certainly. He is attending to Shar. You will find him in the next tent. I will have my guard take you to him but go slowly. As you well know, you must not disturb Shar."

"Indeed, I do, sheik. He has been sorely used!" Jabari's face twisted in anger, his silver eyes flashed, and being young, he could not control his outburst. "If I were a man, I would show Qadir what it feels like to be whipped!" He must have seen the alarm on their faces and quickly calmed down. "I apologize, Sheik Ehsaan. I forget my place." He bowed, waiting for Ehsaan to forgive him. Jalil almost spoke but held his tongue, curious what Ehsaan would say.

"Jabari, it is not wise to voice such threats about a sheik." Ehsaan softened his criticism by adding, "Even if he deserves it. Just remember, Sheik Qadir is a dangerous man, and it would be best if he never learned the name of Jabari."

Jabari nodded sheepishly. "Yes, Sheik Ehsaan."

"By the way, Jabari, how is your sister Kira?" Ehsaan asked with a raised eyebrow.

"Kira? Why, she is fine. I know she misses Adara. She very much enjoyed meeting her and Mukhtar."

"Yes, Adara enjoyed her company as well." Ehsaan glanced at Jalil and then back at the boy.

"If that is all, may I see Amal and Shar now?" Jabari asked.

Ehsaan smiled. "Yes but remember what I said."

Jabari thanked them both and walked backwards, bowing and smiling. When he turned to leave the tent, Jalil stopped him with one more question. "Jabari, how is your cousin, Bassam?"

Jabari froze. "My cousin? Bassam? Uh, um, uh, oh, he is fine, my sheik. He is back at our camp helping my mother. He is a shy boy and does not come out much."

"I am not surprised after hearing what happened to his parents." Jalil smiled. "Maybe the next time you are at my house, I can meet him and your sister."

"Um, well, yes, certainly. If that is all, may I go now? My father will be eager to hear from me."

"Go, Jabari. I am sure we will see each other again." Ehsaan dismissed him with a wave.

After the boy left the tent, the two men continued to talk, both choosing to ignore the mystery of Saad's family tree for the time being. But before long, Jalil began favoring his arm.

Ehsaan noticed. "Jalil, I think we have covered enough for today. Why don't I stop by your tent after I speak with Saad?"

"That is an excellent idea. I must confess, I am tired, and I expect Maryam is waiting to torture me yet again." Smiling, he rose from his chair, bowed to Ehsaan, and took his leave.

As Jalil walked, he thought back to the day at his corral when he had seen the other boy. He tried to reconstruct the image of Jabari's mysterious cousin but found he could only remember a few details, such as a slender form, baggy pants, rumpled tunic, and a rather large headwrap. It seemed like he was missing something important, but at that moment, his arm began throbbing harder, and a shooting pain jolted him back to the present. Cursing his unknown assailant, Jalil vowed to find him and seek justice for the harm he had done to him and Mirage.

Feeling dizzy and needing to get out of the blinding sun, he picked up his pace and returned to the coolness of his tent.

CHAPTER 36

Across camp, Hashem was also cursing, but not aloud. He had snuck into camp under cover of the pre-dawn darkness, and Qadir was now interrogating him.

"What in the name of Allah went wrong?" Qadir growled.

Hashem refused to cower, which seemed to incite Qadir even more. "My sheik, it was Nadim's fault. He spooked the horse, and I could only get a few shots, but I hit both Jalil and the horse. Unfortunately, they were moving too fast, and it was very dark." Hashem had spent his time well while he traveled from the pass to the camp, working out a plausible explanation for his failure.

"That idiot! Where is he? I will cut out his eyes! Bring him to me now!" Qadir was barely in control of his temper, but tried not to shout because there were always ears listening.

"Alas, Nadim is dead. After he killed the guards at the pass, he threatened to reveal your plan to the council unless you paid him for his silence. So I killed him. I could not allow him to report back to the council." It had been the perfect opportunity for Hashem to rid himself of a huge liability. Nadim knew all of Hashem's greatest secrets, but no longer. Hashem had cut his throat and left him for the vultures. Hashem held his breath, hoping Qadir would not see through his lie.

"Did Jalil see you?"

"No, it was too dark. And there were no witnesses."

Hashem, seeing the furious expression on Qadir's face, took a step back. He was afraid that Qadir didn't believe his story, but Qadir's next words put his fear to rest.

"Except for Jalil, you idiot. That son of a hyena knows I cheated. I should have shot him myself. No one would have known." Qadir paced back and forth.

"What happened to Shar?" Hashem was almost sorry that he asked when Qadir stopped to fix his black stare upon him.

"I lost the race thanks to that worthless stallion. I wish I had shot him too," Qadir snarled and slammed his fist on the table, causing his goblet to tumble. "I swear to Allah, I will get rid of Jalil, one way or another. He is the only thing standing in my way. But first, I want that woman."

"What woman?" Hashem asked.

"Oh, I am sure you will hear about her. She attacked me at the finish line. I was trying to punish that four-legged devil. I was exhausted, and she jerked the whip from my hand," he spat, his lips pulled back in a snarl. "Arrrggh! A mere woman!"

Hashem had no words. He eyed Qadir, who was obviously struggling to regain control.

"Hashem, we must move quickly now. I want you to find that woman and bring her to me, but do not harm her. I want to be the one to make sure she pays for what she did to me. You might start with that fat trader, Saad. He is the one who took her away. Also, I wish to leave today, so we will be ahead of Jalil's caravan. They will have to pass the hidden entrance to my kingdom, and Shar will be with them. That will give you the opportunity to redeem yourself. I want Shar killed. I do not care how you do it, just get it done."

"I understand and will obey, my sheik." Hashem bowed and exited the tent, struggling to hide his resentment. He hated having to acknowledge Qadir as sheik.

Hashem was relieved to be away from that madman. Qadir was having more difficulty controlling his temper, and it worried him, but he forgot about Qadir for the moment. He had work to do—he had to find a missing woman before they left and make plans to kill a horse.

After ordering his men to pack up, he slunk through the encampment in search of Saad's camp. With all the activity and confusion of tribes packing and leaving, no one noticed him when he stopped to lean against a palm tree near Saad's tents.

As he watched the camp, he recognized the boy speaking to the fat man by the fire. It was that stupid boy who had performed silly magic tricks at the pre-race feast. The fat man had to be his father, Saad. Hashem could not hear what was being said, but Saad looked pleased and leaned into the smaller tent, evidently speaking to someone inside. Two women emerged, and one left with Saad. The other reentered the tent, followed by the boy.

Waiting until Saad was out of sight, Hashem circled past the kneeling camels and the one horse tied behind the larger tent. The horse pawed the ground and shook her head, but he ignored her. He crept closer until he could lie in the shade of the smaller tent. If anyone looked his way, they would only see a tired servant taking a nap. He waited and listened, and his reward was hearing the woman speaking to the boy.

"Jabari, please help me finish packing."

"But, Mother, why are we leaving so soon? Have you decided to take Kira south after all?"

"Your father has gone to speak with Ehsaan about traveling with his caravan. Now that Ehsaan owns Shar and has asked Amal to take care of him while they travel, we cannot risk the southern road. It will be too dangerous. Until Amal has decided where he wants to be, we must go with him. It is the safest thing to do for now."

Hashem listened harder. *Ehsaan owns Shar? When did this happen?*

"But why did father take Kira with him? Surely it is too risky for her to be seen, especially after what she did to Qadir."

"Jabari, you are asking too many questions. You are as bad as Kira. Your father will explain when he returns. Now, please get to work and start packing up the extra equipment. We must help your father, now more than ever."

"Yes, Mother." The boy sounded frustrated.

Having heard enough, Hashem rose and stretched as if waking from a nap, and walked slowly until he was beyond the palms where he quickened his pace. Qadir would be extremely interested to hear about Shar and, more importantly, about the woman called Kira. There was much to do now, and already a plan was forming in his mind.

CHAPTER 37

Ehsaan hurried to Jalil's tent after his discussion with Saad. Greeting his friend, he said, "Sheik Jalil, may I have a minute? I need to ask your advice on a matter." He needed to speak privately.

"Certainly, Sheik Ehsaan. Let us retire to my tent."

Ehsaan dismissed his personal guards and followed the younger man. While they were getting settled inside, waiting for the servants to set out refreshments, Ehsaan thought back over his meeting with Saad and Kira. Saad asked if his family could come to Ehsaan's kingdom until Amal had decided, and Ehsaan was glad to allow this. Saad also brought his daughter with him to the meeting, and at first, Ehsaan did not know why. That was until he learned the truth about Kira.

When she removed her headwrap, he was stunned by the sight of her shining silvery-gold hair framing a face of unusual beauty. Without her veil, he could see her incredible blue-green eyes, filled with trepidation, and her pale skin beyond the areas that were dyed. When she told her story, he admired her courage and spirit and understood now why Mukhtar had accepted her so readily.

But he feared for her safety, because if anyone in the camp found out there was a foreign woman, especially one so beautiful and possibly still a virgin, she would be in serious danger. She was worth as much as a golden horse. However, if Qadir discovered she was the woman who had humiliated him, she would lose her life. Ehsaan appreciated Saad's honesty and the young woman's bravery at revealing herself to him, but he felt conflicted. He needed to figure out how to protect her until further decisions could be made and decide how much of the story he could, or should, share with Jalil.

Once the servants departed and they were alone, Jalil began asking questions. "Well, how did your meeting go with Saad? Was it what you expected?"

"Indeed, it was. Saad asked if his family could join our caravan and stay at my compound until Amal decides, and I agreed."

"I see. If Amal accepts, you will have a good man. He has a way with horses."

"Yes, and he is the only one who has been able to work with Shar so far. I will need his help to get the horse to my kingdom, and in the future as well."

"Did you ask Saad about the mystery woman?" Jalil leaned forward, anticipation spreading across his face.

"Well, yes. Saad brought her with him. It turns out the woman who stopped Qadir is, in fact, Saad's daughter."

"And what is she like? What did you learn about her? Is she really his daughter? And what of the other boy, Jabari's cousin, Bassam?"

Ehsaan held up a hand, laughing. Jalil reminded him of Jabari. "Jalil, please slow down. One question at a time. I will tell you what I know." He gathered his thoughts, wanting to be careful of what he said next, choosing to keep Kira's real origin a secret until they were safe in his kingdom. "Her name is Kira, but she is not his actual daughter. Saad adopted her. As for Bassam, I do not have any information about the other boy because Saad did not mention him."

Watching Jalil's face, Ehsaan found it surprising to see his curiosity and excitement in learning about the girl. Jalil had never shown much interest in a specific woman. *Why now? Why this girl? Is it because of her bravery in attacking Qadir or the compassion she showed Shar? Or is it because she can handle such a horse?* These questions were flying through Ehsaan's mind, but when he saw Jalil's impatience, he continued talking to forestall more questions.

"As I said, Saad and his family will stay with my tribe until Amal makes his decision, but after that, I do not know what they will do. Maybe they will decide to stay, but Saad also asked me to help him find a safe caravan heading south that they could join. All I know is that for now, they will follow me. I told him it would not be today, though. It is too late, and I want Shar to have one more night of rest. We can leave first thing in the morning if that is convenient for you."

Jalil appeared disappointed that Ehsaan had no more information and shifted to their present concerns. "That is what I would like to do as well. Maryam is insisting I wait one more day before I travel, but I think she is being too cautious. I am sick of sitting in this tent and want to get back on the road. I have been gone too long," he said as he reached for the pitcher of tea.

When Mirage began huffing and pawing behind his curtain, Ehsaan laughed. "It appears you are not the only one ready to go home."

Jalil chuckled in return. "He probably misses his mares."

"I expect he does. Even Mukhtar is acting restless."

"Then we must keep our stallions happy," Jalil said. "And hearing your desires, this might all work out for the best. It would be much safer for us to travel together. Would it be possible for my men to spend a night in your compound before we head to my kingdom?"

"Certainly. I will send someone to notify you in the morning. I expect to leave at first light." Ehsaan rose to leave.

"Thank you, my friend. I will be ready."

Ehsaan nodded and took his leave. While he walked, he wondered how he could keep Kira hidden from Jalil while they traveled. Sighing at this additional complication, he looked in on Shar when he arrived back at his camp. The horse was calm, and Amal assured him the stallion would be ready to travel in the morning. Ehsaan thanked him, returned to his own tent, and sent a message to Saad informing him that Jalil would travel with them and to be ready to leave in the morning.

As he ate his evening meal, he pondered the coming journey, wondering if there had ever been such a strange caravan—a wounded sheik, two wounded stallions, a beautiful foreigner, an eager magician, and a reclusive cousin. His last thought as he fell asleep was that it was going to be a very interesting trip indeed.

CHAPTER 38

It was only the morning of the second day, and Saad's family had already fallen some distance behind Ehsaan. They could not travel as fast, but Saad didn't appear to be alarmed. Ehsaan had suggested the family stay well behind him and keep their distance from Jalil's caravan to ensure Kira remain hidden. Thankfully, it was also an excuse to keep Amber hidden from all of them.

As they plodded along, Kira felt her spirits lift. They should reach Ehsaan's by nightfall, and she was looking forward to a rest. The events of the last few days, coupled with her talk with Ehsaan, had left her emotionally drained. Telling her story brought back painful memories. Of course, she didn't mention Amber, or the hidden valley, and Ehsaan was amazed to hear about Saad finding her lying in the foothills, suffering from heat exhaustion, and wounded by the lion.

She shivered as she glanced at the shadowy outcroppings. The trail wound through rocky foothills, reminding her of the area where the lion had attacked her. Watching Amber walking beside her, she could see her horse was on alert and wondered if that's what was bothering Amber too. Or maybe she was just excited to be back on the trail like Kira.

Perhaps Amber was thinking about the valley. Perhaps Amber thought Kira was taking her back to the valley. It was in the same direction that they were headed, but Kira knew there was little chance of that right now. The family had decided to spend time at Ehsaan's, and there was no talk of going on to Jalil's kingdom. Kira was just relieved she didn't have to decide about leaving yet.

Swaying to the rhythm of her slow-moving camel, Kira rubbed the warm metal of the medallion which she had taken to wearing again. She had replaced the gold chain with an old leather lanyard. The chain was heavy and might draw attention—she hid it in her pack. She debated whether she should wear the medallion, but feeling it close to her heart, she felt a sense of peace. It reminded her of the beautiful secret valley with its clear stream and lush groves.

She thought about returning to the valley, but it seemed impossible now. Even if she wanted to return, she wasn't sure she could find it again. She had a vague idea of where it was, but all she could remember was the steep slippery trail and the dark, twisting tunnel. Her only clue to its location was that it was close to the small oasis Amber led her to after the wreck, but she didn't know where that was.

When her finger brushed against her father's ring hanging from her neck, she forgot about the valley. Instead, she remembered his face, not the one she had seen after the wreck, but the one she had seen when he looked at her and her mother.

Caught up in daydreams of her lost family, Kira failed to see Amber's ears swiveling until she heard her huff and snort. Startled, Kira saw her in full alert mode and busy scanning the surrounding rocks. Alarmed, she looked up the trail and noticed her camel had lagged well behind the others. Jabari was nearing a bend just ahead, leading Amal's camel and not paying her any attention. Saad and Samira were nowhere in sight. Worried, she tightened her grip on Amber's lead rope and urged her camel forward, intending to catch up with the others.

But when Amber suddenly jerked sideways with a loud neigh, she almost pulled Kira from her saddle. Kira could not hold on to the rope and out of the corner of her eye, she saw a horse and rider burst from a narrow opening between the rocks. The man held a pistol pointed straight at her. The gunshot echoed around her, and she felt her camel going down. She hit the ground hard but rolled clear and scrambled to her feet. Amber was dancing around between her and her attacker, and Jabari was fast approaching.

Looking ahead, she felt a wave of horror as Samira suddenly appeared from around the bend, fiercely kicking her camel. She was yelling something, but Kira could not make out what she was saying. When another gunshot rang out, she screamed when she saw Samira falling from her camel. She glanced back to see the black-robed man barreling down on her, and she ran to help Samira, but she couldn't run fast enough. The man jerked her up onto his horse, and when she tried to fight him, he struck her a hard blow. Pain lanced through her jaw and her vision narrowed as she lost consciousness. The last thing she heard was Amber neighing and Jabari yelling, "Stop! Stop! Let her go."

·   ·   ·

Saad was riding beside Samira, enjoying a companionable silence, when he had a strange foreboding. Pulling his camel to a stop, he scanned the trail behind him and was alarmed that Kira and Jabari were nowhere to be seen. Suddenly, he heard Amber neigh and a gunshot echo from the trail behind them.

"Saad, what is happening?" Samira yelled.

"Stay here, Samira!" Saad shouted, turning his camel and whipping him into a loping run. His children were in trouble, and nothing on earth would keep him from going to their aid. As he approached the bend, another piercing neigh rang out, and Saad heard Jabari calling Kira's name, along with the sound of a man shouting.

Unfortunately, Samira had not stayed behind. Her eyes wide with fear, she raced past Saad, whose camel was slower because of Saad's weight, loping around the bend ahead of him before he could stop her.

"Samira, come back!" he shouted, but to no avail. Terrified as he had never been before, he tore after her, and his heart almost stopped when he heard another gunshot. "Samira!" he screamed as he raced around the bend.

When he passed Amal's camel, he came upon a chilling sight. His beloved wife lay in the sand, and her camel stood nearby. A camel lay dying on the ground and another was loping away. Jabari, Kira, and Amber were nowhere to be seen. Throwing himself from his camel, he ran to Samira's side and fell to his knees, pulling her limp body into his arms, "Samira, Samira, come back to me!" Tears coursed down his face and his anguished cries echoed from the stony cliffs. He tenderly smoothed her loosened hair from her brow, and he froze in shock as he stared at her blood-soaked robe and tattered veil. *So much blood! Where is it coming from?* He feared the worst, but when her chest moved slightly and he heard a low moan of pain, he gasped. *Praise Allah! She is alive!*

Easing her to the ground, he pulled her headwrap loose, and caught his breath at the sight of the bloody hair and mangled flesh. Running back to his camel, he grabbed his water skin and returned and drizzled water slowly over the gash on the side of her head to flush out as much dirt and sand as he could. Making a temporary bandage from her veil, he bound it in place with strips he cut from his robe. As he finished, Samira regained consciousness, and her first words were "Jabari. Jabari!" It almost broke his heart.

"Hush, hush, my flower. We will find Jabari. You must not move."

She stared at his face, her eyes rolling wildly. "Saad, what has happened? Where are my children?"

He shook his head and tried to calm her. "Samira, I do not know, but I do not think they are dead. We must hold on to that thought and try to get help from Ehsaan's men."

When she began crying, he knew her tears were not just from the pain of her injury, but he could not stop to comfort her. He had to get help. With strength he did not know he possessed, he gathered her in his arms and lifted her into the saddle of her camel. She couldn't sit upright and immediately slumped forward, her arms dangling on either side. Worried she might fall off, he tied her hands around the camel's neck.

Glancing at the wounded camel on the ground, he recognized it as the one Kira had been riding. That meant the one he had seen running away, its saddle empty, was Jabari's. *Where is my son? What has happened to him? And where are Kira and Amber?* Hearing his wife moaning, he had to make a tough choice, but he knew he couldn't go after the children until he secured help for Samira.

The dying camel on the ground wheezed loudly, and Saad did what he had to do using his knife. He ignored the camels which stood nearby, and the bags on the ground, and climbed up on his own camel and headed toward Ehsaan's, praying he had made the right decision.

CHAPTER 39

Kira woke with a blinding headache. Opening her eyes, she panicked, unable to see, until she realized something covered her eyes. Dazed, she tried to stand but found she could not move her hands or feet. Feeling the bite of rope, and the bitter taste of wet cloth in her mouth, she knew what was wrong—she was bound and gagged. Disoriented, she shivered and felt icy fingers of fear crawling up her back. The air was cold, and the ground was stoney. Beyond that, she had no idea where she was.

Trying to understand what had happened, she reeled as her mind filled with chaotic visions, like bats bursting from a dark cave at dusk in the desert. She remembered seeing Amber rearing and hearing the blast of a gun. She had felt her camel falling and saw Jabari racing toward her. And then another gunshot. Samira! Samira got shot! She shook her head, trying to quell the onslaught of images. The last thing she could remember was being grabbed from behind and lifted in the air and then…pain. The rest was blank.

She struggled against her bonds but stopped when she suddenly felt hot breath and heard a man's cold whisper against her ear.

"Be still, my beauty."

She cringed, feeling a warm wet tongue licking the edge of her ear and a large hand pinching her small breast.

"Oh, you do not like that, do you?" The man hissed menacingly. "Well, if you do not behave, I will do much worse." With those last words, he was gone.

As his laughter drifted away, she prayed her tormentor had left. She waited a few minutes, but desperate to escape, she tried to rise again, only to freeze when she suddenly heard labored breathing, followed by a muted whinny. *What is that? Could it be? Amber?* Her fear turned to anger. *Is she hurt?* Kira had to find out.

Despite having her hands were tied behind her back, she managed to roll over on her side and rub her face against the ground until she pushed the blindfold high enough to see. She seemed surrounded by darkness, but when she looked up, she saw towering rock formations framing a sky full of stars. It was a clear night, and the moon was waning, but there was just enough light that she could make out a person lying nearby. *Jabari!*

Seeing no one else around, she scooted sideways until she could bump him with her knee. She tried to call his name, but the gag muffled her voice. She prayed to God that he was not hurt and continued nudging him until he responded with a soft groan. Struggling, he tried to rise, but evidently his bonds were too tight.

It was then that Kira remembered a trick she learned from one of her tribe members years ago. Ignoring the aches and pains in her arms and legs, she drew her knees up close to her chest and worked her bound hands down her back, over her hips and around to her front. It was awkward and painful, but she finally she got her hands in front of her body. She tore off her gag and whispered close to his ear, "Jabari, it is me, Kira. Do not make a sound." He jerked once, but then stilled. Reaching over, she removed his blindfold and pulled the gag out of his mouth.

He rolled over to face her and whispered, "Kira, are you all right?"

She almost started crying because his first concern was for her. "Yes, I'm fine. What about you? Are you injured?"

"No, but my head hurts."

"Mine too, but we need to get out of here, wherever here is."

Jabari glanced around until he spied what he sought between the rocks across the trail. "Amber," he whispered. "He threatened to kill her if I did not tie her up."

Kira's gaze followed his stare. She could just make out Amber, cross tied between two rocks, with her legs hobbled. Someone had tied a dark piece of cloth around her head, leaving only her nostrils visible. The ropes were so tight around her nose that she could not open her mouth. She was breathing heavily, obviously in distress. Kira longed to run to her and free her, but she knew there was still danger—at least one man was around somewhere.

"Jabari, listen to me. There is a man here. I do not know who he is, but he has already threatened me. I think he plans to take us to someone."

"Yes, I know, and we must escape." He wiggled closer so she could untie his hands.

Once Jabari was free, he untied her hands, and they both bent to untie their legs. As he stood, rubbing his wrists, Kira stared up at him. He seemed to have grown taller over the last few weeks, and she could see in him more of the man he would someday be. Unaware of her thoughts, he reached down to help her stand, and they both hurried to Amber's side.

"Easy, easy, Amber," Kira crooned as she reached out to loosen the ropes binding her head. Amber was agitated, but she calmed and allowed Kira to free her head. Jabari kept apologizing to Amber for having tied her up, but Kira assured him Amber understood why he did it. Together, Kira and Jabari freed her legs. "Shh, shh, Amber, please don't make a sound," Kira whispered, and the horse remained quiet while Kira and Jabari moved closer to her side.

"Jabari, get on Amber. Now! We must get out of here."

Jabari grabbed a handful of Amber's mane and pulled himself up. "Come on, Kira," he hissed urgently, moving forward to make room for her behind him. But before she could reach up, a shout rang out.

"Stop! Stop or I will shoot!"

It was the man with the evil voice, and Kira did not hesitate. She slapped Amber's flank as hard as she could. "Run, Amber!" she shouted. "Run! Take Jabari to Saad!"

Amber did not hesitate and leapt down the path.

•   •   •

Hashem had gone back down the trail to make sure no one else was following and was riding back when he heard voices. Seeing the two captives trying to escape, he rode forward with a shout. The next thing he knew, a bolt of leaping horseflesh surged past him, almost knocking him from the saddle. The boy was going for help and had to be stopped! Instead of giving chase, he raised his rifle—no one would miss a trader's boy. But just as he pulled the trigger, the girl flung herself in front of his horse, causing his shot to go wild, and the fleeing horse was gone before he could take aim again.

Incensed, Hashem almost shot the girl right then and there. His horse had knocked her down and, jumping out of the saddle, he jerked her up by her neck and slapped her across the jaw with all his strength. Her head snapped back, and she fell unconscious to the ground. He never saw the broken chain and silver ring fall from beneath her robe.

Enraged by the chain of events, he tried to calm himself. He had seen Ehsaan and Jalil's caravans pass earlier in the day, but there was no way he could kill Shar. Not with that many men around. He would have to take care of the horse another day. With only one man as backup, it was just too risky. Qadir had insisted he take another man with him, but he made the man wait back up the hidden pass. Hashem did not want any witnesses—he didn't want another problem like Nadim.

When he discovered that Saad's family was not with the others, he was afraid they had not chosen to follow Amal. However, trusting his predator instincts, he waited. His patience paid off later in the day when he spotted the fat man and his unguarded family slowly moving up the trail. He thought that, for once, Allah was smiling down on him when he recognized Kira trailing behind the others.

He shot Kira's camel, but before he could grab her, the other woman had shown up and he had to shoot her, too. It was easy to pick Kira up and sling her across his lap, and a quick blow stifled her screaming. But he did not count on the boy. The little fool jumped on him, trying to knock him from his horse. Hashem threw him to the ground and rode off up the hill between the rocks, thinking he was done, but he had been wrong. The boy mounted the loose horse and raced after them.

The boy's horse was extremely fast and did not appear to tire as it steadily gained on him. Hashem reached the spot where he had left Qadir's man, and turned his horse, forcing the boy to stop.

Thinking fast, Hashem pulled Kira's head back and held his curved dagger to her throat, his threat clear. The boy's piercing silver eyes caught his attention—they were filled with fury, not fear.

"One step closer and she dies," Hashem growled, pressing the knife against her pale flesh. The boy froze, and Hashem considered shooting him. He couldn't risk letting him get away, but having seen the boy's passionate attempt to save the woman, Hashem knew he could use him against her. When he ordered his partner to bind the boy and hobble the horse, the horse would not let the man approach, neighing fiercely and striking at him with her front hooves. Cursing, Hashem sheathed his knife and raised his rifle. "Control your horse, boy, or I will kill it."

The boy looked like he wanted to fight but gave up when he saw the gun pointing at his horse. Hashem's partner tossed some rope to the boy, who soon had the horse tied and hobbled. Hashem chuckled, hearing the boy apologizing to the horse, as if the horse could understand him. *Stupid boy.*

Feeling the woman stir, Hashem yanked her upright and when the boy called out to her, Hashem motioned to his partner, who struck the boy and knocked him out. Thinking back, he should have just killed the boy and the horse. Now they were both gone, and Hashem worried they had gone to get help. At least he had Kira.

Knowing he had no time to waste now that the boy had escaped, he gathered all the pieces of rope and discarded rags he could find and stuffed them behind some rocks. He bound the woman's hands extra tight this time, stuffed the dirty rag back in her mouth, and flung her over his saddle before climbing up behind her. Having sent the other man ahead to let Qadir know he had been successful, Hashem now pushed his horse to the limit, wanting to get Kira to Qadir as fast as he could.

Once he was out of the pass, Hashem pulled up by a small spring to give his horse a much needed drink. Except for an occasional moan, Kira had proved to be no trouble. Aware that Qadir expected him to deliver her in good condition, he roused her enough to half-drag, half-walk her over to the water. Pushing her down, he allowed her a few sips, but when he dragged her back toward the horse, she pulled free and started running. With a harsh curse, he ran after her and tackled her to the ground. She tried to fight back, but he subdued her with another blow to her head. Jerking her up, he threw her back on the horse and took off.

Several guards were waiting just past the spring along with the man who had helped him in pass. "Where is the boy?" the man asked.

"I had to kill him and his horse. He tried to escape," Hashem said, dismissing him at once. After all, he was their captain. They should not question him.

By the time he reached Qadir's house, he saw Qadir waiting on the front steps with a cruel smile on his face. Hashem stopped and slid from his saddle. Kira was moving feebly and moaning, and when he hauled her down from his horse, she collapsed to the ground. Qadir strode forward until he stood in front of her. Groaning, Kira struggled to her hands and knees, but when Qadir gripped her jaw and raised her head to look closely at her face, she fainted away. With a cruel laugh, he let her drop to the sand.

Smirking, Qadir said, "Well, Hashem, it looks like you finally did something right." He turned to stalk into his house, calling over his shoulder, "Bring her."

Hashem sneered in contempt and spat on the ground. He had planned to tell Qadir about the boy, but after that veiled insult, he decided he'd let Qadir deal with whatever happened next. Hashem would have his day, but not quite yet. He still needed to take care of a few details before he could finish with Qadir.

Leaning down, he lifted Kira, threw her over his shoulder, and carried her inside to a small room near Qadir's quarters. Hashem made sure to lock her door, post a guard, and then hurriedly fled from the house.

Thinking back on it now, it seemed his troubles had all started after he shot that stupid golden horse in the desert and found that red-haired witch, Cassie. While Kira distracted Qadir, Hashem was going to arrange for some time with Cassie. She was the source of all his trouble, and it was time to remind her she owed him.

CHAPTER 40

Ehsaan travelled slowly, not wanting to push Shar too hard. Amal was still struggling to get Shar to eat but had made progress in the last twenty-four hours. It helped that the farther they got from Qadir, the more the horse's spirits seemed to pick up.

The worst part of the trip had been on the morning of the second day. Shar became agitated, fussing and fighting against his lead rope. Ehsaan noticed it when they passed the cutoff leading to Qadir's holdings. Amal also recognized the cutoff to Qadir's, having traded there in years past, and urged Shar to pick up his pace. Once the cutoff was out of sight, Shar calmed, making Ehsaan thankful he had asked Amal to come along.

They were close to home now, and Ehsaan looked forward to seeing his beautiful wife and daughter again. It wasn't often they were apart, and he felt their absence keenly. Looking ahead, he saw one of Jalil's men sitting high on an outcropping, and Ehsaan signaled to one of his men, who shot his rifle once in the air. Jalil's man responded with one shot before disappearing behind the rocks. It wasn't long before they came upon Jalil's group resting in the shade.

Jalil rode up to greet him. "Sheik Ehsaan, we await your invitation to your kingdom." He bowed, as was customary when making such a request.

"Sheik Jalil. It is good to see you. Gather your men and follow us," Ehsaan answered just as formally.

Ehsaan thought briefly of Saad's family. They had fallen behind, but he was not worried. Hopefully, they were not too far back.

When they approached the entrance to his stronghold, several of his men rode out to greet him, and his tribe yelled and waved their swords to celebrate his triumphant return and escorted him into his compound.

A huge smile broke out on Ehsaan's face when he saw Issa and Adara standing on the steps waiting to for him. Adara ran out to meet him but stopped short when she saw Amal holding the lead rope of a beautiful coal black stallion with bandages on its face and neck. The horse stood still but was showing signs of increasing nervousness.

"Father, who is that? What is wrong with him?" She took a step towards Shar, her face mirroring her concern.

"No, Adara, you must not approach him. Not yet. I will explain later," Ehsaan said. Adara obediently stepped back.

Ehsaan waited for the members of his tribe to surround them. He dismounted and signaled for silence so he could speak. "Today we have returned, and Mukhtar has once again made his tribe proud. Though we did not win, we finished with honor. Two horses beat us to the finish line. One we all know well. Let us congratulate Sheik Jalil and Mirage. They are this year's winners. The other horse also stands before you. He formerly belonged to Sheik Qadir, and as you see, he did not fare as well. But as the winner of the race this year, Sheik Jalil took Shar as his own and then gifted him to me. Let us all thank Sheik Jalil and welcome him to our fire."

Everyone cheered, and several men left to show Jalil's men where to camp.

Ehsaan looked at Amal and called out to him. "Amal, please follow Baqir. He will find a private stable for Shar, where nobody will disturb him." To Baqir he said, "I will bring Mukhtar myself."

Ehsaan then looked up at Issa standing on the steps, and they exchanged loving looks. Adara grinned and hurried back inside the house. Ehsaan watched her runoff and suspected that she was already plotting something, most likely involving his new stallion. But he was not concerned. Seeing the look on Issa's face, he hurried to take Mukhtar to his corral.

By sunset, Ehsaan was sitting comfortably with his family, enjoying a delicious meal. Jalil had joined them, and they talked and laughed, each sharing stories of the past few days. When the conversation lagged, Adara interjected, "Father, perhaps I might go and meet Shar… tomorrow? I could take him a treat and maybe help Amal."

"Adara, we need to talk about Shar, but not tonight. He got hurt and will need time to recover."

"How was he hurt? Will he be all right?" She was obviously upset.

"I will talk to you later about that, Adara. Rest assured, he will recover in time. Although he has not given his heart to anyone yet, it is unlikely we will ever be able to ride him. So put that thought from your mind. But, come, let us not talk about him tonight. It is a sad story, and I would rather hear about Gigi." Ehsaan tried to divert her attention.

"Who is Gigi?" Jalil asked Adara.

"She is my sand cat, and I am sure that father does not really want to talk about Gigi. He is just trying to change the subject." Adara rolled her eyes.

Ehsaan coughed, choking on his tea. His daughter was much too perceptive. He exchanged a glance with Issa, who laughed delightedly.

"Sand cat? You have a sand cat? But how is that possible? They are wild and reclusive creatures." Jalil said, winking at Ehsaan.

"Oh, Sheik Jalil, they are not so wild, and they can be tamed, if you know how," she answered seriously. "We found her as a kitten in the hills. She was in very poor shape, but I took care of her, and now she is strong and healthy." The young girl took a bite of her dajaj mashwi, a spicy grilled chicken with couscous.

"But how did you know what to do?" Jalil asked, keeping her occupied, while Ehsaan looked on gratefully.

"Well, it really was not that difficult. I made a way for her to drink camel milk until she was able to eat meat. Now she sleeps on my bed and is my protector. I have been told I have a way with animals. I am sure that I could be of help with Shar, too."

Ehsaan thought she had forgotten about the horse, and both men laughed. They had been defeated by a superior foe.

"Adara, Amal and Baqir are quite able to handle his injuries for now. But I promise you that as soon as Amal feels Shar is ready for guests, you will be the first." Ehsaan smiled at her.

"Very well, my sheik. I will look forward to that day," Adara answered formally, her hand on her heart.

Ehsaan smiled at his daughter's words, but part of him was thinking she had given in too easily. He suspected she would find some way to circumvent his wishes and knew he would have to keep an eye on her, as usual.

•   •   •

Jalil smiled at their interplay, enjoying the feeling of family and children, and remembered his own family, the one he had before Akeem had been murdered, and his little brother had been taken from them. His mother still labored to recover from her loss, and he felt something was missing in their home. Looking at Ehsaan's family, he made a promise to himself that when he got home, he would have a long talk with her.

Watching Ehsaan and Issa together, and seeing their affection and mutual respect, stirred unfamiliar feelings, and Jalil felt a sense of sadness and a bit of jealousy. Taking a bite of buttery pilaf, Jalil chewed thoughtfully and wondered what it would be like to have a relationship like that. In the past, he had not given it much thought. Except for a few hours of pleasure, women did not play a big part in his life. After the murder of his father, and Nasira's subsequent withdrawal, he'd had no time to commit to anything other than maintaining the herd, running his kingdom, and training Mirage for the race.

When Adara had to ask him the same question twice to get his attention, he realized he had drifted off. Putting his heavy thoughts to rest, he concentrated on answering her questions about the race and continued enjoying the company of Ehsaan and his charming family. There would be time enough later to think more about his future. For now, he could relax, knowing that he and his men would have a peaceful night and would head home tomorrow.

And that's what should have happened. But just after he had fallen asleep, Jalil was awakened by shouts and rifle shots. He sprang out of bed, grabbed a robe, and ran barefoot down the hall. Racing outside, he saw two kneeling camels. They were blowing hard and were in a bad way. Several tribesmen carrying torches surrounded them.

A large man broke through the crowd and stumbled toward him, carrying a limp form. Ehsaan ran up and together they reached the man as he collapsed on the steps. Ehsaan called for Issa, but she was already by his side. When a guard stepped forward with a torch, Jalil saw Saad and, in his arms, Samira, unconscious, her head wrapped in blood-soaked silk.

Saad looked up at them with reddened eyes, his face streaked with tears. "Help her," he cried hoarsely before falling back, overcome by exhaustion.

Jalil caught him by the shoulders, preventing his head from hitting the ground, while Ehsaan supported Samira.

Issa immediately took charge and ordered two men to carry Samira inside. "Ehsaan, I will take care of her," she said as she ran after them.

Jalil and Ehsaan followed as several men carried Saad to the guest room next to where Samira was being attended. A servant appeared with a basin of water and towels and cleaned Saad's face. Saad's eyes fluttered opened, and he grabbed Jalil by the front of his tunic, something a rational man would never do to a sheik, but he was obviously out of his head. "You must find them! Someone has taken them!"

"Calm down, Saad. You must calm down. Here, take a sip of water, then tell me what happened," Jalil said, struck by the fear he saw on Saad's face.

"Where is Samira?" Saad's eyes darted back and forth between Jalil and Ehsaan.

"Samira is with Issa, and she is going to be fine." Jalil did not know that for certain, but he had to get Saad to calm down if he was going to help him. "Now, tell me what happened? Where is the rest of your family?"

"I…I do not know." Saad paused and gulped more water before continuing frantically, "Samira and I were leading. The trail was narrow and twisted, and the children had fallen behind and were out of sight. I heard the horse neighing and a gunshot. I turned to ride back. I told her not to go! I told her to wait, but she would not listen."

Saad's face filled with such anguish that Jalil flinched. "Who, Saad? Who did you tell?"

"Samira! She passed me, and I could not catch her. She was faster, and I lost sight of her. And then I heard a scream and another gunshot." He stopped, his face pale and his eyes wide and dilated. Jalil shivered at the sight.

Ehsaan grasped Saad by his shoulders and urged softly, "Tell me, man."

"My beautiful flower was lying on the ground… lying so still," he sobbed, "and Jabari was gone. Kira was gone. Someone shot Kira's camel, but Jabari's camel ran off, and Amber was gone."

Watching the man struggling to tell the awful tale, Jalil suddenly realized that Saad had only mentioned two children and had not mentioned Bassam. *And who is Amber?* "What about Bassam?" Jalil was worried about the other boy.

"Bassam? Bassam?" Saad looked confused.

Frustrated, Jalil almost asked him again and wished Jabari were present to answer his questions. But Jabari was missing, and so was his sister! He was ashamed at his own impatience. They were wasting valuable time.

Ehsaan's next question brought his focus back to what was important. "Do you remember where this happened, Saad? How far back on the trail?"

Saad blinked, and his brow furrowed as he tried to think. "The sun was high, and I figured we would be here in a few hours, maybe by sunset. The trail was narrow…there were high rocks…" He was clearly struggling to remember anything else when his face lit up. "Kira's camel! It is still there." His voice wavered, and it was obvious he was almost done for. "Sheik Ehsaan, can you help me? I need to borrow a horse. I must find them!"

"Saad, my friend, I need you to stay here to help guard my house and protect Samira," Ehsaan said. "Leave this to me. I will find your children."

Jalil recognized Ehsaan was being careful not to hurt Saad's pride. A matter like this required speed, speed which Saad did not have in his current state. "And I will help," Jalil said. "Sheik Ehsaan, my men are at your disposal."

"Come, we must go at once. Too much time has passed, and I fear for the safety of the children. The sooner we find them, the better. It will not go well for Kira if she is discovered." Ehsaan and Saad shared a meaningful look, and Jalil wondered what Ehsaan was talking about, but assumed he was referring to her youth and the fact that she was most likely a virgin. She would be worth a great deal on the market—if she made it to market. His stomach churned at the thought of what might even now be happening to her. Eshaan was right. They had to hurry.

Saad fell back against the cushions, his eyes closing. Jalil heard him mumble, "Samira, Samira, Jabari…" before he passed out.

Jalil looked down at him and felt anger freezing his blood. Already running back over the trail in his mind, he looked at Ehsaan. "I think I know where he was talking about."

"You do? Then let us go." Ehsaan whirled, his robe flying, and hurried from the room with Jalil on his heels. On the way down the hall, they stopped by the room where Issa had taken Samira. Knocking, Ehsaan called out, "Issa, tell me. Is all well with Samira?"

Jalil sighed with relief at hearing her answer. "Yes, my husband. Samira will be fine. Have someone tell Saad. He must be distraught."

"I will, my wife. When she awakens, tell her we have gone to bring her children home." Ehsaan directed a nearby servant to notify Saad, then flew out of the house with Jalil close behind, both calling for men and horses.

Within minutes, the air was filled with thundering hooves as they galloped out of the compound. The moon was setting, and the path was dark, but they trusted their desert born steeds. They rode like the wind, intent on finding the victims and, more importantly, the men who were responsible. Jalil prayed to Allah they would be in time.

CHAPTER 41

Kira awoke to find herself laying on a narrow bed in a tiny room. At first, she couldn't remember how she came to be in this room, but slowly, the events of the last twenty-four hours became clearer. She shivered at the memories. *Did Jabari and Amber make it?* She didn't know, and it was killing her now.

Her last memory was of two men. The one who captured her was called Hashem, and she would never forget his face. The other she knew all too well—Qadir. She recognized his dark, soulless eyes from when he attacked her the day of the race and, again, outside his house.

Fighting despair, she determined to concentrate on a better memory. A vision of Jalil's green-gold eyes immediately came to mind. Surprised, but pleased with that particular memory, she longed to feel the strength of his arms again and felt a loss for something unnamed. *Will I ever see Jalil again?*

Trying to think of some way she could escape, she rose to pace back and forth until a pattern of sunlight on the floor drew her attention. Looking up, she was excited to see a window, covered by carved wood lattice. But she realized it was too high to reach, even standing on the bed. In a panic, she attempted to open the door but found it locked. Peering through the gap underneath, she noticed a pair of booted feet just outside. *It must be a guard.*

A wave of dizziness washed over her, forcing her to sit on the bed where she bowed her aching head, closed her eyes, and breathed deeply, willing away a sudden surge of nausea. With her fists clenching the meager blanket, she fought for control. Having survived the wreck, the desert, and the lion, she found her inner warrior, and it strengthened her soul. Qadir would send for her, and she prayed she would be ready. She wasn't going down without a fight.

She didn't have long to wait. Hearing hard footsteps followed by the jangle of keys, she jumped to her feet just as the door flew open, revealing Qadir's tall, lean form clothed in black. His head was bare, his dark, oily hair hung lank around his shoulders, and his hard thin lips twisted in a cruel smile. He leaned against the door to study her.

Feeling vulnerable, Kira darted away from the bed, keeping her back to the wall. Breathing heavily, she raised her fists and glared at Qadir. His eyes were full of anger, but his eyebrows raised in surprise. She flinched when he laughed out loud and took a step toward her, his eyes traveling up and down her body.

Kira was so focused on Qadir, she was unaware her robe was hanging off one shoulder and her sleeves had fallen back, revealing a patchwork puzzle of color. Her face, neck, and hands were brown, but her arms and shoulder were white.

Qadir's eyes widened at the display. "Well, what have we here?" He took another step closer, but stopped when she raised her fists higher, a determined look on her face. He stood with his hands on his hips and chuckled. "Kira, just what do you think you're going to do?"

Kira gasped in surprise. "How do you know my name? What do you want with me?"

"Hmm. You speak my language very well." He smiled slyly, speaking in Arabic. "Why don't we use yours?" He spoke now in English. "As for how I know your name, that is none of your business. As for what I want from you, you will learn soon enough. But for now, you will tell me everything I want to know." His smile vanished and his voice hardened. "Where did you come from? Who do you belong to?" When she didn't answer, he fingered the whip at his side and her eyes flickered in recognition. "I see you remember my whip," he said, stepping closer. "You should not have interfered with the punishment of Shar. I can have you put to death for attacking a sheik."

"You're an animal! You're not worthy to clean his hooves!" She spat at him.

Faster than a striking snake, he slapped her hard across her swollen jaw. Failing to block his blow, she cried out in pain and clutched her face. Taking advantage of her vulnerability, he pulled her robe off and grabbed her hands in a painful grip, transferring both of hers into one of his. Raising her arms, he forced her against the wall, pinning her with his hips.

She kicked at his legs, but he was too strong. He pressed his legs between hers, grabbed her throat with his free hand, and squeezed slowly. Kira continued to fight, trying to buck free, but her vision narrowed as she fought to breathe. Her eyes widened when she suddenly felt his desire through her tunic. Even in her naïve state, she knew what that meant, and she fought harder.

Qadir growled, released her throat, stepped back, and grabbed the top of her tunic, yanking downward with all his strength. The material parted to reveal her pale breasts flushed with her exertions and shaking with every gasp of her breath. She tried to clamp her legs tight, but he pushed her legs apart and pressed up against her.

Kira was horrified by his intimate touch. His raging desire was evident, and she began to hyperventilate. Qadir licked his lips, and his eyes focused on the silvery gold rope of her hair that had fallen over her shoulder. She shuddered seeing his eyes drift farther down her body to her exposed breasts, and she briefly closed her eyes, afraid of what he would do next.

Her eyes flew open when she felt a sudden change in his body. Apparently, his desire was gone. Uncomprehending, she stared at his face, but he was staring at her chest with a look of utter disbelief. Glancing down, she saw what had drawn his attention. Swinging on a piece of braided leather between her pale pink breasts was her gold medallion.

Qadir grabbed the disk and held it up in front of her face. "Where did you get this?" he shouted, releasing her hands but grabbing her throat. She clawed at his wrist but couldn't answer. Her head filled with a loud buzzing, and her vision faded. When he abruptly released her neck and ripped the leather cord over her head, she fell to the floor. She landed in a heap and lay still, only dimly aware when he stomped from the room, calling for Hashem.

Gasping for breath, she mustered enough strength to rise and cover herself with her robe before two burly guards entered the room. They dragged her down the hall to a pair of tall ornate doors where an ancient, wrinkled woman, completely swathed in black, stood waiting. The woman opened the doors and entered the room, and the guards forced Kira inside and departed at once, locking the door behind them.

Kira tried to stay on her feet. She swayed dangerously and would have fallen had not two serving women grabbed her by the arms. They dragged her through an arched opening into an extensive pool area. Disoriented, she tried to focus, and glancing around, she saw half a dozen lovely girls in different stages of undress. A few reclined on silken pillows or benches, and a few lounged in the clear water of the pool. They all looked at her and began talking at once. Before she could speak, the two women removed her robe and forced her into a smaller pool off to one side.

The two women held her tight, as a third scrubbed her roughly, ignoring her cries of outrage. The other girls were staring at her with fascinated looks, and Kira realized she must look quite a sight. Her face, hands, forearms, and feet were dull brown, but her shoulders, torso and legs were very pale. She continued to fight and failed to hear the door open behind her. With a loud screech, Kira finally pulled loose long enough to turn around, but ceased struggling almost at once when she saw who was standing by the edge of the pool. Her jaw dropped in disbelief.

Kira and Cassie stared at each other in stunned silence. "You!" they both yelled at the same time. The servants took advantage of the fact that Kira had stopped fighting and doused her with water before grabbing her once again.

Cassie was laughing so hard she had to sit down to catch her breath.

"What are you laughing at, Cassie?" Kira sputtered, straining to get free.

"Well, if it isn't Kira. Daddy's little girl. What happened to the horse, honey?" Cassie smiled meanly, while availing herself of a glass of lemonade.

"The horse died," Kira lied. She would not give her any information about Amber.

"Oh well. Nature takes its course, wouldn't you say?" Cassie took a long sip then stared at her, blatantly running her eyes over Kira's body. "You don't look too bad, except for that nasty brown color. What is that all about?" she asked with a curious expression.

"None of your business," Kira huffed. "You don't look like you've been suffering." Kira had noticed the older woman's rich tunic, jeweled slippers, and shining red hair. "You always did manage to come out on top, or should I say bottom." Kira couldn't help the small insult. It wasn't like her to be petty, but seeing her old nemesis brought back a fresh feeling of abandonment.

Cassie flinched, and her eyes flashed with momentary anger. "You don't know what you're talking about, you little half-breed. Besides, you'll know soon enough the price I have to pay. And considering your lack of 'experience,' the price will be a great deal higher for you. But who knows? Maybe you'll grow to like it... *if* he lets you live." Cassie helped herself to some refreshments and watched Kira with cruel amusement.

Kira blanched at that thought but controlled her features. She understood exactly what Cassie was talking about. Swallowing thickly, she tried to ignore Cassie while the servants scrubbed and rinsed her body a second time before pushing her into the larger pool.

They dunked her several times but finally relented, pulling her out and drying her off with large cotton towels. Plopping her onto a bench, one woman tried to comb out her long, wet hair until Kira hissed with pain and grabbed the comb away and finished the job herself. Her back was to Cassie, so Kira didn't see her gloating when the women held her down and rubbed her body with oils and dyed her private areas.

The other girls watched in silence, but their sympathy for Kira was easy to see and she noticed them casting suspicious looks at Cassie. Cassie seemed to ignore them as she stripped off her tunic and slid into the warm waters to take her own bath. But she never took her eyes off Kira, and Kira kept a wary eye on her as well.

•   •   •

Fatima had been working on her mending when the servants brought the struggling girl into the bath chamber. When they stripped off the ratty robe, revealing the girl's two-tone coloration, Fatima knew she was a foreigner like Cassie. Surreptitiously casting glances at her, Fatima saw the girl's distress, and it tugged at her heart.

When Cassie entered the chamber, Fatima was quick to note the recognition between her and the new girl. Cassie's scornful response was just as Fatima would have expected, but the new girl's response was surprising. She was clearly terrified but was putting up a brave front, even though it was clear to Fatima the girl knew what she was about to face.

Somewhere deep inside of Fatima, an old feeling awakened, one she had suppressed ever since she was stolen from her family as a child. Fatima had witnessed this same thing too many times, and she was growing angry. Often wondering why First Wife had never come for her, Fatima figured it was because she wasn't as pretty as the other girls and Qadir would never send for a plain woman. It used to bother her, but in time, she came to see it as a blessing from Allah. Eventually, she learned to make herself invisible and accepted the fact that she would never have a husband or children.

As she watched the girl fighting the women who were trying to dye her private parts, she felt a growing sense of wrongness, too. The poor girl was being prepared for Qadir and was about to face her worst nightmare. Just the thought of that made Fatima sick, and she knew she had to do something. Putting down her materials, she rose and strode forward to take the hateful red dye from the servant and push her aside. She looked down at the tear-streaked face of the young girl, startled to see her bright blue-green eyes. *What beautiful eyes!* But the sight of the silvery-gold strands in the girl's hair mesmerized her. *Who is this girl?*

The girl must have seen the compassion in Fatima's eyes, because she suddenly stopped struggling. Lifting the girl's chin, Fatima examined the nasty bruise and swelling on her jaw, and the anger returned. Forcing herself to smile, she said, in English, "It will heal."

The girl's eyes widened, and she gave Fatima a questioning look.

"Yes, I speak your language, but only a little. Can you speak mine?" Fatima asked.

"Yes," the girl answered in very passable Arabic.

"Good. What is your name?"

"Kira. What is yours?"

"Fatima. How did you come to be here?"

"I was kidnapped. I attacked Qadir the day of the race to stop him from beating his horse, and he sent men after me and attacked my family."

Fatima was appalled. "You attacked the sheik? Did you not know what that would mean? It is a killing offense."

"I did not know, and I do not care. What he was doing to that horse was unforgiveable. I had to stop him." Kira's voice rose in anger.

Fatima shook her head. Kira had fought back, something Fatima always wanted to do, but was too afraid. She was in awe of Kira. "You must be careful what you say now…there are ears everywhere," Fatima whispered, hoping Kira understood what she was saying.

Kira cast her eyes left and right before focusing on the soft brown ones before her. "I understand," she whispered.

"Kira, I think you have some idea what the sheik is planning." Fatima paused, watching the horror return to Kira's face. "I am not sure how I can help you except to say that you must try to survive. The sheik has never summoned me, but I have seen many that were. I will not tell you what happened to them, but I can see you are strong enough to get through this. I will tell you the one thing I know about the sheik—the harder you fight, the more he likes it."

"I cannot imagine giving up without a fight," Kira whispered, then confessed, "But I do not really know what is going to happen."

"You mean you have never been with a man?" Fatima looked at her closely.

"Not in the way I think you mean." Kira blushed and looked down at her clasped hands.

Sitting there naked in view of everyone in the room couldn't help but add to the girl's embarrassment, Fatima thought. *Poor, poor girl.* What was about to happen to the girl was the worst thing Fatima could imagine, one she had always dreaded, too. Unable to speak for a minute, not sure what she could even say, she reached down and took Kira's hands in hers. When Kira looked up at her, Fatima said firmly, "Kira, you will survive this. You must, or you will never live to escape someday."

At the word escape, Fatima saw hope flare in her eyes, but before Kira could respond, Fatima hushed her. "You need to let me finish the preparations. First Wife will return soon, and if you are not ready, it will not go well for you. I know this is uncomfortable, but it must be done." She held the dye in her hand, waiting to see if Kira would comply. Kira's face turned as red as the dye, but she allowed Fatima to complete the task.

When she was done, Fatima brushed Kira's hair until it mirrored the late afternoon sun streaming through the skylight. Fatima wove gold wire with pale blue gems into her long locks and dyed her lips a rich plum, then lined her eyes with a dark liquid. After dusting Kira's body with silvery powder, Fatima wrapped a delicate gold chain with dangling gold disks around her slim waist, just above her hips. When Fatima was satisfied with the results, she draped Kira in a tunic of sky blue silk and adorned her throat with a strand of pale blue gems before placing gilded slippers on her feet.

Kira's beauty awed Fatima but seeing Kira standing with her arms at her side, her face without expression, she worried the girl was going into shock. So she led her to a large, polished mirror, and positioned her in front. "Kira, look how beautiful you are."

Watching Kira stare into the mirror, Fatima saw her eyes widen. After a minute, Kira lightly ran her fingers over the long golden hair that spilled around her shoulders. Her skin glowed, and all traces of the brown stain were gone. The sheer silk barely concealed her body, leaving little to the imagination. Blushing, Kira's breathing increased, and she started shaking.

Fatima pulled her away from the mirror. "Kira! Kira, calm down. You need to take a few deep breaths."

Kira seemed to gather her strength and slowed her breathing. She gazed gratefully at Fatima. "Thank you."

"You are welcome. Now, I do not know the last time you ate, but can you eat something now?"

"Oh, no. No, I don't think so," Kira said, clutching her stomach and looking nauseated.

Fatima discarded that idea but insisted she drink something. Everyone knew how dangerous it was to become dehydrated, and she felt better when Kira managed a few sips of sweetened tea.

When she heard the door open behind her, Fatima knew First Wife had come for Kira. As they led Kira from the room, Fatima saw the girl square her shoulders and lift her head. She felt tears in her eyes, awed by the girl's bravery, but saddened by what Kira was about to experience.

Suddenly feeling powerless and alone, Fatima hurried to her own room, where she tried to think of anything but the night ahead.

•   •   •

Kira fought to remain calm as she followed First Wife down the corridor. She felt relieved when they took her back to the little room where she had first been imprisoned. However, her relief faded when

First Wife informed her she would return later to escort her to Qadir, where Kira would be expected to service the sheik.

Once she was alone in the room, she paced back and forth. Fear was eating away at her when she remembered Qadir's face and his threats. But remembering the smug look on Cassie's face, she felt a welcome surge of anger. As she searched for her earlier courage, she clung to the thought that at least Jabari and Amber had escaped and maybe help would soon be there.

Knowing she needed to relax and conserve her strength, she stopped to sit on the bed, but it didn't seem to help, especially when she remembered Fatima's warning. Trying not to dwell on what was coming, she looked down at her chest, still horrified to see her breasts were more prominent thanks to the red dye. The silk was so sheer, she could even see the golden curls at the apex of her thighs. Mortified that her body was on public display, it took her a minute to realize she was missing more than her clothes. The medallion! Qadir had stolen it!

Outraged, she suddenly noticed her mother's fragile gold chain and her father's ring were also missing. She didn't remember having them when Qadir confronted her earlier. *Where could they be?* She had been robbed of the last reminders of her parents. Overwhelmed by the loss of her precious keepsakes and the realization of what Qadir was about to steal from her, her courage fled, and she broke down and sobbed. *Oh no! This can't be happening! What am I going to do when Qadir comes for me? Please God, help me be strong!* Desperate, she continued to pray, holding on to the hope that someone would rescue her before it was too late.

CHAPTER 42

Hashem strode down the hall toward Qadir's chambers, seeing First Wife headed his way. No doubt she had been receiving instructions from Qadir on preparing Kira. Hashem made eye contact with First Wife as she passed, but she didn't acknowledge him—she never did in public. Hashem still hadn't figured out how he was going to get rid of her, but for his plans to succeed, she had to be disposed of.

Hashem had no idea what Qadir wanted to see him about unless it was to chastise him again for his failure to kill Jalil during the race. Resigned to listening to Qadir harangue on about Jalil again, he knocked on Qadir's door. A guard admitted him but exited when Hashem entered.

The front chamber was empty, and Hashem boldly made himself comfortable by sitting down at the table and pouring a glass of tea.

"Please, make yourself at home," Qadir's sarcastic voice rang out.

Startled, Hashem had the good sense to rise and bow. "My sheik."

"Humph," Qadir approached from his bedchamber. "Sit down, you fool."

Hiding his anger, Hashem settled back into his chair and waited for Qadir to speak. He jerked in surprise when Qadir slammed something onto the tabletop. Looking down, he saw what he had never expected to see again. *Akeem's medallion!* He struggled to hide his reaction. Hashem had claimed ignorance of the medallion the day Qadir killed

Akeem and it wouldn't do for Qadir to know Hashem knew exactly what he was seeing.

Hashem had stolen it from Akeem's neck as he lay injured on the mountain trail. He had heard the rumors that the medallion was special, but he didn't know why and had no time to question Akeem. The man was barely conscious and mumbling some nonsense…something about how he had not told Jalil yet. Hashem ignored his ramblings and had hidden the medallion in his robes only moments before Qadir showed up to finish off the sheik.

Qadir was obsessed with owning the medallion—it was the first thing he looked for, and he was furious when he couldn't find it. Hashem listened as Qadir questioned Akeem, but the sheik wouldn't talk. Enraged, Qadir showed him Rayham, lying broken and bleeding in the sand, but still the man did not speak. Then Qadir told him about kidnapping the baby and laughed maniacally at the man's tears.

Akeem cursed and shouted at him, but Qadir just laughed louder and took Akeem's heavy gold dagger and slit Akeem's throat. Hashem had to jump back to avoid the spray of blood. Then Qadir went through Akeem's robes and saddle bag searching for the medallion, and when he could not find it, he screamed in frustration and promptly shot Rayham, even though the stallion was already dead from Hashem's bullet.

Seeing the infamous medallion now laying before him on the table, Hashem felt a trickle of fear. Schooling his features, he reached out and touched the disk, but jerked his hand back when he felt a spark of heat. "What is this?" He looked up at Qadir with an innocent expression.

Qadir was staring at the disk, and he missed any sign Hashem was lying to him. "It is Akeem's medallion."

"But where did you find it?" Hashem asked, feeling a chill in the air.

"The girl had it," Qadir spat and took a big gulp of his wine.

Confused, Hashem fought to hide his anger. *How could that be?* The day they returned from killing Akeem, Hashem had hidden the medallion, intending to save it for the day he took over Qadir's kingdom, but later someone stole it from him. He never figured out who took it. It just didn't make sense. "The girl? How did she get it?" He continued to play his part.

"I do not know." Qadir picked up the medallion and studied it intently. "I am sure it is Akeem's, though. I saw it many times, and he always wore it. But why was he not wearing it that day?"

Hashem was thinking fast. "Perhaps in his haste to find the golden stallion, he left without it. I heard that as soon as he read the message, he did not even go inside to change, but immediately called for Rayham. That must be it." The messenger who delivered the message to Akeem had given Hashem a thorough report.

"But that doesn't explain how she got it."

"Maybe a servant stole it after his death and sold it. Saad could have traded for it, and the girl could have stolen it from him." Hashem's story felt a little thin. "Or maybe the girl got it from whoever stole it, as a favor for a night of pleasure." Hashem was grasping at straws now.

Luckily, Qadir seemed to accept the possibilities. He grabbed the medallion off the table and stuffed it in his robe. "Well, I have it now, and that's all that matters."

Hashem was curious why Qadir was wasting time talking to him when normally he would have been playing with his latest victim. "What are you going to do with the girl?"

Leaning back in his chair with his eyes half closed, Qadir contemplated her fate. "I owe her a whipping, and I think I will have a little fun with her before I decide. Maybe I'll kill her." His smile widened. "But I want her to tell me about the medallion first."

"She might not know its significance." Hashem felt better now that Qadir's attention was on someone else.

"She is just a stupid woman. She probably doesn't know what it means. I just want to know where she got it, and where she came from, and what she was doing in our region. You realize she is a foreigner."

"Really? How can you tell?" Hashem acted surprised, but he had seen her eyes and hair.

"I encouraged her to remove her robe." Qadir smirked. "There was a very pale foreigner under all that brown dye. First Wife is even now helping her to look more like herself, and soon, I will find out what I need to know." He laughed cruelly.

Hashem wondered if the girl knew what was about to happen to her. It was a shame she might not survive long enough for Hashem to enjoy her young body, too, but based on what he had seen of her so far, it was no great loss. He spent another hour listening to Qadir rant about how he was going to eliminate Jalil, but when he started cursing Nadim for the botched attempt to kill Jalil during the race, Hashem made an excuse to leave. While Kira kept Qadir busy, Hashem would spend time with Cassie.

·   ·   ·

Unbeknownst to the two men, First Wife had hastened back to her chambers to listen to Qadir's plotting through the secret door between her chamber and Qadir's. She was worried how she was going to deal with another foreign woman, but hearing Qadir's plans, her fears were put to rest. It was unlikely the girl would be around long enough to become a problem for her. It was Cassie who continued to be an issue.

She chuckled silently to herself now, thinking about her. The redhead was still pretending to be pregnant. First Wife knew it was just a ruse to keep Qadir from using her each night. First Wife used the opportunity to torment her in small ways, simply because she could—she enjoyed making Cassie feel helpless. Each morning, she purposely had a large glass of camel milk was delivered to Cassie, even though she knew Cassie despised camel milk and preferred sweetened tea or lemonade. When Cassie objected, First Wife told her that camel milk was much better for women in her condition, and that the sheik insisted Cassie drink it every day.

With Qadir avoiding Cassie, First Wife could sneak her out every night to lie with Hashem. As much as she enjoyed subjecting Cassie to Hashem's desires, she was more concerned that Cassie get pregnant for real. If Cassie had another cycle and Qadir found out, he would begin using her again, and that would just delay First Wife's plans.

She needed Cassie to get pregnant now, and once the baby was born, she could get rid of Cassie and Hashem. Then Qadir would have his heir and First Wife would still be in charge. Her mind spinning with plots, she scurried off to finish preparing the prisoner to meet her new master.

•   •   •

After Kira was taken away, Cassie exited the pool. After drying off and donning her robe, she stalked from the room, feigning indifference. But she was miffed. She was not surprised that the girl she had left to die in the desert had survived. Kira had always managed to get away with murder, but to see her here, knowing she was about to experience her worst nightmare, was just too rich. Talk about fate. She *was* surprised to feel a stab of jealousy, though. With her young and virginal body, Kira could become Qadir's next favorite and that both bothered her and excited her. If Qadir became obsessed with Kira, Cassie would lose her chance at power, but might be free to put her other plan in motion even sooner.

For a brief instant, she almost felt sorry for Kira. Kira was going to be used and abused in ways she could not even imagine. As a woman of the world with a lot of experience, Cassie was able to deal with Qadir better than most women. Virginal Kira would have a hard time, but she would adapt, or not. Either way, Cassie couldn't afford to worry about anyone else right now.

When she returned to her room, the first thing she noticed was the thick yellowish liquid still dripping down the wall from where she had thrown her goblet earlier. *Camel milk! Yuk. Damn that old woman! And damn Qadir and Hashem, too! In fact, damn everyone in this god-forsaken place.* Having to deal with that crazy old bat every day and suffering through the attentions of that nasty Hashem was becoming too much, and she was at her wit's end. She had grown to hate this land and its people, and every day she dreamed of America. She missed the clothes, the money, and men she could manipulate. One way or the other, she would get out of here. Somehow, she had to convince Hashem to get her far enough away where she could steal a camel or a horse, anything, to carry her to a place where she could get help.

When Qadir was at the race and Hashem on his special mission, Cassie had enjoyed a restful break, and no one bothered her except the old bat. It was almost pleasant around the house. She heard through the grapevine that Jalil won the race and, according to the rules, could take any stallion he wanted, but had only taken Shar. Cassie was glad Qadir had lost his horse. *Serves him right, the bastard.* She thought about Jalil and wondered if she could somehow convince him to help her, but the chances of seeing him again were slim. It looked like she was stuck with Hashem.

Settling back on her bed, she pondered her future. If Qadir found out she wasn't pregnant, she would be right back in his bed, and that was a frightening thought. She didn't know if she could survive his sexual perversions much longer—he was becoming rougher and frequently lost control. Fatima told her that if he grew tired of her, Cassie might be handed over to one of his men. Hashem seemed to think it would be him. Fatima also said Qadir might sell her, but Cassie wasn't afraid of being sold. If that happened, she might end up with a man easier to manipulate and have a better opportunity to escape.

What she was afraid of was ending up like Zahra. That woman had also failed to produce a child, and Qadir had yet to get rid of her. Cassie was frightened at the thought of being stuck there forever.

Bored, she rose and padded over to her trunk. Throwing open the lid, she dug down until she found the small leather bag containing her hidden stash of coins and gems. Satisfied it was safe, she pulled out a small pouch containing treats she made a point of hiding in her robe whenever she was in the social room or bathing area. Nibbling on a date, she considered alternate plans while at the same time, taking a perverse pleasure in thinking about Kira's upcoming initiation by Qadir. Finally, the little know-it-all was getting her just desserts.

CHAPTER 43

While Hashem was galloping away with Kira, Jabari was galloping back to the main trail, praying as he struggled to stay on Amber. His heart was in his throat, and he begged her to stop, but she ignored him. It took everything he had to stay on her back, and all he could hear was the thunder of her hooves and the whistling of the wind as she carried him farther and farther away from Kira. Knowing he couldn't stop Amber, he bent low over her neck and held on tighter. He had to find his father, and he prayed to Allah that Amber would know the way.

Eventually, the trail became slippery and steep causing Amber to slow down to a fast walk, but she was able to quicken her pace when they approached the place where they had been ambushed. Coming out of the tight rocky pass, he knew they'd reached the exact place when he saw the dark form of Kira's camel lying dead on the trail. Grimacing at the sight, he was about to urge Amber toward Ehsaan's, but she was a step ahead of him and broke into a gallop. Holding on to her mane, Jabari prayed to Allah that he could last long enough to find Ehsaan.

His prayers were answered in the form of Ehsaan himself, astride Mukhtar, accompanied by Jalil on Mirage, and a score of armed men. It was still dark, but Jabari could see the silver of Mirage's coat. "Ehsaan! Jalil!" Jabari forgot to call them sheiks in his relief and excitement. "Praise Allah I found you. You must come at once. They have Kira," he shouted as he galloped toward them.

Both men pulled their horses to a sudden stop. "Jabari, is that you?" Jalil called out.

Jabari skidded to a halt in front of them. "Did you hear me? We must go at once!" Waving his hands, he urged Amber to turn around.

"Jabari, stop. Stop! We must talk first." Ehsaan raised his hands, trying to get the boy's attention. He waved two men forward to secure the Amber, but she wasn't having anything to do with them and skittered backward, snorting and huffing.

Jalil called out, "Are you injured? Can you control your horse, Jabari?"

"I am fine, but Amber is not my horse!" he said without thinking.

"Amber?" Jalil stared at Amber and urged Mirage closer.

"Never mind that, we must hurry!" Jabari cried as Amber circled away.

"Jabari, hold on. Who has your sister and where is Bassam?"

"There were two men, and they took Kira up the pass," Jabari said, hoping Jalil would not press him about his non-existent cousin.

"What pass? Where? Can you show us?" Ehsaan moved forward as he spoke.

"Yes, follow me," Jabari cried and urged Amber to gallop back to the scene of the ambush.

Just around the bend they came upon the chilling sight of the dead camel by the side of the trail, attended by two loose ones, and Ehsaan called for a halt. Jabari reluctantly complied and Ehsaan pulled up as close to Amber as she would allow. She did not seem nervous around Mukhtar, but when Jalil approached, she would not let Mirage get near.

"So, this is where it happened?"

"Yes, and we must hurry. They went into the rocks...just over there." Jabari pointed to the cliff side not far away.

"Jabari, my friend, you must go to my house. Your father and mother are there, and your mother is wounded. She will be fine but will need you close by," Ehsaan said. "We can take it from here."

"But I promised Kira I would get help. She sacrificed herself so I could get away."

"What do you mean, Jabari?" Jalil asked, his voice filled with alarm.

"She untied us, and we freed Amber, but when we were trying to get away, the man came back. Kira made me get on Amber first and commanded her to take me away and get help. The man tried to shoot me but missed." Jabari's voice cracked as he tried to control his emotions. *Why won't they listen to me?*

Jalil was quick to offer assurance. "Calm down, Jabari. We must keep our heads. We will find and save Kira!" The strength of his voice seemed to startle even him. Shaking his head, he said more calmly, "But you cannot come with us. It will be very dangerous, and we do not know what we will face."

"I am not afraid, and I must go! I made a promise which I will keep. Besides, you do not know the way." Jabari's voice turned fierce. He would not give up this fight and turned to appeal to Ehsaan.

Ehsaan looked like he was going to agree with Jalil when suddenly, Ehsaan's eyes opened wide and he spoke, "I cannot explain it, but I just had the strangest feeling that we might need Jabari and the horse. It is a risk, but something tells me Jabari will be able to handle himself."

Jalil whipped around and confronted Ehsaan. "Are you sure this is the wise thing to do?"

Ehsaan nodded. "Jalil, Jabari has come through a lot today and has made a promise to his sister. And apparently, he is the only one that can talk to that horse. And the horse is probably the only one that can find Kira. So, yes, I believe Jabari should come with us."

Jabari smiled confidently. He knew they would see the sense in what he said. They needed him, and so did Kira.

"Very well, Ehsaan. I bow to your command," said Jalil.

Ehsaan then turned to one of his men. "Return home as fast as you can. Tell Saad his son is fine, as is the horse. We will take him with us, and we will keep him safe." Ehsaan's man nodded and galloped off. To another he said, "Take the camels and Saad's belonging to my house." The man quickly complied.

Then Ehsaan leaned forward in the saddle to speak to Jabari. "My friend, it seems you are to be our guide. We must make haste, for I fear great harm could come to your sister."

Jabari swallowed hard, remembering the sight of the knife at Kira's throat. He turned Amber toward the pass but held up when Ehsaan asked one more question. "Wait, Jabari, tell me, did you recognize either of the men?"

Jabari thought hard before replying, "No, it all happened so fast. They were both dressed in black, and their faces were covered. One of them shot the camel out from under Kira and when Kira got up, the man grabbed her. I tried to stop him, but he threw me to the ground. Then he shot my mother." Jabari's voice broke, and for a moment he could not speak.

Both men looked at each other again. "Such bravery from one so young," Ehsaan said with a serious smile. "And then what happened?"

"He rode off through the rocks, and I jumped on Amber and followed them."

Jalil piped up, "Ehsaan, we need to get on with it if we are to catch up to the kidnappers. But how will we find the way now? It is too dark to find any tracks."

"Do not worry about tracks, Sheik Jalil." Jabari was once again holding on to Amber's mane. Amber was already on the move, walking briskly toward the trail through the rocks. "Follow me." Jabari's voice floated back to them.

"Well, we have our orders." Ehsaan chuckled grimly.

"Wait," Jalil called, "what about your cousin? Where is Bassam?"

Jabari ignored the question. Focused on saving Kira, he urged Amber forward.

The two sheiks and their men fell in behind as Amber led them up the stony passage. They progressed at a good pace, alternating between a fast walk and a trot. Amber pressed onward, pushing harder until she reached the spot where she had been tied up, and then she stopped to sniff the ground.

"Jabari, why are we stopping here?" Ehsaan asked.

"I think this is where we were tied up." Jabari jumped down to search the area.

"How can you be sure?" Jalil asked.

Jabari ignored Jalil and searched the side of the trail. After a few minutes, he found one of the rags that had been used as a gag. Just as he opened his mouth to call out to Jalil, something glinted beside the path. Bending down, he retrieved what looked like a ring, tangled in a delicate metal chain. Even though the darkness was receding, and dawn was not far off, he could not see them clearly, but he could feel a familiar design on the surface of the ring, and he knew what it was. This was Kira's ring and chain she wore around her neck.

Excited, he ran over to Jalil and held up his finds. "See. I told you so. This is one of the rags they stuffed in our mouths. And this ring and necklace belong to Kira. They are her greatest treasures, next to Amber."

Jalil ignored the rags and took the ring and chain. He appeared to study them for a second, then stuffed them deep into his robe. "I'll keep these safe for now."

Jabari nodded and climbed back up onto Amber.

"I wonder where they went from here?" Jalil asked out loud, but before anyone could answer, Amber trotted off to a steep path beyond two large rocks. Caught off guard, everyone scrambled to keep up. The horse was going fast, considering the condition of the trail, but no one was going to tell her to slow down.

When they reached level ground, Jabari assumed Amber would speed up, but instead, she veered toward a distant cluster of bushes. When he saw the small spring, he called out excitedly. Here the ground told a story—tracks leading to the water.

Jumping down, he gulped some water and as Amber lowered her head to take a drink, searched the damp ground nearby. When Jalil and Ehsaan joined him, Jabari gestured to a small handprint and a crude arrow pointing northeast, scratched into the mud. He looked up with such a smile that all the men had to return it. "Kira!" Jabari exclaimed and climbed back upon Amber. "We need to go."

"Stay, Jabari. We all need a drink," Ehsaan said.

Frustrated, Jabari pulled Amber over to one side and waited impatiently for the others to finish. He was busy studying the tracks when Jalil and Mirage moved closer.

"When is the last time you ate?" Jalil asked, his eyes fixed on Amber, who was obviously not happy to have Mirage so near.

"I do not remember. Yesterday…midday meal, I think."

He watched Jalil reach into his saddlebag and produce a small loaf of bread. "Then catch." He tossed it to him.

Jabari caught it easily and devoured it in seconds. "Thank you, my sheik." He bowed his head.

Ehsaan had mounted back up and rode forward. "Well, Jabari, if you and Amber are ready, we should go."

"Yes, Sheik Ehsaan," he said and grabbed Amber's mane…and just in time. Amber needed no urging and immediately broke into a fast canter.

The early morning sun had crawled over the eastern mountain tops and hot rays of white light revealed the sharp contrasts in the rough terrain through which they rode. Smooth, sandy ground wove between boulders of pink, tan, and beige. The colors blended until it seemed no break existed in the sharp rocky outcroppings.

As the sun reached its zenith, more open terrain became visible. The heat was building, but Amber pushed on relentlessly, setting a grueling pace. Jabari was watching for signs of weariness in Amber, but it was as if she knew exactly how to regulate herself and varied her gaits accordingly. He smiled. *Of course, she knows what she is doing.*

Jabari was thankful that the sheiks had arrived with help. He had a promise to keep and a friend to rescue. Resolved, he tuned out everything but the feel of Amber's muscles beneath had as he raced to save Kira.

CHAPTER 44

Jabari wasn't the only one consumed with thoughts of Kira. Jalil couldn't help but worry about what she might face, and he had to find her. But now and then, his eyes were drawn to the boy riding just ahead. Jabari rode as one with Amber, without saddle or bridle, as if glued to her back. His skill was amazing for one so young.

Amber's strength and endurance astounded Jalil. She didn't seem tired and kept a steady pace. Mirage and Mukhtar could keep up, but the rest were falling behind. Jalil watched her for signs of weariness, but she seemed tireless. He was amazed that a packhorse could perform as well as Mirage.

When he wasn't watching Amber, he concentrated on the scenery flashing by, trying to figure out where they were headed. Based on the position of the sun and how far they had come from the main trail, he had a sneaking suspicion where they would end up. There was only one kingdom immediately to the east of Ehsaan. "Jabari," he called out, "we need to rest and wait for the men."

Jabari nodded in agreement and commanded Amber to stop. To Jalil's surprise, she complied without a struggle. *What an incredible horse! And what stamina. I wonder where Kira found her?* Jalil studied her from the distance she allowed. Her confirmation was excellent, but her color was confusing. Shaking his head, he would have to solve the mystery of Amber later. For now, he needed to concentrate on the task at hand. Jalil moved away from Amber and closer to Ehsaan.

"I have a feeling I know where we are going." He looked at Ehsaan with a grim expression.

"Yes, I think I know too." Ehsaan's face mirrored his.

"Where?" Jabari asked.

Before Jalil or Ehsaan could answer, one of Ehsaan's men approached. "My sheik, may I say something?"

"Yes, Faris. What is it?"

"You know that when I was younger, before I was a member of your tribe, I belonged to another."

"Yes, I remember."

"Well, I know this trail, and we are traveling on that tribe's lands now. The house is not far, just beyond those hills." Faris bowed his head.

"Thank you for that information, Faris. It is what I feared to be true. And Faris, thank you for joining my tribe. You have always been a valuable member." Ehsaan nodded.

Faris bowed his head again and, with a proud smile, returned to his place in line.

"Well, my friends, if Faris is right, we are on Qadir's land, and that means he has Kira. This is a problem I am not sure how to handle."

"Qadir! That loathsome rat!" Jabari interrupted, his voice filled with ire.

"Calm yourself, Jabari," Jalil said sternly. "It will do you no good to get emotional right now. We must keep cool heads and figure out what to do."

"I could send for reinforcements," Ehsaan spoke next. "We will certainly need more men if we are to attack Qadir in his stronghold."

"We can both send for more men, but I'm afraid they will not be here in time to help Kira." Jalil shook his head. He knew Qadir's reputation, and the thought of what the young woman was facing sickened him. He feared they may already be too late.

"It is all my fault. I should not have left her behind," Jabari groaned.

"Nonsense, Jabari. I have heard your story, and I am sure Kira did what she thought was best. You could not have both escaped. At least this way, you both may survive," Ehsaan said.

"Yes," Jalil agreed. "You could have done nothing different. Now, get control of yourself. We need a plan." Turning to Ehsaan, he continued. "Can Faris get us in closer to the house? We need to get a look at what we are dealing with."

Ehsaan called to Faris. "Does Qadir have many guards in his compound?"

"No, my sheik. It is why we were able to come so far without raising alarm. Qadir believes no one would dare attack him." Faris smiled with satisfaction.

"Well then, it seems we might have Allah on our side. Thanks to Faris's information and Qadir's ego, we may just be able to get Kira back without a lot of trouble." Ehsaan looked pleased. Jalil nodded in agreement.

In the end, they sent two men back to Ehsaan's kingdom to gather more men. Amber appeared content to rest and stood off to one side, waiting. Everyone dismounted and gathered around Faris who sketched a layout of Qadir's house and compound in the sand. No one noticed Jabari paying close attention.

Jalil discussed several strategies with Ehsaan, and they decided that Jalil, along with Faris and a few men, would scout the area and gather more information. Ehsaan agreed to remain out of sight with the larger group until they returned. As the sun headed farther west, Jalil motioned to Jabari who was watching and listening from nearby.

"Jabari, if you can keep quiet and control your horse, you can come with me."

Jabari nodded emphatically. "Thank you, my sheik." He ran to get Amber and followed Jalil and Mirage. For once, Amber and Mirage seemed to ignore each other—both horses were focused on the hills ahead—as if they knew what lay ahead.

Eventually, Jalil and Jabari had to leave their horses and proceed on foot. As they eased up toward the crest of the last hill, the sun cast its light upon the compound. It appeared deserted.

All was quiet except for the faint neighing of horses in the distance. The breeze was building and carried the scent of smoke and sand.

"What do you see?" Jalil whispered to Jabari, who lay next to him.

Jabari scanned the area surrounding the house. "I see two guards by the front entrance. One appears to be asleep."

Jalil stifled a laugh. "And what else?" Now was a good time to teach the boy a few things.

Jabari scanned again. "There are three men walking toward the stables on the far side of the house. There are four tents on the southeast corner, but I cannot tell if there are men inside. I see one larger tent closer behind the house and another couple of tents in the distance."

"Very good. I agree, but there is also a man standing by the low wall leading to the back of the house."

"Oh, I see him now. I missed that." Jabari cast his eyes down.

"Do not worry, Jabari. You did well. Let us take this information to Ehsaan. Come."

Together, they carefully inched backward until they could turn and creep away. When they returned to camp, they discovered the other men who were sent to gather information had also returned. As a group, they sat down and shared what they had learned.

Apparently, Faris had been correct in his description of Qadir's security, or rather the lack of it. It was almost non-existent throughout the compound. Jalil hoped the same could be said for the inside of the house. They discussed several options and planned their strategy. Faris suggested they send men to create a disturbance at the main pass and take out the guards, but allow one to return to warn Qadir, in hopes Qadir would send more men to investigate, thus leaving the house less secure. Ehsaan proposed they also send a few men to the stables to release any horses inside and create more confusion.

Jalil proposed to take his men his men on foot and sneak into the house, find the girl, and deal with Qadir. After seeing proof of Qadir's poor security, he felt confident they could overcome any resistance they encountered. When Ehsaan offered to go with him, Jalil insisted he stay behind. He didn't want Ehsaan to be implicated in what he might have to do to Qadir. They argued, but in the end, Ehsaan agreed.

Jabari begged to go along, but both sheiks refused, telling him to remain in the camp. He appeared disgruntled as he retreated to Amber's side, but Jalil thought he saw Jabari hiding a smile. *What is he up to?*

But Jalil had no time to think about the boy as Ehsaan gave the orders, and each group headed out. Jalil and his men rode toward the compound and stopped a safe distance away, leaving their horses with Ehsaan and his remaining men. They would stay close but out of sight and wait for Jalil's men to return, only engaging if necessary.

As the sand absorbed the last rays of light, Jalil and his men crept toward the compound. Jalil's heart raced as he mentally prepared himself for the task at hand. He felt compelled to rescue the woman who haunted his thoughts, so he had to get inside that house, no matter what. Jalil would stop at nothing to save Kira.

CHAPTER 45

After the sheiks had ridden off in the night to search for Jabari and Kira, Amal was so worried about his family, he couldn't sleep. Saad and Samira were both being seen to by the sheikha, so he joined Shar in the stables. As he stepped into the stall to stroke Shar's glossy neck, the big stallion seemed to sense his mood and nudged him with his head. Shar had relaxed considerably, and Amal took it as a good sign.

Amal checked Shar's wounds, satisfied they were healing nicely, but he frowned at the scarring. Such a shame, he thought. Shar was so beautiful. Shaking his head at Qadir's cruelty, he applied fresh ointments and then carefully groomed the stallion. It was a long process, but Shar seemed to enjoy it.

Seeing the pale gray of early morning filtering through the stable shutters, Amal made sure the stallion had plenty of fresh water and grain, and slipped out of the stall, intent on finding something to eat. He found Baqir waiting for him. "Good morning, herdmaster," he said.

"Good morning, Amal. I came to check on you." Baqir's face reflected his concern.

"I am well. I just couldn't sleep. It is hard waiting for news."

"Amal, I am sure that Sheik Ehsaan and Sheik Jalil will find them. But tell me, how is Shar doing?"

Distracted, Amal was about to share his ideas for Shar's rehabilitation when he saw Adara approaching with a purposeful air.

"Baqir, I think we have company," he said and retreated to stand by Shar's stall, where he could still hear their conversation.

"My princess, may I ask where you are going?" Baqir said politely but sternly.

"Oh, good morning, Baqir. I was just taking a walk and thought I would check on Mukhtar's latest foals." Adara smiled innocently.

Amal hid his grin when Baqir answered. "My princess, I fear you have taken a wrong turn. This is not the stable where we keep the foals. I believe you want the next building over."

Amal watched, curious what she would say next.

"Oh, Baqir, I never could fool you," she said resignedly. "I just wanted to see Shar, and I am sure he would not mind a visit from me. And look, I have brought him treats." She held out her small hand to reveal an assortment of sugary nuts and dates. "May I see him... please?" She begged.

Amal could not help but smile. She reminded him so much of Jabari, and he suspected she would not rest until she had met Shar in person.

"My princess, I am considering granting your request, but Shar is still healing from his wounds and may be unpredictable. We must first ask permission from Amal. He is in charge of Shar. If you agree to abide by Amal's decision, we can ask him now," Baqir said.

Amal could see her peeking around Baqir in his direction when she answered, "Certainly, Baqir. Let us ask him." She took Baqir's hand and dragged him toward Amal.

When they approached, Amal stepped forward and bowed. "My princess."

She bowed in return. "Horsemaster, I have come to check on Shar and would like to ask you if I may introduce myself to him. And maybe give him a treat?" She held our hand to show him the sticky fruit and nuts.

Amal considered her request and thought about Shar's condition. The horse was still nervous around anyone other than himself, Baqir and Ehsaan. It would not be wise to push him yet, especially around such a young girl, and that girl being the sheik's daughter. He was about to explain this to her when Shar pushed open the stall door that Amal had failed to latch tightly. Amal stumbled to one side when the stallion shouldered his way into the aisle. Baqir tried to move Adara behind him, but she deftly avoided his arms and stepped forward.

Both men's warnings abruptly died when Shar stopped in front of Adara, lowered his head, and calmly sniffed her all over. Adara was obviously pleased and excited, but she waited patiently. He snorted and blew, and she reached out to lay her hand on his nose. He quivered, and ripples traveled from his neck to his flanks, but he stood still. She began talking to him, telling him how beautiful he was and how she was glad he had come to live with them. Amal felt amazed and relieved as he saw Shar relax and allow Adara to stroke his head.

"May I give him these treats?" Adara politely asked Amal.

Amal smiled. "Certainly, my princess. Just be careful and move slowly."

Adara grinned and held out her sticky offerings. Shar sniffed and blew, then gently took the treats from her little, outstretched hand. Tears formed in her eyes when she saw the whip marks up close. "Oh, Shar, your poor face. Don't you worry though, Amal will make it all better, you will see. Then you can go walking with me in the fields. We will have so much fun together." She continued to stroke his face, avoiding the wounds. He nickered and pushed his nose against her head, nibbling at her hair. She giggled and leaned in to give him a kiss.

Both men were astonished, but Amal most of all. Such skill, especially in one so young, was rare indeed. He allowed her a few more minutes, but then exchanged a look with Baqir. The herdmaster understood and spoke up. "My princess, I believe you have made a friend, but your friend needs more rest. Perhaps Amal will let you come back and check on him before bed tonight?"

"I understand, Baqir. Amal, would that be all right with you?" She looked up at him with her brightest smile.

Amal was hooked. "Yes, my princess." He bowed low.

"Oh, that is wonderful. I cannot wait to tell mother. Goodbye, Shar, I will see you later. Bye, Amal, and thank you." With her goodbyes said, and a final kiss on the horse's nose, she whirled and dashed from the stable. Amal stood amazed when Shar turned and calmly walked back into his stall.

He made sure the door was securely latched before joining Baqir in the aisle. "She is truly a special child."

Baqir nodded. "Yes, she is unique. She has always had a way with animals. Just wait until you meet Gigi."

"Gigi?"

"Her sand cat." At Amal's incredulous expression, Baqir laughed. "Yes, you heard right. A sand cat. But that is a story for another day. For now, I can see you are doing well with Shar. By the way, have you given any more thought to staying with us permanently? We could certainly use a man with your skills."

"Yes, I have decided to become a member of this tribe, but please, say nothing to anyone yet. I need to speak to my brother first." His face darkened. Talk of his brother brought back his concerns for Jabari and Kira, as well as Samira. "Saad has much on his mind, and I am worried about him. When he is ready, I will give him the news of my decision, and then I need to give my answer to Sheik Ehsaan," Amal said seriously.

"I understand completely and will not say a word. And I pray Allah will protect your kin. But know, Amal, that I welcome you with open arms. Our tribe is lucky to have found a man such as you."

"Thank you, herdmaster," Amal said, his voice full of emotion.

Baqir nodded. "Now, I must check on the new foals," he said, waving as he walked from the building.

Upon hearing Baqir's heartfelt words, Amal felt a sense of rightness with his decision to stay. Finally, a chance to have a home, and maybe a wife…and children! He was so close to realizing his dream and wanted to run and tell Saad and Samira. But he did not wish to add to their burden and would wait if he needed to. Resolved, he made his way to Ehsaan's house and stopped at the front door to ask a guard for permission to see Saad.

The guard sent a servant to inquire, and it was but a short time before Sheikha Issa showed up and escorted him to the guest room where his brother and his sister-in-law were recovering. As they walked, she explained Saad was fine, but Samira would need more time. Her head was healing, but she wasn't entirely out of danger yet. Issa cautioned him to keep his conversation light.

Amal thanked her profusely and bowed low when she left him at Samira's door. He entered the room to find Saad sitting by Samira's bed. When he saw her awake and smiling, despite her head being swathed in bandages, he felt a surge of emotion and rushed forward. "Samira, I am so glad you are all right!" Then he laid one hand on his brother's shoulder. "I am glad you are both all right." He wiped his eyes unselfconsciously.

"Yes, brother, thanks to Sheik Ehsaan and especially Sheikha Issa, we are both going to be fine." Saad smiled at his wife. "My flower is tougher than she looks."

Samira was very pale, and it was easy to see her face flush with embarrassment at her husband's praise. "Nonsense, my husband. The man was just a poor shot." She tried to laugh and winced with pain.

"Hush, my flower. Do not talk. You must rest."

"Rest, rest, rest. That is all I hear. What I want to hear is about Jabari." She tried to rise, only to have Saad gently hold her down.

"Now Samira, you promised. We are not going to talk about Jabari. I know we will hear something good soon," Saad said, but despite his brave words, Amal could tell Saad was just as anxious but trying to be strong for Samira.

"I am sorry. I should not have come yet," Amal apologized and turned to depart.

"Stop right there, brother. You are not going until we have had a chance to catch up." Saad was adamant and pulled his brother into a nearby chair. "Tell us about Shar."

Amal smiled, realizing Saad needed his help to distract Samira. "Oh, brother, what an incredible horse he is." With shining eyes, Amal told them about Shar's progress and Adara's breakthrough.

As Amal spoke, his love for Shar was written on his face. When he finally paused and assumed a serious expression, Saad asked, "So, you have decided?"

Amal looked down and then back at them both. He had not expected them to ask yet, but they were both watching him intently. With some hesitation, he explained. "As you know, the sheik offered me a chance to stay and become a member of his tribe."

"Yes, of course, but what have you decided?" Saad asked impatiently.

"Well, I want to stay here, but I have not told the sheik yet. I wanted to talk to you both first. Because as much as I love traveling and trading, I am tired of it. I want to start a family, and I want what you two have."

"Well, my brother, I could not be happier for you," Saad said and embraced him. "You have been the best partner I could have ever had, but you deserve to be here too, and I know Samira agrees as well."

Amal looked at her sweet face and saw nothing but loving approval. "Saad, Samira, I can never thank you enough for letting me be a part of your family for so long. But now I need to ask you both a question... what will you do now?"

Saad looked at Samira, and they exchanged a loving glance. "Samira and I have decided that we want a permanent home, too. We want more children, and Jabari…" He paused, and Amal could see the fear cloud his brother's face. Saad took a deep breath before continuing. "Jabari needs a place to grow up."

Amal forced a smile, hiding his trepidation. "Oh, that is wonderful! Have you decided where?" Amal was hoping they would say Ehsaan's.

"We have not, but you will be the first to know when we do. We will try to stay near you, but that's all I can say for now. But enough of all this, pull up a chair and tell us more about what you'll be doing here," Saad said.

Amal shared details of working with Shar and Baqir, and more about his dreams for a home and family. Soon, they became engrossed in reminiscing about their years together, and Amal felt content seeing Samira's peaceful smile. He thanked Allah he was able to distract her from thoughts of what might be happening to Jabari and Kira, at least for a little while.

CHAPTER 46

When Issa heard two gunshots from the pass, she hurried to the front door and down the steps to see two men galloping her way. As soon as she heard their message, she ran to the guest wing.

Saad and Amal rose from their chairs when she rushed into the room. "I have good news!" she said with a smile.

Samira rose on one elbow, her face full of hope, and cried out, "Tell us! Please!"

"They found Jabari! He is alive!"

"But where is he?! And what about Kira?!" Samira exclaimed, trying to rise, and Saad had to hold her down.

Issa hurried to her side. "They found him riding for help on your packhorse. Kira was not with him, but he said she was alive."

With a painful sigh, Samira relaxed. "So, he is here?"

"No, but keep calm. He is leading Sheik Ehsaan and Sheik Jalil, and their men, to find Kira and bring her back. I am sure they will be successful. When we hear more, I will let you know, but for now, you must calm down and rest." Issa helped Samira take a sip of tea containing some sleeping potion. "Drink some tea and relax. I will sit with you while we wait. The men can talk to the messenger to see what else they can learn."

Amal understood what she was asking and, bidding Samira goodbye, ushered Saad from the room.

Issa watched Samira fade, relieved to see her sleeping potion was working. Soon Samira's eyes closed, and she drifted off. Issa took a cool damp cloth and wiped Samira's brow. *Poor woman.* Issa could not imagine having her child in danger. Just the thought of something happening to Adara was beyond her comprehension.

As she sat watching Samira sleep, Issa thought about lost children and remembered her friend Nasira's tragedy when someone kidnapped her baby so many years ago. Akeem sent for Issa to come and stay with his wife, who was out of her mind with grief. Jalil was just fifteen, Akilah was only six, and Lina had not been born yet. Issa arrived to find a house stricken with grief and pain.

Akeem and Jalil spent months and months searching, looking for any clue that would lead them to the baby. Issa feared for Nasira's sanity, but with the loving care of her husband and her son, Nasira began to recover. The best thing that happened was the unexpected miracle of Lina the year following the kidnapping. The new baby helped Nasira moved on.

Issa felt her own tears now remembering those years. *Allah, be merciful. Send Jabari home to his mother.* Wiping her eyes, she called for a servant to sit with Samira and went to check on her own child. There was no telling what Adara was up to, and she hurried to Adara's chambers where she found her playing with Gigi on the floor.

Adara looked up as her mother entered the room. "Is there any news about Jabari? Is he all right?"

"Yes, Adara, Jabari is fine. He has gone with your father to find Kira. He will be home soon enough." Issa knew Adara was concerned for Jabari's safety. She had been awakened the previous night by the commotion when Saad had arrived with Samira, but Issa had glossed over the details and made her go back to bed.

"Oh, thank Allah. I was worried, but if he is with Father and Jalil, he will be fine," she said with complete confidence.

"Yes, I agree. Now tell me, where did you disappear to this morning? You missed the morning meal." Issa wanted to change the subject.

"Oh, Mother! I went to meet Shar, and I fed him a treat," she exclaimed while waving an ostrich feather back and forth in front of her furry pet.

"Adara! Your father told you not to bother Shar until it was safe to be around him." Exasperated, Issa sat down on a chair by her daughter to reprimand her. "What were you thinking?"

"But, Mother, I was asking permission from Baqir and Amal when Shar just came out to meet me by himself. He likes being kissed on the nose." She giggled when Gigi flipped in the air, trying to get the silky feather.

Issa had no words. Watching her daughter playing with her sand cat, yet another animal that Adara had tamed, she still couldn't understand how she did it. Adara had always had a gift for communicating with wild things. It was scary and something they didn't talk about in their house. She was special, having been born late in their marriage. After losing one baby, many years had passed without children, and eventually, they gave up and accepted their fate. Other sheiks would have taken another wife to produce an heir, but not Ehsaan. He loved only her.

They were overwhelmed with joy when Adara was born. She was intelligent, fearless, bold, and beautiful, a true blessing. In their world, women were not considered heirs, but Ehsaan believed that Adara would be the one to lead his tribe. He trained her like a son and vowed to make sure her husband, if she ever chose one, would be worthy of her and her tribe. But as she sat and watched her adorable child playing with Gigi, Issa was having a hard time visualizing her as the leader of their tribe. She was deep in thought when Adara interrupted her.

"Mother, is Jabari going to live with us?"

Startled by such a question, she had to ask, "Adara, what are you talking about?"

"Well, I know Amal is going to be staying, and I think Saad and Samira would like to join him. Will father invite them to join the tribe too?" She stopped playing and looked at her with a serious expression.

"How do you know what Amal is going to do? He has not spoken to your father yet and will not be able to until he returns."

"Oh, I heard him talking to Saad and Samira."

"And just where were you when you heard them talking?" Nasira's eyes narrowed.

Adara froze. "Um… well, I happened to be passing by their room when Amal came in from the stables."

"So, you just happened to be in the guest hall, by the guest rooms, because…?"

Adara averted her eyes and started swishing the feather again.

"Adara…" Nasira waited patiently for what she knew was coming.

Adara sighed and confessed that she had no reason to be there.

"Oh, Adara, what am I going to do with you?" Nasira couldn't help but smile.

Adara looked up tentatively and grinned. "So, Mother, what about Jabari? I would love to have a brother, and Jabari loves horses as much as I do!"

Issa's smile dimmed. "Let us not talk about him right now, at least not until he is safe and back with his parents. And I do not know what his parents will do, and we must not talk about Amal's decision until he has met with your father. Do you understand?"

Adara assumed the same serious expression as her mother and nodded. "Very well, Mother. We can talk about this when the sheik returns." With the matter put to rest, as far as she was concerned, Adara waved the feather faster.

Issa sat for a few more minutes, enjoying being with her daughter without the drama of missing children and wounded friends. But soon enough, she had to return to her duties. With Ehsaan gone, it was her responsibility to rule in his stead, so she hurried to find Fahad. Together, they needed to put a plan in place to protect their kingdom.

The day was advancing, and soon it would be time for the evening meal. With so many gone, including her husband, she decided she would have it in her chambers with Adara. She would also have meals sent to Saad's family, too. And inform the guards Amal was also welcome in the house.

As she passed the front entrance, she noticed the westering sun and worried anew for the safety of her beloved husband. Standing in the golden light, she prayed silently. *Allah, please protect him, help him find Kira, and send them home safely.*

CHAPTER 47

Jalil wasn't the only one who had his own agenda. Jabari had the information he needed to set his own plan in motion. He had a promise to keep and a friend to rescue.

As soon as the men had disappeared, Jabari sprang onto Amber's back and directed her on a circuitous route toward Qadir's house. She wanted to run, but he held her back. "Amber, we're going to find Kira, but we cannot let the others hear us," Jabari said. Amber bobbed her head as if in agreement and slowed her pace. Her ability to walk as quietly as a sand cat amazed him.

Together they made it as close to the rear of the house as he dared while still having cover for Amber. Slipping off her back, he bid her stay while he forged ahead. Even less cover existed from that point forward, but he was small enough to take advantage of the few clumps of bushes scattered about, and the darkness of the night provided the last bit of cover he needed.

Remembering the man near the back of the house, he paused and looked for him, relieved to see he had disappeared. Scared but determined, he walked toward the low wall surrounding the house, controlling his pace to appear as if he was just a member of the tribe going about his business.

When he reached the wall, he heard voices raised in argument coming from the large tent he had seen earlier. He had been so focused on getting to the house that he had forgotten about that tent. Panicking, he scurried forward and, seeing no one about, climbed over into the courtyard, keeping the wall between him and the tent. He was about to continue when he heard a man inside the tent say Kira's name. Acting on instinct, he crept along the wall intent on hearing what was being said.

•   •   •

Hashem couldn't believe his ears. He had been lying there after satisfying himself with Cassie when she mentioned Kira. His good mood disintegrated. "You know Kira?"

"Yes, Hashem, I know her. She's a scheming little brat," Cassie snarled loudly.

"Shh, keep your voice down, Cassie."

Jabari froze. He recognized that evil voice. It was the man who had kidnapped them! *So, his name is Hashem.* He crouched lower and listened as Cassie continued to rant.

"Kira's part of the reason I'm stuck in this god-forsaken part of the world. I told you about the plane crash. She was also on the plane. I left her with that dying horse in the desert. I thought they were both dead," Cassie said petulantly.

"What horse?" Hashem felt the hair on the back of neck rising.

"That golden horse she insisted on saving."

"A golden horse? What was wrong with it? Did it die?" He grabbed her by the shoulders.

"Stop shaking me! How do I know? There was a lot of blood, and it looked dead to me, but Kira was giving it all our water! That's when I decided I'd be better off without her, and I took off. And then you found me. God, I hate that bitch! I'm glad she's going to get what she deserves. Qadir will be summoning her any minute!" Cassie laughed triumphantly. "But I don't want to talk about her. I want to know when you're going to get me out of here!" Cassie said, her voice rising perceptively.

"Shut up, witch! I am getting tired of having to drag you out at night when I want my pleasure. I should be in that house! It should be mine, not my brother's!"

Out in the courtyard, Jabari's ears perked up at the man's angry confession. *Hashem is Qadir's brother?* He stilled his thoughts, waiting to hear more.

"Hashem, did you just say Qadir is your brother?"

Hashem went completely still. *Did I say that aloud?* Now Cassie knew what no one else knew, that Qadir was his brother. Not even First Wife had that information. He hated to think what she would do if found out.

First Wife had ruined his life. Hashem watched her seduce his father, who was captain of the old sheik's guards. The old sheik had never produced a child and when she presented the old sheik with an heir, Qadir, the old sheik made her First Wife, and she became the real power in the house. It was then that she rid herself of the old sheik…and Qadir's real father.

Hashem remembered when his father died. His mother suspected poison, but no one would listen to her. First Wife couldn't risk any loose ends, so she sold her lover's wife and son to slavers. Their life became hell on earth, and he never forgave her and swore he would get his revenge someday. When he had returned years later to worm his way into Qadir's confidence, he was secretly amused that she never figured out he was her lover's other son.

His attention was drawn back to Cassie when she moaned and stretched, and his eyes drifted over her lush, naked body. She was a beautiful creature, and he found himself wanting her again. *Will I always have this strange desire to tame her?* He thought he would eventually steal her away from Qadir and, when he tired of her, sell her to someone far away. She would bring a nice price. But now, as he looked at her flushed face, bright green eyes, and lovely pale skin, he realized he wanted her too much to let her go. She could prove handy in the days ahead, and he needed an ally to help him get rid of First

Wife. In that moment, Hashem chose to share his knowledge with Cassie and take her on as a partner. "Yes, Qadir is my brother."

"How did this happen? Is First Wife your mother?" Excited, Cassie propped up on one elbow, distracting Hashem when her breasts swayed invitingly with her abrupt movement.

"No, that witch is not my mother."

"Then Qadir's father...," she started to ask, but he quickly cut her off.

"Was not the old sheik." He turned on his side to watch her reaction.

"Then you share a father, and Qadir has no legal claim to rule." She abruptly lay back down and stared up at the ceiling of the tent. "But that means neither do you."

"Yes, but no one knows any of this except..."

Cassie rolled back onto her side, her eyes wide. "First Wife! No wonder she makes sure no girl gets pregnant. If a woman gives Qadir an heir, First Wife would lose her position and her power. Unless she can control the child and get rid of the mother and the real father."

Hashem was ever amazed at how smart Cassie was and how quick she figured things out. Yes, she could prove very helpful indeed, but he hoped she wouldn't find out that First Wife didn't know who Hashem really was. It was his greatest secret. Seeking to distract her and feeling his own arousal, he trailed his hand over her soft belly, and he stroked her until she moaned, and her hips began to rise.

But then he had a new thought—he was becoming obsessed with her physically. He suddenly realized he was falling into the same trap as his father and abruptly withdrew his hand. She groaned in frustration and turned toward him, reaching for his manhood, but he pushed her away.

For a second, they shared an intense look, like a lion meeting a tiger at the watering hole, two predators who normally avoided confrontation...unless necessary. She backed off and acted like she understood, but he could see she didn't like it. Rather than get into anymore arguments, he hustled her into her robes. It was time to get her back inside.

•   •   •

When their conversation stopped, Jabari leaned back against the wall in shock. *So many secrets!* If they knew he had heard, his life would be in grave danger. He should take this information back to Ehsaan and Jalil at once. But hearing what Cassie said about Kira, he knew he had little time to save her from whatever was about to happen. Jabari didn't know exactly what Cassie meant when she said Qadir would be summoning Kira, but he knew enough about Qadir that whatever it was, it would not be good. All he knew was he needed to save Kira, like she had saved him.

Reaching deep for the courage he needed, he crept nearer to the house, only to stop again when he heard the same voices, but this time much closer. Pressing low against the wall, his heart pounding, he watched the man he now knew as Hashem, drag Cassie by the hand, climb over the low wall, and hurry to the back of the house, where he stopped between two short columns. A dozen of these columns ran the length of the house, supporting huge clay basins that could be filled with wood and used as torches. And the entire back wall of the house was carved in geometric patterns and arches.

Jabari watched Hashem run his hand down the wall, apparently searching for something. Rising just enough so he could see, he watched in wonder as a small section of the wall swung inward. Hashem shoved Cassie through the opening, and the wall closed behind her. Jabari saw Hashem pause, look around, and walk off in the direction of the stables.

Breathing a sigh of relief, Jabari slid down to catch his breath. He knew what he had to do. Feeling his pocket to make sure he had his dagger, he pulled his robe tight, and gave silent thanks to Allah for having shown him the way.

CHAPTER 48

When Qadir sent word from the feast hall for First Wife to bring the new girl to his chambers, she knew she had very little time. She needed to make sure everything was in place for her plan to work that night.

In a hurry, she wished she could use the little door between her chamber designed to give the ruling sheik access to his sheikha. But Qadir had no use for it and kept it locked, and he had the only key. Another door existed between their chambers—a hidden door, carved like part of the wall panels. It was one of her oldest secrets, known only to herself and the old sheik who she had murdered long ago. Not wanting to risk Qadir finding out about it, she entered his rooms from the main corridor.

Placing an ornate silver goblet and a pitcher of wine on the table nearest the bed, she lit the oil lamp next to it, along with several others around the room. His whips lay on the table—his favorite one and another made from a carved piece of ivory from which dangled long thin strips of leather. She saw his prized gold dagger on a crimson cloth beside the whips. Glancing over at the bed, she saw the cords attached to each bedpost. All his toys were ready.

Noticing how quiet it was, she hurried to his bath chamber to peek inside the musicians' alcove hidden behind elaborate carved panels on the far wall. It was empty. Apparently, Qadir did not want any witnesses tonight. Maybe she might not have to worry about this new foreigner for long—he might dispose of the girl after all. That would make her life easier. She had enough drama dealing with Cassie and Zahra. Satisfied everything else was in order, she returned to her chambers.

Picking up a smaller goblet she had prepared earlier, she scurried to the prisoner holding room to fetch the girl. When she approached the door, the guard looked at her warily. First Wife knew no one liked her, and no one trusted her. Her skill with poisons was well known, and everyone did as she bid if they wanted to see another sunrise.

"I have come for the girl. Assist me." Waiting impatiently for him to unlock the door, she held the goblet tightly. She had prepared an unusually strong potion. A few sips would ensure the success of her plan. As the door swung open, she stepped inside.

•   •   •

Kira jumped when her door creaked open to reveal First Wife. She sat on the bed and gripped the blanket tighter.

"Get up. Your sheik summons you," First Wife said harshly and stepped forward, the goblet in her hand.

"Go away," Kira growled. "I'm not going anywhere with you. And he is not my sheik!"

First Wife took a deep breath, apparently rethinking her approach and her wrinkles transformed into a gentle smile. "Now, now, you must not fight this. Our sheik will have you brought to him, one way or another. It will go better for you if you come peacefully," she said, her voice full of false sympathy.

Kira hesitated, then remembered Fatima's words. Qadir liked it when you fought back. *Well, I'm not going to give him any enjoyment at all.* She slid to the edge of the bed and placed her feet on the floor. Standing, she squared her shoulders and stood stiffly, with her arms tight to her side. It was the bravest thing she'd ever done.

First Wife's smile diminished, and her voice hardened. "That is better. If you are smart, you will survive this." It was an echo of Fatima's words, and Kira paid more attention. "Come, I brought you something to give you courage. Take a sip to steady your nerves." She held out the jeweled goblet.

Kira eyed it suspiciously but seeing the apparent kindness in the old woman's eyes, she complied. She took the goblet and raised it to her lips. Pausing, she sniffed, but not detecting anything other than a sweet smell, she took a cautious sip. Swallowing, she waited, and still tasting nothing but very sweet wine, she took a bigger sip. Feeling stronger and braver, she drained the goblet.

First Wife's eyes widened, but she quickly composed herself. She took Kira's hands, tied them together with a silken cord, and led her from the room. The guard followed closely.

Trying not to be too obvious, Kira paid attention to every detail. Looking left, she saw the hall continue until it disappeared around a corner. When they turned right, she looked ahead and spied a set of gilded doors at the far end. As she walked forward, she scanned the walls, but only saw one other door. The guard who followed them stepped forward to open the gilded doors.

The sight that met her eyes reminded her of an oil painting she had seen in Cairo of an ancient caliph's palace, opulent and mysterious. Kira stopped to gape at the spacious chamber covered in luxurious rugs and hung with black and red silk panels. Polished oil lamps, some sitting on tables, and some suspended from the carved ceiling, cast flickering pools of mellow light on golden silk cushions and gilt-edged tables. On the far wall, she saw an open door and could just make out a pool surrounded by benches, like the harem's bath chamber, only smaller. If she hadn't been so scared, she might have appreciated the scene.

A sudden movement drew her attention to the double doors on the near wall. Qadir stepped into the doorway, wearing nothing but a long black silk robe, his feet and head bare.

Kira took a step backward and found herself flat up against a locked door. First Wife and the guard had slipped away. Swallowing hard, she fought her rising panic and summoned her fighting spirit. She raised her fists, but suddenly everything seemed surreal, and she swayed and shook her head. Her vision was becoming blurry. *What's happening to me?*

·   ·   ·

Qadir watched her like a predator—his eyes unblinking, and his body tensed, ready to strike. Seeing her defiance, his smile grew. *Oh, yes, she is going to fight after all.* When he first saw her enter the room, he thought she had succumbed to her fear. But when she raised her arms higher, the light from the lamps shone through the pale blue silk of her tunic. Seeing the darkened tips of her breasts and the soft curls bunching the silk at the top of her thighs, Qadir was immediately aroused. He continued to look at her body and smiled when he saw her eyes widen and the blood drain from her face.

Kira was more beautiful than he first thought, and Qadir could not help comparing her to Cassie. But where Cassie was lush, Kira was toned. Cassie was fiery, like the desert, and Kira was cool, like an oasis. Staring at the golden hair cascading in soft waves around her body, he couldn't wait to have her, but first he had to punish her.

When he took a step toward her, she anticipated his strike and darted toward the bath chamber. Unfortunately for her, he was closer and faster. He slung her, screaming and struggling, over his shoulder, carried her to his bed and threw her down.

Kira scrambled across the silken covers and tried to get away, but he reached out and grabbed her ankles, jerking her down to the foot of the bed. When he let go of one foot and grabbed the cord from the nearest bedpost, she kicked at his face, and he knocked her leg out of the way. Sitting up, she tried to kick him again. He hated to do what he did next, but only because he wanted her awake for the next part of his plan. He struck her with his fist, and it was enough to knock her down where she lay stunned.

He secured her ankles, spreading her legs wide and grabbed her wrists and tied them to opposite bedposts. She was coming out of her daze and tried to pull loose. He stood back and watched her struggle, laughing aloud as her eyes filled with anger.

Feeling almost drunk at the sight, he turned away, not wanting to rush. While she thrashed and moaned, he walked over to the nearest table and reached for his goblet. Taking a large sip, he swallowed, savoring the cool sweetness. Feeling more in control, he picked up his favorite whip and turned to see her watching him with narrowed eyes. She was panting and trembling but had stopped fighting her bonds.

Moving to the end of the bed, he stared at her body splayed before him. She was stretched so tight that she could barely lift her head, but he could see her eyes watching the whip. "Do you recognize this, Kira?" From her expression, he knew she did. "Perhaps you will enjoy it more than Shar." She was panting harshly now, and her face drained of color.

Chuckling, he laid the whip down on the bed between her legs and leaned forward to stroke the soft flesh of her neck. He could feel the light moisture forming on her skin. When she tried to turn her head away, he grabbed her swollen jaw and jerked it back. She moaned in pain. Holding her jaw with his left hand, he reached with his right and grabbed the top of her tunic. With one harsh pull, he ripped the gossamer silk garment down the front, exposing her body to his view. She cried out once, but bit her lip, trying to remain quiet.

Keeping her in suspense was part of the fun, and he left the bed to take another sip of his wine. Picking up the other whip, knowing she could see what he was doing, he caressed its long tails, but she showed no fear, so he placed it back down. He looked at the dagger with the engraved gold horses—Akeem's dagger. He remembered killing Akeem and felt a pleasurable tingle. When he picked it up, he heard her sharp intake of breath. It would seem she was more afraid of the dagger than the whip.

"Kira, where did you come from? And what were you doing with those traders?" His questions appeared to catch her off guard, but she was still eyeing the dagger. When he moved to the head of the bed, she glared at him, refusing to answer. "You will tell me everything… eventually. If you tell me now, it will go easier for you." He fondled the dagger and tested its edge. She was sweating now, pulling at her restraints, and her breathing increased tenfold.

He placed the dagger on a table by the bed and picked up the medallion he had torn from her neck earlier. "I have one more question that you need to answer." He leaned down and shoved it closed to her face. "Tell me where you got this!" he hissed through clenched teeth, his lips twisted in a snarl.

Kira froze, her eyes locked on the medallion. Then she appeared to wipe all expression from her face. "I don't know what that is," she slurred and glanced away, but she was not fast enough.

He saw her eyes and knew she was keeping something from him. "This is mine, you hear me? Mine! Where did you get this? You had better tell me. It is mine! It should have always been mine! Jalil will never have it now." He slammed it back on the table, walked back to the foot of the bed, and gazed at her body, taking his time and letting his eyes roam.

He saw now she was not only afraid, but ashamed as well. He reached over and stroked her belly, allowing his fingers to slide down until they rested between her legs. She moaned in fear and jerked. Curious, he probed her body and laughed aloud. Watching her face as she cried out, he pushed once just to see her flinch, but then withdrew, being careful to leave the barrier in place. He would take care of that soon.

He was about to stand until he saw the scars on her thigh and stopped to trace them with one long finger. She whimpered and pulled at her restraints. "What happened here, Kira?" He was truly interested. Using four fingers, he slid them down the parallel grooves, and it suddenly came to him—it was the mark of the desert lion. *How did she survive this?* She was full of secrets, and he wanted to know the answers to all of them, but first, he had more important things to do.

Making sure she was watching him, he stood and removed his robe to stand before her, tall and lean, his desire on full display. Her eyes were so wide, he could see the whites. Her pupils dilated, and she breathed rapidly. As she watched, he stroked himself, finding he was already so close. "Kira, are you sure you don't have something to tell me? There is still time."

She only spoke once. "Go. To. Hell."

Filled with a sudden fury at her continued defiance, he grabbed the whip laying on the bed, and she started screaming.

"Kira, you can make all the noise you want. No one will save you tonight." He laughed manically, his lips flecked with spittle, and leaned down until his face was inches from hers. Kira ceased screaming and Qadir saw a decision cross her face.

"Oh, don't stop on my account, Kira. I like it when you scream." He stepped back, and the whip fell open, uncoiling like a dark serpent down his side. "There is so much we have to talk about, but first you must be punished for daring to attack me."

When the first stroke fell, her body arched upward at the stinging pain, but she refused to scream.

He smiled in satisfaction when he saw the rising red welt traveling up her thigh and partway across her firm belly. Waiting until she caught her breath, he added a matching welt on the other thigh. When she remained silent, he dealt her several more blows, and a few broke the skin.

He could see her struggling not to make a noise and was excited when she finally let out a loud scream.

He was having a difficult time controlling his desire now. Qadir was finding her more entertaining than he expected and decided he would not kill her, at least not that night. She would be a welcome distraction until Cassie had borne his child and was available again. Maybe he could even take the both of them at once? Just thinking about that increased his desire, and he threw the horse whip aside and grabbed the shorter one. It would be as painful, but it would not break the skin.

He continued whipping her, but when she quit screaming and stopped responding, he tossed the whip on the floor. Perspiring heavily, he grabbed his goblet and drained it. Feeling strangely lightheaded, he lurched back to the bed and crawled up on top of her, ready to complete the act. He rose on his elbows and looked down into her eyes, which were fully dilated—the turquoise eclipsed by black. And though she was looking directly at him, he knew she wasn't seeing him.

Impatient, and wanting her to be aware so he could watch her reaction as he took her, he slapped her face. But she failed to respond—the fight had gone out of her. His desire peaking, Qadir couldn't wait any longer. But when he raised his hips, he felt a wave of extreme dizziness roll over him. He fell onto her body, his hips pressing down on hers, and slipped into unconsciousness, unaware that she had already passed into darkness.

•   •   •

As they lay together in the dim glow cast by the sputtering oil lamps, neither was aware of the woman watching from next door. First Wife had seen the last few minutes of Kira's punishment through the peephole in her bedchamber, grimly satisfied to see another foreign woman getting what she deserved. As soon as she saw her son collapse, she grabbed a small jar and a rag and entered the room through her secret door. Knowing that no one would dare disturb the sheik when he was taking his pleasure, she had plenty of time to complete her task. When she pushed his naked body off Kira, she was gratified to see her suspicions were correct.

Working quickly, she smeared the contents of the jar on the intimate parts of the girl, careful to spread some between her thighs and on the silk tunic beneath her. She also applied some to her son's body in similar places and replaced his goblet with an identical one that held a few drops of unpolluted wine. Satisfied, she returned to the safety of her own chambers.

Once she had locked the door, she sat down in her front room to catch her breath. No doubt Qadir would fall for her ruse, thus making her plan successful. He was an egotistical fool and would never question the traces of blood on himself and the girl. He would think he had done the deed. Coupled with the damage from his whipping, First Wife knew he would leave the girl alone until she healed. He liked it when they fought back. Smiling, First Wife knew she would have time to get rid of her. It would be simple to make it look like she escaped, and she already knew who would help her with that.

As she prepared to retire, she thought about Cassie. If she failed to get pregnant by Hashem, First Wife would have to secure another to assist in her plans. Then she remembered another woman in the harem—one who had never been summoned. Fatima. Qadir had never shown an interest in her, something that had always puzzled First Wife. Perhaps she could convince him to be intimate with her, at least once. Then she could let Hashem try, but lately she was thinking it was time to get rid of that upstart Hashem. He knew too much and had become a liability she could ill afford. It wouldn't be difficult, and she already had another who would be glad to help her—for a price.

Her head full of schemes, but tired from her work that day, she filled a glass with sweetened tea from the pitcher on her table and took a long refreshing drink. Swallowing, she paused and licked her lips and her brow furrowed. The tea tasted odd. Something wasn't right! With a growing sense of horror, she glanced into her goblet and saw an oily sheen on the surface of the tea. She only had time for one final thought before falling dead to the floor. *Who?*

CHAPTER 49

Fatima paced in her chamber, listening to the faint screams coming from Qadir's quarters. Increasingly agitated and sick to her stomach, she couldn't stop thinking about Kira. Her heart went out to the girl who had shown such courage and spirit, and Fatima felt she could no longer stand by and do nothing. She had become complacent and was ashamed of her own cowardice. But what could she do?

Without a clear plan in mind, she headed to the harem pool. Just as she entered the bath chamber, she saw Zahra disappear through the door to her chambers, but she ignored her—she didn't have time to figure out the puzzle that was Zahra. She was undoubtedly up to no good. Fatima hurried forward through the social chamber to listen at the main doors, but all was quiet. The thought of why was terrifying.

It took Fatima but a second to retrieve the hidden key. Fatima had seen the old crone use it once. It had been a day when one of Qadir's enemies had tried to take over his kingdom, not long after Fatima had been taken from her home. First Wife had rushed into the social room along with several guards to secure the harem, but she had forgotten her keys. Fatima had seen her open a bit of the carved panel on one side of the door and remove the key to lock the main doors. Fatima suspected one other knew of its secret—Zahra.

When she reached the point where several corridors joined, Fatima's heart began to pound. Not far away was the main entrance…and freedom. It was dark, and she knew few guards would be posted. Here was her chance! But remembering the young woman in pale blue, her brilliant eyes filled with tears—and courage—she couldn't do it.

Moving silently, she paused to peek around the corner to the corridor leading to Qadir's chambers, relieved to see it empty. Still unsure of her next move, but having a strange feeling that she must hurry, she tiptoed toward the tall doors at the end of the hall. When she heard a sound from First Wife's chambers, she glanced about frantically. If she was discovered out of the harem, the consequences would be severe. Seeing a small door on the right, closer to Qadir, she ran to it, desperate to hide. Thankfully, the door was unlocked and soon she was running down a narrow hall that ended in another smaller door. It was unlocked as well, and a quick look revealed an empty narrow room. She eased inside and carefully closed the door.

Stopping to catch her breath, Fatima took stock of her surroundings. In the dim light, she saw a few unlit oil lamps hanging from the ceiling and large flat cushions piled along one wall. Light glowed dimly through the carved panels that made up the wall to her left. She tried to peek through the scrollwork, but it was carved in such a manner she could not see much. And then she realized where she was. The room was exactly like the one found in the main hall, which was designed for people to listen without being seen. It was undoubtedly for the musicians who often played for Qadir's pleasure. Based on the stories from the women who had been used by Qadir, she knew his bath chamber was just outside the room, and suddenly, she had a plan.

Hearing nothing but her own breathing, she inched her way along the panel, feeling for what she hoped would be there, just as it was in the main hall viewing chamber. Her heart stopped when she triggered the hidden release. The snap of the metal sounded loud in the quiet chamber, and she froze.

At that moment, Fatima faltered. *What am I doing here? What if he catches me? What will I say?* Praying for strength, she summoned her courage and eased the panel open, but was seized with dread, afraid of what she might see. Trembling, thinking she would be discovered at any moment, she peered out, but the pool area was empty. Soft light streamed from the door leading to Qadir's front chamber. When the silence remained unbroken, she walked around the pool and paused at the door, but seeing the next chamber was also empty, she edged her way to the arched doorway she knew must open to his bedchamber. The light of the burning oil lamps revealed two bodies on the bed—neither one was moving.

Petrified, but determined, she called out, "Sheik?" It was the bravest thing Fatima had ever done. Expecting to hear some response, she hesitated, but when all remained quiet, she swallowed her fear and inched closer to the bed. She was unprepared for the sight of Qadir lying on his back, naked, his private parts on full display and spotted with blood. He breathed deep and appeared to be asleep. Holding her hand to her mouth to muffle her gasp, she hastily averted her eyes and tried to concentrate instead on Kira lying next to him, still tied to the bed.

Long red welts crisscrossed her torso, and a few appeared to be bleeding. Kira's jaw was again marked in purple, which had spread up her cheek, and the swelling was worse than before. She was wearing the remnants of her blue tunic, and Fatima could not help but notice the blood on Kira's thighs. Fighting nausea at what had happened, she knew what she had to do. Her hands shook, and it seemed she'd never get the cords untied, but she managed. While she worked, she watched Kira's face for any sign of consciousness, but she never woke.

One of Kira's arms and one of her legs were pinned beneath Qadir's heavy body and extracting them was difficult. Fatima held her breath in fear that he might awaken, but he was sleeping the sleep of the dead, except the dead didn't snore, she thought with grim amusement. Amazed at herself for making a joke at a time like this, she felt her courage returning. But now she had to get Kira out of the room, and she knew the safest way would be to take her through the musicians' alcove.

Thinking fast, she grabbed a black robe that was draped over a nearby chair and laid it on the floor. As gently as she could, she slid Kira off the bed, dragging her ruined tunic with her, and eased her down onto the robe. Kira stirred but made no noise. *Thank Allah. She is still alive!* Fatima tugged the robe with the girl on it through the bath chamber and into the alcove. Once there, she closed the panel and dragged her through the room, down the empty halls and into the dark, deserted harem bath chamber.

Stopping to catch her breath, Fatima looked up at the skylight, grateful for the stars. They provided just enough light to see by. Knowing that the sun would be up soon, and with it, everyone in the house, including Qadir, Fatima needed Kira to wake up now. Desperate, she could think of only one solution. Tired but determined, she dragged Kira to the pool, removed the torn tunic, and pulled her into the water.

Kira's eyes fluttered, and she cried out. "Amber! Amber, where are you?"

Startled by Kira's cry, but encouraged, Fatima whispered, "Kira, Kira, you must wake up. Come on, Kira, we need to leave now." She waited anxiously to see if her words had reached the girl because she most certainly had been drugged, as had Qadir. Fatima had seen the effects before, and she suspected First Wife had a hand in this, though she could not think why. Grasping at straws, she tried again. "Kira! Wake up! Amber is waiting for you." Fatima had no idea who Amber was or why Kira was calling for her, but she had heard the longing in Kira's voice and knew Amber was someone special to her.

Kira's eyes fluttered, then gradually opened. She squinted up at Fatima's face. "Fatima?" She tried to stand, but floundered, and Fatima held her securely.

"Yes, it is me. Easy, Kira, easy. That's right. Put your feet down. You are in the bathing pool. Stay calm. You will not drown."

Struggling, Kira submerged briefly then jerked upright, coughing and sputtering.

"Shh, you must be quiet," Fatima whispered, helping her up the steps and to a nearby bench. She risked lighting a small oil lamp, praying it would not draw attention, but she needed it to find some towels. Locating a few close by, she draped one around Kira's shoulders, then removed her own wet tunic and dried herself off with another.

When Kira started shaking uncontrollably, Fatima recognized she was in shock. Wrapping Kira's long, wet hair in a towel, Fatima twisted it up on her head and began to dry her body. Kira flinched and moaned, but she allowed Fatima to do what needed to be done.

Finding several tunics discarded earlier by the harem girls, she slipped one on and grabbed another for Kira. "Hold out your arms, Kira. We need to get you dressed. I am taking you away from here."

Kira's vague expression finally cleared, and her eyes filled with hope. "Away? You can get me out of here?"

"Yes, but we have very little time left. We must be outside before the sun rises. We must get you dressed," Fatima said as she pulled the wet towel from Kira's head. Kira dutifully raised her arms, allowing Fatima to slip a dark blue tunic over her head. "I cannot do much with your hair at the moment, but I can braid it and tie it back." Seeing Kira nod, Fatima quickly finished the task.

"What is your plan, Fatima?"

"I know of a way out. It leads into the mountains, but I do not know where to go from there. And we have no food or water, and no time to find any before we must leave." Fatima hesitated, realizing how little thought she had given to what they would do if they made it out of the house.

But when she looked into Kira's eyes, she saw fear and trauma but also determination and strength, and Fatima felt her own courage return.

Kira smiled grimly at Fatima. "If you can get us out of here, I can take care of the rest."

Fatima tried unsuccessfully to hide her skepticism, and Kira must have noticed because she added, "Trust me, Fatima. We can do this. Just show me how to get out of here."

Fatima nodded, but as she led Kira across the room, Kira stopped by the torn blue silk on the floor. She picked it up and stared at the red stain halfway down.

Fatima took it from her, crumpled it up, and shoved it into her pocket. "You don't need to see that." She couldn't explain why she wanted to save Kira's ruined tunic, but it did not seem right to leave the evidence of what Qadir had done to her behind for others to see, especially Cassie.

"What is that? Why don't you want me to see it?"

"Kira, it is nothing. Things happen, things we do not plan. It is not your fault."

"What things, Fatima? You need to explain because I'm not going anywhere until you do."

Fatima had never known a woman like Kira, and she stared at the girl, awed by her bravery. In her heart, she knew Kira deserved to know and also knew that if anyone could handle the truth, it was Kira. She would find out later anyway. *Allah forbid if there is a child!*

"Kira, you do know what a virgin is, do you not?"

"Yes," Kira said warily.

"Well, you were a virgin, but you are not anymore. That is your blood on the tunic. A woman always bleeds with her first man." Fatima hated to be the one to tell her, and she felt tears in her eyes at the horrified expression washing over Kira's face.

"My blood?" She looked down at her body as if seeking confirmation.

"Yes, when I found you and Qadir, the evidence of what he had done was on you, on him, and on your tunic." When Kira wavered, Fatima had to ease her back onto the bench.

"I don't remember much. Not after the whip," Kira said, then suddenly she stiffened, and her eyes widened. "Oh my God! No, no, no, not him! Not Qadir!" Overcome, she leaned over and lost the entire contents of her stomach.

Luckily, Fatima was sitting next to her and not standing in front of her. Holding Kira by the shoulders until she had nothing left to throw up, Fatima grabbed one of the discarded wet towels and wiped Kira's face, before dropping it on the floor, effectively covering the mess. *The servants can figure this out tomorrow.* Aware time was growing short, she pulled Kira to her feet. Still reeling from having heard that Qadir had violated her, Kira staggered and tried to sit back down.

Fatima was having none of it. "Kira, we must go now! Stop feeling sorry for yourself. You can do that later. If we stay here any longer, neither of us will live long enough to regret this night. Now, come on!" She half-dragged Kira from the room, and together they stumbled down the hall, passing Cassie's room. Intent on escape, neither of them heard the door opening behind them.

At the end of the hall, Fatima stopped at the door to a room used for storage. Kira huddled close behind her. They slipped inside and Fatima grabbed two of the black robes and headwraps laying on top of a trunk. It took but a minute for them to don the dark garments. She also found a pair of durable slippers, and luckily, they fit Kira.

Walking to the back of the room, Fatima pulled aside an ancient tapestry exposing a section of block wall. She reached down by the floor and a sharp click sounded. Kira's eyes widened in amazement as a small section of wall swung inward, but before she could marvel at the ingenious bit of engineering, Fatima hustled her through the door, following close behind. They found themselves standing outside. Behind them was the house, and in front of them was a slim berobed figure, brandishing a dagger.

Fatima tried to step in front of Kira, ready to do battle, but several things happened at once. Gunshots rang out in the distance, causing them to jump. More gunshots rang out from around the house, and they heard men shouting. The faint glow of the sun in the east was threatening the darkness, and the two girls rushed forward, knocking down the figure blocking their way.

As she ran, Fatima heard growing thunder and looked up to see riderless horses racing around the corner of the house. More gunshots rang out and, eager to get as far away as they could, the girls struggled over a low wall and raced for the hills they could see in the distance.

Running as if being chased by a desert lion, Fatima quickly outpaced Kira, only slowing when she realized she was leaving the wounded girl behind. She turned to run back and felt alarm when she saw the person who had surprised them at the door grabbing Kira from behind, causing them both fell to the ground.

•   •   •

While Kira struggled with her unknown assailant, Qadir was regaining consciousness. His mind filled with inky darkness until two points of light appeared, growing larger and larger, becoming luminescent pools of blue-green that came closer and closer until he felt like he was being submerged in their depths. When he was suddenly surrounded by silken, silvery-gold strands waving around him, he reached out a hand to touch them, only to see them waver and disappear like a mirage in the sand.

Gasping at the pain in his head, he opened his eyes and struggled to focus. He moved his head gingerly, looking around, trying to determine where he was. As his senses returned, he felt the soft silk beneath him and knew he was naked, and when his sight sharpened, he realized he was in his bed... alone.

Memories of the evening came rushing back then, and he remembered Kira's pale body and could feel the whip in his hand and the pleasure of seeing the marks on her thighs and breasts. He tried to rise, but his arms and legs were like jelly, and his stomach roiled. Closing his eyes, he fell back with a groan. Licking his dry lips, he tasted a strange bitterness and gasped again, this time in anger, when he recognized the taste. *Someone drugged me!*

Hearing a shuffling noise, his eyes flew open to see a familiar face leaning over him. He attempted to call out but felt a tearing pain in his neck, and his shout turned into an ominous gurgle. Staring upward into a pair of evil eyes, he tried to speak, but only managed a garbled whisper. "You!" His last sight was of a sneering smile, and the last thing he heard was the satisfied laughter that faded away as his killer left the room.

CHAPTER 50

When Cassie had heard faint screaming coming from the sheik's rooms, part of her cringed, but part of her relished the idea that Kira was being punished. That girl deserved to be brought down a notch, and what better way than to lose her virginity to a man like Qadir. She figured he would have his hands full tonight because Kira was a real fighter. So, it came as a surprise when the screams abruptly stopped, and even she was chilled by the thought of why.

When she heard a noise in the hall, she rose, thinking it was First Wife finally coming to bring her nightly drink and to lock her in after her visit to Hashem. Standing near her door, she listened, but when no one approached, she sat down by her table, drumming her fingers on the lacquered top, letting her thoughts drift to her evening with Hashem. She fully intended to use his secret to her advantage. *How can I make this work to my benefit? How can we get rid of First Wife?*

When she heard approaching footsteps, she rose, thinking the old woman had finally come, until they passed by her door without stopping. That got her attention. Unable to control her curiosity, she padded silently to her door and eased it open. The click of the handle echoed loudly, and she looked into the hall in time to see two women disappearing into the storeroom. Dressed in silk tunics, they were obviously harem girls. Their backs were to her, and the dim light in the hall made identification impossible.

Determined to find out what was going on and hoping to gain information she could use to her advantage, she waited a few minutes before darting to the storeroom door. But she was too late. The room was empty, and the hidden door was closed. *Who were they, and where were they going?*

Torn between wanting to expose them, but worried that First Wife would find her out of her room, she decided it wasn't worth the risk. The women would have to return the same way, and she would listen for them from her room. As she turned to leave, she caught herself as she slipped, and looking down, was puzzled to see wet footprints. Another mystery she didn't have time to solve. Worried now, knowing First Wife might show up at any minute, Cassie dashed back to her room.

Just as she closed her door, she heard distant gunshots, but assumed it was a figment of her imagination, or perhaps a tribesman guarding the herd. What else could it be? But then she heard more gunshots, this time closer. *What is going on?* Alarmed and unable to concentrate, she snuck from her room intent on investigating once more.

She was on her way to the bath chamber when she heard gunshots again. Someone must be coming in the pass, she thought as she entered the room. A small oil lamp sputtered on a bench across the room, and she saw a pile of towels on the floor in front of another bench. The feeble light revealed several puddles of water by the steps to the pool. *Was someone taking a bath in the middle of the night?* Cassie only knew of one person who was allowed to do that. Walking over to the towels, she reached to pick one up but hastily backed away, gagging at the horrible smell. Someone had been very sick here recently. She shook her head, thinking the night was getting stranger and stranger.

Disgusted, she crept into the social room. It was empty, so she continued over to the main doors leading out of the harem wing. Detecting no sound, she mentally crossed her fingers and turned the handle, shocked to find it unlocked. Heart pounding, she opened it and waited, listening. She knew she was risking punishment if she got caught, but she could not help herself. She leaned out to glance down the long hallway, but it was empty. *Where is everyone?*

Gambling on the fact she was known as Qadir's favorite and the mother of his future heir, she squared her shoulders and walked through the doors as if she had every right to be in this part of the house. At the next corridor, she turned right, intending to make her way to Qadir's chambers. She expected to see at least one guard, but again, no one was in sight.

Emboldened, she continued walking and stopped by the first door on the left. It was open, and she looked inside to see an empty room with a small bed and shivered as the cold night wind moaned through the window high on one wall. Hashem had mentioned that Kira was being kept in a small room near Qadir. This must be it, she thought, but where was she? Qadir never kept a woman in his room after he was done with her. Even Cassie was not granted that honor. Cassie's temper flared. *Kira must still be with him!*

Growing angrier by the minute, she stalked past a small door on the right and down to the next door, the last one before reaching the tall ornate doors of Qadir's chambers. Remembering the one time she had been through this door, she shuddered. First Wife's chambers. It had given her the creeps, seeing the dry withered plants hanging over the long scarred worktable, its surface covered with twisted glass bottles and crusted ceramic jars. It had smelled strange too.

Stopping at the door, she listened intently, but all was quiet—too quiet. She felt something touch her neck, like an icy breath, and she felt a trickle of fear. Feeling exposed, she looked at Qadir's doors and knew he had to be in there with Kira, but she couldn't understand why it was so quiet. *Maybe they're asleep? But how can that be? He never sleeps with any woman. Dare I interrupt?* Her mind searched for an excuse, and suddenly she had it. *He will want to know about the strange things that have been going on tonight, especially the harem girls sneaking outside.* Her mind made up, she walked toward the gilded doors but stopped in her tracks when she heard more gunshots. *Are they closer?* Nervous, she glanced once behind her and then dashed forward. Pressing her ear to one door, she could not detect any sound. Taking a deep breath, she tried the handle, and finding it unlocked, she opened it slowly to see a few lamps were lit, but the room was empty.

Stepping inside, Cassie looked across the room and saw his bath chamber was dark. Encouraged by the continued silence, she stepped farther into the room and looked through the open doors to his bedchamber. By the light of the lamps, she could make out the shape of his body on one side of the bed. There was no sign of Kira.

She whispered his name, but he did not stir. Recognizing the whips on the floor and the cords dangling from the bedposts, she shivered and whispered his name louder, "Qadir?" When he still failed to move, she edged closer, and her hand flew to her mouth. She froze. Blood was everywhere—sprayed across the headboard, pooled on his chest, and dripping down the side of the bed. His eyes were open, and his lips set in a frozen grimace. Seeing the bloody handle of a large dagger protruding from his chest and his throat sliced open from ear to ear, she gagged and turned away from the gruesome sight to stumble back into his front room.

Time seemed to slow, and she leaned with her hands braced on his table, her eyes clenched shut, breathing heavily and swallowing convulsively. She didn't know how long she had been standing there when loud gunshots echoing down the hall startled her. Her eyes flew open, and she heard men yelling, the noise drifting through the carved shutters of a window high on the wall. Panicking, she looked for a way to escape. Hearing the increasing noise outside in the corridor, she ran back into the bedchamber, frantically scanning the room for a door or a place to hide.

Then she remembered the intricate scrollwork on the wall in his bath chamber. How many times had she lain on that bed listening to the horrible desert music coming from the alcove hidden behind that wall while Qadir tormented her? *The musicians had to get in and out somehow! Maybe there's a way in!* But before she could flee, she heard the sound of someone entering the front room. She panicked and scrambled into the corner to crouch behind a massive ceramic pot overflowing with lush greenery. Holding her breath, she waited to see who had dared to enter the sheik's chambers and prayed it wasn't First Wife.

CHAPTER 51

Kira was running as fast as her pain would allow and was totally taken by surprise when she felt someone grab her from behind. She cried out in pain when they both fell to the ground. Moaning, she struggled, but when she turned to face her attacker, she cried out in joy. "Jabari! Is it really you?" No one she knew had eyes like that.

"Oh Kira, I cannot believe I found you. Jalil will be so proud of me," Jabari exclaimed.

"Jalil? Jalil is with you?"

"Yes, Jalil and Ehsaan, and all their men, too. We are here to rescue you!" He scrambled to his feet and was helping her to stand when Fatima ran up.

"Let go of her!" Fatima yelled at Jabari and grabbed Kira's hand, tugging her toward the hills. "Kira, hurry. We must go now."

"Wait!" Jabari was still holding Kira's other hand and pulled back just as hard. "Who are you?"

Kira moaned out loud at the pain from their rough handling. "Please stop, both of you," she gasped.

"Let go of her, boy," Fatima yelled. "She is hurt!" Fatima ceased tugging but held Kira's hand tightly.

"Fatima, it is okay. This is my brother."

Jabari ignored Fatima's look of disbelief but dropped Kira's hand at once. "Kira, are you hurt? I did not mean to cause you any pain," Jabari said, his voice fraught with worry.

Kira rushed to put Jabari at ease. "Jabari, listen to me. I will be all right, but I can't walk much farther."

"Oh Kira, you will not have to walk. We have someone here who can help." He gave a low whistle and waited.

A moment later, Kira heard hoofbeats and gasped aloud when she saw her beloved Amber galloping toward them. Fatima stumbled backwards, obviously afraid of the charging horse.

When Amber slid to a stop, Kira threw her arms around the horse's neck and cried, "Oh Amber, I was afraid I would never see you again."

Jabari tugged on her sleeve. "Kira, we must go. Qadir's men will be searching for you."

Kira wiped her face and sniffed loudly. "But Jabari, how are we going to get out of here? Amber cannot carry all of us."

Before Jabari could answer, Fatima cut him off. "I am not riding a horse. I have never ridden a horse. Kira, it is simple. You will ride the horse. I will run." With that, she dashed toward the hills.

Kira called to her, "Wait. Wait. Come back, Fatima!" She grabbed Jabari by the arm. "We need to stop her."

Dumbstruck, Jabari stared at the departing woman. "Kira, we cannot. We need to go."

"We have to help her!" Kira was desperate. If only she could think of a solution.

Amber's loud neigh startled them both, and they heard another set of hoofbeats approaching. A small chestnut mare cantered up, her reins dragging and her saddle empty, and stopped beside Amber. Jabari immediately turned to Kira and motioned for her to put her foot in his clasped hands. Kira tried not to think of the painful ride ahead and climbed upon Amber. Jabari snatched the reins of the chestnut mare and sprang into the saddle. His horse danced nervously, but he easily controlled her, reminding Kira of Jalil.

Together they galloped off to catch up with Fatima and Jabari circled in front of her, forcing her to stop.

Panting, Fatima tried to catch her breath as she looked up at the two riders. "What are you doing?"

"We are saving you." Kira pointed to Jabari's horse.

Fatima looked at the horse and at Jabari. "I do not think that this is going to work."

"Nonsense," Jabari said, slipping his foot from the stirrup. He scooted backwards, giving her the saddle, and extended his hand.

Fatima looked at his hand and looked back at Qadir's house. The dark of night was losing its battle with the dawn, and they could all see riders circling the house. Squaring her shoulders, Fatima grasped his hand and climbed up awkwardly in front of him. "How will I stay on?" The quiver in her voice gave away her fear.

"I will hold you." Jabari grasped the reins in one hand and wrapped one arm around her waist.

Fatima stiffened at his touch then relaxed. "Thank you, Jabari. I will try to stay on," she said, griping her knees and holding tightly to the front of the saddle.

As Kira watched Jabari take charge of Fatima, she was filled with pride. This was no boy playing with magic tricks. This was a young man, strong and brave. She was staring at his handsome profile when he glanced at her with a smile and a wink of a silver eye.

"Are you ready, Kira?" he said.

If she wasn't so racked with pain, she would have laughed aloud. But she didn't have to answer. Amber was already on the move. As the two horses raced to safety, Kira held on and prayed to God for His help.

CHAPTER 52

Jalil ran inside the house with only one thing on his mind—Kira. According to Faris, Qadir's chambers were down the left corridor and he raced forward. The ornate doors were not locked, and he kicked them open without a thought.

"Kira!" he yelled as he strode into the room. "Where are you?" Seeing the room was empty, he dashed into the bed chamber where his eyes were drawn to the body on the bed. It was Qadir and even from where he stood, Jalil could see the hilt of a dagger protruding from Qadir's chest. Before he could investigate, he heard a rustling behind him, and turned, bloody sword raised, ready to do battle, only to see the beautiful redheaded woman who had danced at the pre-race meeting.

She walked slowly forward and stopped at the end of the bed. "Jalil." Her voice was husky, and he felt her eyes on his body.

"You!" he exclaimed harshly. "Did you do this?" He pointed at Qadir.

"Wha... What? Of course, I didn't. I heard Kira's screams and was coming to help her," she said, her face showing nothing but deep concern.

"Who are you, and where is she?" Jalil shouted at her.

"I'm Cassie. And I don't know where Kira is. Qadir summoned her, and from what I can see, he was doing what he always does with women." She glanced at the horsewhip on the floor. "Poor Kira. He must have used it on her. It's what he liked to do, you know," she continued, looking up into his eyes. "I heard he was going to punish her for making a fool of him at the race." Shaking her head, she lifted the cord hanging from the nearest bedpost. "But it looks like she escaped. She was always clever that way. Probably her Indian blood."

Jalil didn't recognize the word "Indian," but he did recognize the whip. It was the same one Qadir used on Shar after the race, and the sight of it sickened him. Staring at the cords made him feel worse. But as he watched her face closely, Jalil saw her mask slip and thought her voice had a touch of contempt. Before he could question her further, he saw her looking down at the sheets.

"I bet Kira killed him. After what he did to her, I wouldn't blame her. First the whip, and then…" she looked pointedly at Qadir's exposed manhood, still showing streaks of red, but quickly looked away as if embarrassed by the sight.

Jalil blanched. He knew immediately what the woman was suggesting. It was as he had feared—Qadir had used Kira and taken her against her will. The thought of what Kira must have gone through filled him with anger. But he didn't believe Kira killed Qadir. Somehow, he knew she couldn't have done such a cold-blooded act, but he wasn't going to tell Cassie that. Instead, he stood up for Kira.

"If she killed him, then good for her. I only wish I could have been the one to cut his throat." He stepped closer to the side of the bed and smiled grimly, seeing Qadir's torn throat and the blood-covered dagger buried in his chest. The dead sheik's eyes bulged, and his lips were stretched wide as if he had died screaming. It looked like Qadir had suffered and Jalil couldn't help but feel a small curl of satisfaction.

Dismissing the redhead, and anxious to continue his search for Kira, he turned to leave but felt his boot tangle in something on the rug. Looking down, he saw a leather cord and lifted it up. When he saw the gold disk dangling from it, he gasped and stumbled back against the wall, stunned. As he steadied himself with one hand, he studied the disk by the light of the oil lamp, watching it turn slowly, and immediately recognized the turquoise stones and sparkling golden gems. Tears filled his eyes when he realized exactly what he was holding. *My father's medallion!* He looked at Qadir, then back at the disk. *Is this the man who murdered my father?* When he looked back at the dead sheik, Jalil was filled with fury.

Cassie's whine interrupted his thoughts. "What's the big deal? It's just that old medallion of Kira's." She stood with her hands on her hips, her face filled with disdain.

In a flash, he was across the room and grabbed her arm. "What do you mean, Kira's medallion?" he ground out, his voice deep and fierce.

Cassie paled. "Let go, Jalil. What is wrong with you? Kira's been wearing that thing ever since the plane crash. It was her father's. He bought it in Cairo. When he died in the crash, she took it." Cassie pulled free and shrunk away from him.

Jalil's head was spinning. *What is she talking about? What plane crash? How did my father's medallion get to Cairo?* Completely confused, he needed time to sort this out, but he knew this was not the time. Jalil needed to gather his men and return to meet up with Ehsaan. It was clear Kira had escaped, and he felt certain she was no longer here. Somehow, he knew she would not have stayed in the house if she could get away. And it was time for him to do the same. Slipping the leather cord over his head, he tucked the medallion inside his tunic, where it could lie close to his heart. Taking one last, hard look at Qadir, he ran out of the chamber, leaving Cassie without a backwards glance.

Dashing through the front doors and down the steps, he leaped over dead bodies, pulling his sword as he ran. Faris was fighting off two guards, and Jalil threw himself into the fray. Together they dispatched both of Qadir's men, then looked around for any other foes, but the compound was empty. Jalil paused to wipe his blade clean on the robe of one of the fallen men.

It was Faris who spoke first. "Did you see Qadir?" He also bent to clean his blade, but his head flew up at Jalil's answer.

"Yes. He is dead."

"And the girl?"

"She is gone. I feel she is no longer here, but don't ask me how I know."

"I did not see any woman leave through this door, but there are hidden exits in this house. Maybe she found one of those," Faris said hopefully.

"Perhaps, but we must go." Jalil bolted in the direction of their camp. Faris followed, and they ran toward the place where they had left their horses. Jalil was relieved to hear a familiar neigh and see Mirage come running, his silver mane streaming in the wind, trailed by Faris's horse. Mirage slowed and Jalil ran alongside and swung up into the saddle. Faris mounted his horse in like fashion, and the two men galloped off to find Ehsaan.

CHAPTER 53

When Jalil left, Cassie was stunned that he had not offered to take her with him. Furious, she dashed after him. As she ran down the hall, she noticed that someone had kicked in the door to First Wife's chambers, and she stopped to look inside. She was stunned to see the old woman's body on the floor, her unseeing eyes frozen in death, and a silver goblet by her side. Chilled by the sight, she dashed toward the front door, intent on escaping, but the sound of fighting caused her to run to the harem's quarters instead.

The bath chamber was in total chaos. Servants ran through the room, and harem girls huddled in groups, crying and whining. She couldn't help but notice the one calm figure sitting on a bench by the pool. It was that bitch Zahra, sipping a drink and smiling. When their eyes met, Zahra laughed aloud. Unnerved, Cassie ran on to her room.

Once safely inside, she tied her bag of valuables to her waist, then grabbed a spare tunic and a pair of sturdy slippers, which she rolled up in a light blanket, along with the bag of treats. Clutching her bundle, she headed to the storeroom and soon she was stepping outside into the growing light. The back of the house was deserted, and she ignored Hashem's tent, climbed over the low wall, and ran toward the hills without looking back.

Exhilarated to be free, she stumbled when she heard hoofbeats growing closer. Before she could turn to see who was following her, she was grabbed from behind, lifted in the air, and flung over the front of a saddle. She howled in fury when she heard the familiar voice.

"Just where do you think you are going, witch?"

"Put me down, you barbarian!" Cassie screamed at Hashem.

"Oh, no, witch. We have business to attend to, and I am going to need your help. So quit yelling unless you want someone to kill us both."

The saddle dug into her hips and her breasts were pressed against his hard leg as she struggled to get free. "Stop this horse and put me down. Now!" she yelled louder.

Hashem chuckled and slowed his horse to a walk. Surprising her, he dumped Cassie on the ground where she landed squarely on her soft behind.

"Ow!" she screeched and scrambled to her feet, in a full-blown temper and shaking with rage.

He circled his horse around and stopped in front of her, grinning, and burst out laughing.

"What are you laughing at?" she hissed, rubbing her abused posterior.

"Why you, of course. Here we are, trying to avoid being killed by Jalil's men, and you are doing everything in your power to get their attention." He sat calmly on his horse with arms crossed and one leg thrown over the front of the saddle.

She straightened her robes and checked to make sure her bag of treasures was still tied to her waist. Her eyes narrowed as the heat of her rage hardened into icy anger. "How do you know those are Jalil's men?"

"It was not hard to figure that out. But what I would like to know is, did Jalil rescue Kira?"

Cassie thought back to her earlier confrontation with Jalil. "No, I am pretty sure she ran away before he got there."

"Did you see her?" Hashem slid off his horse and stepped closer.

"I heard her screaming, so I know she was with Qadir, but when I got to his room, she was gone."

"And what did Qadir say?" He raised an eyebrow, waiting for her reply.

"You mean, you don't know?"

"Know what, Cassie?" he said without emotion.

"He's dead."

His eyes widened, and he approached her. "Dead? How did it happen? Did you see who did it?"

"I don't know how it happened or who did it. When I got to his room, he was already dead. And then Jalil came in."

"Did he see you? Did you talk to him? What did you tell him?" He grabbed her by the shoulders as he spoke.

"Hey, that hurts. Let me go, Hashem. Yes, I spoke to him. He said he was glad Qadir was dead, and he was looking for Kira. That's all he talked about until he found that stupid medallion. Then he ran out."

"The medallion? Jalil found the medallion?" He shook her hard.

Cassie had finally had enough, and jerking out of his grasp, she started running again. Cursing loudly, he jumped back on his horse and chased her down. This time, he jerked her onto his lap and rode back to the house, not stopping until he reached the front steps where he slid off, pulling Cassie with him. She was still fighting, but seeing all the dead bodies, she stilled and averted her eyes.

Hashem stomped forward, dragging her along, and it was all she could do to keep up. When he turned toward the sheik's quarters, she knew what he wanted to see. He paused at First Wife's chambers. The door was ajar, and he pushed it open with his boot, his free hand resting on the hilt of his sword. When he saw the old woman on the floor, he burst out laughing. He looked at Cassie. "Did you do this?"

"No, you idiot, of course not. I'm not a murderer like you."

He stared hard at her and gripped her chin. "You need to watch your words, Cassie. I am no idiot, and you will do well to remember that."

Cassie jerked free of his hand and pointed to the goblet on the floor by the woman's hand. "I don't know how to make any poison...yet..." she said with narrowed eyes.

Puzzled, he looked at the goblet and then gave her an inscrutable look. She maintained eye contact, refusing to look away. Finally, he continued to Qadir's chambers, still holding her arm. Once they entered his chambers, he stopped by the table in the front room, shoved her into a chair, and released her with a warning. "Do not run away, my pet. We still need to talk." He waited until she nodded before walking into Qadir's bedchamber.

Curious, Cassie rose and followed him, but stopped in the doorway to see what he would do.

Hashem walked to the side of the bed and stared down at his half-brother. "All the years of living in your shadow, *brother*, being your henchman, having to serve at your beck and call, while at the same time having First Wife's threats hanging over me." He laughed and spat on the body. "All gone in a single night." He leaned over Qadir and took a long look. "I want to remember this forever."

She watched him pick up one of Qadir's hands and remove a ring from a finger. She winced when he grasped the dagger sticking out of Qadir's chest, slowly pulled it out, and casually wiped the blood off using the silk panel hanging from the corner of the bed. He held the dagger up to the light and turned it back and forth. Now that it was clean, Cassie thought it looked like one Qadir had used to threaten her on several occasions. She remembered seeing the blue stones and yellow gems embedded in the hilt and the pattern of running horses inscribed on its blade.

When Hashem turned to face her, she let out a gasp at the look on his face. She had seen him in many moods over the past months and thought she was familiar with all his expressions, but she had never seen him like this. His eyes had hardened into flashing chips of black ice, and his lips were curled in a grim smile. He looked satisfied and triumphant, and she saw Qadir's massive gold ring, inlaid with black onyx and blood red rubies, on his finger. She had a bad feeling when he picked up Qadir's favorite whip, coiled it tightly, and tied it to his waist. He spied her where she stood in the doorway, and she swallowed hard at his next words.

"Bow before your sheik, Cassie."

Seeing him like this, Cassie was horrified, but not surprised, especially now that she knew about his parentage. A million thoughts flew through her head, but foremost was the thought that this could work to her advantage. Recovering quickly, she bowed to him. "My sheik. How can I be of service?"

"Rise, Cassie. I am glad to see you have come to your senses. Now, there is much to do. We need to let the world know that Qadir has been murdered and that Sheik Jalil is responsible. He must pay for his crime."

Cassie reeled at this pronouncement when she realized what he was planning. She was the witness that Hashem could use to destroy Jalil. That was both a good and bad thing, depending on how she played it. She might be able to use it against him, but right now, Cassie wasn't going to take any chances with this new Hashem. She would do whatever he asked until she had another plan. "What do we need to do, my sheik?"

He gave her a sinister smile. "We will find one of the guards. Surely, they are not all dead. We will tell him of Jalil's treachery and let him see Qadir's body. Then I will round up the rest of the men and let them know Qadir is dead and that I am the rightful successor."

"How do you know they will believe you?"

His smile grew, and he held up Qadir's arm and pointed to the strange purple mark on his upper arm.

"So?" Cassie had seen it many times during her sessions with Qadir. Puzzled, she stared at him until he slid his own sleeve up, revealing a similar mark.

"Oh!" Cassie had never seen Hashem completely naked, and she grinned slyly as all the pieces fell in place. *A birthmark!*

He smiled evilly. "Yes, now you understand. My father had one as well. Now, come, we have work to do." He strode from the room and Cassie followed without protest, inwardly gloating. Finally, she just might make it out of this hellhole.

CHAPTER 54

When Jalil and Faris returned to their temporary camp, Jalil was relieved to find that every man had been accounted for, and only a few would require the skills of a healer. Unfortunately, no one had seen Kira. Eager to find her, Jalil hurriedly reported the story of what he had found inside the house.

Ehsaan listened patiently, then touched his friend on the shoulder. "Jalil, I am sorry, but we must go. Qadir is dead, and his men will think we did it and will be looking for us."

"No, Ehsaan. I cannot give up on Kira. She is still in the area, I am sure of it. You get everyone to safety. I will stay and find her."

"I understand, but you do not know what you will find."

"That is true, but I must try."

Ehsaan nodded and signaled to his men to mount up and prepare to leave.

Jalil was giving final orders to his men when he realized someone was missing. "Where is Jabari?"

Ehsaan looked around with alarm. "He was supposed to stay here. Did anyone see him at the house?"

Everyone looked confused, and when no one could shed light on the missing boy, Jalil turned to Ehsaan. "I will find him, too."

Ehsaan simply nodded and said, "Be careful, my friend."

Jalil was preparing to mount Mirage when one of the men gave a shout and pointed in the direction of the compound. Two horses were approaching at a steady canter. The lead horse carried one rider, and the second bore two.

To Ehsaan's relief and Jalil's joy, Jabari rode up with a woman mounted in front of him.

Ehsaan chuckled heartily. "Leave it to Jabari the Magnificent to pull a pretty woman out of thin air."

Everyone laughed except Jalil, who was staring at the other horse, who bore a small figure swathed in a black robe and headwrap. The person was having trouble sitting erect. When the horse stopped close by, the growing light drew Jalil's attention to its coat. Streaks of shining gold peeked through smears of brown, and curious, he stepped closer, but he was startled by a soft moan. Glancing up at the rider, he was mesmerized by a pair of pain-filled blue-green eyes. She smiled weakly and promptly fainted. Jalil caught her as she fell and knelt with her in his arms.

Ehsaan dismounted and ran to his side. "It is Kira, but what is wrong with her?"

Jalil felt for a pulse at her neck and sighed with relief. "She has a pulse, though it is faint."

The woman with Jabari quickly explained. "She was severely beaten. She needs help."

Galvanized by her words, Jalil struggled upright with Kira in his arms and carried her to Mirage. Ehsaan held her until Jalil was in the saddle and handed her up to him. Jalil wrapped one long arm around her, holding her in his lap, and grabbed Mirage's reins with his free hand.

When Amber showed increasing signs of increasing agitation, Jalil suggested someone put her on a lead rope. But Jabari dismissed the idea at once and addressed the assembled men. "There is no need for that. This is Kira's horse, Amber, and she will follow us. Fatima will ride with me."

No one said a word as, apparently, Jabari had already decided what would happen. Even Jalil, as concerned as he was about Kira, had to smile. *That boy. What is it about that boy?*

With a wave of his hand, Ehsaan turned to lead the men back to the hidden pass. They maintained a steady pace, and there was no evidence of pursuit. Jalil glanced back to check on Jabari. The boy was doing well and appeared to be at ease, riding behind the slight woman. *What did he call her? Oh, yes, Fatima.* She was a brave little thing and holding her own, but she had a death grip on the saddle, and he expected she would need Issa's services by the time they returned to Ehsaan's.. Undoubtedly, she would be sore.

Occasionally Kira would stir and moan softly, but she didn't wake. Concerned, Jalil was careful to pick the smoothest path. Carrying her was not straining Mirage, and Jalil found she felt comfortable in his arms—almost as if she belonged. But his heart ached for her, and he was devastated by the thought of what she must have endured. Over his shoulder, he could see Amber following, as Jabari had predicted. *That horse cares about Kira as much as I do.* The thought surprised him—not that Amber could care so much, but that he could.

Once they made it through the treacherous pass and back to the main trail, they stopped to rest. Jalil would not let anyone else carry Kira, and he laid her down in the soft sand in the shade of the tall rocks. Mirage moved away, but Amber sidled closer. Jalil stepped back to watch her lower her head and sniff Kira's still form. Raising her head, Amber exchanged a look with him before moving away, allowing Jalil to return to Kira's side.

Kneeling, he took a cloth from his saddlebag, dampened it, and tenderly bathed her pale face. A few strands of silvery gold escaped from beneath her headwrap, and he caught them in his fingers, awed by their silky texture. He dribbled a few drops of water on her lips, hoping she would respond. Watching her lips part, he was encouraged to see her swallow. With a sigh of relief, he did it again. This time, her tongue slipped out to capture the drops.

Disconcerted by a strange feeling, he tore his gaze from her lips and studied the tiny freckles sprinkled across the tops of her cheeks and nose. Reaching out to touch one, he suddenly found himself falling into twin pools of clear blue-green. Kira looked at him and her eyes widened, her lips parted, and she sighed. He froze and stared at her, afraid to move. She smiled, a tentative smile, a gentle smile, and then passed out again. Swallowing hard, Jalil was still staring down at her, unaware of his surroundings, when Ehsaan walked up and touched him on his shoulder. Jalil jerked, as if awakened suddenly, looked up and smiled.

Ehsaan stared at his face with a curious expression, patted his shoulder, and said, "It is about time."

"What is it time for?" Jalil asked, truly puzzled.

Eshaan chucked and shrugged. "Nothing, my friend. Come. We must go."

They rode onward, stopping only once more for water, and it was late in the evening when they reached Ehsaan's kingdom. Men rode out to meet them and escorted them to the compound. When they reached the front steps, Issa was already there, along with Adara, Saad, and Amal.

"Kira!" Adara called out when Jalil approached the steps with Kira in his arms.

"Hush, Adara, stay back," Issa said, grabbing Adara to restrain her.

Saad rushed down the steps with Amal when Jabari came into view. "Jabari! My son! Are you all right?"

"Yes, Father, but we must help Fatima." Saad held the horse's bridle while Amal lifted Fatima down. Fatima protested, insisting that she didn't need anyone's help, but as soon as she was on the ground and tried to take a step, she groaned and collapsed. Amal caught her in his arms and lifted her as if she weighed nothing, and Issa pointed to the house.

Jabari slid to the ground, and Saad, his eyes wet with tears, pulled him into a fierce hug. "My son, my son. Thank Allah you have returned." Jalil's heart warmed at the sight.

Several men rushed forward to help Jalil with Kira, but once again, he wouldn't let anyone else carry her. Following Issa to a guest room, he gently placed Kira on the bed and stood nearby, worried about her condition. He was strangely reluctant to leave her, but when the serving women began to remove her robe and tunic, he hastened out the door. Needing answers, but unsure who to talk to, he went in search of Ehsaan.

He found him just outside. "Jalil, I just directed my men to help set up a temporary camp for your men. Your men will be provided with food, and their wounds will be tended. And now, how are our guests?"

"I am not sure, Ehsaan, but your sheikha has assured me all will be well."

"If Issa has said it, it will be so," he chuckled.

"Yes, I know Kira is in good hands. Ehsaan, I need to talk to you. I have many questions, and I think you might have some of the answers," Jalil said as they walked into the house.

Ehsaan sighed and nodded his head. "Jalil, there is much to discuss, but please, not tonight. I am tired and hungry, and I expect you are too."

Jalil wanted to talk, but what Ehsaan said was true. "You are right, I am tired, and I would like to get something to eat, too, but I must check on Mirage first."

"It is already done. Baqir and Amal are seeing to Mirage and Mukhtar. Even Amber is being taken care of. Your men and their horses have food and a place to sleep. Now, go and take a bath. I will have a meal sent to your room. Our talk can wait until tomorrow."

Jalil conceded defeat and headed for the bath. It felt good to forget everything for a while, and he looked forward to his first restful night in quite some time.

CHAPTER 55

The sun had cleared the hill tops when Jalil woke the next morning. Stretching lazily, he lay still, enjoying the cool morning breeze and the muted sounds of the distant herd. Golden beams of light shone down through the carved lattice covering the window, creating geometric patterns on the creamy stone wall across the room.

Watching pale dust motes swirling like desert devils in the air, he was reminded of the silvery-golden strands of Kira's hair. *What would she look like riding on her golden horse with her silk robe clinging to her body and her hair flying in the wind?* He closed his eyes as if that would help him see her lovely blue-green eyes, soft and clear as an oasis pool, and the tiny golden freckles sprinkled on her face like the gems on his medallion. His eyes flew open with surprise when he felt a surge of passion.

Disconcerted, he jumped out of bed and reached for a pair of tan trousers. A polished mirror on a tall table reflected a man that looked like he had barely survived a sandstorm. His hair was askew, and a heavy shadow covered his jaw. He knew he needed to shave, but it would have to wait. Splashing his face and hair with water from the basin on the table, he dried himself dry with a soft, cotton towel and dragged a comb through his tangled mane, which he secured with a leather cord.

When his eyes were drawn to the gold medallion resting on his chest, he lifted it up and studied it, remembering his father's face the last day he had seen him alive. Thinking how his father had worn this medallion and that now it had returned to him, he felt a shiver at how fate had played a hand in his life.

Shaking off the eerie feeling, he threw on a simple white tunic, tucked his trousers into his leather boots, and strode from the room. He needed to check on Mirage and also wanted to check on Jabari and Kira before meeting with Ehsaan.

Mirage was in a private corral along with ceramic basins of water and grain. Seeing his horse taken care of, Jalil went to look for Jabari. He found the boy in another corral, caring for the chestnut mare he had found at Qadir's. Jalil stood by the fence and watched him tend to the horse, who nibbled at a small pile of grass while Jabari cleaned her hooves. When Jabari finished with the last hoof, Jalil called to him. "Jabari, come here for a minute."

Jabari walked over and slipped under the fence to stand next to Jalil. "Yes, my sheik?"

"You are doing an excellent job with that horse, Jabari."

"Thank you." Jabari looked back at the pretty mare who had wandered off toward her water basin. "Do you think that Sheik Ehsaan would let me keep her?"

"Well, considering you are the one that captured her, you do not have to ask his permission. She already belongs to you and to you alone," he said, smiling down at the boy.

"Really? Oh, that is wonderful news. I have always wanted a horse, and though Kira lets me ride Amber, she belongs to Kira." He smiled as he gazed back at the little mare. "I will name her Sarii."

"Sarii, huh? That would mean you are saying she is fast."

"Yes, she is small, but she is swift."

"I see. Well, then, I think Sarii is a good name." Jalil nodded.

"Thank you, my sheik. But tell me please, how is Kira? I tried to see her earlier, but no one would let me in," Jabari said, his voice laced with concern.

"I do not know. She has suffered greatly, but I am confident that Sheikha Issa will help her recover." Jalil prayed Jabari would not ask him any specifics about her injuries.

"It is all my fault, sheik. If I had not let Amber take me away, maybe I could have stopped that man from taking Kira." He frowned and hung his head.

"Jabari, you must let that go. Sometimes things happen for a reason. It is the will of Allah." Jalil laid a comforting hand on his shoulder.

Jabari seemed to consider Jalil's words for a moment. "So, maybe the lion was supposed to attack Kira, and Kira was supposed to find Amber, and Amber was supposed to find me."

"Wait." Jalil stopped the boy. "What lion?"

"The one that attacked Kira in the foothills. Kira was in a very bad way, and if Amber had not come to find me, I do not think she would have survived."

Jalil's head was spinning. Every time anyone talked about Kira, some fantastical story would emerge. "What happened to the lion? How did Kira get away?"

"Well, it is a long story, my sheik. Perhaps we could find something to eat, and I could tell you all about it?" Jabari looked hopeful.

"Jabari, I think we can find something to eat. I have not yet had my morning meal either. Come. Let us find Sheik Ehsaan and beg something from his table." Laughing, he grabbed the boy by the shoulders and turned him toward the house. Jabari waved goodbye to Sarii, and together they went to look for Ehsaan.

Ehsaan did, in fact, give them something from his table where they were invited to share a meal with Issa and Adara. After Jabari recounted the story of the lion and they ate their fill, Adara begged her father to allow her to take Jabari to visit Shar. Issa voiced her concern, but Ehsaan just laughed and sent the children on their way.

"Issa, when has that girl ever listened to me? Besides, she is the daughter of a sheik. She can take care of herself," he said proudly as he poured a fresh glass of lemonade.

Issa just smiled and took her leave, hurrying off to check on her patients. Jalil was left alone to talk with Ehsaan.

The next few hours were very illuminating for both men. As Jalil listened to Ehsaan tell Kira's story, he was filled with admiration for her. She had to be the bravest woman he had ever met. When Ehsaan finished, Jalil shared what had happened in Qadir's chambers, including how he found the medallion and his conversation with Cassie. He chose to omit exactly what he saw in the bedchamber of Kira's personal tragedy. Afterwards, they sat in silence, digesting the details and events of the past few days.

Finally, Ehsaan looked at Jalil. "I am sorry I did not tell you everything at first, but many things I told you were given to me by Kira in confidence. I would appreciate it if you would be careful with that information."

"I have also shared some intimate details and would ask the same," Jalil said and wondered again about his burgeoning feelings for a girl he barely knew.

Ehsaan nodded in agreement. "But Jalil, who do you think killed Qadir?"

"Well, I did not do it. That Cassie woman seems to think Kira did, but I know Kira would not have done it. And I do not trust Cassie. I cannot put my finger on it, but I believe she is hiding something. Besides, for all we know, Cassie did it. But then, Qadir had so many enemies. He spent his life ruining the lives of others, and his brutality was extreme. It could have been one of his own men, a servant, or even a woman from his harem." Jalil felt the certainty of his words even as he said them.

"I agree, and I also do not think Kira did it, even after what he did to her. I wish I knew who did do it, though, so I could thank them," Ehsaan said with a twinkle in his eye.

Jalil burst out laughing. "As would I, my friend, as would I."

He was considering a visit to check on Kira when Ehsaan asked him another question. "Jalil, would you show me your father's medallion?"

Without hesitating, Jalil reached into his tunic and carefully pulled it from around his neck and handed it to Ehsaan.

Ehsaan studied it closely. "Yes, this is indeed your father's. I never saw him without it." He fell silent for a minute, then handed the medallion back to Jalil. "Your father was a great sheik. He was so proud of you."

Jalil placed it around his neck and smiled. "Thank you for those words, Ehsaan. Truly, there was no one quite like him."

"Did your father ever tell you where the medallion came from?" Ehsaan looked at him intently.

"Where it came from? What do you mean? I thought he had it made just for him." Jalil was intrigued.

"Not that I am aware of. I think it was passed down to him. He started wearing it when his father, your grandfather, died."

Jalil leaned back to consider this information. "Well, I know I will never take it off, not until I have a son to pass it on to. But what puzzles me is how it got to Cairo."

They shared a look, trying to figure out the mystery that was the medallion. Ehsaan nodded, as he would often do when he had discovered a truth. "Jalil, I think that if you can find that out, you will find out who murdered your father."

Jalil's eyes narrowed, and a smile spread across his face. "Ehsaan, my friend, I intend to do just that. And now I know who to talk to."

Ehsaan laid a hand on his arm. "Be careful with her, Jalil. Ever since the plane crash, Kira's life has been anything but easy. She has suffered many losses. You would do well to remember that."

"I will be careful, Ehsaan. I am not a cruel man, and I will give her a few days, but I intend to get answers." When Ehsaan nodded, Jalil thanked him for the meal and the talk and took his leave.

As he walked through Ehsaan's house, Jalil pondered all he had heard. So many questions. Who murdered his father? How did the medallion get to Cairo? Where did Amber come from? Who killed Qadir? So many mysteries, but the greatest mystery of all was Kira. Something told him they were all related. *What is the connection?* He didn't know, but he was going to find out.

CHAPTER 56

Kira had been awake for a few hours before Jabari stopped by to check on her and give her an update on Amber, as well as Shar. She was pleased to hear the stallion was doing well. Of course, Jabari also had to regale her with tales of his new mare, Sarii. It was enjoyable to watch him talk and laugh, his silver eyes full of joy and life.

They were having a good visit when his new partner in crime showed up. Adara burst into the room with her usual energy and stole him away. Evidently, she needed someone to help her take Shar for a walk. Kira smiled, seeing them both run out the door together. She was happy to see Jabari had found a friend. Maybe he and his family would end up as part of Ehsaan's tribe, too. Saad mentioned the sheik had invited them to stay for a while. Kira was saddened by the thought of her adopted family retiring from the road, but she knew it was what Samira dreamed of, and if anyone deserved her dreams to come true, it was Samira. *Will Samira ask me to stay? Will Ehsaan ask me to join his tribe? Do I want that?*

The past few days had been filled with pain and nightmares and Kira tried not to think of what happened at Qadir's and concentrated instead on getting well. She did everything Issa asked of her, drank the potions she was given, and allowed the serving women to apply healing ointments to her wounds.

Since arriving in this country, Kira had learned a great deal about the people and culture. Their language was complicated and musical, and their writing was an art form, beautiful and magical. The people were tough because they had to be. They lived in a land of contrasts, not unlike her American southwest—a land of rocky mountains, burning deserts, and cool, hidden valleys. A reflection of their land, the people were strong and fierce. They could burn as hot as the desert and be as cool and gentle as an oasis.

They reminded her of her grandmother's people, who respected the land, didn't try to change it, and lived as part of it. Although she didn't always agree with their rules and beliefs, Kira had come to respect and love the people who lived by them.

Kira loved living here, but watching Ehsaan with his family made her long for a family of her own. Bored and feeling restless, she felt a need to get out of the house. She had been shut inside long enough, and she wanted to see Amber. With an hour yet until midday meal, it was the perfect time to sneak away.

Before leaving the room, she retrieved her old travel bag. Thank God Saad had recovered it the day of the ambush. Opening it, she was relieved it appeared undisturbed. Her father's money belt lay on top of her old robe. Pulling out Jabari's old pants, a small leather pouch fell onto the bed. She looked inside at the gold chain she had removed from her father's medallion and remembered Qadir holding the medallion in front of her. *He stole it from me!* Her eyes grew moist when she realized it was lost to her forever, just like her father's ring and her mother's necklace. Except for this chain, her only connection to her parents was gone forever. She took solace in the fact that another medallion existed, buried in her secret valley, even if she might never see it again. Sniffing, she wiped her eyes and buried the pouch in the bottom of her bag.

Wanting to clear her head and longing to see Amber, she removed the tunic Issa had given her to wear and let it float to the floor. Reaching for her pants, she froze when she glimpsed her nude body in the tall, polished mirror standing in front of one wall. Stunned, she traced one thin, pink stripe running from the side of her breast down and across her flat belly. Another one started at her hip and snaked its way down her thigh to just above her knee. Issa had warned her there might be scars, but Kira had not registered that fact until now. The marks were healing, but no doubt traces would remain.

Her eyes were drawn to the four grooves on the outside of her thigh. They were an ugly reminder of her encounter with the lion, but she could live with them because they had led her to Samira and her family. The new scars were worse—they were evidence of her downfall, and she was thankful no one would ever see them.

Lately, Kira had begun to doubt her faith. Ever since the wreck, her life had been fraught with danger and pain, and she wondered why God would allow her to suffer so much. She had tried to live a good and decent life, striving to help others and doing the right thing whenever possible. And she tried to respect all people, and nature, too. So why was He punishing her? At times she felt herself sliding into dark depression, and all she could think about was escaping back to the secret valley where she would not have to deal with any more pain and suffering.

Fighting not to feel sorry for herself, she sighed and raised her eyes to study her face. At first glance, she looked the same, but the longer she looked, the more she felt like something had changed. Her eyes were still the same blue-green, all traces of the hateful dye were gone, and her skin was clear, except for the few freckles scattered high on her cheeks. Thanks to Issa's conditioners, her hair was luxurious, the gold more pronounced, and it cascaded down around her shoulders and curled around her breasts, falling almost to her waist. But she looked different, older, maybe.

When she glanced down at her thighs again, her face flushed, and she felt sick. He had touched her there. Tears welled in her eyes when she remembered Qadir's hands on her body, and for just an instant, she imagined she could see red smears on her thighs, and she bowed her head in shame.

Her mother had told her that one day she would find a man to love, like her mother loved her father, and that it would be up to Kira to choose whom to share her body with. But Kira knew that could never happen now. Qadir had taken away her choice. Clenching her eyes tight, she felt her nausea replaced with rising anger. When she opened them, her eyes were filled with new resolve. She may have lost her family and future, but at least she still had Amber. Perhaps God had not forsaken her completely.

Donning Jabari's old clothes, she combed and braided her hair, coiling it around her head, and covered it with a headwrap. Checking herself in the mirror, she saw that Kira the girl was gone, and Kira the woman was staring back at her. Nodding grimly at her reflection, she made her way outside.

As she passed several men on their way to various duties, she heard thundering hoofbeats approaching. The men watched in admiration as Amber raced toward her. Kira ran to meet her, grabbed her mane, and mounted her on the run. In a flash, they were gone, galloping out of the compound. Behind her, the men shook their heads, watching until horse and rider disappeared behind the house.

•   •   •

Jalil had risen at first light and was checking on Mirage when he saw Amber running through the pasture behind the stable. He had watched her the past week and was becoming as obsessed with her as he was with Kira, wondering where she came from. He suspected Kira knew the answer.

After sharing a light breakfast with Ehsaan and Issa, he went to check on his men. They were ready to leave, and frankly, so was he. Spending time with Ehsaan and his family made him long for his own. His mother had sent him a message, urging him to come home as soon as everyone was fit to travel and suggesting that he invite Saad and his family for a visit. Jalil decided it was a good idea because the invitation would include Kira as part of Saad's family. The more he thought about it, the more he liked the idea of Kira and her golden horse coming home with him.

Before the sun reached its highest point, Jalil joined Baqir and Amal in the stallion stable to check on Shar and, afterwards, stopped by the corral to watch Jabari working with Sarii. After the midday meal, he returned to his room, and in the process of washing off the stable dust, he leaned over the basin and the medallion slipped from inside his tunic. He took a moment to study its mysterious design, and once again thought of all the unanswered questions that surrounded it. Impatient again for the answers, he decided he would try to talk to Kira now. *I will not pressure her. Surely, she will not object to at least talking about it.*

Tucking the medallion under his tunic, he made his way to the guest wing. He knocked on Kira's door and when she didn't answer, he called out, "Kira? Are you there? This is Jalil and I was hoping we could talk?" But there was still no answer.

He was about to knock again but was interrupted when Samira peered out of her room next door. "She is gone, Sheik Jalil."

Jalil whipped around to see Jabari's mother, fully dressed and wearing a simple bandage around her head. "You should not be up, Samira." He was concerned after hearing more about her wound from Ehsaan.

"I am fine, Sheik Jalil. Sheikha Issa has said that I will live." She chuckled softly. "And if the sheikha says it is so, then it is so."

Jalil could not help but smile. "Yes, so I've been told. Do you know where Kira went?"

"No, but one of the servants said she left a little while ago." She smiled encouragingly. "Perhaps you should check with Amber?"

Of course! Why didn't I think of that? He smiled sheepishly. "Thank you, Samira. I will do just that."

On the way to the stables, Jalil spied Baqir by the corral, watching Mirage.

"Greetings, Sheik Jalil," Baqir said with a bow. "I have been admiring your Mirage. He is a fine stallion. You are indeed a lucky man."

"Thank you, Baqir." Jalil nodded before asking, "Baqir, have you seen Kira or Amber this morning?"

"I have not, but my men reported seeing the two of them headed toward the hills behind the house not too long ago. Is there a problem?"

"No, not really. I just need to talk to her about something. Perhaps I can persuade this lazy stallion of mine to take me for a ride."

Mirage let out a snort as if he understood the insult but didn't care, and pranced over with an eager expression.

Baqir laughed. "I think that you have offended your horse, and he is about to prove you wrong."

"I hope so. If anyone needs me, tell them I will be back soon."

Jalil was soon riding out of the compound in the direction that Kira had taken. As he raced across the land, he worried about Kira riding so soon after her ordeal. Concerned for her safety, he urged Mirage to go faster.

•   •   •

Kira was hanging on to Amber and trying to forget everything but the sun on her face and the wind in her hair. She didn't want to think about Qadir and the events of that night in his chambers. Thankfully, she could only remember up to a certain point and was spared the memory of his final act. It seemed First Wife had actually done her a favor by giving her the drugged wine.

Feeling Amber's muscles bunch between her knees, rhythmically churning as the horse's powerful legs drove them onward, she let go of the memories and cleared her mind. She didn't know where Amber was taking her, nor did she care. Holding on tightly, she tucked her head down, letting the horse fly, unaware of the approaching stallion.

When Amber slowed, Kira was startled by the sudden appearance of Jalil astride Mirage. Their eyes locked, and seeing the excitement and challenge in his, she laughed out loud and urged Amber to go faster. Mirage needed no urging and burst forward with renewed speed. When Amber pulled ahead, Kira glanced back to see Jalil's eyes widen, then narrow with excitement. He leaned forward and Mirage inched closer to Amber until they were running head-to-head.

It could not last for long though—the terrain was becoming rocky, and Kira could feel her strength ebbing. She signaled to Amber, who snorted and tossed her head, but heeded the command, slowing to a fast walk. Trembling, Kira struggled to maintain her seat, but as soon as Amber was walking more slowly, she slid off. Her legs promptly gave out, and she stumbled to her knees.

Jalil leapt off Mirage and ran to her side. "Kira, are you hurt?" He reached for her shoulder.

"Don't touch me!" she yelled as she scramble away.

"Kira, what is wrong? Let me help you." He stepped forward.

"No! No, stay away!" She was afraid but didn't know why.

Amber sidled close and lowered her head, and when Kira looped her hands around Amber's neck, Amber slowly lifted her up until she could stand. Afraid and breathing harshly, Kira leaned against her, keeping her face tucked against Amber's warm, silky neck, as she tried to still her racing heart.

Jalil remained quiet and stood by Mirage, his eyes wide, and his face reflecting immense concern. When she turned her tear-stained face toward him, he gasped out loud. "Kira, I am so sorry. I did not mean to frighten you."

She stared at him, and for a minute, he seemed to fade, and in his place stood a huge, dark form, swathed in black. She didn't recognize him or her surroundings. Praying silently, she closed her eyes tightly until she felt her control return. Wiping her sweaty brow, she opened her eyes to see it was just Jalil, his face filled with confusion. Mortified, she took a deep breath. "It…it's okay, Sheik Jalil. I'll be fine in a moment. I just need to be alone."

When he averted his eyes and pretended to tighten his saddle and adjust a stirrup, she felt like she had to apologize. "I'm sorry. I don't know what happened. Please, forgive me," she said.

Jalil glanced at her. "I understand," he said, but his face was strangely blank. When she didn't respond, he continued, "Well, I must get back. We are planning to leave in two days, and I have much to do."

She turned away without expression, but when she struggled to mount Amber, she felt a pair of large hands on her waist, lifting her onto Amber's back. Disconcerted, but knowing she couldn't have managed on her own, she grudgingly thanked him.

He merely nodded and vaulted up on Mirage. "Then if you do not need me, I will see you later," he said with a nod and cantered off.

Watching him ride away, Kira couldn't help but admire his wide shoulders and long legs and the way he rode as one with his horse. Bewildered by the warm tingling that spiraled through her body whenever he was near, she thought about Jalil as she rode back to the house. Still shaking from her reaction to being chased and subsequently seeing a dark vision, she couldn't imagine someone like Jalil being attracted to her—not now. She had been kidding herself, thinking she had recovered from her ordeal and that the only scars she would carry were the ones from Qadir's whip.

Jalil had mentioned he was leaving in two days and Amal was staying at Ehsaan's, but Saad hadn't said yet what his family would do. Where did that leave her? Would she be able to stay at Ehsaan's? Should she try to go home to America? Did she even still want to go home? The unanswered questions swirled in her mind, like dust devils in the deep desert—appearing out of nowhere and disappearing in a blink of an eye, only to re-form just as fast. Blinking at sudden tears, she let them fall, and Amber, as if sensing her mood, walked more slowly into the light of the westering sun. By the time she reached the stable, Jalil was nowhere in sight, and Kira was no closer to any answers.

She kept to herself the rest of the day and declined to join the family for dinner because she did not think she could face Jalil yet. All she could think about was she had one more day and then Jalil would be leaving.

CHAPTER 57

The next morning, after a light meal and a visit to Amber, Kira found herself back in her room sitting at the table. Having become used to a more active lifestyle traveling with the family, the lack of routine was driving her crazy. She jumped when she heard a knock on the door and opened it to see Samira carrying a small basket. "Come in, Samira."

"Thank you, Kira. I just want to see how you were doing. Can I help you with anything? Are you still having any pain?" She still wore a bandage, but her head was healing nicely.

"Samira, please sit." Kira gestured toward a chair. After they sat down, Kira said, "I am doing much better, and you look like you are excited about something. What is going on?"

"Kira, it is good news! Jalil has invited Saad to join his tribe! We will leave with him tomorrow. I cannot wait. Just think, Kira. I will have a home with a proper house. Saad will work for Jalil, and Sheik Jalil said Jabari could help their herdmaster, Sakhr." Samira sat on the edge of her chair, leaning forward in her excitement.

Kira was filled with joy but, at the same time, she felt a stab of pain deep in her heart—Jalil had not asked her to join. Masking her tears of sadness with tears of joy, she hugged Samira gently. "It is indeed the best of news. It is what you dreamed of. I am so happy for you." Sitting back in her own chair, she noticed Samira's smile fading and knew Samira had sensed something. Kira averted her eyes and sought to distract her. "What have you brought me, Samira?" She gestured to the basket.

"Oh, well, it is just some extra ointment I put together last night for you to use," Samira said hesitantly. "It will help heal your skin and lessen the scars."

"Wonderful!" Kira said with obvious delight. "You are so talented. Thank you, Samira. I will use it diligently." She rose and carried the basket to her bedside table.

When she rejoined Samira at the table, she could tell she hadn't pulled the wool over Samira's sharp eyes—she must have seen Kira's look of rejection. "Kira, I am sure that Jalil meant to include you in our invitation."

"I don't know. He hasn't spoken to me. And after everything that happened, perhaps he doesn't want me at his house. He risked a great deal rescuing me, but he may regret his actions before it is over. I just wish it had never happened." Kira was remembering her night with Qadir again.

Samira must have seen something on her face because she suddenly looked very serious. "Kira, you have not talked about it yet. I would like to help you if I can. Maybe if you…" She stopped in mid-sentence when Kira cut her off.

"No, Samira. Please. I just want to forget it. Talking about it will solve nothing. Please."

"If that is what you wish," Samira said, but her face mirrored her doubt. "So then, what will you do?"

"Issa stopped by last night and said she would help me get a message to my grandmother. And that I was welcome to stay here until I decide what to do."

"Is that what you want?" Samira asked.

"I guess it might be the best thing for me… and Amber. She's comfortable here, and Adara has already made friends with her."

Samira smiled. "Adara could make friends with a desert lion, I expect."

Kira laughed. "That is probably true. But really, I think it is best that I stay for now. I may even have the opportunity to join a caravan soon and travel to a coastal city. I'm sure I can find someone there who will help me get a message to my family."

"Well, at least you will have another friend while you wait. Issa has discovered Fatima's amazing embroidery skills, and Fatima will be helping with the robes and tunics they make here."

Kira was relieved the former harem girl would be staying. Fatima had saved her life, and Kira had a special connection with her. She encouraged Samira to tell her more of their plans, successfully diverting further conversation about her own lack of plans.

Later, after the evening meal, Kira sat at her table, applying ointment to her arms when she heard footsteps stop outside her door. She thought it might be Saad or Samira until she saw the black boots under the edge of her door. *Jalil!* Holding her breath, she waited for him to knock.

"Good evening, Kira. Can you spare me a moment to talk?" Jalil stood in the doorway, his tall, muscular form outlined by the light of the lamps in the hall.

"Yes, certainly, my sheik. Come in." Kira gestured.

"Thank you," he said and settled into a chair.

His face was devoid of expression, and Kira couldn't tell what he was thinking. She waited for him to speak first.

"We missed you at evening meal."

"I am sorry, my sheik. I was not feeling well." Kira steeled her expression, not wanting him to see her blatant lie.

"I am sorry to hear that. Are you feeling better now?" he asked politely.

"Oh, yes, much." She let her eyes roam around the room, looking everywhere but at him.

"That is good. Well, I just wanted to let you know we are leaving at first light. I hear Issa has invited you to stay here. If that is so, I expect Samira will be sorry you will not be going with us."

Kira stared at him now. *Are you sorry, Jalil?* She couldn't help thinking it but didn't say it aloud. When he didn't continue, she said, "My sheik, I never got a chance to congratulate you on winning the race. And I have to thank you for rescuing me, too."

"Thank you, and you are welcome. I am just glad we found you when we did. I wish I had come sooner." After he said it, his face fell as if he realized he had said too much.

Kira blanched but quickly recovered. "I am alive and safe, thanks to you. And there is nothing you could have done to change what happened."

She was startled when he suddenly stood up. "Kira, I must go now. I have much to do. But I want you to know how much… I mean, I want to tell you…"

Seeing him struggle to put his thoughts into words, she came to his rescue. "I understand, my sheik, but it is getting late, and I am very tired."

She rose, thinking to escort him to the door. But she couldn't take her eyes from his. She suddenly sank into their green-gold depths and as if drawn like a moth to flame. He seemed to be just as caught up in the moment until they were both startled by the sound of approaching footsteps in the corridor. They both fell silent and waited until they passed.

Jalil cleared his throat while Kira blinked rapidly. He started to turn away and then stopped. "Oh, I forgot." She watched as he reached into his robe, pulled out a small turquoise-leather pouch, and held it out. "This belongs to you."

Curious, Kira took it, loosened the golden drawstring, and dumped the contents of the pouch into her hand. Out tumbled what she least expected—her father's ring and her mother's gold chain. "Oh, Jalil!" she cried out. She was in shock and stared at them in disbelief. Her eyes flew up to his and her face broke into a huge grin even as her tears began to fall.

At first, his eyes widened with worry until he saw her grin. He grinned back. "Jabari found them in the pass."

Kira continued to stare at him until he squirmed slightly, as if embarrassed. "I hope you are not mad. Look, I even had it fixed." He pointed to the chain.

Numb, she held it up, and when she continued to focus on it without speaking, he reached over and took the chain from her hands, placing it around her neck. The ring settled against her chest where it belonged. Jalil's face was close, and Kira's heart began to pound. Inhaling his scent—warm sandalwood, leather, along with something else unidentifiable—she sighed and closed her eyes. When his fingers touched her neck, her eyes flew back open, and she shivered. He inhaled sharply and jerked his hands back, and the moment was lost.

Glancing down at the ring, she clutched it tightly as tears ran down her face. Looking back at Jalil, she smiled. "Thank you, Jalil." It was all she could say, and she wasn't aware she had not used his title.

His eyes widened at her words, but he just nodded, apparently at a loss for words as well. Neither spoke, and when the silence grew uncomfortable, Kira stirred and steeled herself for what she had to do. There was no reason to prolong this. Jalil had his own life to live, and she was not worthy to be a part of that. "My sheik, thank you for returning my father's ring. And for saving my life."

"Again, you are welcome. And now I must retire," he said as he opened the door. He paused, his hand on the handle, and turned back to say one last thing. "Kira, I hope you find your way home."

Kira could not answer without showing how close she was to tears again. She simply nodded and watched as he left the room, closing the door softly behind him. As soon as she heard his footsteps fade, she fell on her bed with a sob.

Later, lying in the dark, she thought of the valley. It had been her home for a while, and Ndee and the herd had been her family. Life was simple there, with no troubles, no pain, and no tough decisions. Maybe that's where she needed to go.

With no idea what the future would bring and knowing she would have to face Jalil in the morning after what had just happened, she spent the rest of the evening thinking about her options. But as the hour grew late, she was no closer to making any decisions. Exhausted and wishing to think no more about it, she closed her eyes, cleared her mind, and prayed to God that she would not dream that night. Thankfully, her prayers were answered once again.

Kira woke the next day with an unusual sense of calm. Though she hadn't come to a decision yet about returning to America, at least she knew she had a home with Ehsaan and Issa as long as she wanted.

She gathered with Ehsaan's family on the steps to bid farewell to Jalil and his men. As they assembled behind their sheik, Kira could see how proud they were to be part of his tribe. She had personally thanked each of them in the past week for having risked their lives for hers.

She could hardly look at Saad and Samira sitting on their camels, reminding her of the wonderful days she had spent on the trade route with them. And she tried not to cry when she saw Jabari, sitting proudly on Sarii next to Jalil's warriors, waving at her and smiling.

When Jalil gave her a last, long look, she nodded but quickly looked away, missing the brief sadness that flashed in his eyes. She heard him shout a command and looked back to see him spin Mirage about and gallop toward the pass. Ehsaan's men yelled and fired their guns in a farewell salute. Ehsaan and Issa turned and walked back into the house, and little Adara skipped toward the stable in search of Shar.

Kira stood and watched as Jalil disappeared from sight, and for a second, she felt a stabbing pain in her heart, until she heard a familiar neigh ring out across the compound. She turned to see Amber running toward her, with her shining mane and tail flying in the breeze. When she turned back, Jalil was gone and so was her pain.

Feeling the sun warming her robe, she breathed deep, savoring the scent of horses and wood smoke and, underneath it all, the clean, sharp scent of sand. She had been so worried about finding a home, but she didn't have to worry anymore. For now, her home was anywhere Amber was. As for her future, it was as mysterious as her secret valley. She would trust in God to take care of her.

Smiling, finally at ease, Kira looked at her best friend. Her smile grew, and she hurried forward. The future could wait. Today was all that mattered.

ACKNOWLEDGMENTS

At first, I seriously considered not adding any acknowledgements. I mean, how do you thank the many people who are responsible for the creation and publication of my book? I had no idea how to even start, but then something compelled me to try. Maybe it was hearing my mother's voice again: "Did you send a thank you note?" (Both a question and a warning.) So, consider these my thank you notes.

Thank you, Celeste Ramirez, for months and months of listening to every word of this story. Part of you can be found in many of the better adjectives. If you hadn't gone snooping in my office, this tale of mystery, intrigue, murder, love, magic, and general tomfoolery might never have been completed.

To Linda and Trish, my extraordinary sisters (and friends), thank you for a lifetime of love and for believing in me, always. Whenever my life got rough, and I was sure I was going down, y'all were there, reaching out to lift me up. The spirit of sisterhood echoes throughout my stories, thanks to y'all. You are both amazing teachers and wonderful readers.

Oh, and thank you, thank you, thank you, Mary Ellen Bramwell, Editor Extraordinaire. Your insight, your commitment, your editing skills (technical and content) are, for me, without equal. You're stuck with me now, so hold on tight! I have a lot more stories to tell. Get ready for those pesky timeline and continuity issues, not to mention the adverbs. And I am sorry if I missed any of your recommended changes. I take full responsibility for any errors that I forgot to correct.

To my publisher, Black Rose Writing, thanks are just not enough. Y'all took a chance for which I am eternally grateful. I am so glad I found y'all. A shout out to Lone Star Literary Life for having listed Black Rose Writing as one of the top ten publishers in Texas.

Did I mention Larry (a.k.a. Mr. Wonderful)? My rock, my split-a-part, my soulmate…you know how I feel. Best husband ever!

Almost done.

Have any of you ever experienced that wonderful feeling when you create something? It could be a painting, a story, a pillow, a new dessert, a new way to tie a fishing fly…the possibilities are endless. Whatever it is, did you wonder, "How did I do that?" Well, when that happens to me, I don't have to wonder. I know I'm just holding the pen and someone else is "telling" the story. For me it comes from my God. So, thank you, God.

Finally, last but never least, I must thank you, my reader. If you are reading this, you must have read the entire book. I hope you found something in this story to inspire you or comfort you, make you laugh or make you cry, or just help you escape into another world, if only for a few hours. Because that is why I write.

And if you want to know what happens to Kira and Jalil, learn who killed Qadir, find out if Amber and Mirage ever get together, and discover what happened to Bassam, look for the second book in the Desert Born series: *Desert Bold*. It will all be revealed!

For now, keep calm and read on.

And please drop me at line at gincoleman.com. I'd love to hear from you.

ABOUT THE AUTHOR

Gin Coleman was born in the United States but calls no state home. A story-telling tumbleweed, she currently parks her trusty computer in the wilds of Mississippi where she surrendered her garage to her husband's beloved bass boat but maintains a She-Shed for her riding mower. A lifelong lover of horses and dogs, she grew up in the Ozarks, was raised by wolves, and her favorite car is a truck. It was said that the night Gin was born, her mother reported a green light at the window and a crop circle in the back yard. Gin is the proud mother of the *Desert Born Series* and will soon give birth to the *Lost and Found in the Lone Star State Series*.

NOTE FROM GIN COLEMAN

Word-of-mouth is crucial for any author to succeed. If you enjoyed *Desert Brave*, please leave a review online—anywhere you are able. Even if it's just a sentence or two. It would make all the difference and would be very much appreciated.

Thanks!
Gin Coleman

We hope you enjoyed reading this title from:

www.blackrosewriting.com

Subscribe to our mailing list – *The Rosevine* – and receive **FREE** books, daily deals, and stay current with news about upcoming releases and our hottest authors.
Scan the QR code below to sign up.

Already a subscriber? Please accept a sincere thank you for being a fan of Black Rose Writing authors.

View other Black Rose Writing titles at www.blackrosewriting.com/books and use promo code **PRINT** to receive a **20% discount** when purchasing.